Darque Legends:
The Black War Begins
Book One

Derrien Relyea

What readers are saying about the first book in the *Darque Legends* series:

"If you like dragon lore, you'll love this book! The author's attention to detail paints a world where you can see and feel, what they see and feel! Follow along, as their legend begins!"   —Charles D

"Any fan of dragons or warrior mindset can wrap themselves up in this book and get lost in another time and place. I would love to see a movie of this!!!!!! Ready for more from this author!!!!!"
                                                            —Paul C

"…intriguing… full of fantasy and one of the main characters is a dragon they don't just occupy the background. In the end all the little strings are tied into a bow with one of the tails leading for the next sequel."   —Vanessa B

"Derrien is a passionate, prolific writer. Reading the book is addictive, I can't put it down."   —Uriel B

"… dragons and damsels in beauty and distress… battle maidens abound… with sages to assist them… The sword is for freedom and peace in this book. The book stretches your mind and imagination and makes you want to join in the action. There is a sub-underlying message in this book and it grabs you in the real world of today. This is a great fantasy of very high caliber for the author, Derrien Relyea. It is right up there with Lord of the Rings, IMO! I trust the author will bring us more in this series."
                                                          —Mildred L

"Fast read, great characters and fantastic journey into the magical realm of flying serpents! LOVED IT. A must read. Can't wait for the sequels."   —Terry H

"If you love fantasy writings with a heavy dose of Dragons, magic and yes dungeons you will love this read! This adventure is destined to be

Table of Contents

Acknowledgements

For endless hours reading, listening and assisting me to edit, my heartfelt gratitude goes out to Paul, Lori, Rocky ("we had one good day together"), Erica, Uriel, Anthony, Zemira, Bebe, and my niece Tirza, I love you all. Please don't leave me now, I need you. The second book in the series is already begun.

To Authors Howard Flomberg (http://tinyurl.com/CC4LR2Y) (Baruch Dayan, chaver) and Ariel Frailich (http://ginsengpress.com), who taught me how to do what I am now doing and helped me format the book (I am not a geek), words fail me (imagine that?).

My thanks also to Elliott, David, Lewis and to many other friends and relatives for their support. Some went beyond and I want to recognize them for encouraging me along this new journey in my life, but there are honestly too many to name individually. You know who you are. I also send out my thanks to the people I used to work with at LMMC (Tara, you'll like Chapters 17 and 18) and Livingston Physical Therapy. Please forgive me if I've left anyone out, this has been a wild ride.

To the many adventures to come, my friends.

Long live Darque and the Dragon Clan!

A Most Disturbing Vision

TEN WINTERS PAST

In Legend Song they'd praise our stand,
tell how we fought the End of Man.
Come with me now and you will hear
of how the Evil One drew near.
Too long the warnings were ignored.
With just a few left to stop the Hoard,
know 'tis the truth that you will learn,
when these pages you do turn.

"AMA!" Darque cried out into the shadows, waking herself from the recurrent nightmare. Sitting up, she glanced at Storrm lying alongside her. Her little sister jerked in response to the cry and sluggishly lifted her head off the pillow. Darque covered Storrm's eyes with one hand and pushed her down, gently brushing the lids closed again. Singing quietly in her high pitched youthful voice, she lulled her back to sleep the way she'd done every night for the last full moon.

Pulling the blankets up to her chin, questions ran unbridled through her mind. Night after night it woke her gasping, her heart pounding in her chest like the battle drums in the Training Pits. Something horrible was happening that she hadn't the power to prevent. 'Twas not fear she suffered, but a deep despair and frustration, a sense of failure that grew with imminent loss. But great passion and purpose prevailed, setting her a'Flame with the need to engage. Recalling what the Elder Warriors had taught her, she recognized the emotions. 'Twas Battle Lust. She contemplated the elusive nightmare, determined to uncover what was causing her such turmoil. What had she cried out? "Ama?" She paused to think how long it had been, and felt shamed when she couldn't immediately remember. How old was Storrm? Darque had seen seven winters now, the sleeping child beside her had seen six, and Aalanna had been missing without a trace since just after Storrm's birth. She could scarcely recall her mother's face, her voice, her touch, but at least she had some real memory, whereas Storrm had nothing but Darque's memories to share. And share them, she did. Storrm wouldn't grow up not knowing their mother. Darque wouldn't allow that to happen.

Wide awake now, she laid upon the down stuffed mattress filling the far corner of the tiny room. The shutters of the single window were open, and the cool night breeze carried the fragrance of early spring, as she stared silently at the ceiling in the pitch black of the night. She and Storrm were blessed with excellent hearing and night vision, and they needed not the torch in the hanger at the doorway. They were alone as usual, for their father was working, but they were safe. He'd probably return by dawn, or mayhap the following evening for supper. If not, the sisters would go to the village and visit with Kallyr and Shayla, or shadow the kitchen staff in the Den, or almost anywhere, even to wander the back alleys of Port O'Drekinn. They were the daughters of the Battle Commander and they were well known. Anyone causing them harm would answer to the entire Dragon Clan. Besides, she and Storrm had already begun their fighting curriculum, including weapons and survival skills. They'd been riding the War Horses since birth, and as often as not could be found sleeping with the huge War Dogs in the kennels. Although young, they were rapidly becoming a combined force with which to be reckoned. Even the Elders felt the air of authority when in their presence, but they'd not admit to such, after all, they were just two little girls. Still, there was something different about them that none could ignore.

Darque believed she could protect them both, even though they were the same size. The Masters reported their progress in Battle Training near daily to the Commander, comparing their skills to true Gifts. Darque seemed especially competent, having little difficulty with her Training and taking great care with tutoring Storrm. Since their mother's disappearance, and with their father often absent, she'd taken responsibility for her sister and no one dared to make challenge.

She sighed deeply, and as she had since the nightmares began, concentrated on trying to recall the specifics. So far this effort had proven fruitless, but tonight she'd cried out a word as she'd awakened. Mayhap this heralded the breakthrough. Her attention upon the bare beams above, she noted a slow swirl of muted color appear afore her eyes, floating just out of reach. Random drifting became focused intent while the rafters vanished. 'Twas not her first, but only one with the Gift of Sight had Visions. She'd not divulged this knowledge to Kallyr, as he might try to Claim her as a Clan Seer, and she was most certainly not going to be a Seer. She'd be a Warrior of the Dragon Clan. Her fingers strayed to the scar upon her right thigh. She couldn't remember when or how, but she knew she'd been so marked and 'twas her destiny.

The swirling colors resolved further, revealing a palatial Fortress the like of which she'd never seen afore. Blood splattered 'cross her path as she was swept along through the Keep, up a grand staircase, and down a long hallway. There she was dropped abruptly atop a heavy oaken door just torn off its hinges, falling open afore her astonished eyes. Inside the Tower room her father stood in front of a tiny woman backed against the far wall. Darque knew he couldn't see her standing there, and he seemed preoccupied with someone she couldn't see. The woman was instantly recognizable, although she appeared older. 'Twas her mother. A mighty battle had taken place here, but where was, 'here'?

In the blink of her eye the Vision morphed, and despite her thirst for more knowledge, to stay with Aalanna, she was suddenly flying through the air o'er a raging battle. "How," she mouthed to herself, her eyebrows furrowed together in consternation. Flying was merely a dream state and 'twas impossible in reality. Glancing down, she saw herself astride a huge blue Dragon with glistening scales. Off her right hand flew Storrm, riding a great green beast of her own. Bearing down upon the Dragon's Den from on high, she saw Flame belched forth by many Dragons as they fought ferociously in the air o'er the castle, her beloved Drekinn Village was rubble, and the smoke billowed upward as Dragons and Warriors fought viciously upon the ground. There were Warriors battling against the King's Forces, and other Warriors riding Dragons as were she and Storrm, fighting together as a Team. Without her unique senses, she would've been hard pressed to know who fought for whom. In a sweeping glance she took in the glittering scales, the rivers of blood pouring forth, and the flash of fangs, claws and broad swords. She could hear the grunts and groans of massive effort, the screams of pain and defiance, the singing of cold steel slicing through the early morning air. Darque's eyes grew wide as she realized she and Storrm might have arrived late to this horrendous battle, but she was the ranking officer. Her father must have Passed the Veil, and her friends, Warriors and Dragons both, were depending on her to take Command and turn this tide of defeat into victory. Soaring down from the heavens, her Dragon Flaming at full stream, she bellowed out her Battle Cry and heard her sister's voice echoing her own as they entered the fray, "Fight for the One! Fight for the Clan! From here to the Veil, 'tis free we'll stand!"

The Vision shifted again and the battle was done. With the Evil Dragons and the remnants of the King's Forces in retreat, she dismounted her massive beast and ran 'cross the bloody battle grounds where many now lay in agony, a slow death awaiting them. She knew not how the Clan had come to be enemies of the Crown, but she had no time to ponder this, for she must use her power to save the dying. Reaching deep within herself, she pulled from that place she'd discovered winters past, and grasped firmly onto the warm tingling substance without substance. With her Dragon's Magic to boost her own, she slammed a mighty Shield of Protection o'er her forces, ruthlessly excluding the opposition, leaving them to the Fates. She shook with her efforts to keep them all alive. There were so many. Breaking out in a sweat, she wouldn't be able to maintain this Shield for long. She was being drained, her power depleting substantially by the moment. Near falling to her knees with the exertion, she grit her teeth and resolved not to weaken. They had to survive, they counted on her, and as Commander, 'twas her responsibility. She couldn't, wouldn't, let them down.

"Darque." She heard the strangled voice from just behind her, followed by the gurgling intake of a ragged breath. Turning, she saw the Warrior lying in the muck created from his own blood. His Dragon lay beside him, her great jaws clenched, her eyes near black and flashing with the intensity of her effort to maintain her Magic, trying desperately to keep them both alive. 'Twas obvious they'd soon Pass, for they were old and gruesomely injured. He looked familiar, and slowly the sun dawned upon her as she realized 'twas Tannyr, her Swordsmanship Trainer. But this Vision bespoke the future and he was old even now, in her 'present'. He'd retired from active duty winters ago, he should have been teaching at the Den. The gravity of this battle upon Clan soil hit Darque so hard, tears welled up in her eyes.

The pain he suffered thickened his accent as he struggled to speak, his words coming slowly and with hesitation. "Darque. 'Twas good to see you take Command. And you did a fine job of it, lass. But you must know, me Dragon can't Heal herself, let alone me. Her effort is barely enough to keep us from becoming entrenched in the Fade. If you don't let us Pass soon, 'twill be our fate. 'Tis the severity of our wounds that drain you so. Without us, you can Hold the others. Don't force us to the Fade to be lost forever. Please girl, let me go." Tannyr sucked in another shallow breath, noted the indecision upon Darque's face, and continued, "'Tis our time, me destiny has been well served. Now our thread in this tapestry is cut, and yours just being woven in. Do you still not understand? You shall bring the Races of Kadoor back together and reestablish the balance. The prophesy unfolds as it should, to a new beginning." The Elder Warrior coughed weakly and stopped to take another choking breath. He wanted to say more, but couldn't. The pain and fatigue of holding on was taking its toll, and 'twas clear they'd run out of time. She was forced to make the difficult decision to let them Pass, or she would indeed, lose them all.

Relaxing the pair out from under her umbrella of Protection, she placed his sword in his limp hand, holding his fingers tightly around it, as he had no grasp. Then with the barest smile upon his bloody lips, he shifted his focus to his Dragon, who laid her great head 'cross his chest, gratefully taking her last breath with his. Peace surrounded her the very moment they Passed the Veil, and although 'twas still draining her power, the struggle to maintain the Shield had become noticeably easier. But she refused to let anyone else go. Angry, frustrated with having to make such a decision, she realized she'd have to face him in the Pits at dawn, knowing his future... and hers. What was she to do?

With these rapid fire revelations, the Vision began to dissolve and Darque reached out trying to hang onto it physically, but 'twas like holding water in her little hands. Slowly but surely it disappeared and was gone. Momentarily weighed down with the hard core emotion evoked, she knew she had to tell her father about this. The Clan would be drawn into some kind of alliance with the Dragons, and she'd never even seen a Dragon afore. Her mother was still alive and Grifynn would find her, but she knew not the outcome of the rescue attempt. They were approaching a war and many would Pass the Veil in a bloody battle on their own soil, but there'd never been a battle upon the homeland. No one would dare such. And what had Tannyr said about a prophesy? The Vision had been so detailed, she wasn't sure how to prioritize the knowledge so imparted, and 'twas not clear victory resulting. She struggled briefly, attempting to organize it in such a manner as to make sense to her youthful mind. Surely she'd not Seen the end of the Dragon Clan!

She turned her head quickly to a sound coming from 'cross the room, and noted a raven had landed upon the narrow windowsill. 'Twas his claws clicking as he hopped along the smooth stone, and when he saw her he stopped and stared. Abruptly he leaped forward, and shifting into a Man in mid-air, he landed lightly beside her bed. Even so startled, she made a grab for the blade lying under her pillow, but the Raven/Man was faster. 'Twas Magic he used of course, as he hadn't even lifted his hand to touch her. He merely had a glazed look to his dark eyes, and she suddenly found she couldn't move. She watched him carefully but was unable to challenge, and she could only pray the need for defense wouldn't arise. Darque was not afraid despite the Magical Hold, and yet 'twas so surreal, she wondered momentarily if 'twas some kind of extension of her Vision.

"You Hear me little one, 'tis so?" The Raven/Man Spoke to her in a deep, calming voice that came not from his lips. Hearing his Voice in her mind, she tried to blink her eyes to say yes, and he Spoke again, *"I am no Vision. Do not fear, I shan't harm you. Ahhh, I see you are not afraid. Fascinating."* Raising his eyebrows, he stepped closer and continued, *"I am called Corbyn. I am of the Fay."* His entire face lit up with amusement when he saw the unexpected lack of reaction in her eyes. *"I see you already know of my Kind but that could be dangerous, child."*

Sighing, he sat on the edge of the bed next to her. He was tall and lean, hard muscled and finely sculpted. His voice was mesmerizing, his face rugged, with the look of a predator in his narrowed eyes, which she likened to black clouds in the night. Flashes of lightening she saw there, and she had to break eye contact or risk being drawn into their depths, never to return. His hair was long and fell in layers past his shoulders, the multicolored strands of deep rich chocolate to near black. When he tilted his head, shaking his hair off one ear, she saw they came to a short, thick point fanning backward, like miniature wings. His shoulders were broad and square, and he wore some kind of cloak made of ebony feathers that shone iridescent in the moonlight coming through the window. But the most remarkable thing was his skin, what skin she could see that wasn't covered by the cloak. 'Twas evenly tanned, smooth and flawless, and he had a warm golden glow that emanated from within, making him appear as a heat mirage on the sands of the Dragon's Breath. But try as she might, everything about him seemed to alter, 'til she wasn't certain just what he looked like, and wouldn't have been able to describe him to anyone other than to say, he was incredibly masculine. For a girl usually surrounded by Warriors, that was saying something.

He leaned in closer. *"Mayhap you are the answer to the prophesy; I must say I'm truly amazed at your Gifts. The One True Liege divulged to me eons ago, you'd be capable of such and more. He asked me to keep you in my Sight but I've been quite busy of late, so when these Visions began I placed upon you a Spell to end them."* He laughed softly. *"But you're a clever child and created a way around it, which I found truly wonderful. You converted them to nightmares. Quite inspired, but I was figuratively and literally tied up at that time, another story, mayhap I shall tell you one day."* Flipping his hand in the air in a gesture of dismissal, he continued. *"Whatever, the easiest fix was to alter your memory of the nightmares, but once again, you managed to circumvent my Magic."* Corbyn was charmed by the girl's rapt attention to his narrative. *"I am impressed. But, the One has asked me to erase this Vision, which I will do as a favor to Him, although you're not entirely His. No, you're something else, something new. No matter, you won't recall any of this night, but there will be no damage done. We can't have the prophesy modified, now can we? You must do what you do, little one, without prior knowledge. All shall then unfold as it should."*

With that, he placed his hand gently o'er Darque's eyes, and the last thing she heard was Storrm's soft breathing, as her sister managed to sleep through the entire ordeal.

The Fay stood back and watched silently as the little girls slept. The younger would one day be his Mistress's namesake and The Morrigan would be pleased, for he Saw that Storrm would be a great Warrior. Mayhap he'd just not tell the holder of his Curse this revelation, 'twas good to keep such secrets for his own purposes. His gaze then rested upon the elder sister; she was beautiful indeed. There was something particularly intriguing about Darque. Even her name was mesmerizing. 'Twas an ancient name, a name of Power within the High Races, and he knew it had been provided for her father to bestow upon her. Thinking back to the Gathering marking the Retreat just prior to the Last Holocaust, he recalled how he'd debated unsuccessfully for the return of Mankind to the Counsel of the High Races, along with the Fay, the Dragons and the Elves. The Fay, being considered the most Powerful of all the Magic Bearers, had led the Counsel since the beginning of Time. Corbyn had been in line for the succession when the War began, but so much had changed. He grimaced. He didn't like being reminded of the past, but he knew Man must return to their rightful place, for without them, the Balance and the War, would be lost.

Oh, what he'd felt when he touched her. He was certain 'twas innate Magic manifesting. 'Twas no other explanation, she must be the answer to the prophesy. Lifting the blanket, he noted the scar upon the pale skin of her right upper thigh. The Dragon shaped mark was placed upon her by the High Prince of the Highland Dragons himself just after her birth, announcing to the world that they protected her. 'Twas proof they also believed she was the one. He recalled when she was so marked, and how she'd been without fear. There was not a tear shed when the Prince laid talon upon her, blooding her. And yet he'd complied as the Mighty Blue had requested of him, and subdued the memory of that event.

Musing o'er the past, he whispered into the night, "And there will be a girl child born to the Race of Man, of Dragon Blood and Dragon Seed, with flaming red hair and piercing blue eyes, who will take up the Sword to lead the Races from near extinction, into a New Beginning." There was more to the prophesy, but 'twas mostly descriptive of that initial statement. Mere details. 'Twas interesting, and he did know every word, but he didn't have time to consider it now.

Not surprisingly, he felt the urgent Call of the one he now Served. 'Twould be soon for her. The end was always bitter sweet. 'Twould be great loss, for he grew to love them all, but then there'd be the release 'til his Mistress sent him to Serve another. Turning toward the window he hesitated, and then turned back once again to the little girls. This child he'd definitely keep in his Sight. Leaning o'er them, he touched Darque lightly upon the forehead with the tip of one finger, imparting the tiniest spark of Magic to help protect her, while Pushing the Suggestion that she hide her Gifts from others. The Evil One also knew the prophesy and she'd be hunted. If she allowed others to know of her Gifts afore she was able to properly defend herself, she was doomed. She could use all the protection she could get, but he was walking a fine line. One did not fare well if one managed to alter prophesy, he knew from personal experience. What was Told, must come to pass.

The Call now panic stricken, he turned, took one long step, and launched himself through the window head first. Shifting back into Raven form, he took wing into the night.

The sisters slept on.

CHAPTER 1

Day of the LifeBond

As blinding pain forged through my body, I clenched my teeth and concentrated on breathing, to keep from dropping to my knees. 'Twas insanity and I was dumbfounded that Mankind was once again upon the brink of extinction. The Evil One had returned, but this time the Dragon Clan would be prepared. This time, we'd take advantage of the only chance we'd have, to defend ourselves and our people. 'Twas the offer of life itself, how could we resist such? Most people still had no idea what was happening around them, and those who'd discovered through first hand observation, had done so while being Flamed. Dead people couldn't report what they'd finally realized was fact. Such was especially annoying to a Warrior, where information ruled.

I must admit, even I was skeptical, when the offer was first laid upon the table and 'twas not many days past. Soon though, I'd conceded the truth, given the vast evidence being presented. But I'd never envisioned myself standing naked at midnight, upon sacred ground, amid all the Dragon Clan Elders, and the Ancients of the Highland Dragons themselves, with a huge Magical fire leaping toward the sky in their wake. Fully armored, or mayhap in leathers, my sword strapped at my back and blades in my boots....but not like this. My fingers were numb, I felt like I was on fire, my head was near ready to burst. I heard my heart pounding rhythmically with the pumping of my blood, as it trickled slowly down my leg from the slash on my thigh. Everything appeared in slow motion. We were thirteen Warriors standing a few paces apart, semi-circled facing the fire, and yet I couldn't see any of my brothers or sisters in arms. I was mesmerized, unable to move a muscle as the Elder drew forth the sacred blade with the jewel encrusted hilt. 'Twas three hands in length, and could slice through bone with ease. Through the Battle Trials I'd earned the right to receive the First Cut. All the while, the Dragon Ancients droned on, chanting in their grunting and growling language as they Brewed their Magic. Drawing the Life Force from every living thing on and near this sacred ground, they charged the very air we breathed. Heat permeated my muscles, settling the gooseflesh from the chill of the early winter air. A tingling rush coursed through my body, finally centering in my low gut, as he waved the ceremonial blade toward the starlit sky in deference to the One True Liege. Bringing the razor sharp edge to the scar on my thigh, he laid open skin, fascia and muscle with a mere touch.

I had a high pain tolerance even for a Warrior, but I freely admit, when the ceremony was explained to us, I was slightly concerned. By the Flame, I'd only recently achieved Warrior status and had never suffered a true battle injury. 'Twas energizing to discover I was worthy after all, taking the pain with little outward sign. Of course, we were warned at the Cleansing Ritual, any sound we made during the Calling would most likely be our last. That might've had something to do with my present stoicism. But mayhap I've led you to underestimate my headstrong and competitive nature. Let me make this perfectly clear: 'twould be a cold day in Hades afore I'd fail.

<div align="center">~~~~~~~~~~</div>

I prayed to m'Liege, the Elders couldn't Hear my thoughts, as the pain sent me spiraling back in time. 'Twas near mid-morning a fortnight past, and Storrm and I were caring for our weapons at the Blacksmith's forge near the heart of Drekinn Village. We sat in the sunlight off the threshold, hoping this approaching winter wouldn't be as vicious as was the last. Being theoretically jobless since we'd yet to deploy, we scraped and bartered for every extra blanket, weapon, and bite of food. Not that we did badly, mind you. We were extremely resourceful, and by cleaning the other Warriors' weapons and tack, we did rather well for ourselves. That, and working with the War Horses for Ian the Stable Master, and the War Dogs for Teaka the Kennel Master, kept us quite busy outside of our daily schedule. In truth, we were well known for our ability to train the huge animals to do whatever we desired, and there was a long waiting list for our talents. "'Tis as if you actually speak their language," Teaka told us when we'd first started working there, but knew not how close to the truth she was. I smirked afore noticing the growing haze to the east.

"Storrm, there," I murmured, as I barely lifted the tip of my sword and my gaze to the horizon, where a great black cloud was forming in the distance. 'Twas moving rapidly toward us from o'er the far mountain range know as the Raptor's Talons. Adding a few more drops of oil, I continued running my sword edge along the whetstone.

"Noted," she stated quietly, while rubbing a dull sheen onto her knife with a fine grit sandpaper. Teasingly she added, "I was beginning to think you'd been rendered blind, it took you so long. The great Darque, who sees all and knows all," My disapproving scowl sobered her mood, and she finished contritely, "but me thinks we shall discover all too soon what 'tis to be."

Recently the very air had been thick with tension, and only one person felt it more than Storrm and I. Kallyr, the Clan Seer, had been shaking his graying head and looking anxiously at the cloudless skies for days. 'Twas rather disturbing, considering the man didn't predict weather patterns. Kallyr's strength was Seeing events. Something very bad was stirring and we'd no idea just what 'twas. But bad things always held great potential for battle, hence we prepared for the worst.

"Those clouds aren't moving as any formation I've seen afore. See, Darque, they wax and wane." We stood and openly watched them darken, moving in hard and fast.

"The Elders gather at the Lodge. And they wear War Leathers." I pointed to the far side of the village square, 'cross Drekinn Well. In Battle Dress, they muttered solemnly to each other near the huge, ornately decorated oaken doorway of the Clan meeting hall. Our hearing acute, we listened intently. Very soon, most of the villagers were milling about, or standing 'cross the thresholds of their homes and shops, craning their necks to the darkening skies. Uncertainty laced the air, and the horses in the stables behind us began to stamp and paw at the ground with increasing distress. These skittish animals didn't include the Stallions we'd ridden into town, but were those stabled by travelers, or waiting to be shod by the smith, or belonged to villagers who hadn't the space to keep them at their homes. War Horses wouldn't put up such a fuss, as a nervous horse was useless in battle, and dangerous to all around them.

Realizing no one else would be aware of their growing anxiety, 'twould be up to us to take the appropriate action. We couldn't allow the horses to hurt themselves, or worse yet, break out of their stalls and cause damage in Drekinn.

"To me," I began, but she was right at my shoulder, understanding what I'd thought afore I'd said it aloud. Sheathing our weapons, we dashed through the alley serving as a shortcut to the stables at the back of the shop, to settle the frightened beasts.

As one, we came to a sudden stop midstride when a hard gust of wind whipped up the dirt all around us. 'Twas as if at least twenty Dragons were trying to land all at the same time in the middle of the village square. This of course, when we finally could see, was actually the truth of the matter. 'Twas quite puzzling. They were huge, represented a rainbow of colors, and appeared very old. Although we'd never actually met them, 'twas plain they were the Highland Ancients themselves. This was a diplomatic entourage to the Clan, with a proposal some would come to think of as simply insane.

Storrm and I had seen a Dragon once, four winters past, but by no means imagined to see so many in one place, and certainly not here. Near speechless, which was truly odd for her, she finally found her tongue and sputtered, "Darque? Have you ever?"

"Not that I know of," I answered. My hand strayed to the scar on my thigh, and once again I had the distinct feeling a memory was just outside my consciousness while adding, "No Dragon has visited the Clan in generations."

Kallyr brushed past. "You two stay here, I'll want your thoughts on this matter as soon as I am free. This is bad. This is very bad," he mumbled to himself quietly, shaking his head as he hurried along his way to the Lodge to join the others.

We glanced at each other incredulously, and leaving the horses in the capable hands of the Smith, returned to our work. "Leave now? Does he think to jest?" I grinned at Storrm and she punched me in my arm. "By all of Hades, Darque, does nothing frighten you? If we hadn't been together near every day of our lives, I'd swear you'd been touched by prophesy." Her words gave me pause, as I drew my sword and began sharpening again.

Curiously we watched as the Ancients somehow managed to stuff their collective bulk into the meeting hall. For all of its enormous size, able to comfortably hold the entire village, half the outlying farmers and the Elders during Session, the Dragons were a large Race and there were twenty of them. But mayhap through some form of their Magic, they all fit. As they entered, I was struck by a sense of familiarity; there was a parallel in my memory, if only I could bring it forth. However, there seemed nothing we could do, as together they secreted themselves for what seemed endless marks. While we waited, we cleaned and sharpened not only our own weapons, but several others as well.

'Twas in the dark of pre-dawn when finally they exited the Lodge and as one, swept up and away toward the rocky ledges near the horizon. Their flight pattern, and the ease with which they'd arrived and departed, made me wary. Drekinn was easily defensible from any ground attack, but what would happen if the attack came from above? The village was built entirely upon a raised, plateau-like outgrowth extending from the Great Plains into the Sea of Dreams, in the Midwest part of the land mass of Kadoor, leaving us more than half surrounded with shoreline. Along the northwest and western face was sheer cliff wall riddled with caves, providing perilous purchase for attack from without. Port O'Drekinn was situated at the southern edge within Drekinn Sound, and the barrier reef kept the traffic well controlled. For several marks ride to the south, east and north, farmland gave way to grassy plains, and rocky steppes gave way to rolling hill country. The landscape transitioned to Byndynn Forest and then the mountains known as the Raptor's Talons beyond in the north and east, and to several forested areas, afore the mountains to the south, giving an approaching enemy force no cover close enough to surprise the Clan. The foothills in the distance in all directions were full of caves, ledges, canyons and rivers. The Razor's Edge to the south bordered the Ocean of Fears along the Southern Slippes and surrounded King's Gate Village, wherein stood Evanntyr Castle.

I couldn't see the Ancients clearly from this distance, but I knew they gathered on the ledges o'er which they'd so recently arrived. 'Twas ominous they'd not simply returned from whence they came. Soon enough, the now disheveled Seer returned, and beckoned us to follow him home.

Kallyr was dazed and weak. Considering he and Shayla, the Clan Healer, our 'adopted' parents, we'd spent enough time together to be familiar with his position, and understood what he'd endured. Since Aalanna had mysteriously disappeared and was subsequently presumed dead shortly after birthing Storrm, they'd taken us into their home and their hearts. Ensuring our education went above and beyond what was otherwise offered, 'twas equal to that of either of their professions. A Seer was born to the Sight and usually the Gift would manifest itself within the bloodlines, however Kallyr and Shayla had no children of their own. Sometimes the Gift appeared randomly, and when a child showed signs of such, they were publicly offered by the local Clan to be Claimed by any who might have need. None had ever been without at least one Seer, and near a decade past, Kallyr had a Vision leading them to Walkyr, the youngest son of an Outlander, whom they'd Claimed at his weaning. Although he'd only seen six winters now, the boy promised to be one of the most Gifted Seers of all time.

I went to the fireplace to draw a mug of soup, kept warm in an iron kettle near the fire. Kallyr sat in his ladder back chair, and with shaking hands, he took what I offered. As he sipped, using his fingers to dip out bits of meat and root stock, we waited respectfully to hear his account of the historic meeting.

Sitting at his feet on the wide stone hearth, he slowly began to tell us what had transpired. Shayla listened intently, leaning against the doorframe of their bedroom to one side of the fireplace. Walkyr was supposedly sleeping in his tiny cot in the back room, but somehow I felt he was paying attention as well.

In a slightly trembling voice, Kallyr began. "Five days ago I received a most disturbing Directed Sight from the Highland Dragon Ancients. They haven't Spoken to Man in so long that this initial communication was pictorial. In point of fact, I'd never connected with them in my span of days. Of course I relayed it immediately to your father."

In most Clans the Leader was chosen or elected, but being a War Clan, the Battle Commander was considered Leader as well as running the Warrior Training Program, and thus had the most decisive powers. Next in line were the Clan Elders, a group of the eldest and wisest of the citizens (usually retired Warriors) who assisted the Battle Commander as needed.

The Warriors of the Dragon Clan were the world's peacekeepers. We'd always prepared for War, had always been a War Clan. From time immemorial we'd studied and trained, and although there hadn't been a major war since the Last Holocaust, we knew the time would come and we stood proud and ready. There were those who doubted us, but none who could best us.

Kallyr sighed as his strength began to return from what little sustenance he'd managed to consume, and clearing his throat he continued. "This communication led to many others, all of them more and more frantic. They pleaded for audience with the Battle Commander and the Elders. They Spoke of a terrible danger that would affect us all."

I tried to imagine to what 'terrible danger' they could be referring. We'd always fought for what was good and right. Most Warriors were employed by the King in his Forces, either at Evanntyr Castle, or deployed throughout Kadoor. Surely we would've heard about any opposition, being considered the hub for all such information. I racked my memory for anything recently reported that might be pertinent. The only notable exception to the normal routine was that we'd not heard from many outlying villages in the last few moons. Not necessarily unusual, but given this new information, I began to extrapolate.

Kallyr continued, stronger as he gained his second wind. "The Ancients told of one of their own, whom they dared not even name, for fear of his gaining more power through so doing. Known as The Black Dragon, an evil 'bad seed', he's been wreaking havoc and their very existence is now threatened." He gazed into my eyes and seeing the questioning look upon my face he asked, "How is this Man's problem, you may wonder?"

"You misread me Kallyr, I merely gather the facts." Allowing my 'intuition' to guide me, I continued, "'Tis no question this is our problem. Even I know that the Evil a creature like The Black represents, won't be satisfied with decimating his own Race. He'll also target Mankind. 'Twouldn't be long afore the extinction of the Dragons would be ensured, and when that happens, we are doomed." His expression changed from uncertainty to pride, as he took in my calm assessment of the situation.

"Your battle logic is as always impressive my child. Continue, please."

Glancing at Storrm, I was bolstered by her conspiratorial wink. "They're more powerful than Man, but if our intelligence is correct, there are far fewer Dragons, since they don't procreate as quickly. Even so, as much as I pride my fighting skills, there'd be no contest against this 'Evil One' without their assistance and we'd be inundated despite our best efforts. Another very important point is that they're omnivores, their hunt including damn near anything organic, but there's been no history of them including Man in their diet. I believe they're indicating The Black has crossed that line. If 'tis truth, we'd provide them little more entertainment than the herd beasts in the fields and would be hard pressed to avoid extinction ourselves."

I paused, waiting impatiently for him to confirm I was on the right track. A barely noticeable nod was my cue to conclude my summary. "It takes a Dragon to fight a Dragon, but that would leave them evenly matched and given the current circumstances, 'tis apparently not good enough. Nevertheless, they wouldn't have come to us, if they didn't have a plan."

"Yes, they have a plan, if you want to call it that." He sighed, and the fact that he didn't confirm or deny The Black's current menu, spoke louder than his next words. "You're aware we're the only Clan in all of Kadoor who knows for certain of the existence of the Dragons. 'Twas a'purpose, since the Last Holocaust, to keep both our Races safe. And to keep their secrets the Dragon Clan has signed binding treaties in blood. Now they offer a scheme they feel is their only chance at survival, as well as ours. Their decision to approach us was twofold. We know of them and we know of War."

Kallyr set his half full mug of soup upon the stone. His deep sigh broke through the quiet of our anticipation as we watched his face. "You are correct, Darque. They're in dire straits. Since the Last Holocaust, their numbers have decreased dramatically, due to several factors. Recently The Black has decreased those numbers further, for which they have just concern, and they fear spillover to Mankind. In point of fact, according to your father's sources, this spillover has already begun."

His words made me shiver. Pausing, he met my eyes and continued, carefully phrasing his thoughts. "They're near desperate for us to join with them, proposing age-old Magic to create a 'LifeBond' 'tween a Dragon and a Warrior. Through the millennia the Dragons drifted apart, living solitary lives, coming together rarely and then only to mate. Without any natural predators and with near immortality, they've lost their fighting edge. With the LifeBond they will gain our human stubbornness, our will to live and fight for what we believe, what we call 'gut instinct'," and suddenly I felt self-conscious as he stared at me, acknowledging my Gift of insight afore he continued, "as well as our breeding and training. For the Warriors, the 'Bond will enhance reflexes, strength and speed. The degree and type of Gifts so imparted will vary, however 'twill also provide near immortality. Sharing their accelerated Healing will allow you to survive most any injury, with exception of the complete loss of your head or heart. These would be fatal injuries even a Dragon couldn't survive, and therefore neither would you."

During his narrative, I'd actually sucked in my breath and realizing I was still holding it, I sat up straighter and sputtered, "But their lifespan is measured in eternity, while we can only expect mayhap forty or fifty winters as a Warrior..." at which point Storrm chimed in and waving her hand o'er my shoulder she interrupted, "Depending on how good we are," as I continued, "...with an additional fifty to teach and or procreate," while Storrm added, with an impish smirk, "The reward for being good!"

Kallyr grinned at her antics despite the gravity of the situation being discussed. "Yes, you are correct. 'Twas revealed they must abandon their immortality in order to balance the difference in life span, still, the 'Bond will match your span of days, giving you the potential to live for centuries. So, you can still be forced Past the Veil, or eventually you will 'wear out' as you age, similar but much slower, to how our bodies age now."

Kallyr regained his serious countenance. "And that brings me to one final issue. If you survive the Magic that is Brewed that night, and if you succeed in making the 'Bond, you'll be tied to each other, Dragon and Man, for the entire span of your days. When one reaches their Final Sleep, so will the other; if one is killed in battle, so the other will also Pass."

My excitement was tempered only slightly by these revelations. "'Tis honorable. They've chosen to make this attempt, knowing if they fail, we all die. And either way, 'twill greatly shorten their own life spans." At this point Kallyr could no longer look me in the eye and gave another barely noticeable nod. Tears began to slide down his cheeks and he wiped them away without a word.

'Twas obviously not an easy decision for the Highland Dragons and 'twas deserving of great respect. Together we would fight Evil, together we would stand or fall, and regardless of the outcome, together we would be, in life and death. There'd be no backing out or changing our minds once we took the 'Bond. This was forever. A frightening thought for the average child of seventeen winters, but I was not average. I was a Warrior. In Kadoor, there was nothing more to say. Still, I knew what Kallyr was thinking. 'Twas as clear to my senses as if he'd said it aloud. Storrm and I would be first in line to make this outrageous attempt and added to all the stress and strain and gloom and doom of this day, he believed he was losing his own daughters.

His exhaustion was palpable and we stood to take our leave. Gently I said, "I know you have much more to tell us but you need time to rest. Your Gift this night has taken a heavy toll. 'Tis late, get some sleep. We'll do the same and return in the morning." Hugging him, we then left for the Barracks, although I seriously doubted we would get any sleep.

<center>~~~ LESS THAN A MARK LATER ~~~</center>

We'd returned quickly, but spent much time combing our Horses' long manes, tails and forelocks. Thinking to enjoy the pre-dawn silence, we sat for barely a moment afore we heard the clamor of a runaway horse charging headlong up the trail nearby. Capturing the frightened animal, we discovered he was carrying an incredibly filthy, and quite dead, Runner. "Flame it all, he's Passed the Veil," I spat in frustration. Together we managed to settle the beast as we untangled what was left of the reins from around its front legs. Obviously the Runner had lost them some time ago and did not, or could not, stop to collect them. We had to break the boy's fingers to loosen his snarled grasp in the short, thick mane. His body was so covered with dried blood we couldn't determine the extent of his injuries. The tattoo upon his shoulder confirmed he was a Runner for Kaddart, a small and very distant farming village, although only a Warrior would know this rank system. Searching his bag, we found no Report to provide the reason for his Run, no food or water, which bwas very odd, and no clothing changes or camp gear at all, which was even stranger. No one left without supplies for such a long Run. Mayhap he hadn't planned on this destination? No, a Runner's horse is trained to travel where his rider directs him, despite being frightened. "'Tis apparent the boy meant to arrive here, but the Run was not planned. Mayhap he was fighting or being chased…" and glancing at Storrm with a look that told her we'd have to change the way we thought about everything since the return of the Dragons, I continued, "…or hunted. We need Shayla to tell us his true injuries."

~~~~~~~~~~

She was cooking breakfast when we arrived. Stepping into the pre-dawn light as soon as she heard three horses riding in, the boy strapped o'er his own, she directed us to the examination table in the back, where she practiced her medicinal arts. There we placed him and it didn't take long for her to confirm what I'd already determined. "He is of Kaddart, a Runner, as I am sure you've already noted by his tattoos." I tried not to appear surprised; Shayla's knowledge seemed infinite at times. Standing up and wiping her hands upon her apron, her gaze bored into mine. "Now for what you came here to learn. I knew this boy, he was called Tonn. I believe he Passed within the last few marks. He has multiple wounds consistent with battle injuries, and some clearly inflicted by methods of torture." The disgust on her face was evident, and the fear she tried to hide, transparent. "All of these are healed, mayhap within the last moon. It appears he was starved and beaten sometime in the last few moons as well. Then there are some unhealed injuries, a fortnight at most. Knowing how far away Kaddart is, I am led to believe he received them about the same time he left for this Run." She turned back to the table.

Aloud, I summarized this information. "'Twould appear he was taken captive, tortured, wounded again during his escape and managed to flee."

"Yes, 'twould appear so." The Healer considered her words. "There's more. You should know this afore anyone else gets wind of it. Although he is severely malnourished, death was due to lung damage, loss of blood and dehydration, all caused by burns. But these aren't ordinary burns. They're not from exposure to a normal fire, from field or forge. These burns reek of Flame."

"You believe they were inflicted by a Dragon?" And although I'd suspected this, I couldn't help but wonder how Shayla would know Flame wounds when she saw them.

"Yes Darque, that's exactly what I'm saying. Do you know any other creature who hunts with Flame? Girls, I know what happened last night, but you're missing a piece of this puzzle. What you don't know are Walkyr's Visions. I don't trust the Ancients. Why can they not rein in their own Kind? Mayhap they're in league with The Black." Her voice had grown softer 'til she barely whispered. Was she afraid of being heard?
~~~~~~~~~~

Here in her home, with no one around? What, or whom, would she so fear?

Shayla shook off the uncharacteristic mood and told us Kallyr was already with our father. Vaulting onto our horses, we steered the massive beasts back to the Barracks to report to the Battle Commander all that had happened this morning. He was a brilliant strategist and he'd fully understand these events. We might even pick up some new details. I could sense my destiny rising, could almost taste it. As was my habit when excited, my fingers strayed to the scar. I couldn't feel it through my leathers but it calmed me to acknowledge its presence.

The Ancients had given us a mere few marks to make our decision. Tonn's death, mystery though 'twas, would be a turning point.

~~~~~~~~~~~

"Come, Warrior. Tell me what you know," my father said, as I barged into his office. Sitting behind his heavy oak desk, I noted Kallyr in the chair 'cross from him.

"I know little, and much." Pointedly, I turned my gaze to the Seer as I continued. "I know Kallyr managed to miss us as we were in route to his home, seeking the Healer." Wincing slightly, I sounded suspicious to my own ears, but I couldn't help wondering, and details could make or break a battle. I was nothing if not detail oriented and besides, 'twas protocol for the Battle Commander to confirm 'twas safe to report with someone else present.

Clearing his throat, Kallyr stated, "I didn't go to sleep after you left. The Commander sent a message to meet him at the Lodge. We spoke briefly with the eldest of the Ancients and then we rode here. We just arrived afore you." Thankfully, he wasn't offended by my suspicions. He knew me well.

Stepping forward I made my report, relating all that had happened from the time we'd departed the Seer, to the time we arrived at this office. It didn't take long. I was thorough, yet succinct. My transition to Battle Mode was flawless and I was rewarded to note the corners of Grifynn's mouth turned up slightly. Facing Kallyr he barked, "Gather the Elders. Call the Dragons. We meet at the Lodge in one mark." Hardening his expression, he turned to his daughters and said simply, "We take this offer of the Dragon Ancients, I send forth a Call for Warriors by dusk. Do you answer that Call?"

Without hesitation, nor even a glance in the others' direction, we exclaimed in one voice, "Yes!"
~~~~~~~~~~~

THE BLACK WAR BEGINS

<div align="center">~~~~~~~~~~</div>

Once our respective Elders finalized the agreement, the Call was cast. The Commander chose to field fifty fighting men and women of the Brotherhood, eliminating to a chosen thirteen, the number the Ancients requested for the ceremony. Afore the day was done we began the process leading to our attempt to 'Bond with the first batch of thirteen Highland Dragons. There'd be more flying in from various points hither and yon but there was no guarantee they'd be available in time for the ceremony, as we learned they were already engaged elsewhere against The Black. My gut churned at the obvious implications.

The winter solstice was deemed necessary to provide the best chance to succeed. Since a LifeBond hadn't been accomplished in these Ancients' span of days, they'd be working from their Memories, and therefore no one knew if we'd make the 'Bond or even survive. Theoretically, they could perform the ceremony on any night but neither side was willing to take the chance for this initial attempt. We'd all be stumbling in the darkness and we needed every advantage we could muster. The first to take the 'Bond would also shoulder the greatest risk and I intended that position to be mine. From my experience the following Dragons would gain insight, and I felt 'twas my duty to my fellow Warriors.

We didn't want to lose anyone Beyond, but more importantly, we needed as many Teams as we could create, as quickly as possible. The Black was gaining momentum and his minions were joining him from around the world. Travelers and merchants from distant villages brought tales with increasing frequency of some atrocity or other and it made my blood boil. I was hungry to engage, but I was a strategist like my father. I knew the odds were against us unless we succeeded with our plan. I held my tongue and tried to be patient, taking out my aggravation in the trials to ensure my place.

<div align="center">~~~~~~~~~~</div>

O'er the next fortnight we fought for the right to join with Dragonkind. Our physical and emotional strength was stretched to the limit as we battled our own in the Training Pits. 'Twas too dangerous to hold these trials in the field as the Black's rising tide of terrorism was creeping ever closer. All available Warriors had set out, their mission to locate the Hoard lair, learning his minions were loosely gathered and mostly untrained. Our strategy focused on diversionary hit and run tactics to prevent them from knowing what we were doing as well as to keep them away from our ancestral lands. The War had already begun, even though 'twas undeclared, and we were literally in the line of fire. Clearly, 'twas only a matter of time afore all of Kadoor knew The Black had returned.

While we were battling, our people were preparing for siege. Every Clansman pitched in, male and female, old and young. Our single goal was survival, and no complaints were heard, only shouted directions amidst the soft roar of hundreds working together. As the fifty dwindled, each of those eliminated added to the recognizance efforts in the field, or to help with the siege preparations. There was much to do; doubling our supplies, preserving and stockpiling food stuffs, water (the Well had never failed but there was always a chance it could be fouled), preparing herbs for medications, curing leathers, setting perimeter alarms, traps, anything to slow down an enemy force if they chose to besiege the Den. Although no one believed 'twould happen, we did expect to have 'guests' from other regions, refugees to care for and protect, and we'd be ready. Silas's forge within the Den began to operate under siege conditions, with every available blacksmith, Master and Apprentice alike, keeping the fires burning non-stop. The rhythmic pounding and ringing of hammers on anvils throughout the day and night, added their voices to the Battle Drums. Thus providing melodic background to our labors, they turned our contests into a macabre Great Hall dance. Our Warriors were ready for battle at a moment's notice and 'twas amazing we lost not a man through those uncertain days.

My sister and I continued to fight our way through the fifty, the winter solstice rapidly approaching. As the days passed, we gazed 'cross the plains toward the ledges where the Dragons held vigil o'er our efforts. More flew in near daily and I could make out the big Blue, his scales sparkling in the sun, who'd been here since the beginning, speaking with the Elders. The others seemed to hold him in deference but he was obviously not an Ancient and had no noticeable identifying markings. They didn't wear clothing or adornments but I'd noted some intricate scars like tattoos. I couldn't imagine how they'd been able to create them, as from what I knew of the Healing, 'twould be near impossible. The markings reminded me of rank designations but as far as any of us knew, they were a solitary, peaceful Race. Apparently at one time they'd been warlike. Must've been centuries ago, and I wondered if mayhap my Dragon would share their history with me one day.

Of those who first approached us with their daring scheme, the Blue was the only one who would be participating in the ceremony. Catching snippets of their conversations, I ascertained his Elders were quite agitated with that idea. 'Twas a mystery that wouldn't be solved in the immediate future, as Dragon Tongue wasn't decipherable by human ears and they often used a form of telepathy, Speaking to each other through the MindLink rather than speaking aloud. 'Twas obvious they also spoke Common Tongue as I'd understood them when they approached the Clan Elders, but why then had they needed Kallyr to interpret through the Link? 'Twas confusing, but I had no time to ponder this phenomenon while I concentrated on the eliminations.

My sister and I had gone through Warrior Trials early in our lives and were still the youngest. Because of this, we'd not been allowed to deploy or seek employment, as we'd yet to reach our full growth. So, for the last four winters we'd continued to Train with the Elders and other new Warriors at home. We were good. We were very good. But we were still untried in actual battle. We were twelve and thirteen when we joined the Brotherhood, now of age at sixteen and seventeen. The Battle Name bestowed upon me when I took the Oath was The Dragon, after the mighty Dragons that our Clan always knew existed. Mayhap 'twas ironic, but under the current circumstances, I held this name as a good omen. My sister's Battle Name was The Morrigan, after the ancient goddess of Fate, War and Death. The goddess was characterized by ravens, and during the trials we'd been blessed to see a raven daily. He'd sit on the wall watching us, or fly high above the Pits. Whenever we looked, he was there and he'd turn to gaze at us as if he could Hear our thoughts. It became so obvious even Shayla remarked about it, and once we heard her talking to him in the hallway, calling him 'Corbyn'. Even though 'twas unnerving at times, the raven was another good omen.

~~~~~~~~~~

We'd survived, our time had finally come. We now stood afore the Elders on sacred ground, the Magical fire dancing brightly toward the stars glittering in the clear skies above. Naked as the day we were born, we were unashamed. Velvet o'er steel, we were well muscled from daily training and just plain hard work, yet there was no mistaking our gender. My youthful breasts were high and firm but they'd become more than a handful as I'd passed through puberty and when I fought I kept them tied flat to my chest with a width of leather, which I wore even under my tunic. My sister and I were graced with the fair coloring of most of the Dragon Clan, with shocking blue eyes and thick, flaming red hair. The only truly remarkable characteristic I had was my lack of height and everyone, including my younger sister, towered o'er me. When I was a child, Kallyr claimed 'twas a blessing and insisted 'twould make me a better fighter. He'd even revealed he'd Seen
~~~~~~~~~~

one day 'twould save my life. Mayhap I'd realize the truth of that Vision afore I leave this world.

'Twas the winter solstice, the night the Dragon Elders would bring forth their ancient Magic to Brew the LifeBond. Two become one in a powerful ritual entwining our Life Forces, one beating heart tying us together for the rest of our days. By now no one doubted 'twas the only way to defeat the Evil One and his Hoard, but I also knew the War wouldn't end with The Black's demise. Evil was loose again and although it could be lorded o'er at times, 'twould never be completely eradicated. Warriors would always be needed on Kadoor.

At this point, my reverie of the past met the present. After fighting so hard, I wouldn't foul my chance to achieve a full, live 'Bond with a real Dragon by not managing a little pain. I stared as the Elder made the cut with a skilled flick of his wrist and my Life Source spurt forth to run down my leg and 'cross my foot, soaking into the coarse sand upon which we stood. My Blood Call released in a burst from deep inside and I watched in stunned amazement as it plunged into the blaze. As if I could actually see the powerful notes of the Song of the Call dancing through the air, it rippled and undulated its way from the fire toward the line of Dragons waiting expectantly upon the far ledges. It fanned out and softly covered them like a mantle of sparkling mist. So quickly I could scarcely believe my eyes, it lifted from each of the beasts, ebbing and flowing as if alive to gather itself to just one. 'Twas the Blue, the biggest and baddest of them all, now enveloped in a mist of my internal being. Roaring in acknowledgement, he rose off his haunches to his towering roof top height, spread his wings to a span that more than doubled his length, took a single step, and launched himself off the ledge. The Call vanished like the mist o'er the ocean when kissed by the sun and I locked eyes with him 'cross the red and gold flames as he flew directly at me. Stepping forward afore I even knew what I was doing, I had to brace myself against the rush of wind from the back-beat of his great wings. Then he thrust his forepaw deep into the flames licking higher and brighter, reaching a hundred arms to the sky.

Compelled to respond, my right hand lifted of its own accord, and grasping forearm to forearm, he yanked me into the inferno. Surprisingly, I felt no more than a slight warmth, I heard naught, and even with my eyes wide open, we were surrounded by a void of nothingness. The beast's sharp talons pierced my skin as he struggled to drag me to the other side of the fire. 'Twas as if he were pulling me through mud against an opposing force. Instinctively I recognized if either of us lost our grip, 'twould be the end. I prayed he wouldn't rip my arm off entirely, as I did everything I could to help him win this tug of war.

Somehow, layered o'er the reality of the struggle to pull me through the flames, came another, slower, gentler reality, as if I existed in two places at the same time. Accepting that on some level I was fighting to keep my arm attached to my body while the Dragon was tugging as hard as he could, I focused upon this new level, leaving the other behind me for the moment.

Now came a Voice rushing ever closer, 'til the roaring in my ears was so loud, I feared for my sanity. 'Twas Dragon Tongue and as a delicious tingling sensation swept through my body, I understood every word. *"You are the one, the answer, so beautiful... and now, you are MINE."* The tingling grew, and 'twas warm and wet, and I became conscious 'twas the Blue licking the blood from my body. His incredibly agile tongue encircled my arm, moved 'cross my ribs, my hips and o'er my flat belly. With long, erotic strokes he lapped downward 'tween my thighs. Gasping slightly as he nudged me to shift my weight, I widened my stance while he lingered there for the span of one long breath. With his powerful tongue, he lifted me up by my leg, pulled me closer and continued his sensual exploration. Licking the back of my knee gently afore moving downward, I wasn't certain I was still breathing by the time he'd completed his task. Melting against him, 'twas not the heat of the fire that surrounded me, 'twas the skin of the beast, as his wings wrapped my bare body tightly against leathery scale with the intimacy of a lover. Skin to skin, his powerful Magic permeated my very essence, changing me forever.

Time seemed to have no meaning within the flames, but 'twas in reality a mere few breaths afore I was jerked clear. With the ritual raging on in the distance, I was now standing with my bare feet on the cold stone of a rocky ledge, silent and alone but for the Dragon in front of me. Although fully aware of the dual roles I'd so recently played, 'twas abruptly insignificant. The pain in my thigh had vanished, the slash completely healed, and the remaining scar had returned to its former appearance. Quickly performing field triage, I was amazingly free of bruises, burns or talon scratches, and vanity preserve me, not a single red hair on my head was even singed.

Glancing up, my attention riveted upon the Blue, with his massive tail curled around his feet, his great wings folded and laid tightly against his flanks, and I was suddenly beset by the fact that I knew little about him. Staring into his bejeweled eyes I heard his Voice again, just as during our struggles. My brow furrowed trying to recall yet another time, deep in my past, but I couldn't draw the memory. Entranced mayhap, I listened to the beautiful language as he Spoke to me and I Heard him in my mind. I saw his speech as if reading a parchment, I felt it in my soul. I sensed his emotions, his desires, his anxiety. No wait, I thought as I shook my head. Those were my emotions, my desires, my anxieties. Weren't they? 'Twas confusing, and my head began to swim. With little warning I was ashamed, I was mortified, I was sick. Everything began moving in circles as I collapsed to my knees. By all the fires of Hades, my head was going to explode. Holding onto the hard flat surface, I fell in slow motion to my side but the spinning didn't stop. Finally I managed to roll onto my back, spread eagled upon the cold stone in front of the cave, trying not to fall off the pitching ledge. I'd imbibed heavily in mead afore but that sensation held no comparison. Holding my breath, as breathing seemed to make things worse, I realized my eyes were closed and considered trying to carefully open them. Mayhap one at a time, I thought. I didn't like being naked of both leathers and weapons, leaving me totally exposed, with a stranger snuffling me. My head jerked and my eyes popped open when I felt puffs of air blow softly 'cross my belly. The beast was so close I could only see one of his beautiful eyes as he leaned o'er me, making his examination. His nostrils flared, his breath warmed, but 'twas somehow soothing. The ledge became still and solid once more while he licked my eyelids with the tip of his sensitive tongue. By the 7th Egg, I thought I'd survived this night! Was I to be eaten now? Surely this wasn't all a trick for a midnight snack?

"Better you are? I grieve you suffered so for my ignorance." Through telepathy his words seemed crisply formal. What had happened to the sensuality? Knowing he understood my thoughts made me blush as I recalled my blatant sexual response in the fire. Mercifully, he didn't increase my discomfort or confusion and simply continued aloud, "Stay here, I'll return soon. We've much to discuss." And with these cryptic instructions he spun his massive bulk, spread his great wings, and dropped off the rocky ledge to sail swiftly toward the Dragon Ancients at the Magic fire, where the ceremony continued into the night. I barely had time to register these events, a multitude of unfamiliar emotions all clamoring in my mind for my immediate attention, afore I lost consciousness.

CHAPTER 2

The Raven's Curse

PRIOR TO THE LIFEBOND CEREMONY, DURING THE TRIALS

"Who is it? Who did you come for?" Shayla near spat her questions as she blustered through the Great Hallway surrounding the Training Pits, following the flight of the Raven. After losing him briefly, she spotted the iridescent gleam of his black feathers where he perched upon an elaborate silver candle sconce providing the only light within a tucked away alcove along the far wall. Breathlessly she approached, praying to the One True Liege that he wouldn't take wing again, and looking deeply into the beady black eyes of the bird she exclaimed, "You must tell me, Corbyn." Her apprehension was evident but she maintained eye contact.

Days past, when she'd first spotted him flying above the Pits, she'd made every attempt to gain his attention. She knew that bird was Corbyn, why had he ignored her? There was no mistaking the Power emanating from him, it practically made her skin crawl with his proximity. 'Twas as if she was about to be struck by lightning. To her senses, he literally reeked of Magic.

Corbyn knew she'd recognized him. 'Twas not that difficult, given her unusual talents. Even so, he'd done his best to delay as long as possible. Finally he'd been forced to acknowledge her, in order to avoid a potentially awkward scene. Moments ago, he'd diverted his observation flight and made his way in here, to face the admission he knew he could no longer evade. Why did he indulge these humans so?

'Twas even more awkward when he sighted the Warrior sisters walking toward them in this very hallway. Admiring their beauty, having observed first hand their battle skills, he actually felt some regret that he'd not returned to see how they'd fared, since that night nearly ten winters past. As usual he'd been occupied and besides, his presence might have brought the Evil One sooner. 'Twas no matter, they lived and thrived. They'd not heard all of Shayla's words and they wouldn't remember him, but he chastised the Healer, his Voice deep and commanding, *"And you must lower your voice. They heard you call my name."* With resignation, The Raven hastened to perform damage control and Pushed the sisters to move away, none the wiser to what had taken place in this alcove. Immediately, he'd felt something odd. He could've sworn by the 7th Egg that Darque had actually Pushed back. Casting his senses, he realized the young Warrior wasn't even aware she'd done this, however, the ability was out of the ordinary for Man, making him even more certain she was the one for whom they'd all hoped. He tucked away the knowledge of her blossoming talents, for she was not his present concern and his time was limited. Still, he thought, her Gifts were growing, although untrained, and mayhap she wasn't aware of any of them. Pondering this further, he longed to See her destiny rising but 'twould have to wait, and shaking his head to clear his mind, he returned to the present. *"They will fear for your sanity soon, thinking you're talking to an ordinary bird, and I wasn't planning on doing that type of work this trip."*

Corbyn's mood had lightened. Was he ever serious for any length of time? Shayla knew much about The Raven but there was much she didn't know. And she wasn't certain if she could trust him but she didn't want to alienate this one, he was far too powerful. There was no telling what he could or would do under stress and although she'd not felt a lack of commitment to their alliance, she knew not his true fealty. No, pushing him too far would never do, but still, he was here early and that meant only one thing. He was not here for them. "Forgive me, m'lord Corbyn. 'Twas just such a shock to see you again this soon. Not that I don't want to, or that I don't appreciate what you've done and continue to do for us, but…." Shayla trailed off as she tried to gather her scattering wits.

"'Tis not like you to grovel, stop. You know why I'm here. And I'm sure you've guessed for whom I've come. I have no choice." Corbyn added the last statement stoically, without blinking his gleaming ebony eyes.

Ignoring the rebuke, she continued, "Could she not have sent you for another? Could you not be mistaken?" She desperately tried to uncover some loop hole within the Curse she was aware he endured.

In a Voice that would've commanded attention from those within the chaos of the Fade, Corbyn stated firmly, *"Do not make this any more difficult than 'tis already. You know I must Serve. She has sent me here, to this time, for this Warrior. 'Twas ever thus and cannot change."* Nodding his feathered head, he preened his left wing as he waited tolerantly for her next question. 'Twas not a game he played, but 'twould seem he was as reluctant to name this one, as she was to hear her so named.

Shayla couldn't hold back, she needed confirmation. "Who is it this time? Who did she send you to Serve?" Fighting back the tears, her voice trembled as she glanced o'er her shoulder nervously to ensure they'd not gained a new audience.

Corbyn lowered his Voice and stated with astonishing empathy for one of a Race notorious for a lack of feeling, *"I will keep her alive as long as possible."*

He hesitated once more. The tears in Shayla's eyes spilled as the sun dawned upon her and she sputtered, still trying to negotiate the Curse. "But she's so young, this cannot be. She's not really a Warrior; she's never even been in a true battle!" Then anger took her and she hissed, "The Morrigan must be wrong this time. She couldn't have sent you to Serve a child!"

The silence that followed was unnerving. For what seemed like ages, Shayla fought to calm herself. The Raven continued to stare at her, seemingly devoid of emotion once more, his grooming complete. Finally, her heart still racing, she respectfully asked to hear the name that in her heart, she already knew.

"Storrm." Speaking succinctly, leaving Shayla shaking with emotion, The Raven took flight, returning to the Pits to keep vigil o'er his latest charge. He began the cycle of his curse once again. How long this time, he wondered?

CHAPTER 3

Taking the Link

MORNING AFTER THE 'BOND

"The Ancients called you Gunnarr. I heard some of them speaking with the Elders when you first arrived." Something about that conversation still didn't sit well, but I shook off the peculiar impression. I was quickly learning to bank my questions like a fire amongst a growing pile of coals, for later stirring. 'Twas not enough time to do otherwise. Receiving no response, I stepped closer and peered into his eyes. "I am called Darque, by family and those few who know me well." Once more I hesitated in this monologue. Gunnarr didn't appear to be paying any attention to me whatsoever and a bit miffed at his apparent lack of interest, I briefly pondered the concept that mayhap this was how Dragons slept. His eyes looked open but he hadn't so much as twitched since I'd been standing here and he didn't seem to be attentive on anything in particular. His incredibly beautiful, crystalline blue eyes, were currently glazed and unfocused. Those eyes… drew me like a moth to the torch. Like a statue frozen in time, he sat 'cross the ledge from where I remembered losing my mind and my dignity last night. Cautiously I stepped closer. I'd awakened beside a small pile of glowing coals, a blanket spread o'er my legs as if casually dropped, with the most delicious, mouth watering aroma wafting through the air. 'Twas surprising, I'd never afore slept this late. The sun was already breaking o'er the horizon and the early winter chill made the air crisp. Still naked, I'd wrapped the blanket around me and now stood staring at 'my' Dragon. The scent of cinnamon reminded me why I'd awakened and sniffing the air with growing excitement, I sought out the tantalizing aroma. Since early childhood I'd been drinking the hot, black, bitter liquid, and the addition of cinnamon had always been my personal favorite. Better to be honest with myself, I didn't just like kaafy, I lived for it. Grumpy if I missed out, 'twas scarce to a Warrior, and it had been awhile since my last mug. Where had it come from, I wondered? And just who had made it? And since I was asking, what the Flame had happened last night after I'd lost consciousness? Admitting to that, I grimaced, shaking my shoulders in repugnance. Trying to move beyond that distasteful reminder, I returned to wondering who'd made the fire. No, that was an easy one, since Dragons breathed fire. They could literally walk through it, if they protected certain parts of their anatomy, like their eyes and leathery wings, being two of their most vulnerable. But breathing fire wasn't their only talent. Consider Flame, a Magical substance Brewed in one of their guts and exhaled within their fiery breath.

For all of their massive bulk and animalistic appearance, Dragons were a sentient Race. As a Warrior, I'd been privy to all known intelligence on the other sentients of Kadoor. That would be Mankind and Dragonkind, at least as far as we'd been told. Storrm and I knew there were others, but we'd yet to prove their existence. We saw, felt and heard things in our youth we'd never dared tell anyone, not even our father.

But, back to the intelligence on Dragons; Man really knew very little and I remembered our Trainers as they'd recited to us by rote. We'd glanced at each other out of the corners of our eyes and tried not to smirk, as that would most definitely get our butts tossed into the scullery for days of hard labor. All summed up, we knew more than they, but not being in a position to reveal how we'd obtained our knowledge, we'd wisely kept our mouths shut. "Dragons are Magic Bearers. They breathe fire and Brew Flame. They Heal quickly and are near impossible to kill. They live apart from each other, rarely coming together, reclusive even within their own Race. They stake huge territories for hunting, they have no known predators, and their span of days measures to eternity." This last had always been a mystery. If they lived forever, did they not procreate? And if they did, how often, and how many were born? From Legend Song we knew they hatched from eggs, but how did that happen anyway? No one had ever seen Dragon eggs, or a Dragon mating afore. 'Twas obvious they were of different ages, surely they hadn't just stopped. And forgive me my skepticism, but after an eternity of living on the whole of Kadoor together, we didn't have more information than this? Something was just not right.

"DARK? YOU ARE NAMED FOR THE TIME WHEN THE SUN IS SLEEPING?" All but leaping out of my skin, Gunnarr's thunderous Voice boomed in my head.

"Stop that, I near pissed myself! How do you do that? I Heard your Voice in my head and 'twas LOUD." Snarling, I leaned forward and pointed my finger at him to emphasize my point. I'd never liked being put on the defensive. I'd always been an offensive fighter.

He cocked his head quizzically. *"Is this better?"*

Prepared for a confrontation, his calm demeanor caught me off guard. My indignation deflated, I sighed, "Much. I still want to know how you do that." Curious as to which one of us would take the Leadership role in this Team, I added almost as an afterthought, "Please."

Gunnarr looked me straight in the eyes without blinking. While I wondered if they even had eyelids to blink with, his stare became glazed again and he fell silent. 'Twas a bit peculiar as well as agitating. My patience was coming up short and 'twas not all that long to begin with, after all, I am my father's daughter. But the Ancients preserve me, I'd even said please. I wanted answers, I wanted to learn to fly, to fight a'Dragonback, and I wanted my weapons. I felt more exposed without them, than I did without my clothes. Give me a sword and I could defend myself. Of course, I didn't even need a sword, as I recalled the long marks spent Training with Elder Warrior Regynn, who taught hand to hand. With the clothing on my back, I could snatch my opponent's hand, or foul his weapon….and so my thoughts wandered as I waited for Gunnarr's attention to return.

"And no," I grumbled, as I was forced to submit to the lengthening wait and turned toward the fire in an attempt to rescue the now burning kaafy. "Not DARK, as in the lack of light there, biggun, DARQUE, as in, 'ancient family name, mighty Warrior of old'. LONG afore the Last Holocaust, for your esteemed information, and by the Dragon's Breath, one would think you'd have more intelligence on Man than this. You could've at least learned our names! But then I wasn't really told yours, now was I?" My rant ended as sarcastically as 'twas begun.

Wrapping the corner of the blanket around my hand, as I could find no other material in sight, I reached into the edge of the fire and grabbed the handle of the kaafy pot. Trying not to set myself ablaze, and with the metal at near Flame heat, I struggled to move it far enough away from the coals to set it down safely, at which time I realized I'd nothing to pour it into. I couldn't drink it straight from the pot without burning the flesh from my lips. By the Ancients, this was absurd! My emotional status was uncharacteristically out of control. My hands fisting, I was about to scream out in frustration when I Heard Gunnarr again. *"Do all Warriors have such short tempers? If not, then mayhap I chose my rider poorly."*

That did it, I was incensed! Spilling the kaafy rushing to gain my full height, every inch of my short, naked frame was bristling. I swirled like a wind devil rising from the desert sands of the Dragon's Breath, and dropped into Battle Stance. Locking eyes with the beast who now stood on all fours and loomed o'er me, I bit my tongue to keep my mouth shut. "I will not ruin this, there's no turning back," I chanted quietly to myself. "I cannot fight with my partner." Knowing for fact that such behavior would return to bite me in the ass, 'twas still a struggle to regain my composure.

Suddenly I felt gut punched, my head was exploding once again and I let out a forced breath. 'Twas as if a floodgate opened within my mind and I slapped my hands firmly o'er my ears, trying to quiet a tumultuous rush of Voices, all Speaking at once. Desperately, I tried to keep my wits about me. With growing dizziness and disorientation, I was down on my knees again to increase my stability, for the second time in less than half a mark. Squeezing my eyes tightly shut, I Saw places I'd never been, Heard Voices I knew not, languages I couldn't begin to decipher. I Felt strange emotions, while new and pungent scents permeated through the chaos. My nerves were raw, my senses inundated as all this flashed simultaneously, and 'twas too much, it must stop!

As nausea began to swamp me, resentment quickly followed. Declaring an end to this onslaught I chanted, "I am a Warrior of the Dragon Clan. No outside source can defeat me. I can only defeat myself." Slowly I sorted through the confusion. Think, breathe, be calm. Rational thought returned to me. Tediously, I pushed the rush of sensations from the forefront of my mind and instinctively Searched for one Voice. I Heard it in the jumble like my father's 'cross the chaos of the Training Pits. 'Twas Gunnarr, and I forced my focus there. Somehow amidst the pain, I knew 'twas a turning point for us as a Team and if I failed this test, I wouldn't get another chance.

"To me, Darque of Man. Hear my Voice and follow. You must Push aside all else." Gunnarr Spoke urgently, encouraging me to fight my way out of this mental maze.

Methodically, I gained upon my prize. Building a massive door in my mind, I managed to entrap the still clamoring multitude of sensations behind it, 'til all I could See and Hear was the big Blue.

The respite provided with the silence was short lived, as with it came suffocation. Discovering I couldn't breathe, I struggled through the depths from the bottom of the Ocean of Fears, pulling and kicking as hard as I could. Rising rapidly, I saw the light above the waves just a little farther o'er my head. With one final kick, I reached out with both hands, broke through to the surface and gasping, I grabbed onto Gunnarr.

Still naked, I was also still dry and standing upon the ledge once again, face to snout with the massive beast, my hands on either side of his muzzle, my lips pressed against the skin 'tween his nostrils, as I stared up his long nose, deep into his glittering eyes. Skin to skin, the Magic tingled throughout my body. His hide was leathery and o'er most of his neck, body, and tail, excepting only his head, a small area on his low belly, and the insides of his massive legs where they joined his torso, his thick skin was covered with scales so hard they were impervious to near every weapon. They sparkled in the sunlight and the multiple shades of blue matched his bejeweled eyes. Up close, I could see he had a double eyelid, the inner one much thinner and more delicate than the leathery outer covering, which would most likely protect them from weapons and fire alike. The inner membranous lid was almost clear, his eyes still visible even when he blinked to moisten them, making it appear they were always open. He could even sleep with just this inner lid closed, and most would be no wiser, however, they were so luminous, they would be like a lighthouse beacon in the dark. He had a single row of viciously sharp teeth along the sides and back, with front fangs longer on the top than on the bottom, the upper set extending slightly past his lower jaw even when clamped tightly shut. His muzzle was long and wide, and tapered gracefully to a small beak in the middle of his top lip, reminding me of the raptors of the forests, though not nearly as prominent. His wide set nostrils had a hard ridge that seemed to roll around and taper up his muzzle, and they flared and smoked slightly with each exhalation. Whether if 'twas from the chill in the air or the distress radiating from his very soul at my near death experience, was uncertain. His huge eyes were set even wider, with hard ridges 'tween and above them like brows, sweeping gracefully upward into short horns. His ears were aside his head, under and slightly behind his eyes, and there was a ruffle of leathery skin that half encircled them, fanning backward.

Caught up in admiring his good looks, I was slightly startled to Hear his hearty exclamation. *"You're quite the stubborn one, my little Warrior."* 'Twas followed by a deep rumbling growl, and with the emotional turmoil abruptly spent, he laughed at me, Saying, *"You will do!"*

"I hope so," I Stated cryptically, then added, *"You will enlighten me as to what just happened, correct? And where are my weapons?"*

"M'lady, you bring tears of laughter to these eyes. I haven't laughed in so very long, but I have cried an ocean of tears. I knew you were the one when you were birthed, and together we cannot fail." Approval was clear, but I was saddened for the truth revealed in his admission.

"Good for us. Weapons?" As still as stone, I hadn't even blinked when I suddenly registered the entire exchange was telepathic. Not only could I Hear Gunnarr, but by the 7th Egg I was now projecting my thoughts to him.

"Your sword and other fighting accoutrements are lacking for one of your station, but they will serve for now. Soon we'll Draw pure Strength from the heavens for you."

Just what had he meant by my 'station'? If not a reference to our 'Bond, was there something else? And to what specifically did 'Draw pure Strength' refer? So many questions to ask, so much to learn.

Gunnarr was full of mischief as he continued, *"You don't seem to mind you are still uncovered. I was under the impression most of Man prefer to be clothed. Are your weapons the only items you wish returned to you, m'lady?"*

His mirth shone brightly, as I acknowledged he was quite correct. Still naked, I hadn't even bothered to reach for the blanket. Recalling the intimate touch of his bare skin to mine, the delicious pressure of his wet tongue 'tween my thighs, I was slightly confused. Was it getting warmer? Loosing my grip upon his snout and stepping back to see more of his massive bulk, I Spoke, *"Very funny, yes, I want my leathers. Are they 'lacking' as well? How long do you expect me to stand here naked while I wait for you to supply me with something more suitable?"* Raising my eyebrows, my hands on my hips, I struck the most serious pose I could, under the circumstances. With heavy fatigue setting in, I saw his eyes darken intensely and begin flashing. He raised his thick brow ridges and cocked his huge head in challenge. His gaze burned leisurely from my long red hair now falling o'er my shoulders, down to the junction 'tween my legs, where his eyes darkened even more and the tip of his great tongue slid out 'tween his lips. After a moment's hesitation there, he drew his tongue back in and his gaze continued downward to the tips of my bare toes. Raising his face to mine with a smirk, he made it clear he knew exactly what I'd just been thinking, and I tried to redirect the conversation to cover my embarrassment. *"And when are you going to supply me with an explanation of what just happened? And while you're at it, how about going o'er what happened last night."* Waving my hand in dismissal, I concluded my run of ideas. *"You can skip o'er the part where I got sick."*

But that very dismissal brought me back to the ceremony and I realized I hadn't even asked about the others. Had everyone survived, had Storrm 'Bonded? How could I forget such important information? We were entering a war, and I was bantering about whether or not I wanted to get dressed. What was wrong with me?

Unexpectedly, Gunnarr tore his gaze away, and as I watched him back up, I felt a dangerous transformation in his attitude. By now 'twas obvious the changes in his eyes meant deepening emotion. Gone was the playful teasing. *"Your people arrive soon, bringing weapons, provisions, leathers. You will dress and eat. I'll not return 'til they leave."*

"But, but, wait! I have more questions!" I Sputtered, to no avail. I couldn't imagine what I'd done to make him angry. Ignoring me, he twisted about, threw his tautly muscled body off the ledge and soared through the mid-morning skies without looking back. As I watched him fade into the eastern horizon, I counted twelve others joining him in flight. All the Warriors were now alone. Wondering why, I glanced toward the plains, catching sight of the clouds of dust from the direction of the village to various points 'cross the steppes. Stunned, I realized my vision was much sharper than possible, and I was clearly seeing at least two or three mark's ride. I knew where I was, and I should just be able to see their dust trails from this distance, but not the War Dogs ranging near and fro, the Warriors riding escort to the wagons following, obviously bringing provisions to all the newly 'Bonded — and was that my father? While I stood there, astounded at my new found visual acuity, I couldn't help but note the supplies packed on the mules following the wagons. Not only had they begun their journey very early this morning, they must think to supply half the Clan!

My enhanced vision had come at a price, and when I tried to return my focus to the ledge where I stood, 'twas blurred, making me queasy. With some effort, the nausea subsided as clarity returned. Obviously a 'Bond benefit, but shifting focus would take practice to achieve proficiency. The challenges were stacking up, but it only fired my spirited nature. I was more confident than ever that I would succeed.

Trying not to think about the food in those packs made me acutely aware of how hungry I was. I spent the time awaiting for their arrival by tending the fire, gathering more fuel, and exploring my present living arrangement. I hadn't eaten anything for the last two nights and the more I tried not to think about it, the more I thought about it, and soon my stomach was growling loudly enough I feared they'd hear it at the Den.

Gunnarr Snorted. *"M'lady, I feel your hunger. I wish you to lack for nothing, but I left these first provisions to your Elders, as I'd not enough knowledge or time to do an adequate listing. Let your people satisfy themselves that you are well, then eat. All your questions can be answered when I return. Whatever you want or need, will be provided, but from this day forward we shall complete your supply runs together, by flight,"* Gunnarr Spoke possessively.

"'Tis well Gunnarr. I'm certain I'll have plenty in my larder. But will you do me one favor?"

His mood lightened with my response and he began to relax. *"Anything for you, m'lady."*

Laughing, I Insisted, *"Please stop calling me that. My name is Darque. No one has ever called me, 'm'lady', and I dare say I do not fancy the title. I am a Warrior, not a lady."*

To which I Received a hearty, *"Yes, m'lady!"* 'Twas followed by robust laughter! At least it seemed like laughter. Apparently even Dragons had a sense of humor, and this one in particular enjoyed teasing. It made me giggle, and the more I thought about it, the funnier it became 'til, doubled down in gales of laughter of my own, tears spilled o'er my cheeks. By the Ancients, when had I lost my mind?

But I didn't have time for more questions, I had supplies to sort and I was still naked. "Dragon dung," I muttered to myself, the first words I'd said aloud since the 'lesson' earlier this morning and it felt awkward. 'Twas strange how the MindSpeak had become so comfortable so quickly. Grabbing the blanket, I wrapped it about me, tying it as best I could. One small field blanket covered my entire torso, but the other Warriors were bigger than I, and since we had the same blanket I knew 'twould barely cover their essentials. Of course, Warriors usually walked about the Barracks half naked anyway, but not in front of the residents of the village. Their certain discomfort made me snicker as I jogged out to meet my people. Finally, I had work to do, something I could understand completely, and 'twould give me purpose. This whole ceremony had given me too much down time. I'd rather be working or fighting, or working at fighting, and I knew my brothers and sisters in arms would feel the same. Soon we'd learn to fight a'Dragonback. Soon we'd be flying.

That brought me to a dead stop in the middle of the trail. My eyebrows rose almost involuntarily. "Flying?" The last time we'd attempted to fly, I'd seen what, seven winters? My little sister in tow, drawn by some sense we'd been given the Power, we fearlessly leaped off the formidable wall surrounding the Training Pits. Landing in the soft sand beneath, miraculously without even a broken bone resulting, we suffered a few minor lacerations that near gave our father a heart attack. As a result, we'd sworn never to 'fly' again.

"Darque!" My father shouted out in joy, and I was astounded as I slipped from one sense of confusion into yet another. He hadn't called me by my given name since I was a toddler. Although he knew every Warrior personally, he held a double standard with his own daughters in his attempt to harden us, and to avoid any outcry of kindred favoritisms. There really was no need, as we were fine Warriors and had earned our right to stand shoulder to shoulder with any in the Brotherhood. Hiding the shock on my face, I ran to Konann, his dappled, dark gray War Stallion.

Expecting to be greeted in standard fashion of linked arms, he rapidly dismounted and yanked me into a bear hug, nearly crushing me in his enthusiasm. 'Twas as if he'd thought never to see me alive again.

"Commander… uh… Commander?" My feet dangling, I could barely breathe, my face smashed against the leather tunic o'er chain mail covering his heavily muscled chest.

"You are well," he said in a more normal tone. Letting go reluctantly, he set me down on my feet in the grass. Inspecting me at arm's length, he searched for non-existent injuries. Not even allowing me time to answer one question afore he asked the next, he near shook me as his voice rose. "You are not injured? You are not in pain? You are not bitten or scratched or burned? Have you been well cared for? Answer afore that big blue one returns. I will hear it in your own voice. Swear you have been forced to no deed, and you are still in your own mind!"

Confused by his manner, I thought 'twas wise of the Dragons to leave us alone, as I tried to reassure him. "Commander, I am well. I have clearer vision than any can claim. I've had little time to explore the benefits, but so far there's nothing bad to report." Searching his face I saw, for the first time in many long seasons, what he truly needed to hear. Quietly I told him, "Father, I know you love me. I love you, too." Blushing slightly, he harrumphed and pushed me away. Then he turned, barking orders to unload.

Loudly enough for everyone to hear, he said, "We brought everything one needs for long perimeter watch duty. 'Twas the only similar circumstance to which I could compare. If you find anything deficient, tell that dragon, and he will get me the information." Then softly for my own ears he said, "I do love you, you know, and your sister. I've always loved you. I feared for your lives last night, while I feared for your loss in mine. I've seen so much loss…." With antiquity draping his muttered words he trailed off, but the puzzling sensation dissipated and he continued, "I suppose now that I find you well, 'tis only the latter that proved truth. I always knew this day would come. You've made me proud." Then in absolute delight, he boldly stated, "Oh, and as I see the question in your eyes, yes, Storrm did 'Bond. She went second to you, taking the second largest Dragon." With a superior twinkle in his eye, he finished, "You took the largest and 'tis rumored these two have very high status with their Kind. All of the Warriors made the 'Bond, and all are well, as far as I've heard. Kallyr and Shayla are with the supply team traveling to Storrm. I will get thee information as soon as I can."

Suddenly my father vanished, leaving the brusque Battle Commander in his wake. "I expect you to report soon. Keep the stealth. Stick to the Code." His face was stern, his long, rich auburn hair was ruffled by the cool breeze, the loose curls blown in all different directions giving him the appearance of a wild animal, and his deep blue eyes betrayed an emotion with which I was unfamiliar.

Emboldened by the events of the past fortnight, and never having been one to keep my mouth shut to spare another's feelings unnecessarily, I stepped up. "Sir, 'tis alarm I sense from you. If you fear something, we need to know." To my knowledge the Commander had never feared anything in his life, certainly not in mine. Having his daughter accuse him of such wouldn't go well. Sadly, I had to admit, the Highlands had my primary fealty now, even though I recognized this notion bordered on treason. Attempting to push him into saying what was obviously on his mind, I spat forth with undisguised sarcasm, "Do you think The Black and his Hoard might be working together with the rest of the Dragons against Man?"

'Twas a barely concealed insult, and the fact that he didn't even flinch was disquieting. I just managed to contain my emotions as he continued. "I think you know the Runner died from Flame. I've sent a Team of Warriors to Kaddart to investigate. I've also sent a Team to Evanntyr." Bordering on rage he hissed forth, "I will know what Dragon killed the boy. Upon whose side do the Highlands stand? I want you to do that for which you've trained all your life! You have one full moon afore their return from the castle. You are a Warrior of the Dragon Clan, you have sworn Oath to fight for Mankind!"

Gooseflesh rose on my arms, and I caught my breath afore he noticed the utter distaste that flowed o'er me like an ocean wave. Had he really just challenged our allies? 'Twas betrayal to them he sought from me. The Oath I took upon entering the Brotherhood was not to 'fight for Mankind', 'twas to maintain the peace, to fight for what is right and good. The rush of emotion was gone almost afore it could be identified. Gunnarr had Heard the entire conversation, and our feelings had combined. Clearly, we had a lot of work ahead of us in order to control the Link, to allow our private and public conversations, and all the emotions layered therein, to carry on simultaneously, none the wiser. And due to another benefit of the LifeBond, I knew my father was wrong about the Highlands. We held no secrets from each other. We each knew the other's entire life, every emotion, every event, every thought. 'Twould take a long time to sort through all of the information; 'twas as if we had a huge new library at our disposal, but even now I knew the Highland Dragons were honest and trustworthy, yet leery of Man's honesty. Truth be told they were right; because we didn't MindSpeak, we kept secrets even from ourselves.

"Gunnarr, I'm concerned about Grifynn sending a Team to Evanntyr. I trust not King Shytin." I Spoke assertively as was my nature, then shifted with less confidence. *"I'm not sure what's happening to me. I Feel misplaced emotions, I See unusual places, I no longer take everything my father says as absolute truth. I question my Oath to the King and to the Dragon Clan. I am ashamed."* Glancing self-consciously to the dirt at my feet, I licked my suddenly dry lips.

"No, Darque. What you're experiencing is simply the backwash of establishing the MindLink. Your emotional control will return as you gain strength in our 'Bond. There's much you don't as yet comprehend. I admit I made a serious tactical error with the plan. I knew not that Man used no overt form of MindSpeak, that your Gifts rose no further than 'instinct'. As soon as I touched you, when you reached out to me through the fire, I realized you'd never Spoken with another. I had much work to do, and quickly, to lessen the trauma when your minds opened to us. I Blocked all incoming Speak, which caused you to be so ill. I was shocked when you couldn't open your thoughts to mine. While needing to Heal you, 'twas my responsibility to inform the Ancients, so appropriate steps could be taken to ease the burden upon the others. Placing you in a deep sleep, I studied the problem and discovered you and Storrm were quite different from the others, although they all had their difficulties learning to Shield. You actually had an innate Link of sorts, unacknowledged and untrained. While teaching you to accept the Link, I had to protect you from the onslaught of foreign sensations and Voices, or lose you o'er the edge of sanity. But your personal strength and stubbornness made you your own worst nightmare. Amazingly, you alone continued to fight the Link long past when the other Warriors managed to accept theirs. I couldn't provide your Shield much longer and in the end I had to force you to create your own. 'Twas not a pleasant experience, I know. You were the test my little one, but you fared well. From now on, we can prepare the human half of the Teams in advance, teaching them what to expect so they don't fight the Link, so they can take it efficiently."

"The Shield being the 'door' I created in my mind?" I Spoke, and received his affirmation. This exchange took place in the blink of an eye. Not only words flashed through my mind, but also the emotion and subsequent full understanding of what was being conveyed. 'Twas an interesting mode of communication and 'twas for me quite exhilarating as

well as fatiguing. Instantly, I understood Gunnarr, that the fatigue would disappear as soon as I became more proficient. But the awesome implications of using this on the battle field didn't slip past me. Gunnarr was pleased.

"I chose my Rider well," he Approved, and stepping away from my father, I directed the unloading of the supplies upon the ledge afore the shallow, low ceilinged cave that was my temporary home. Taking careful stock of how long they'd last, 'twas nothing out of the ordinary, and I wondered how Gunnarr's appetite would be appeased. Locking forearms and pulling in close, I stood upon my tiptoes, my left hand on his bulky shoulder to bid him farewell. Unsure of the next time we might see each other, I whispered this parting advice as my instincts suggested, "Look to Walkyr, keep him close." Then I sent him home, assuring him I'd keep my Oath, even though I was unsure myself. Yes, I was a Warrior of the Clan, but my primary allegiance had shifted. For now, the LifeBond Teams were a solitary fighting force outside of the chain of Command system in which I'd been raised and trained, and I would filter my reports despite his orders. Any sense of betrayal to my people was dampened, knowing my new primary mission was to prevent the annihilation of both our Races. Furthermore, 'twas a given the situation wouldn't sustain itself and we'd soon be working together again. I felt certain my father would approve of my reasoning, although I was not quite so sure the same would be true of the Commander.

CHAPTER 4

Each One Hides One

DAY TWO OF THE 'BOND

"Kallyr, tell me again of your Visions," Grifynn spat with a scowl. He glared at the aging Seer, sitting 'cross from him at his desk. He hadn't liked the tone of voice, the urgency in his daughter's whispered words about Walkyr, and was at a loss as to why she'd made the demand to keep him close. Thinking she meant to convey something ominous, he searched for a clue to decipher her secret message, as she'd never shown such emotion. She must be in trouble, what was he missing? Near sweating as he obsessed o'er the verbal exchange, he made a conscious effort to keep from slamming his meaty fist upon the desk in sheer frustration.

Kallyr took a deep breath, sat slightly forward on the natural leather cushion of the massive wingback armchair, and leaned his elbow against the edge of the desk for added support. "As I have mentioned afore, they were not my Visions, m'lord. They were the Visions of young Walkyr." He was the only person in all of Kadoor, with the exception of his life mate Shayla, who could correct the Commander and get away with said action. Many winters past, he'd been granted a personal Vision and much to his surprise, discovered how she managed to gain the Commander's tolerance. Reluctantly, he chose to keep the knowledge to himself. If they'd wanted such to be public, 'twould have been so. And he'd always suspected she was older than he, although she appeared much younger. 'Twas most likely why she'd not conceived. No, he'd not muse on such, he loved her dearly, she was the light of his life, and he'd never regretted their vows. Still, it pained him that she'd not confided her secrets. But, as Clan Seer, discretion was primary and he'd betray not his Oath. Suddenly, he became conscious of the fact that he envied Grifynn's relationship with his mate.

Grimacing yet again, he shifted in the ornately carved chair. His back hurt. His feet hurt. His head hurt. When they'd returned last evening, he barely stabled his horse afore being called to this office, and they'd been going round and round o'er what had been said, or rather, what had not been said.

Kallyr couldn't remember when he'd last slept. He was too old for this kind of work. Most of his long life had been in service to the Dragon

Clan, but there'd not been a war in all that time, and he had no practical experience whatsoever in Battle Mode. Resting his heels on the ball and claw chair legs, he found 'twas as difficult to get comfortable as 'twas to remain awake. He ran his fingers through his thinning strawberry blonde hair, and tucked the long strands firmly behind his ears, recalling with amusement how Shayla had begun teasing him about the gray around his temples.

Kallyr was a good Seer with fairly strong Sight, and after Seeing Walkyr's birth, Shayla had made the long journey to the Outlands, far from the domain of the Dragon Clan. There she'd Claimed the child for the King's service, shortly after he'd been weaned. Most such Claims didn't happen 'til the child was in puberty, when he could actually tell everyone of his own Gift, or the family would make it known to the Elders.

But Walkyr's parents were happy to present him, even with his Gift yet noted, as he was the last of thirteen children and faced much hardship. Traditionally, the family business or farmland would be deeded to the eldest, and the other siblings were welcome to stay, but only to work. If anything happened to the eldest, the Claim passed to each sibling in succession, according to their birth order. But odds being what they were, the younger siblings with their spouses and children, would be forever dependent upon their elders. Their only option was to leave home and seek work or an apprenticeship in some other profession. Even so, they could end up working for someone else for endless winters, hoping to save enough to purchase their own farm or business, or mayhap to inherit if the Master was without kin. This led many to go into the wild, attempting to carve a living with a subsistence farm. Extremely dangerous, these farms were outside the King's authority, and Warriors were unable to assist them against marauders. Although Walkyr's family would probably never see him again, at least they didn't have to worry about his safety. 'Twas certain he'd be well educated, have his needs met, and be provided with most of his desires, since the Seer was in the upper class of the Clan hierarchy.

Walkyr was not only the youngest Seer Claimed in the history of the post apocalyptic world, but as far as Kallyr could tell, might prove to be the most Gifted. Not for the first time, Kallyr wondered if one had anything to do with the other. Training, after all, needed to begin as early in life as possible, for proficiency in any undertaking. He'd seen near fourteen winters afore he'd been recognized. But the clarity, frequency of Sight, and absolute raw power the boy held, near gave him gooseflesh. He shuddered at the idea his Gift might be misused. What if the Hoard got hold of him? What would they do to the boy? Walkyr was small for his age, but he was beautiful, even for a male child, and the perversions associated with the Hoard were becoming well known. Still, the youngster wasn't one to be casually tossed aside and he'd already shown a fighting talent, even against odds. Once he set to, he was a veritable raging windstorm blowing wild upon the plains. Unfortunately, unless he grew much bigger, he'd not escape bullying without injury. Kallyr thought of the last several moons, and even though the boy appeared older and wiser than his number of winters, he was still young and needed to be around other children his age. Instead, he'd become more withdrawn as time passed, hadn't left their home recently without Shayla, and didn't relate well with the other children. Of course, now that he thought about it more, he realized why. Even being well versed in the importance of the Sight, he was still considered 'different' by the Clan children. He was unusual, even for one with the Gift, and being all born and bred Warriors-to-be, the other children teased him about his appearance as an Outlander. He'd already been forced to defend himself when running errands for Shayla or traveling to and from classes at the Den. 'Twas no wonder he often chose to stay home alone. Somehow, despite his growing responsibilities, he'd have to find more time to spend with the boy.

Since he'd still not received any response from Grifynn, he continued, stating succinctly for what seemed to be the hundredth time, "Walkyr Saw Evil return from the Void to Kadoor within a huge black Dragon. There were 'others' with him, not of the Dragon Race. He Saw an apocalypse. He Saw many generations Pass the Veil. He Saw the Highland Dragon Ancients approach the Dragon Clan for help. He Saw us delve deep into Magic, joining them in a great War against these 'evil' Dragons, led by this same Black along with the 'others'. Walkyr shared these Visions within mere moons of his Claiming, near three winters past. Visions I shared with you my friend, when they were had." Lifting his eyebrows and smirking slightly, he finished his rote report once again and pushed away from the desk. 'Twas going to be another long night.

The two had been comrades as well as family for so long, he could tell what Grifynn was thinking. The aging Warrior had seen much battle in his younger days, along with his father and grandfather afore him, although he wasn't sure where. Grifynn wasn't that much older than he was and his eyebrows furrowed as he tried to clear his muddling thoughts. He didn't understand why, but whenever he reflected upon Grifynn's youth or predecessors, his thoughts tended to become hazy. Aging memory he supposed, shrugging away the odd notion.

Because of Grifynn's fighting prowess and savvy leadership, the Dragon Clan was now the exclusive supplier of the King's most elite fighting forces. One out of a hundred candidates might come from the Outlands, but only one out of a hundred of them actually made the cut. Trainees were chosen on characteristics such as honesty, good sense, strength, and reflexes. No one was rejected strictly due to a lack of fighting skill, since the Clan's Trainers were the best in all of Kadoor, and skill could be taught if you had the rest of the desired qualities. In their entire history, no Trainee had quit prior to taking his Oath (not considering untimely death), and no Warrior had ever betrayed that Oath.

According to Legend, sometime after the Last Holocaust, the first High King (usually just referred to as "the King") had granted the first Dragon Clan Commander the title of 'Ri', or 'Lesser King'. Conversely, the Battle Commander declined to use the title but kept all of the associated rights. 'Twas about the same time they'd relocated from King's Gate to Drekinn.

The Clan consequently had its own castle, known as the Dragon's Den, and had the right to collect taxes for construction and continued maintenance. Even so, instead of leveling those taxes, Grifynn's ancestors funded the castle through Warrior wages paid by the King. Therefore, through a most bizarre twist, instead of the Dragon Clan paying tithe to the High King, the High King literally paid the Dragon Clan. Clansmen who were not Warriors or working for Warriors, were raising Warriors, or farming for Warriors, or were in other associated professions to care for Warriors. In this way they maintained independence for Drekinn Village, even from the High King himself. Everyone was employed and earned a fair wage. 'Twas a simple yet effective system. You worked, you lived well, you took care of your own. 'Twas not so in other Clans, as they mostly relied on the feudal system linked to sub-servitude, but Grifynn had always been brilliant. Of course, brilliance often borders on insanity. 'Twas a fine line.

If need be, the Den could withstand an endless siege. Grifynn had enough coin, precious gems and metals stashed within the ramparts, the dungeons, beneath the stone and sand of the open Ward and Training Pits, that if the King stopped paying wages this very day, they'd never again have to work. 'Twas a concealed treasure trove that had taken generations to stock pile. He and his forebears had invested wisely in the development of their economy, and the castle itself was actually a huge training garrison with, among other things, kitchens and larders large enough to feed the entire Clan, barracks, offices, kennels and stables with arenas. The Den was nearly as large as the village proper and the Battle Commander and his family lived there, as did all the Warriors working at the Den, or on respite, or 'tween duty stations keeping the Peace. And once a Warrior always a Warrior. When he or she retired, if their skills matched the Fates and they actually lived long enough to retire, they either took a mate and moved into their own cottage or lived out their span of days at the castle. If they'd been wise with their pay, they'd not want for much and there was always work to be had, teaching, archiving, maintaining weapons, or in animal training and husbandry. There was no time to be idle.

One more interesting bit of trivia, there were actually two wells in Drekinn. The village well was typical of most, situated in front of the Lodge in the middle of the square. The second however, was not typical. 'Twas found deep in the heart of the dungeons, in the bowels of the Den. There was only one other known well in such a position. 'Twas found in the dungeons of Evanntyr. Not many knew of the existence of either, and there were rumors they were haunted. Of course, no one really believed those stories.

Every village throughout Kadoor had a well, but no one knew who'd built them, how or even when. They just existed, were clearly ancient, mayhap even pre-dating the Last Holocaust. Built in layers of rock native to each area, they rose up as if grown from the depths, of mortar and method otherwise not found anywhere in the world, yet similar to each other no matter how far apart. 'Twas obvious they'd been designed and built by the same architects. The wells had survived harsh weather, winters beyond measure, and natural disasters, and would probably survive any physical attempts to tear them down. Not that anyone had ever tried to do such a terrible thing. For decades, even centuries after the Last Holocaust, living conditions were so harsh that without these wells, Man might have perished. To this day, they continued to be the single most valuable resource for any village.

History recorded the well in the dungeons of the Dragon's Den was uncovered during excavations, while breaking through to the caves that honeycombed the land upon which the village was established. The fact these caves were so extensive was also a closely guarded secret, and like the well, not many knew the truth of their existence. During the construction, the caves were somehow blocked off from the dungeons to prevent access by the enemy, but there seemed to be no entrance, not even a trace of how they'd been blocked. But if the rumors were true, they connected all the way to the cliffs along the Sea of Dreams. Nevertheless, if truth, and the caverns did open to the Sea, the surrounding cliffs presented a formidable climb and difficult access. Although, now came the Dragons. Considering briefly how they could fly to the caves, he decided 'twould still present major challenge, and brushed the notion aside. Dragons were too big to get through the maze of tunnels and hence not a threat.

Once the dungeon well was cleared of some surface debris, 'twas found to be in perfect working condition. As was the case at Evanntyr, the dungeons were then built around the well. This kept it safe through drought or siege, and always available. All wells ran crystal clear, cool, fresh water with unknown depth. The best swimmers in the Clan were Grifynn's own daughters and they'd not been able to reach the bottom of either of them. They had however, felt a strong colder current pulling them under, and with some difficulty, they'd been tugged back to the surface by the ropes tied around them. The Clan Historian concluded the wells were all connected to an underground river flowing to the Sea of Dreams.

Kallyr sighed again. So much had been lost, and maps were a major loss indeed. We knew so little about the land mass upon which we lived, let alone that which surrounded us or lay beneath. The Last Holocaust had actually been the decisive finale of the last great war of their ancestors, although there'd been no 'winner'. 'Twas a relatively short conflict, the people not even aware 'twas happening 'til, as they used to say in ancient times, 'all hell broke loose'. But the result was so devastating, the topography of the land and even the shorelines of the oceans had changed. Near half of all animal life was lost, massive earthquakes and volcanic eruptions altered the mountain ranges, and most of the great forests burned to the ground or were buried by mud, ash and debris in massive slides and volcanic eruptions. The survivors struggled and finally grouped together, somehow managing to forge a new society. Through many generations the forests returned, and abundant animal life once again flourished. If Kallyr hadn't been a Seer he would've enjoyed being Clan Historian, as he felt knowledge was sacred. Although he had to concede that given the current circumstances, understanding one's history didn't necessarily mean one wasn't doomed to repeat it.

"Flame it all Kallyr, what in Hades was she trying to tell me? If those Dragons have deceived me again, I'll slaughter them where ever they flee!" An eerie light shown in his darkening eyes, and a sheen of sweat broke out upon his forehead, causing Kallyr to shiver involuntarily. Deceived? Again? Too tired to speak aloud, he mused o'er what he'd just heard, then returned to staring at his hands folded in his lap. A passing thought that

Grifynn may be sick crossed his mind but was rejected. Sickness and most of the ravages of the aging process itself had been nigh on eliminated since the Holocaust, one of the few positive consequences. It seemed that while nearly destroying Mankind, most forms of disease were also destroyed. The end result being, of those who'd survived the harsh aftermath and formed the base of their present population, there were few illnesses and no inherent fatal diseases, which actually lengthened their lifespan. From reading a few ancient manuscripts, Kallyr learned that Man had only about seventy winters to them, and only about forty were productive. Incredible! They could now boast a century of good living, if not killed in battle of course. And this brought his thoughts back to Grifynn, who'd never appeared to age. Warriors kept in good shape and the man hadn't slacked off as he'd gathered his winters. 'Twas normal to wait 'til they retired to have children, and Grifynn had waited even longer than most, due to the time restraints of his position. Surmising further, at sixteen and seventeen, his daughters were of age and that meant Grifynn was… he gasped! His friend had to have already seen at least a hundred winters or more! How had so much time passed without his notice?

His eyes darted toward the Commander when he heard the dull thud. Grifynn was slumped in his chair, his head upon the desk. Swiftly, Kallyr ran to him as he called for the Standing Guard outside the door, but he couldn't lift the big man's torso to assess the damage. The guard crashed into the room without a moment's hesitation and pushed Kallyr aside, effectively taking charge of the situation. He quickly lifted the unconscious man into the cradle of his muscular arms, and leaving Kallyr in his wake, he hurried to Grifynn's waiting War Horse. The big stallion was the only one that would carry him now, although no one knew why. 'Twas not as if no other was strong enough, and 'twas not that Grifynn didn't know his way around Horses. Something had happened when he was out on long patrol near seven winters past and upon his return, animals spooked when he drew near. Soon after, Grifynn left all the husbandry to the Masters. Taking a new born colt to train, he formed a special relationship with Konann. The Guard mounted with his Commander still in his arms, charged through the halls of the Den, past the Barracks and Training Pits, through the huge domed, double oak doors with the massive iron hinges, and o'er the draw planks of the main entry. Steering the mighty animal away from the castle, he aimed straight for Kallyr's home in town. The echoing of Konann's heavy hooves resounded through the Den as Kallyr followed him on his own mount, pushing his much smaller horse for more speed.

He finally arrived home to find the Battle Commander lying on his mate's examination table. Shayla was already working on him as he came stumbling in, breathing hard from the race through the village. Grifynn had yet to revive, and she was waving some liquid under his nose that he knew was noxious enough to wake the dead. With quickened insight, Kallyr understood, this was why Grifynn had tried so hard o'er the past seven winters to get them to move into the castle compound. He'd claimed with a hearty laugh that he needed his Seer close and his Healer closer. But Kallyr realized now, he'd been jealous of their 'relationship', avoiding the move as long as he could, and since nothing had ever happened to the Commander, he'd felt justified in his stubborn refusals. Now near panic as his lifelong friend lay upon the table comatose, he stood restlessly at the doorway, watching and agonizing. He speculated if 'twould have made a difference if they'd been able to treat him sooner. What was wrong with the man? This simply couldn't be how he'd reach his Final Sleep.

The guard stood o'er his Commander, trying to stay out of the way of Shayla's ministrations and failing miserably, making the Healer elbow him aside as she hastily went about her business. The man was so agitated he was nearly growling and Kallyr only realized he was holding his own breath when unexpectedly, Grifynn's leather clad chest expanded, jerking his torso up off the table, then slammed back down. With a stuttering gasp, and obviously disoriented, he slowly opened his eyes.

As soon as he regained consciousness, Shayla turned the astonished guard away from the table. Catching her fingers 'neath the lower edge of one metal studded leather cuff laced solidly against his huge biceps, she twisted him afore he had time to stop her. 'Twas evidently a technique she'd employed successfully in the past. Still off balance, she pushed his leather clad backside firmly o'er the threshold, forcing Kallyr along in front of him. Then she slammed the heavy wooden door shut, locking it loudly, leaving them standing in the adjoining room in shocked amazement. They simply stood there for several moments, staring at each other incredulously, afore in unison they turned to stare at the closed door. Momentarily, the guard straightened to his full height, walked purposefully to the door, knelt beside it, and pressing his ear against the keyhole, listened intently. Kallyr barely breathed, allowing the other to hear as much as possible.

"You're fortunate he brought you here so quickly. I slipped the Life Crystal under your tongue when they weren't looking, then used the smelling salts to appear to revive you, for their benefit." Shayla nearly hissed at the groggy man clumsily trying to maneuver to the edge of the table. Grabbing his outstretched hand, she helped him to a sitting position while she continued chastising him, her accent thickening with her temper. "'Tis not the first time ye've collapsed m'lord, but 'tis the first time ye've done so in other company than me own. What would your death do for Aalanna?" The Commander grimaced with the mention of his missing, and much beloved mate. Shayla looked gravely at him, and holding nothing back she said angrily, "Long I have treated ye in secret for this injury, m'lord. Ye know it. I know it. 'Tis your heart. The sword wound ye sustained did much damage, and 'tis taking a heavy toll. Ye've lived far longer than even I thought was possible with such a wound. I almost lost ye just now. The Clan almost lost ye! I cannot keep ye alive much longer like this. Your heart cannot stand the strain of this coming War. Ye must stand down." Shayla spoke emphatically, her eyes filling with tears.

"I cannot!" Nearly roaring his response, he glanced to the closed door with the ornate wrought iron hinges. He recalled long ago, when he'd ordered the design of those hinges as part of his betrothal gift to them, and assisted Kallyr to hang the heavy door. He licked his dry lips, took a calming breath, and lowered his voice. "I cannot stand down while I know not what's going to happen with me daughters and these dragons. You and I have been through this afore. You know what we face, what our people will endure, what could happen. There is no Healer more skilled than you, Shayla. You can and will keep me going, at least for a little while longer. You know I must see the Clan into this War, if not through it."

Pursing her lips and gaining slightly more control o'er her speech, Shayla threw her hands in the air in resignation. "Then at least take better care of yourself! This lack of sleep and proper food will take the decision out of your hands, and soon. 'Twould seem lately the Crystal is doing less to keep your heart rate even. I believe this is caused by the stress you've been under," she told him, and glancing away she continued, "but in truth, I know not. I need me laboratory and I haven't had access for many winters." Shayla turned away, not able to look into his darkening eyes as they began to sparkle, a sure sign he was losing control. "You must name your successor, so that when the time comes…." Trailing off, she looked back at him, the tears streaming down her face. Impatiently, she wiped them away with the back of one hand. As she watched his eyes, she'd thought she'd never see this day; they'd both lived through so much. Seemingly eons ago, he'd made her swear to force him Past the Veil if he ever fell o'er that edge of sanity. Could she make good on her promise? By the One, please don't let it come to that, she prayed.

Grifynn stood and stepped closer to her, weaving a little. Squeezing her shoulders gently and staring into her eyes, he let her see the sparkling effects diminish as he regained his control. Then he leaned in closer still and whispered in her ear, "You'll not fail me if the time comes, but I have no plan for that to happen in the near future. All the same, I've never been able to say no to you and since I can do naught else, I'll try to do better, me lovely." And kissing her on the cheek, he stepped back, transforming into the gruff and efficient Clan leader once again.

CHAPTER 5
Housekeeping and Homework

DAY ONE OF THE 'BOND; DARQUE ON THE LEDGE

The first thing on my mind was filling my empty belly. In a language all its own, it made me perfectly aware of the rude results that would occur if I waited much longer. Eagerly I searched through several sacks, and as frustration grew, I inhaled deeply and realized 'twas what I should've done to begin with. My senses were enhanced and I needed to start using them. Upset for being such a slow study, I closed my eyes, Cast forth gradually so as not to be inundated with irrelevant information, and concentrated on the multitude of aromas with which I was surrounded. Unfamiliar with my new scent perception, I spent some time identifying as many as possible for future reference. 'Twas common knowledge all creatures in the animal kingdom had higher olfactory clarity than did Man, but this was truly fascinating. However, my mouth was watering and my stomach grumbling, so I locked onto the one scent for which I longed. Keeping my eyes closed, I let it lead me unerringly through the haphazard stacks of supplies to the far side of the ledge, afore opening them again. 'Twas intriguing and remarkably similar to 'Threading', a tracking game all Clan children are taught as toddlers, increasing in skill and challenge levels as we progressed. A Trainer would unravel a great length of fine thread, while weaving, reversing, burying and hiding it through shops, stables, the village square, people's homes, the Den, advancing to the meadows and plains, wherever he thought we could be lost. Rolling it up in a ball as we went along (the tie breaker was the number of breaks in the thread) we'd follow it to the end where there'd be treats awaiting the victors. The only difference now was this 'thread' was a scent I followed with my nose as clearly as if I was using my hands and eyes, and the 'treat' would be my long awaited breakfast. The amusing memory brought a fleeting smile to my lips, but I returned quickly to the task at hand.

Squatting upon my heels, I grasped the nearest bag tied with twine. The oiled cloth used to make the bags was a type of heavy, moisture repellent canvas also used to make sails amongst other items, and helped to keep the carefully preserved foods from spoiling. I was certain this one held what I wanted, and my stomach growled even louder. Without thinking, I ripped apart the twine with my bare hands, letting the top flaps fall open. Several smaller bags were inside and I pulled one of them out, opening it with a bit more finesse to allow for retying of the twine. Grabbing a piece of the jerked meat laid neatly inside, I gnawed off a hunk with barely controlled enthusiasm. I savored the salty flavor as it rested on my tongue, making my mouth water. This would soften the jerky, but I was hungry enough to eat it completely dry. Chewing thoughtfully, the tangy juices running down my parched throat, I valued the moment. After living the lean life of a new Warrior awaiting deployment near four winters, I'd learned simple pleasures were often the best. Biting off another large piece, my olfactory sense told me what the other bags contained. There was a variety of dried fruit and fish, as well as more of the jerked red meat, a bag each of fresh roots, grains and flour, and to my delight, I found a full bag of the ground beans used to make the kaafy I so craved. Quite satisfied, I rummaged for the water skins.

Quickly finding the life sustaining liquid, to my utter surprise, 'neath them was a bag of mead. The unique scent of Shayla's handmade soap was pungent, and with no other scents upon this bag, 'twas clear she must've used great care to sneak it into my supplies. I loved that woman!

Relocating my food stuffs to the back of the cave area would keep them fresher longer. There they'd be in a consistently cool environment, and with the cave being so shallow 'twas also dry. The rocky ledge still held the sun's heat from the day for several marks and then would get quite cold, as the curtain of the night dropped. 'Twas still early in the season, although this winter was starting off rather mildly, and I wondered if 'twould herald any patterns that might later affect us adversely in battle. Mayhap the Dragons could predict the weather? 'Twould be most helpful if my new found senses assisted me. I'd always been able to forecast rain and snow from the scent as well as the 'feel', which was harder to explain. Storrm shared this Gift, but our 'predictions' were merely a few candle marks ahead of the knowledge of most and considered lucky guesswork, or they'd rant about our close ties to the Seer. Prudently, we allowed them to suggest we obtained our information from him. Something told me 'twas not wise to brag about our special talents. Still, sensing weather changes had proven helpful occasionally, but could we now do more? Time would tell, I supposed. Shrugging, I moved on to the task at hand.

I hadn't sorted the supplies as I directed their unloading, and things were a tad haphazard o'er the ledge. Gunnarr wouldn't return 'til the Clansmen were well away, and I felt a growing urgency driving me to distraction. Biting my lower lip, I pondered where he might've gone.

Organizing everything efficiently, I made sure 'twas carefully packed and safely stowed to protect from animals as well as extreme temperature changes. I even had time to make a rather comfortable bed with the extra blankets provided. How did Dragons sleep? I rather doubted I'd have to be much concerned about animals trying to steal my supplies, as the not unpleasant scent of Dragon permeated everything, and not even a fox had I seen this day. Not positive the two were related, but realizing it might prove to be a potentially serious problem in the battle effort, I added it to my list of 'need to find out soonest'.

Now that my belly was no longer growling obnoxiously, I located the package certain to be clothing. Inside were new Warrior Leathers appropriate for battle. Having abandoned my own simple work leathers upon the sands during the Cleansing Rites, I fully expected to receive them back again. These new leathers would've taken at least a sennight to make, and the workmanship was unsurpassed. Snatching the bottom of the bag and shaking it upside down, I dumped its contents at my feet. Holding up the first item off the top of the jumbled pile against me, 'twas obvious 'twould fit me well. Pulling on the loose sleeveless tunic considered suitable for everyday work wear, 'twas unlike the rough, worn and natural work leathers I'd left behind. 'Twas made of the finest leather, with the soft absorbent suede left intact against my skin. Very supple and buffed to a dull sheen after being dyed a burnished bronze, almost black, in a process known only to the Masters of the Clan, 'twould make me near invisible under any conditions. The tunic fell to mid-thigh, slit up the sides to my hips, and I could wear it alone or with britches and boots. These leathers were stoutly made and would last many winters. I picked up each piece for closer inspection, then refolded it neatly, creating a new stack. Included in the assortment were two long widths, one of which was worn as a breast tie under a tunic. Most female Warriors wore such a tie, often alone, especially when 'twas very hot. The other strip was used as a belt, into which could be tucked an extra blade or two, or a water bag. The slits close to one end of each leather width, allowed the threading of the opposite end to pull through for tying.

The short sleeveless chemise fit snugly from just beneath my ribs to just o'er my breasts. This one opened in the front and had long thin strips of leather for ties which laced in a crisscross pattern from navel to mid-sternum and could be tied or left hanging loosely. This piece varied in style and was usually worn 'neath a tunic to provide another layer of protection to our mid-section or to retain body heat in the coldest weather, but could be worn alone. It also tended to be more comfortable as well as sensual, than a plain leather width. No one but Storrm knew how acute was my hearing, and I smiled when I thought about the conversations among the male Warriors in which they discussed their preferences for female Warrior dress. The most appreciated were widths or a tight chemise holding our breasts up firmly, with the laces loose, braided with beads and feathers. Shaking my head, I couldn't understand the fuss about beads and feathers. By all the Ancients, no one wore that kind of decoration into battle! Even so, most obliged the males while in the Barracks. My sisters in arms seemed to do so because of the overt admiration they received. Personally, I found the less I wore the more comfortable I was and the better my fighting skills, so I often wore little else a'top than a chemise or a tie. Had I been trying to attract attention? No, I didn't think so, and shaking my head I decided 'twas simply more practical in the heat, and provided me full range with my sword arm during Training.

Next from the pile was a tunic with long sleeves that cuffed to the elbow, also for colder weather or for battle, and forearm and biceps vanguards to provide added protection. Such were usually worn against one's bare skin but could be laced o'er long sleeves. Early in my Training I'd found having them laced o'er my sleeves was restrictive, and always wore mine against my skin. In my opinion the vanguards and braces kept my arms warm enough, and no tunic was needed if actually engaged in fighting.

Two pair of britches that fit me like a second skin, were included. The leather as supple as the chemise, even as snug as they were, I still had total freedom of movement. And much to my surprise, my final discovery was a pair of new boots. My father was amazing, but there'd been something dark within him when we'd last embraced and then 'twas gone as if a door had closed upon a memory. 'Twas as this door closed I was compelled to warn him to keep the boy Seer close. Walkyr's Visions would be important in this War. Sighing, I also knew I'd confront my father again all too soon.

Trying to ignore the increasing uneasiness associated with Gunnarr's absence, I scurried about, ensured my new leathers were stored properly afore dragging out the rather large, wood framed, canvas covered box with leather hinges I recognized as a field class Weapons Hold. I frowned for since 'twas so light I need not drag it as I'd always done with my Hold in the Barracks, I thought 'twas empty. In fact, I was able to hoist it with one hand. Suddenly remembering my enhanced strength, I laid it back down near giddy with excitement. Trembling, I knelt beside it, opened the latch and lifted the lid to reveal, "By the 7th Egg!" My jaw fell open as

I exclaimed this aloud. 'Twas the largest assortment of fine weaponry I'd ever laid eyes upon, excepting the shop of Alric the Weapons Master of course, and I had to use my hand to shut my still open mouth. The blades were the hardest, yet most flexible steel, folded and hammered and folded again by Silas himself, in a process I'd watched often but never managed to duplicate, despite having tried. Laughing, my attention was momentarily diverted by the memory of Silas trying to teach me how to fold steel. 'Twas early in my 'training' and I'd somehow caused him to set fire to his own apron. That part of the memory had always been a bit hazy, and I could never quite remember what actually happened, but he'd yelled and jumped up and down and tried to pat it out with his big calloused hands, while I'd grabbed the bucket of water beside the forge. Because I was so small, I had trouble lifting it, and in trying to get the bucket himself, we clashed, banging our heads together, which made me lose my grip on the handle of the bucket and drop it, spilling the precious contents upon the packed dirt floor. Without hesitation, I snatched the ties of his apron as he stood up holding onto his aching head, and yanking as hard as I could, I loosed the bottom half. The jerking release of the ties caused the now off balance Smith to fall forward, allowing me to hastily pull the neck piece o'er his head. By then he had no chance to regain his balance, and as he fell on his face in a cloud of dirt, I tossed the now heavily smoking leather as far away from us as I could. I watched in fascinated horror as the soaring apron burst into flames mid-air like a Phoenix rising. The fact that it landed in the wood bin was not my fault, although I accepted full blame. The Battle Commander had taken the news with dignity, offering compensation for the destruction, and in order for me to pay off the debt I believe I didn't see the outside of the kitchen scullery for a full moon. Needless to say, 'twas my last formal lesson at the forge.

Still laughing to myself, I returned my attention to the Hold. On top of the array of weapons was a small blackened steel shield. 'Twas functional, designed by Alric himself, and forged by Silas in a Clan secret, well-guarded process similar to the one used for battle leathers, that ultimately produced a lightweight shield, flawlessly camouflaged. Warrior Shields were highly sought after, but none had even appeared in the Black Market of the coasts. I'd never possessed my own shield and I had little in the way of my own weapons. Scarcely breathing, my eyes sparkled with excitement as I pulled forth each new treasure. The shield fit well against my arm; the grips fit my small hands perfectly. Laying it aside, I picked up the carved hilt of a short boot blade from a stack of four. 'Twas odd. The blade felt warm to my touch, as if it had been recently handled. Surely I was mistaken.

I only had two boots, and fought with no more than two blades available to me at a time, three if you considered my sword. Not willing to leave any good blade behind, I'd have to alter my boots to allow me to carry on both sides. 'Twas true War pending, and I was certain there'd come a day when I'd be very thankful to have all four blades at my hand. The hilts were intricately carved bone, the guards inlaid with Mother of Pearl and Fire Opals, and the flats were etched with Dragons, each depicting a different fight scene. The Dragon was streaming Flame on one side and roaring his defiance upon the other. The quality indicated they'd been commissioned at least several moons past. Since 'twouldn't be like my father to offer such as mere reward, did his prescience proclaim my current need? I suddenly had to wipe my wet face with the back of my hand, as the smoke must have gotten into my eyes.

Setting the blades aside, the gleaming edge of a sword caught my notice. Raising it o'er my head while rising fluently, I stepped back into battle stance. Slowly, I began to swing the long sword in a circular pattern in front of me, and to each side. Moving it around and behind me, I switched hands, swung again and switched in front, and again o'er my head, making this circuit several times, gaining speed with familiarity. The cold steel sang as it sliced through the air, the resistance barely noticeable, the balance perfect in my grasp.

One final circuit and I brought my new weapon to rest, knelt down again, and continued my exploration. Finding a beautiful leather and metal scabbard, designed to strap 'cross my back, I sheathed the sword to protect the edge. Tucked under the scabbard was a second one, designed to fit my low back or hip, and held a short broadsword. Searching further, I uncovered two more daggers, along with matching sheathes to fit at my thigh and forearm. Amazed at what my father had managed to accomplish o'er the past fortnight, all I could do was shake my head. Raising my eyebrows, I couldn't help but be staggered, as I considered the purchase price of these treasures. By the Dragon's Breath, he had to have expected this end result for many moons. He knew we'd need these weapons, these leathers, and he must have had foreknowledge of the 'Bond as well as who'd survive the trials. These were not standard issue, all were custom to me, perfect in length, balance, fit, and etched with my Dragons. Where did he get his information? Kallyr wouldn't have kept such secrets from us, so how had he known? And while I was grateful, my instincts told me he'd done the same for all of us. The man had uncanny insight, but he'd insisted from my earliest memories, mine was the true Gift. Incredible.

Moving on, I located the cooking supplies, fed the coals, and set a pot of kaafy o'er the fire on a proper grill. Then I finished my morning meal of dried fruit and meat. In all my memories, I'd never eaten breakfast so late, and 'twas delicious. As I sat on the edge of the rocky outcropping, my bare feet dangling above the brush and grassy hills below, Gunnarr rejoined me. Gliding in slowly, I covered the mug of kaafy to keep it from sloshing out and burning my fingers when he landed.

Jumping up, the unease of our separation melted away like a bad dream one couldn't quite recall upon waking. I chugged the last of the kaafy and quickly cleaned up, banked the fire to last through the day and then finished dressing. I knew what was coming, and I was excited as I donned my weapons. So armed, I felt complete. The air was clean and crisp and the sun warmed me as I made quick work of braiding my hair, and pinned it up using the wood picks I'd also found in my Hold.

Warriors were as often female as male, and both usually kept their hair long. Not all, but most. Mayhap long hair was not practical for some, but 'twas a statement. Having long hair meant we'd not fallen or been taken captive in battle, for the first thing the enemy did was cut your hair. The shorn locks were used as proof of capture, and for negotiation. Conversely, if a captive's hair was short, 'twas considered they might not be worth ransom, but 'twas still common practice to either shave their head, or use a body part or roll of skin to prove capture. Of course no Warrior had ever been taken alive by any force, no matter how large, and therefore our long hair was considered by some to be egomaniacal. Were they correct? Almost certainly. But keeping our hair long was not entirely nonfunctional. Clansmen had course hair, which could be braided quite easily into extremely strong twine. Among other things, the braids could be used for fishing or horse hobbles. Storrm and I had created small animal snares when we were but children, as had most of the Clan, survivalist skills being foremost in early education.

The picks were also used as weapons, and were made from wood, metal, or the strong long bones of animals. Some were quite intricate, carved and decorated with all manner of inlaid metals, shells and precious gems. Stories flourished of their opportune use in a fight to the death. The picks I had now were unadorned wood, but the grain was lovely. However, I'd no time or desire at this moment to stare at a hair pick. In fact, I'd never cared for decorative picks, believing the inlays might catch in my hair, making them dangerous if needed quickly. I'd always chosen the simple ones. Apparently my father remembered.

"Are you ready to begin?" Gunnarr Questioned, and turning my left side toward him, I drew my sword from o'er my shoulder, and dropped into Battle Stance in reply. No sense in waiting any longer, I'd not Trained in two days. I could lose my edge and that would never do.

Without warning, Gunnarr 'attacked', his great jaws slicing toward my neck in an arc of flashing white teeth. Instinctively I brought up my sword to block his incoming fangs, but he was faster. Caught off guard by the unfamiliar speed and force of my own swing, I missed the strike, but twisting quickly, I recovered in time to face him. Crouching to avoid another near collision, I swung again. My initial concern, that I might injure him, was completely forgotten in the first few moments as I came to the solid realization I could never outfight a Dragon by sheer strength or speed, despite my enhancements. This knowledge was obviously one of Gunnarr's primary goals for today and he was pleased with my skills and how quickly I learned. Victory o'er the Hoard could only be secured through skill. Given this understanding, my usual offensive battle strategy would be much to my advantage.

As the lesson progressed, I struck fangs multiple times only to discover how unyielding they were. I'd have to find another strike region in order to do any real damage. Aiming for a Dragon's great maw was proving to be a waste of time, not to mention his scales were near impervious to any but the most direct, hardest hits I could manage. Even then, what would have sliced cleanly through the heaviest War Horse, made only the slightest scratch, and when my blade did glance off them 'twould actually cause a spark. Given the Healing, I stood in near shock while he allowed me to watch my best efforts simply disappear. 'Twas after all, a learning experience, and Gunnarr turned out to be a very good teacher.

I didn't go unscathed myself, but barely acknowledged what should have caused me great pain, and stopped me cold prior to the 'Bond. Gunnarr forced me to look upon the bruising and blood from the multiple lacerations I sustained, barely avoiding his fangs and talons. Fascinated, I watched in awe as they Healed. Had to be Battle Lust that numbed me, for I felt no pain.

Many things did my Dragon teach me this day, and I learned much about his Race. The secret to forcing them Beyond was to negate the Healing. Healing was a function of Magic. Magic must be fed and nurtured, and its strength and complexity could be affected any number of ways, but Gunnarr maintained his teaching focus this day upon how to kill a Dragon. Decapitation, or the destruction of the heart, were the only ways to force a Highland Dragon Past the Veil. Fangs and talons could slice through scale, but the damage had to be fast enough and severe enough to beat the Healing and get through their tough hide. The heart and the brain were required to Brew the Magic, therefore any injury to those organs was a major distraction. And if he were so distracted by assault on his brain that he had to focus on Healing and couldn't properly defend himself, then 'twas possible that Flame could get through the scale covered hide to destroy the heart. There were few places on the massive beast where a sword could penetrate, and nothing Man made could slice through scales. The 'sweet spots' included the eyes, small areas where each leg attached to the torso, and the groin, as well as a small, tapering region from his groin to mid-belly where there were no scales.

Damage to these organs was required to assist in the kill, but 'twould be difficult to accomplish. Of the two, the brain was the easiest to reach, situated at the back of the skull 'tween their wide set ears on either side of their broad head, at the top of the neck. Even so, 'twas protected all around by thick bone. The heart was mid chest, basically situated where a Man's heart would lie, protected by a massive ribcage, the scales of the chest, back and legs, and a rather longer than arm's length distance from said scales. 'Twould take a substantial effort and pinpoint precision for a sword strike to pierce the thick hide in that tiny area unscaled at mid-belly and plunge into the heart. 'Twould also have to be exceedingly fast, as the Healing would capture the sword and quite possibly cut off one's arm if still inside, unless the heart was sufficiently damaged in the initial plunge to distract the beast, providing opportunity to affect the kill.

Gunnarr also revealed that the skull was such, that even a solid strike through the ear canal wouldn't hit the brain, ending up in the back of their throat. But if I managed a direct, straight plunge of my sword upwards through the roof of his top jaw at just the right angle, I would pierce the brain. I could use a similar strategy by going through the eye, which was physically closer, but actually making either of these strikes would involve not only great skill but extreme luck, and I knew 'twas not wise to count on luck. Of course, I also knew I had the skill.

Being a Dragon, he'd never used a sword or any other type of weapon, and knew little of how they were wielded, and this training session was teaching him much as well. But as I added all I'd learned to my arsenal of information, I speculated as to just how I was supposed to affect these strategies.

Of further interest, I found some wrestling and hand to hand techniques held true even against an enemy as large as a Dragon. That is, if one could manage to get close enough and to secure certain holds. It seems they shared a fatal trait with one of their non-sentient animal cousins, the large lizards found in certain rivers, in that they're not nearly as strong opening their great jaws, as they are closing them. 'Twouldn't be easy, but if chance allowed, any ordinary Man might be able to hold the beast's mouth shut just long enough for the Fates to provide another form of escape. Of course, their lethal talons would most likely tear you apart as they pry your grip away, unless you were able to keep them otherwise occupied.

Yet another fact of note was in learning that like Man, their bodies followed their heads and tails. In other words, if one was strong enough (and fortunate enough) to be able to push a Dragon's head toward his belly for instance, he'd roll forward. Logically that would involve rolling o'er the one doing the pushing, so I couldn't imagine how that was helpful in any way at all. Also, if one could pull a Dragon's tail 'tween his legs and up his belly, he'd literally roll o'er backwards. I spent yet another moment of speculation upon just how I was to accomplish that feat. Apparently Gunnarr was telling on himself, as he chuckled when he made these revelations. I sighed, as I realized not all of the information imparted to me this day would prove practical, and briefly wondered whether or not this last information was merely humor on his part. No, Gunnarr was proving to have a depraved sense of wit but he was not a liar. In fact, I discovered no Dragon was capable of outright lying. Now, that information would prove to be quite helpful, I was certain.

For what seemed many candle marks, I strengthened my technique against Gunnarr's attacks. We trained 'til near dusk afore I finally admitted to fatigue. I'd been struggling for awhile but was driven by the headiness of my increased reflexes. I could barely see my own sword path through the air even with my enhanced vision, and I moved in the blink of an eye. Through the 'Bond, I knew exactly what and where his next move would be, almost afore he made it, and I began to meet his every attack. 'Twould prove a blessing in battle, but would be more so if I could Hear the other Dragons and not just the one to whom I was in 'Bond. These thoughts ran silently through my mind and although I knew Gunnarr understood them, he answered not, leaving me wondering if 'twas possible.

Although Gunnarr was much faster and stronger than I, he held back just enough to challenge me, and although I worked harder than I ever remembered working afore, 'twas exhilarating. Still I was disappointed; I'd never called a practice afore. 'Twas always my opponent who'd capitulated to me, either to mock death blow, or eventually just being injured or worn out. The idea that my next fight wouldn't end in a 'mock' death blow was sobering, and Gunnarr's enthusiastic Voice startled me. *"Your tenacity is impressive, Warrior. I knew you were the one when you were birthed."* 'Twas not the first time I'd heard him make this unusual declaration.

Grateful for the respite, and struggling to catch my breath more than I cared to admit, I Replied, *"Gunnarr, what does that mean? I wanted to ask last night afore I, well, afore I, you know."*

"Fell asleep involuntarily?" Gunnarr flashed his jewel-faceted eyes in his version of a wink.

"Have you ever been told you have a wicked sense of humor?" I Spoke, as I sat limply on the ledge, my heart rate slowing and the adrenaline spike of Battle Lust dissipating, leaving me unexpectedly exhausted.

"I am vaguely familiar with that concept, but I am learning much from you." Sitting on his haunches beside me, he curled his great tail around his feet. With his eyes glazed again, I determined 'twas the indicator of when he was in Link with another. Feeling slightly jealous and immediately ridiculous, I couldn't understand what had happened to my usual stoicism. I was normally calm in all situations. I couldn't say I wasn't an emotional female, or that I was not impatient, but I was the master of my feelings, and as a Warrior this trait had served me well. I was known to keep my head in any disaster, making quick rational decisions even in the heat of Battle Lust. I'd been groomed to take my father's position one day, if I proved myself in the field. Now everything had changed. I thought about Storrm and how she was faring with her Green. I wondered what he looked like, and fervently wished I knew his name.

"He is ugly and lazy. Green is such an unbecoming color. Blue is much better," Gunnarr snorted aloud. Then as I broke into the giggles he Spoke, *"Mystynn. He is my second brother. His fighting skills are exemplary. I was his Teacher, after all. He is also larger than any other, except me of course."* He was proud of his brother, and in his Voice I heard feigned ego. Gunnarr was not a braggart. He said what was truth only, and then only when asked.

Quietly I said, "Gunnarr, you've managed to avoid the majority of my questions. Don't think I'll let you get away with that forever. I have many questions. Know that I'll accept nothing less than full answers, and soon."

"Agreed." He growled grudgingly. "What is it you wish to know?"

Not giving him a chance to bow out this time, I immediately replied with something that had been bothering me, and that I needed to understand in order to perfect our MindLink. "Do you Hear every thought I have, when I have it, and do I Hear all of your thoughts?"

He hesitated briefly, considering how to proceed. Since 'twas obvious I didn't Hear this process, I felt justified in my curiosity. *"Yes and No. Our Minds are Linked at all times however, 'twould be impossible to function if we shared all of our thoughts continuously. Recall if you will, the chaos you experienced afore you learned to Shield. The Human mind doesn't operate upon the same plane as the Dragon mind. Therefore, you know what I am thinking, when you 'ask'".* In response to the puzzled look upon my face, he attempted to explain further. *"You can Speak to me and I you. 'Tis accomplished by the Push. You Push the thought into my mind and I you. 'Tis similar to asking a question of someone aloud. You Push the thought into the open, expecting an answer. You've done this very well, and in fact, you've used the Push since you were very young. Do you not recall how you seemed to understand what others were thinking? How oft times you were able to get others to do your bidding? Ahhh, another story for later. But you Feel me in your mind always, correct?"* I nodded my affirmation, and he continued. *"You Know I am there. 'Tis not an emptiness you sense, and 'tis the same for me. We each Know the other's location, if danger lurks near, if we are happy, or sad, or... aroused."* Gunnarr smirked once again and I knew exactly what he was thinking.

"Ok, I get that. Simplistically stated, I only have to actually wonder, to Hear you." And Listening at that moment, I blushed and then laughed. "And your thoughts are as wicked as your sense of humor!"

Gunnarr returned to my previous statement, "Has anyone told you, that you are a mighty Flame Spitter in a tiny package?" His great leathery face contorted in something akin to a smile. I knew that 'Flame Spitter' was old slang for Highland Dragon, and I knew he meant this as a sincere compliment. I was honored. 'Twas odd though, to hear my own language emerge from the throat of this beast.

"Beast? We shall see... but I will answer that as well." His mood became more serious and he began again. *"Eons ago we spoke the same language, for we shared the world openly. This is Ancient History but I have perfect Memory, as do all Dragons. The Highlands stayed behind through the Last Holocaust, to ensure the survival of Mankind. We attempted to save as many as possible, relocating them where they might thrive after the destruction of so much life. Initially we stayed close, nurtured and protected, then as the winters gathered, Man turned their backs on their past, and on*

Dragonkind. We became more reclusive, our numbers dwindled, and we did not speak with Man as we once had, maintaining contact only with the Dragon Clan. Man, in the meantime, lived many generations, struggled to create a new society, a new way of life, and even your language altered. When we began to communicate again, 'twas with the Seers, as their Gifts allowed such contact with the most ease. Although I have knowledge of your One True Liege, I felt his presence strongest through those dark decades, guiding and protecting both our Races. Once, He Called to me..." Gunnarr trailed off, his Voice softening and looked deeply into my eyes, *"He told me much about what was, and what is yet to come, cautioning me not to attempt to alter the Plan. We Spoke for some time. He does not interfere. He expects the best, and has Seen the worst. As have we all."* Looking away, he peered into the heavens above for several moments. I sat quietly and mulled o'er his words, knowing there had to be more to that story, but grateful for what the Dragons did for Man, and for being able to live my life and reach my destiny. My destiny! "Please tell me what you meant when you said you knew I was the one when I was birthed." My hand strayed to my scar, intuition telling me there was a relationship here.

Gunnarr took a moment to make his decision afore he quietly began again. *"Your life was Told in ancient prophesy. Maahayyel, the Last Dragon Matriarch herself, bade me go and lay talon upon you, when you were birthed. By so doing, I gave you the protection of my Race, and laid claim upon you for the first LifeBond."* Gunnarr stared at me with his crystalline blue eyes, needing no special sense to feel my distress. Again, 'twas clear he wasn't telling me everything.

"You mean, you knew my Blood Call would be yours, or that you made my Blood Call yours?" I Said hesitantly. Surely this was wrong. If he'd made something happen that shouldn't have, wouldn't that anger the Fates? Was I one of the things the True Liege told him about? Had he attempted to circumvent prophesy? But if he'd tried and 'twas not to be, our 'Bond wouldn't have happened. Did that mean he was supposed to 'lay talon' upon me, and that was actually part of the prophesy? Just what did the prophesy say? By the gods, I was more confused than ever.

"You are the prophesy, Darque. How do you explain hearing my name spoken prior to the LifeBond? You told me you heard the Ancients afore we entered the Lodge. My sweet, do you not realize yet, that no human ear can decipher Dragon Tongue?"

I'd heard his name stated clearly among the Ancients that day, but surely I wouldn't have understood if 'twas spoken in Dragon Tongue. I was still skeptical. *"Could you not be mistaken? Could they not have been mixing Common when I happened to hear your name?"* But even as I made this protest, his explanation rang true.

"How do I convince you?" Gunnarr questioned himself quietly, and then came to his conclusion. Forcefully he stood and leaned o'er me. *"Come my Warrior. Share the image in my mind's eye, and you'll See it clearly. I Show you Evanntyr, the King's castle. Follow as I take you o'er the drawbridge, through the Ward, into the Great Hall of the Keep. Gaze above you, upon the many floors entering into the Great Hall from the Grand Staircase. Examine the ancient tapestries covering the walls of the landings."* Gunnarr hesitated, allowing me to catch up with the rapid pace he'd set in this dream-like journey, afore insisting, *"Tell me what you See."*

His Voice Drew me forth, his Vision became my own, as the scene was laid o'er what my eyes told me was actually there. 'Twas similar to the swirl of color produced when I'd stirred dye into the great vats for the Weavers as a child. Carefully, I scrutinized the wall-hangings, seeking the answer. *"There are a multitude of tapestries. Close to the top of the stairs, kept in the shadows, is one that appears to be very old, one of the oldest in the collection."* With a trembling voice and dry throat, I fought the knowledge being set afore me. *"The scene depicts two young girls with long red hair. They chase 'cross a meadow, climb to the timberline, and discover a Dragon. They're distinctly illustrated and... I know them. But this can't be real Gunnarr! It's me and Storrm the day we went afore the Counsel. We'd been playing in Far Meadows and heard the Dragon's Song. We rode hard to the hills, and after a perilous climb, we found the great beast. We were very careful to avoid being seen, and rushed back home to make report. 'Til that day we hadn't truly believed in Dragons, as we'd never seen one, and although we feared they'd think we were lying, we refused to stray from the truth. Thus we proved our integrity and were recommended for Trials. But that was only four winters ago. How the Flame...? It cannot be!"* Shaking my head, I sputtered in disbelief.

Gunnarr responded by Drawing me deeper into the Vision. *"Seek the evidence you require, Darque. Open your mind to the truth, and believe."* As Gunnarr Pleaded with me, I squeezed my eyes shut to increase my concentration. Suddenly there 'twas; the Dragon scar upon my thigh, in the portrait skillfully woven centuries afore my birth!

CHAPTER 6

More Than They'd Bargained For

THE NIGHT OF THE 'BOND; KADDART

"No," the young man growled under his breath to the elder Warrior. "You must keep going. We stay together!" His alarmed expression was clear to his partner, and couldn't be hidden behind a mask of bravado. "I'll help you," he huffed, and still attempting to catch his own breath, he scrambled back to assist the other to his feet from where he'd stumbled again, this time lying sprawled in the muck that surrounded them in the aqueducts. The tunnel was just large enough for them to run near side by side, crouched to avoid hitting their heads and ramming their shoulders against the stonework in the flickering light of the torch. But 'twas evident the elder of the Team couldn't continue, and the young man couldn't carry him within these confines for long. Neither of them was built as ruggedly as the rest of the Brotherhood, as they weren't of the Dragon Clan by birth, having both come from the Outlands. Tall with long lean muscle, they wouldn't have been as effective in their specialty had they been brawny. Stealth was their forte and now speed was of the essence. Racking his memories, he was desperate for a solution that didn't involve leaving his partner behind. 'Twas simply unacceptable.

"You go, I'll catch up. I will find you!" The man wheezed, knowing full well this could be the last time he'd ever see the boy again, but if he didn't leave now, neither of them would have a chance to get back to the Den and make report. Painfully, he pushed up on his elbows, scooted on his butt through the mud and slime that had been his downfall, 'til his back wedged against the wall. "I have to rest, but you go on. If he knows where we are, where this system opens, we're damned and our flight will have failed. Surely he'll scent us soon and our refuge will be compromised. If you stay, 'twill be impossible for me to hide, and for you to make good your escape. Don't worry about me, go, hurry!" He had to drop his gaze afore he'd completed his sentence and 'twas his undoing.

Bastyen said quietly, "You aren't going to make it, are you?" Seeing the answer in his mentor's expression, he sighed and stepped closer. "I won't leave you here alone." Keeping his own gaze averted, he knelt beside the exhausted man, leaned his makeshift torch against the wall, and applied manual force o'er the slash in the other's thigh to stop the bleeding.

THE BLACK WAR BEGINS

The pressure bandage he'd hastily applied earlier was again saturated, and Graasyn wouldn't be able to sustain function if he lost much more of his Life Source. At least the Agent who'd done the deed would never again swing a sword against a Warrior, or anyone else for that matter, as Bastyen had secured that one's passage Beyond. After fighting the four swordsmen who'd attacked him, forcing each of them Past the Veil in rapid succession, he'd come to assist his partner who'd successfully managed to handle the other four assailants, but had been wounded by yet another, sneaking up behind them in the alley. This one had swung in under Graasyn's lanky frame and long arm, and made the strike as Graasyn's sword cut down his comrade. Bastyen was a candle drip too late, but gutted the bastard for his effort. They'd just vacated the bloody alley, leaving nine bodies in their wake, when the Hoard Dragon arrived. Since then, they'd been playing a most dangerous game of cat and mouse.

The fight in the alley had occurred around midnight, and 'twas near dawn now. They'd been aided surprisingly by the very blood they'd spilled. For reasons unknown, it seemed to confuse the Dragon who chased them. There'd been no lack, after all, nine of the King's Agents had spilled their Life Source, covering both of the Warriors with the sticky abundance. And the Dragon himself had been splattered with blood as well, apparently having just left the arena. Mayhap that had lent itself to the stupor in which he functioned. During the long marks they were hunted, Graasyn theorized the Hoard Dragon was not as astute as the other Highlands, who were at this very moment participating in the LifeBond ceremony back home, and would soon be fighting against such as these, alongside the Clan. 'Twas the winter solstice and they'd hoped to be present to witness the Magic, ushering in a new era of battle to help them as they entered the Black War. Still, 'twas frustrating that given all his theories, he couldn't be certain what was affecting this Dragon, making him appear so different from the others. Was the entire Hoard like this one? Grifynn desperately needed their information, including conjecture.

Bastyen had always thought of Graasyn not only as his mentor, but as a father figure. He'd not known his 'real' father, abandoned in the Port District no more than days old. He'd been accepted and raised collectively by a group of tavern owners along the docks, where he'd been found. Not belonging to anyone in particular, his rather large 'family' did their best to care for him. Still, growing up in this manner he'd had no one person to call his own, no one family to consider as his or to answer to, and feelings of rejection led to much rebellion in his youth. He discovered he was very good at picking pockets and general theft, although he always gave his 'gatherings' back to their rightful owners. His early life experiences made him tough and resourceful, and he'd learned every nook and cranny about the Port O'Drekinn. All children of the Clan are provided with standard childhood education and he'd attended, erratically at first. After some effort to uncover his personal interests and talents, he'd been encouraged toward Stealth, after which his attendance took a definite rise. He'd done well in Survivalist Training and shined in Hunting and Tracking. However, Swordsmanship was just barely good enough to keep him from being forced Past the Veil too early in a fight. Hand-to-hand was quite decent and Warrior Regynn's classes held his rapt attention, with his unique strategies of using whatever was available as a weapon, including your hands and feet, and survival without a sword, which made most Warriors shudder in horror. And then the day arrived when Graasyn had filled in for Regynn's classes for a moon, while he'd been on sabbatical. The Warrior saw something in Bastyen and nurtured it, even to the point of tutoring the boy 'tween other classes to get his swordsmanship up to par, and then sponsored him to enter into Warrior Training. The day Bastyen took the Oath and joined the Brotherhood was the best day of his life to that point, but the day after, when Graasyn adopted him as his Claim Son, outranked even that honor.

Since that day near nine winters past, the two had been Grifynn's most effective Stealth Team. As well as being battle hardened, they specialized in interrogations, covert operations, and investigation techniques, and were ready to fight any and all enemies of Clan and Crown. Often going undercover as father and son, since they were of similar builds and appearance, they also had pretended to be all manner of skilled Master and Apprentice. Frequently, they'd not a true weapon 'tween them, other than the usual traveler's dagger, and 'twas fine with them. Their fights occurred in remote, dark, tight places, where they quickly and quietly dispatched their enemies. 'Twas more important that no one was the wiser when it came to their business, and they had no problem being known as 'ambushers', 'backbiters', 'throat cutters' or 'the Whisper of the Veil'. Neither of them had taken a life Beyond that was not necessary. Recalling the majority of their battles, there wouldn't have been room enough to swing a full sword arc, even if they'd been able to carry one in, keeping with their undercover assignations.

When they'd received orders to investigate the Kaddart Runner's death, they thought 'twould be rather routine. Still, they were equipped for all contingencies, no less so now that they'd seen the return of the Dragons, not something either of them had ever thought to experience. They already knew a boy was found dead on his horse near the Barracks, the night afore they received their orders. 'Twas a Runner's horse with Runner's tack, and his body was taken to the Healer by Darque and Storrm, the sister Warriors and daughters of the Battle Commander. His identity was quickly confirmed, as his two elder siblings were of the Brotherhood. The eldest, Tannyr, was currently retired from active duty, a Swordsmanship Trainer in residence at the Den. Daayn, the middle brother, was deployed but notified, and should be there by now to assist with the arrangements. Tannyr made claim to the body and had him placed on ice. They'd have to wait for Bastyen and Graasyn to return with their full report afore they'd be allowed to take the boy home to Kaddart, and if this delay was too far extended he'd be cremated at the Den. They were disappointed this recognizance mission had taken so long, as they knew they'd be too late to allow the brothers to perform the cremation ceremony on Tonn's home soil. Had the boy been a Warrior like his two elder brothers, the Den would've been considered his home soil, and there wouldn't have been any such conflict.

They began with the mystery of Shayla's extended knowledge. How had she known the boy's name? If she hadn't, they'd have had a much more difficult time locating his family, but how could she have known about an Outlander? Shayla had made few trips outside of Drekinn in their entire lives, the most recent to Claim the boy Seer. Tonn's professional tattoos would only identify his position as a Kaddart Runner. This system of rank was begun by the very first Battle Commander and wasn't considered common knowledge. Of course, 'twas likely the Healer learned this system, given her line of work, but that still didn't answer the question of how she knew his name. Names were only tattooed on Warriors, and then only the Battle Name bestowed upon them when they took the Oath.

The pair rode hard the first few days, their War Horses eager for an adventure. Tying along their smaller stock horses for approaching the village, they set a fairly quick pace. After leaving the flatlands they entered the hill country, and riding at night, staying in the shadows and woods, they began to use more caution. However, the closer they came to Kaddart the more their mounts protested. 'Twas yet another mystery. War Horses were not prone to being nervous, even in full Battle Lust, and this behavior could only be described as such. They'd need to confirm their suspicions about the cause of this distress. They noted the War Horses had been wary when the Highland Ancients first arrived and although similar, this behavior was more pronounced. Were there Dragons nearby?

They'd be recognized if they rode the massive beasts into the village proper, so leaving them to free graze farther away than they'd planned, the two men removed their heavy tack and stowed it under cover of a quickly made but sturdy lean-to of brush. Changing their leathers to coarsely woven cotton tunics, wool wraps and cloaks in grays, greens and browns, they armored up with everything well hidden and reloaded their custom saddle bags to the smaller horses, effectively disguising them as traveling merchant pack animals. Even riding part of the way, it still took them another day and a half to get to the village.

War Horses were highly intelligent beasts taught not to wander, and the Warriors knew they'd be safe. Afore the return of the Dragons there were few creatures big enough to injure, let alone kill a War Horse, and they were fearsome fighters in their own right. If not reunited with their handlers within a fortnight they'd unerringly return to their stables at the Barracks.

After making their way through the hills and the virgin woodlands, they finally crossed the bridge o'er Clear Water Creek, surrounding the lush fields of Kaddart. Walking boldly into the village proper, they made arrangements for their horses at the stables, and took up temporary residence at the Clear Water Inn. Their disguises gave them access to most of the village and provided them with due cause to wander about the region under pretense of marketing, without drawing too much attention from prying eyes. All traveling merchants would do the same and they'd played this role many times.

The Clear Water was centrally located, small but clean, with a few scattered tables downstairs and a large stone hearth in the middle that divided the kitchen area from the dining room, serving the entire structure for heat as well as cooking. A handful of sleeping rooms were upstairs and all were empty, except for the one at the end of the hallway, where the owner, his mate and their daughter all stayed together.

Graasyn and Bastyen forgot nothing, no matter how small an observation. Therefore, the fact the inn was empty, prompted them to search the other available shelters at which travelers might be staying, and found no one but themselves currently in town, even though the stables were full. The next thing they noted was an overwhelming aura of apprehension. 'Twas not a normal distrust of visitors, 'twas a strange dread in the air with no obvious cause. The people were reserved and their attempts to strike up even a social conversation, were strained. Added to this, there was no music or laughter in the taverns. In fact, there was little customer traffic anywhere. 'Twas frankly odd, even for such a remote village. They'd fallen into a deeper well of intrigue than they'd originally expected and so they kept to themselves, feigning travel fatigue. Quietly they'd observed, then set forth in the dark of the night to learn the lay of the village, and could find their way anywhere within a few candle marks. Returning afore dawn, they'd uncovered more mysteries than answers and 'twas most disturbing.

They'd seen much o'er the course of their professional lives and had learned nothing was sacred, so when the daughter of the tavern owner (who'd taken a liking to Bastyen) slipped him a note the following evening with their ale, urging them to beware the King's Agents, they took the warning to heart. During their prowling the prior evening they'd established there were no travelers in the village because they'd all been 'detained'. 'Twas disconcerting at the least, as they'd made every effort to locate them, without success. Where were they being kept, why had they been taken, and had the Runner been involved?

With all haste the two made their way back upstairs without the few villagers at hand noticing, and packed their things into their saddle bags, their multitude of small arms worn at all times. Leaving a fair amount of coin upon the bedside table, they'd climbed out the window to disappear into the alley under cover of the shadowy dusk, not to be seen by the villagers again. 'Twas fortunate timing, as they just missed the King's Agents breaking down the door into their room.

Altogether, they'd been hiding for near a sennight, with slightly more than that same amount of time from starting their mission, to their escape through the upstairs window at the Inn. That meant that tonight should be the winter solstice.

During their time in concealment they'd been forced to steal food and had lost their horses, as they couldn't claim them with a price on their heads. They'd refused to involve the girl anymore than she was, and were truly relieved when it appeared she'd also left the village and that her deceit had gone unnoted. They'd acted as the Whisper of the Veil for two of the King's Agents, retrieving as the victor's spoils the swords they'd used in the alley, and had managed to stay always one step ahead of their enemy. But they'd not simply left the village, as they could easily have done, because they could almost taste the truth simmering under a thin layer of lies.

And uncover it, they did. Just after dusk turned into deep night, they traveled once again to the far edge of town where the Agents were barracked. Scouting around, they made ready to spend yet another night listening for some clue or unexpected drop of information from the many men milling lazily about. Initially, they were appalled at the deplorable state of their general condition, their living quarters, and the obvious lack of discipline. Of course, this very lack was most helpful to them and they found 'twas not too difficult to eavesdrop and observe the comings and goings. Not once had they seen the Agents work at anything. There were no drills, no exercises, no weapons care, nothing but sloth and gluttony. They appeared to be getting their food from the villagers, who came in the night to deliver and were in great distress, as they were often abused. 'Twas distasteful and most unsettling, which was why they kept returning. They knew the secret of Tonn's death would be found here.

Quite by accident, within mere moments after they'd settled in, they heard a conversation that made their blood boil. Battle Lust quickened their hearts as they listened intently.

"I wanted time to play with that pretty one afore they messed her up," growled one of the Agents disgustedly to another. Standing at a fire pit outside the Barracks, he gulped noisily from a bag of mead. They were changing o'er the guard, which was a laughing matter, as 'tween the two of them they couldn't have detected the heat in the fire, let alone an incoming enemy.

"I don't care what they do with 'em, as long as I get me share," the second man sneered obscenely to the first, grabbing the mead from the incoming relief and guzzling what was left, then wiping his face on the back of his hand and up his tattered cloth sleeve.

"But ya gotta admit, that dark haired beauty was special," the first man replied, reaching for his mead. But realizing 'twas empty, he dropped to his butt in the dirt. "And she'd have kept this man's bed warm for many nights," he finished with an evil leer.

Bastyen prayed they'd not been talking about the pretty girl with the most remarkable black hair and silver gray eyes, who'd warned them at the Clear Water Inn. And 'messed her up' couldn't be anything but bad. He hadn't even realized he was rising in his anger 'til he felt Graasyn's hand staying him, which brought his focus back to their present danger.

What was wrong with this scenario, thought Graasyn. 'Twas insanity. He'd trained and served beside Agents in winters past, and they'd always been honorable men. This was just wrong. Everything about this was wrong. These men were dirty, drunken, slovenly and loud. They were disrespectful, and apparently allowed a young girl to be abused in some manner about which he was very much concerned. He didn't need his gut instincts to confirm something horrible was happening here, and the villagers were being drawn into the mess, unable to defend themselves.

'Twas nearing midnight and the Ancients would be Brewing the Magic at the sacred grounds of the Clan. But he couldn't think on that right now. He had to find out more. He decided 'twould be their last night here. After this, they dared not try to stay. They had to return to deliver their report, and that meant make good their escape afore dawn broke 'cross the hills. What they'd discovered about the condition of the village, the atmosphere, and the King's Forces stationed here, was enough to warrant sending out a full company at the very least.

Hearing approaching footsteps and adjusting their positions, they saw a group of hooded villagers being dragged along, tethered one to another, up the long path from the village to the Barracks.

"Here they come. Do ya think we can take a couple for ourselves this night, afore the Dragons get to them? I hate using their scraps," said the first one again.

"Not a chance in Hades, are ya daft? Do ya have a death wish? They're still angry with Bekkat for letting that Runner escape, and there're no more travelers to give 'em either! If they discover those last two got away…" and the second man picked up the empty mead bag and staggered off, leaving the first one still sitting in the dirt. Soon a few others gathered around the warmth of the fire and the two Warriors crouched deeper into the shadows, eager to hear more.

Graasyn wondered what was happening to the villagers and what the Dragons were doing with them. He had a vivid imagination though, and wished with all his might he'd not eaten that stolen pie earlier. The references about the travelers, Bekkat, and 'letting that Runner escape' hadn't passed o'er deaf ears, either. The hobbled and hooded ones being led up the path were moving quite slowly, even with the 'encouragement' being offered by their captors, and the men surrounding the fire pit were becoming loose tongued. Through the ensuing conversation they learned the Runner had been held not far from here after being caught listening in and observing the 'arena rapes and bloodings'. The boy had attempted to report to the local Captain of the Guard but to his surprise, he'd been beaten and imprisoned. Shortly thereafter the 'events' had been stepped up and any travelers who'd stayed more than one night were taken to add more bodies, as well as to keep the Dragons' affairs secret. After some time, the guards grew lax and the youth took advantage, effecting his escape. They thought he'd been wounded, for one of the Dragons had Flamed him for sure, but he was quick and still managed to outrun them all, losing his pursuers in the forest. 'Twas evident even to these men, that the Dragons always avoided the heavy growth of trees. They'd been forced to search the surrounding areas for days to no avail, but then they hadn't really tried that hard, believing he'd died of his burns somewhere in the woods. This would be valuable information for the Commander, but there was a much more important question still to be determined. Was this tragic farce a fringe group of anarchists working independently, or were they under Royal Decree?

The guard didn't hail the incoming party and there was no exchange of recognition 'tween them, as they finally passed each other. The only sounds came from the shuffling steps of the prisoners. They disappeared through the alley 'tween the Barracks, followed eagerly by those around the pit, leaving the lone guard muttering to himself about being left out.

With a sudden rush of wind from o'er their heads, Bastyen and Graasyn looked up. Through the tree branches they saw the silhouettes of Dragons upon the black on black monochromatic sky, their heavy bodies banking to land on the far side of the Barracks. Almost as soon as they lost sight of them o'er the roofline, they heard screams of panic followed by pain, a skirmish of monumental proportions, and lewd comments bellowed forth from a multitude of throats. The attack had begun.

Desperate to help, they slipped past the drunken guard and found themselves alone within the alley. Concealed in the shadows, it took little time to realize there were none left to assist. The alley opened into a small clearing with raised benches and torches all around. What they heard now was appallingly ghastly with moans, heavy breathing, crunching and horrible sucking sounds. Then came the voices of the King's Agents, low and angry, some bitter and impatient to 'get one of 'em afore they're all gone'. 'Twas obvious they spoke of the young girls presented in this depraved, ritualistic, mass rape and slaughter. Moving closer they saw the Dragons blooding their victims, most of them mercifully Past the Veil, brutal wounds evident even in the flickering shadows of the torchlight. The two had witnessed cruelty in their careers, corruption, battle injuries, all manner of abuse, but this was butchery they'd never forget. Body parts were spread everywhere, some still dangling from Dragon fangs, so that they couldn't have identified one from another even if they'd known them all their lives. And the sexual abuse! By the Dragon's Breath, how could they do that to a human? Graasyn watched in stunned disbelief at the debauchery and with nausea rising, he saw the girl twitch. By the gods, she was still alive. He swallowed hard to avoid losing what little had been on his stomach of late. He hadn't the heart to stop Bastyen when the youth stood up, pulled the experimental crossbow from under his cloak and let fly the first long dart at the Dragon's exposed appendage. His aim was true as always and didn't require the bestial scream of agony for confirmation. The second was for the girl, sending her Past the Veil, for there was no chance of her survival. Dropping the crossbow, for it would have taken too much time to replace it, they turned as one and ran. Within a few strides they faced eight swordsmen just entering the alley, seeking to discover the cause of the Dragon's painful screams. In full Battle Mode they cut them down in ghostly silence, their signature methodology. 'Twas when Graasyn received the wound now causing them so much trouble.

Bastyen was disappointed he'd lost the new weapon. 'Twas a shame really, he had high hopes for its use in their profession and mayhap the others would take to it for battle. 'Twas made by Regynn from research he'd done in the archives, and he knew of no other like it. He hoped it could be reproduced and that 'twould not end up in the hands of the Hoard, as 'twould give them an advantage they could ill afford to lose. But their report was more important than the loss of any weapon, and so they fled.

They'd zigzagged their way through the village, the vicious beast always a step behind, 'til they'd finally reached the aqueduct unseen, which would lead them undercover to the creek. Exhausted, desperate and uncertain for the first time in their careers, they wondered whether or not they could complete their mission.

Their heads jerked up in unison when the dark stranger came striding toward them from out of the shadows, but 'twas the last movement they could muster. No words came from their throats, their bodies wouldn't obey them, they couldn't even blink their eyes. A tingling warmth spread o'er them from the tops of their heads to the tips of their toes. 'Twas the mantle of Magic under which they were caught. After such heroic effort to avoid capture, 'twas infuriating to be thwarted by Magic. Graasyn observed as the stranger came closer, wishing only that he could tell his son how much he loved him. The boy had made his life worth living. He'd never taken a mate and had no known children, although he'd been plenty active as a youth. He could've asked for no better son of his own seed. He'd thought to spend many long winters with the boy, not have him watch them die like this. The Fates were certainly twisted.

Bastyen saw what was happening but could do nothing to prevent it. How maddening! They were helpless, with not a chance of survival. They could do nothing to stop this man or whatever he was, from doing whatever he was going to do. Bastyen had regrets in his life but the biggest one was not being able to tell his father how much he loved him, just one more time. Even though it had taken being abandoned at birth and raised in the Port District, he could have asked for no better father, no better life. He just wished he could get their information to the Battle Commander to honor Graasyn and to finish their mission afore....well, afore all was lost!

"'Tween the two of you, your Thoughts are louder than that disgusting Hoard display." The deep voice of the stranger penetrated the fog o'er their minds, lying thicker by the moment. Vaguely the two Warriors thought they heard sympathy in the voice, but distaste overrode that impression. "I had no trouble whatsoever, with your trace. 'Twould have been much easier had you vacated when I sent the girl to warn you. Now things are a fine mess. But what I'd really like to know is how you became MY problem." As he stooped o'er them, his long hair fell in a wispy curtain about his face, but 'twas too dark to get a good look at his features. He gazed into nothingness while he spoke, but their vision must have been compromised, for he thought he'd seen silver flashes in the shadowy depths of his eyes. And as the voice began to fade, he wondered if this was how they'd be forced Past the Veil, simply to fall unconscious, never to reawaken. If only he could get his hand on his blade, at least he'd Pass with dignity.

"The beast is upon you and I cannot frustrate his efforts much longer, as the Magic being Brewed this night elsewhere is so strong, 'tis making it difficult for the rest of us." He waved one hand in the air o'er his shoulder toward the west, in an obvious reference to the LifeBond Ceremony. "He'll find you if you stay here, and given the way you're fumbling about, 'twill be soon. And I can only keep those inept humans occupied for so long. AND I suppose those were your horses wandering the hill country? You're fortunate 'twas I who found them, and that I could get here without being seen or missed from my other obligations. Still, there isn't much time. Why do you humans complicate everything? If I allow your return, you may alter the prophesy, and prophesy does run deep through the Clan. What will happen must happen as 'twas told long ago. Yet I cannot alter everyone's memories of your existence, too many have been involved. I either have to present your blooded bodies or... you cannot be found." He stood up again in his anger, but somehow he wasn't angry at all, and he sighed heavily as if trying to make a painful decision. 'Twas difficult to understand, but he seemed almost apologetic.

"All will not be lost. But for a time, you will be." And with these odd words, he lifted his hands in front of his face. Crossing them palms outward, he pressed them slowly and forcefully through the air toward the Warriors, as if against a heavy load. Just afore they lost consciousness they felt a whisper of cold air and then... they were Pushed.

CHAPTER 7

No Time To Sleep

NEARLY A MOON FROM THE 'BOND;
GUNNARR AND DARQUE AT HOME

Finally stealing a moment to rest after a traumatic day in the field, I laid on the ledge and fixed my eyes upon the sky. Minute pinpricks of pure radiance glittered through the curtain of the night. Slowly, disappointment faded and catching a deep breath, I pondered the day's events. 'Twas my habit to review everything, to glean whatever might be of benefit to our efforts in the field, and 'twas my duty to pass this knowledge along. But the 'Bonded were still operating solo and I knew we must alter our methods soon or fail.

We'd begun our day as usual, taking wing afore the sun rose. After training and a hearty breakfast, we went in search of the Hoard. We'd seen none yet but we could smell them, and in several near misses, we'd stumbled upon the results of their rampages. The others reported the same frustrating chain of events. What were they doing, why did they not stand and fight? It made little sense for them to keep such a low profile. We'd had no success in finding their lair, or any location they might be using as one. Although originally they'd been scattered and fractioned in their attacks, often working apart or even against their own, their tactics were becoming more organized and I was exasperated. We were doing too much searching and not much fighting. Truth be told, we didn't even know how many we faced.

Drawn to a heavily wooded area more by the visible smoke than the sense of disaster, 'twas a gruesome sight that met us. Although the attack might have appeared disorganized to the untrained eye, a brief look around told me 'twas far from truth. The barn was the initial target, which to a family of subsistence farmers meant everything. Their animals kept their meager larder filled and when the barn was Flamed they would've come running out of their small thatched roof cabin to see what was happening. They'd been as a smorgasbord laid afore the evil creature, but I was somewhat confused at the ensuing sloppiness. Such a plan seemed well thought out, initiated and then apparently abandoned. Another thought plagued me. Why had he not simply chosen to fire the cabin? He could've roasted his meal, not risking anyone being the wiser for some time. Did the beast want us to know of his deeds? And 'twas as if he'd preferred torture to feasting, and had chosen the humans o'er their animals as well. What was the point? Terror factor mayhap? Certainly not merely to assuage his hunger. The bodies had been mutilated, as if they'd been grabbed mid-flight and shaken to bits, the remains simply discarded. They'd been blooded, with a vastly insufficient amount of their Life Source anywhere to be found. No, they hadn't bled out in death, and in fact the beast had left so little of his victims' blood he must have flown off drunk on the elixir. In my exploration of the surrounding fields I stumbled 'cross the lower half of a small child and lost my breakfast then and there. Our rescue attempts had taught me something. I was no longer too proud to openly wretch.

As was proving typical, it took far too long to gain the survivors' trust, to allow us to help them in their time of need. Carrying a water bag full of Gunnarr's thick saliva had become common practice for me of late. Dragon spit held Healing properties and so stored, reduced to the color of fine aged whiskey. This tint was due to the slow deterioration of the Magic, which began the instant the ooze contacted the air. Interestingly enough, I had firsthand knowledge that it also carried the scent, taste and end result of imbibing in such, and I may choose one day to reveal that tale. However, this characteristic explained why Dragons who are undernourished or dehydrated, drool golden spit and smell like the inside of a whiskey keg. Not necessarily unpleasant, but since the 'Bond, the Teams had been having difficulty with separations and I was fairly certain they weren't hunting as they should. So when I'd accidentally discovered this phenomenon, I immediately shared with the rest of the Warriors. 'Twas proof of the health of their 'Bond and necessary steps would be assured.

Applying the golden 'salve' to the wounds would stave off infection and boost the healing. The source had to remain unbeknownst to them of course, for they'd never have allowed me to treat them had they known. Although 'twas not as effective as fresh from the tongue, 'twas a foregone conclusion, as I have mentioned, that the survivors of a Dragon attack were not likely to allow another one to lick their wounds.

Once all the injured were triaged and treated, we'd assisted them to gather what was left of the bodies, both human and animal, and fired the pile to ash. The cremation served dual purpose, in helping the survivors to achieve closure and to avoid disease. With the assistance of the youngest of the three, I lashed together a makeshift cart with timber Gunnarr supplied from the ruins of the pole barn. We gathered the last of their possessions, everything they could find that could be useful or repaired, packing it along with what food stuffs they'd scrounged. On top of that, I loaded their two critically injured Mastiffs on a pile of slightly smoky straw, with the remaining cow hooked up to help pull. Two goats had survived by fleeing the area at the onset of the attack, and were tied to the back of the cart. After ensuring they knew how to use it, I gave them the sling I usually kept in my belt, to supplement the few tools they'd managed to salvage, which would help them hunt along the way. Then I steered them toward Drekinn, as 'twas our practice not to send anyone to King's Gate 'til we heard from the Team sent there. Thinking about that Team gave me gooseflesh, as they were due to return any day and there'd been no communication at all. 'Twas an eerie silence from Evanntyr. After setting the refugees on their way, we spent the rest of the day seeking the Dragon responsible for this butchery, alas to no avail.

By the time we took flight toward home, 'twas well past dusk. I made a mental note to check the progress of the refugees periodically 'til they arrived safely. At the very least, their dogs were fine animals. The two intact males gave them something with which to barter, and would provide a respectable start-up stake. I knew good lineage when I saw it, and Teaka would be quite pleased with these boys. If they survived their wounds and the journey, they'd be an excellent addition to the War Dog bloodlines. Given good care, they had a fair chance.

Discouraged, 'twas clear we needed to manage ourselves differently. Fortunate thus far, we'd been skating on thin ice and 'twas only a matter of time afore the Fates noticed. I'd been asked to take Command but refused, due to lack of experience in the field, and was chosen unanimously to gain my father's concurrence. 'Twas felt the umbrella of martial organization under which we'd worked as Warriors, would give us needed rank and direction. My hands pillowing my head and my best friend stretched out beside me, we stared at the shimmering sky of our temporary living quarters.

So much to do, so little time. I could feel an approaching storm gathering, but name it I could not. With enhanced vision, the domes of glistening multi-colored sheen were clear to my eyes, like the sun reflecting off a line of soap bubbles floating 'cross the steppes. I'd been amazed these protective Spheres couldn't be seen by anyone outside the 'Bond. Creating a miniature Void, similar to how an air bubble beneath the water literally pushes the water out of its space, the Spheres could not be penetrated by Magic, making us invisible and without scent. But if we were stumbled upon, physically touched by another Magic Bearer, these would simply collapse like the bubbles they appeared to be, a mere camouflage only. I wasn't satisfied with these arrangements. We were too vulnerable out here.

'Twas Gunnarr's own Magic that kept the Spheres o'er all thirteen Teams. But the effort was taking its toll and he couldn't keep them solid much longer. He was the strongest of the thirteen, although not the eldest, yet they deferred to him. Patiently, he waited for me to take action.

Sighing, I knew they were right. 'Twas time to make some decisions. Petulantly, I'd avoided my father, as he'd made his wishes very clear. He wanted us to move into the Den, but I'd opposed that plan. At first I'd seriously considered it, but rejected the idea secondary to an innate sense of insecurity. Danger lay in that location. Was that notion unbiased? 'Twould make no difference, I must learn to trust my intuition and base my decisions upon them. And it told me I had to approach my father. Soon.

With a flash of inspiration, I made my first leadership decision. We'd relocate this very night. The Teams would make their base lair in the caves riddling the cliffs of Drekinn. There we'd find security. At ease with this decision, Gunnarr organized the others and within a single candle mark we gathered at the edge of the rocky sea cliffs to claim our new homes.

A few days later we stretched out on our ledge, fronting the cave we'd chosen as our permanent living quarters. Still in my leathers, I hadn't even helped to remove Gunnarr's strap, too exhausted to even think. 'Twould have to wait. Besides, Gunnarr didn't seem to notice. He could've removed the strap himself, if he'd wanted, but he had difficulty untying my knots without cutting through them with his razor sharp talons, and he didn't want to bother using Magic.

We'd worked long and hard helping the others transfer and getting our own gear moved in, but we'd not slowed down our other efforts. We'd also run checks on the refugees, who should arrive in less than a fortnight. They'd lost the cow but managed to nurse both the Mastiffs to good health using the 'salve' I'd provided them, and had banded with another pair of refugees they'd run into along the way. With them came two extra goats, a horse and some laying chickens. The horse proved well enough to pull the cart, which they'd enlarged using parts from the others' ruined wagon. This enabled them to combine all their goods and get the occasional ride, which made travel much faster. The cow was no serious loss as they were also getting fresh goat's milk, but the eggs did much to supplement their meager resources.

Gunnarr had added a new twist to our training regimen, but I couldn't possibly make yet another attempt to Cast into the cosmos Seeking distress energy tonight. I glanced o'er my shoulder and he was as fatigued as I. His leathery wings tucked tightly against his flanks, and the strap still dangling off his neck, he slowly closed the outer lids of his great luminescent eyes, leaving me in total darkness. Scooting closer, claiming his foreleg as my pillow, he gently unfolded his wing, curled it around me, and pulled me tight to his side. I gazed once again at all the stars glimmering like pin pricks in black velvet above. Pleased with all we'd accomplished o'er the past several days, I slowly relaxed. Ticking off my duties in my mind, the discussion with the Battle Commander was my next priority. Closing my eyes, I had but a few marks afore the sun's rays broke o'er the horizon.

Just as sleep beckoned me come, a Cry of anguish resounded through my senses. Startled fully awake, I barely avoided Gunnarr stumbling o'er me as he raised his massive bulk and prepared to take wing. Battle Lust granted me second wind as I secured my sword, tucked my blades in my boots and mounted up. Soaring off the cliff and leaning hard against the salty airstream, I Cast in all directions, unable to locate the source of the Call. Gunnarr gnashed his fangs in frustration, for not even a thread could he find, to give us a bearing. We'd been awakened by a female Voice desperate for another's rescue. Had she been silenced? Unexpectedly, from out of the cosmic hush, came a male child's Voice yelling for someone to help 'the girl', streaming 'cross the heavens as he ran blindly out of his house, unseeing, unknowing, a horrible fate awaiting him. 'Twas impossible, yet I knew that Voice. Confused, I screamed into the wind in answer to the Call, "WALKYR!"

CHAPTER 8

The Battle of Kaddart

EARLIER THAT SAME NIGHT;
THE HOME OF KALLYR AND SHAYLA

"Me'Shayla, I can't sleep. The dreams come again." Walkyr sighed, as he peered around the edge of the doorframe at his Claim Mother, lying in the middle of the big bed. She always slept alone now. Kallyr hadn't spent a handful of marks at home for more than a full moon. He pursed his lips. 'Twas since the ceremony that had taken several of his Warrior friends away as well. And although Walkyr had never slept soundly due to vivid dreams, since the Magic of the LifeBond he barely rested. The Visions were increasing in frequency as well as becoming more specifically violent and twisted. They should've frightened a child of his age, but instead they made him sad, aggravated and exhausted. The people needed help and he had none to give. He was just a little boy, why did they Call him anyway? Could they not tell he was too small to do anything? He wanted so much to be a Warrior, to do more than just tell his mother about the dreams. But for now he resigned himself to that, for 'twas all he could manage.

The Healer ignored his shortening of 'Ama'Shayla' to 'Me'Shayla', which was more common in the Outlands for what one called their mother. She'd never seen the point of using the more formal wording, though he did call her Ama at times, but rarely with her name, which was proper. She had to shake her head to keep from laughing. The child was quite unique in all ways and 'proper' would hardly be a term used to describe him. "Tell me about them, Walkyr. What did you See?" Sitting up, she scooted to lean against the hand carved headboard, patting the edge of the bed. Walkyr climbed in and she pulled him close, wrapping her arm around him and tucking him under the covers. He needed more than she had to offer lately, but everyone was so busy. Her hands were full and she spent much of her time at the castle, with many long nights treating injured refugees. Even though a formal state of war had yet to be declared, for it took the Battle Commander to do so and he'd been mysteriously distant to the entire mess, 'twas truly upon them. O'er the last full moon, (by the Dragon's Breath, had it only been that long?) the Teams had been working to control their 'Bond enhanced strength, speed and Healing, and also learning the intricacies of MindSpeak. She'd heard they were running patrols and there were rumors about Hoard encounters, but so far no actual skirmishes were confirmed. In fact, there'd been little contact with the 'Bonded since the supply runs, and she didn't like being so ill informed. All of her information came from the refugees the Teams directed to the Den, where they'd shared phenomenal rescue stories, along with increasing and disturbing details of the depravities and viciousness of the Hoard.

She also knew they'd sustained many injuries, some of them believed to be rather severe. Occasionally one could observe them upon the plains, but being so far away 'twas difficult to see much. 'Twas the flight Training, which was the most spectacular to watch. At every opportunity she stood with her head tilted back, her hands shading her eyes from the glare of the sun, marveling at the aerial acrobatics. Crowds gathered afore she could break away and return her attentions to her patients. Early in the practice sessions she'd witnessed a Rider fall off her Dragon and plummet toward certain death. Afore she caught her breath, the Dragon swooped around and dove for the falling Rider, soaring under her to break the fall just afore she hit the ground. The Rider was completely limp during the plummet, telling Shayla she'd been unconscious, but she'd seen nothing prior to the fall to account for this condition. The Rider had landed on top of the Dragon in a heap and she was certain the maneuver had involved a broken bone or three.

She'd immediately raced to the stable, expecting to ride out to meet them coming in for emergency treatment. Tossing her saddle o'er Blush, her strawberry roan mare, Grifynn confronted her afore she'd even tightened the girth. He'd told her in no uncertain terms, the Teams took care of themselves, for they shared the Healing with their Dragons, and they'd not need her talents for such a simple thing as a broken bone. His assertion hadn't set well with her but there seemed little she could do at the time. She'd felt an almost unrecognizable emotion when he'd made the announcement. 'Twas as if he was worried, and was that jealousy? For certain not. More likely 'twas his own stubbornness set in since the 'Bond, and his daughters hadn't visited the Den yet. She'd suggested he make the first move, but he'd steadfastly refused.

In the meantime, she kept her eyes and ears open. He might be Battle Commander, but she was Clan Healer and she, like Grifynn, had seen battle afore. 'Twas very long ago but she'd never forgotten. She'd set up a triage area within the castle walls, directing many of the now homeless refugees as her assistants. 'Twas obvious she'd need to begin training more Healers very soon. She was trying to cope with the needs of everyone around her and had little time or energy left for young Walkyr. With her fingers, she swept his long mahogany hair off his face and looking into his pale blue eyes she asked him again, "Walkyr, what did you dream?"

He snuggled into her shoulder, the air chill in the back room, and began in a clear voice, "'Twas a village with many people. 'Twas not Drekinn, not Clan. They had dark hair, not like us." Shaking his head up and down, he turned and stared at Shayla, reaching for her thick red curls with his small fingers, making reference to the Clan's fair coloring, mostly red headed or blonde with blue or green eyes. Walkyr had rich brown hair, tanned skin with a sprinkling of freckles and pale blue eyes, but he still considered himself one of us, and so he thought of himself as fair. "'Twas raging fire with much smoke and many people screaming. I could scarcely See through. Then a little girl ran out of the smoke away from the village. 'Tis her goal to cross the open fields and enter the forest." Walkyr sounded older than his six winters when he spoke. Shayla could tell he was deep in his Vision, staring straight ahead, but 'twould seem he was transitioning to the present, giving her goose flesh. This wasn't a common Gift and it made her shiver with the Power he wielded. His fluid shifts from past to present to future were disturbing at times. Only recently they'd used his Vision as a kind of map, following the boy as he walked through a world only he could see, 'til real time caught up, leading them unerringly to locate the lost and injured. Anyone would appreciate how useful his abilities would be during War time, and mayhap the One True Liege had provided precisely for that purpose. But she also knew 'twould make it very difficult to keep him safe. If the Hoard got hold of him, she didn't want to think of how they would misuse the Gift, let alone abuse the child.

He'd been quiet too long, and nudging him to continue revealed he was truly upset. Examining his face 'twas clear his reality fluctuated 'tween her and the little girl. "We're being chased by a Dragon. He's a big one, not as big as Darque's or Storrm's, but close to the third one!" Shayla shivered again thinking about the size of Ragnyrr, the third to take the 'Bond. He was huge. She wouldn't want to face such a mighty beast alone. Walkyr became more anxious as he narrated his Vision. "He's hunting us. We're hiding, ducking in and out of the rubble of the village, we have to make it 'cross the fields, we have to get to the forest! The beast won't follow us there! FLAME! The Dragon turns us with Flame! He plays with us, wants to feel our fear, torture us!" Walkyr's reality returned to

Shayla, while he anxiously searched her face. "He means to kill her! She needs help, she needs help now! Ama, this happens now! She'll soon arrive in the burning village, she'll soon face the Dragons and the Flame!" Frantically pulling himself free of the heavy bed linens, Walkyr jumped off and ran for the door. Afore Shayla could untangle herself and give chase, he dashed into the pre-dawn shadows as fast as his little legs could carry him. Yelling for him to stop, he gave no indication he heard her, nor that he was even aware of his present surroundings, seemingly chasing after the girl himself.

Shayla rushed after Walkyr, screaming in her mind for someone, anyone to help him. She could actually feel the frenzied waves of energy he was Pushing into the darkness, as he ran blindly 'cross the square. Without warning, a dim shadow on shadow passed o'erhead, followed instantly by a great rush of wind, knocking her to her hands and knees on the cobblestone. Looking up, 'twas a huge blue Dragon swooping down upon the child now running headlong toward the village well. Walkyr didn't know how to swim and if he stumbled into the depths of the well he'd surely injure himself in the fall and most likely drown. All appeared in slow motion as the Rider slid around the Dragon's neck and ducked under his wing, hanging onto a single leather strap with one hand. Using her muscular thighs she squeezed tightly against the leathery scales and stretched out her free hand. Enthralled, Shayla held her breath, mutely watching the action unfurl. The Rider grasped the fleeing boy by the back of his nightshirt and yanked him to her side just as they approached the well. Shayla inhaled sharply, fearing the oncoming collision would smash both Rider and child, but the Dragon pulled straight up at the last moment, climbing vertically into the sky with the sharp talons of his hind feet barely grazing the wooden edge atop the stone wall. Leveling off, using a maneuver that seemed to help them right themselves upon his neck, he secured his passengers and disappeared into the darkness.

Shayla could only gasp at the daring of such a feat. Quickly standing, she brushed the dirt off her nightdress. Somehow she knew the boy was safe, but couldn't stop her heart from hammering in her chest, as she set off at a fast jog to the Commander's Office to report his daughter was making fine progress in the art of air travel. The in-flight rescue was both fearsome and thrilling, but she desperately needed to find out where they were going. She wondered what was happening to the little girl in his Vision, as she must be in great danger and needed help without delay. Breathlessly, she approached Grifynn's office as these thoughts ran through her mind.

~~~~~~~~~~

"I have him! Hurry, my friend!" The wind whipped harshly 'cross my face, making my eyes water. Hugging the boy tightly to my chest, Gunnarr Cast for the little girl's distress energy, but 'twould take precision. And now that he was in 'Bond, his ability to share another's Sight was sluggish and we didn't have time for that. We'd have to do this together, and through the Link I could Share the boy's Vision with clarity. 'Twas the only way. I yelled aloud o'er the roar of beating wings amid furious flight, "You must Link with me Walkyr! Do you fear the blooding?"

"I trust you Darque, blood me! We must save the girl! I can help!" He shivered in my grasp, but whether 'twas from the cold or from fear, I knew not.

Shifting his slight body, I hung onto him with one arm and drew one of my boot blades, as I followed Gunnarr's directions for establishing this, my first Link outside the 'Bond. Leaning o'er him, my lips close to his ear so he could hear my next words, "You must be brave, my young friend! I cannot let go of you, I have no extra straps, and I have to make the cut with my other hand! Can you do this?" I felt, rather than saw his head nod in consent. "Hold out your arm!"

Walkyr instantly lifted his small arm o'er his shoulder, giving me easy access, then took a deep breath afore I made the cut on the inside of his wrist, loosing his Life Source. Suckling gently, his blood sang to me, as I closed my eyes and sought entry to his thoughts.

His Vision became my own so quickly and with such clarity, I nearly lost my grip on the strap. The heat and the acrid odor of Flame permeated my senses 'til my eyes and throat began to burn, but I recognized the surrounding forest, the fields, the bridge o'er the creek that meandered lazily around the area. I'd visited this remote region southeast of Drekinn, in my youth. 'Twas Kaddart, from whence the murdered Runner had come. The King's Agents here were barracked and rotated every other winter, since Shytin had deemed the farmers had no need for real Warriors. But within the Vision there was no evidence of them, nor any indication they'd been present during the attack. These people apparently had no defensive forces against the Hoard. Keeping Walkyr's wrist to my lips, his blood hot upon my tongue, I Searched for the girl, for anyone left alive. We could sort out the events later, my first priority was rescue. But to my utter disappointment, 'twas apparent this one little girl was the sole survivor of the entire village. At least, I hoped she yet lived.
~~~~~~~~~~

"Hurry Gunnarr," I Spoke, once again grateful for the 'Bond as I gave him the reference coordinates to Kaddart.

"She is in my Sight." My heart leaped with the energy of Gunnarr's Voice. *"Prepare yourself for the carnage. All but the child have been forced Beyond. There were many Dragons, no Riders. The others departed, leaving just one in their wake to finish the girl. What is your wish m'lady?"*

I knew what he Asked. *"Rescue. We can do nothing for the village or the people there. We cannot fight and rescue at the same time. There will be another day, and the people of Kaddart will be avenged."*

"As you will," Gunnarr Spoke. *"We'll take her aboard as we did the young Seer."* After what seemed an eternity, we neared the village. The beautiful countryside was marred by scorched patches, and huge black plumes of smoke filled the early dawn skies. 'Twas nothing more to learn from Walkyr. Gently I swiped my tongue o'er the cut to stop the bleeding and prevent infection, then dropped his arm and tied my strap around his waist. 'Twas my desire he not fall off if we had to engage the Hoard. Ensuring my primary weapon was still strapped on, I was relieved 'twas in its scabbard and I'd not lost it in the maneuvers to rescue the boy. Drawing the long sword, I consciously controlled my Battle Lust so I'd not lose rational thought. I fisted the hilt and squeezed tightly 'cross Walkyr's chest, hugging him close, thinking to calm him. But my senses were clear with skin to skin contact through his ripped nightshirt, and I was assured he shivered not from fear but from excitement and the cold of flight.

"There!" I Spat forth, my eyes studying the southern border of the village. *"She runs out of the thicket edging the fields."* At the same time Gunnarr looked to the east and Spoke o'er me. *"There! The Dragon who torments her. We must face him to save the girl."*

"We cannot fight with Walkyr aboard!" I tried to reason, but he was correct and I resigned myself to the inevitable. Rattling off a series of questions, I adjusted our plans to include the upcoming conflict. *"You're certain the others have fled, but are there any close enough to Hear who might return to join their comrade? How many do we face?"*

"'Twould appear this one is concluding their business solo. I Sense no others. Are you ready for this, Darque?"

Softly, mayhap not even with the intent to Answer, I declared to myself this moment of truth, *"My Legend Song begins in this moment."* Crouching, my fingers gripping the edges of his neck scales for balance, I crawled o'er Walkyr, placing myself as a shield 'tween him and the coming battle.

With a snort of smoke Gunnarr gathered himself, his muscles bunched 'neath my feet, and without further warning we were flying faster than ever afore. The Hoard Dragon was skimming the ground, ignorant of our presence above him, focused upon his victim. I could see her now without enhancement, as we plummeted toward the Evil creature, Gunnarr's lethal talons bared and ready. The winter crops had been Flamed, providing the girl little cover. If his attention remained focused on her 'til we were close enough to engage, I thought, we could make this rescue and leave afore we were confronted with backup from his comrades.

Suddenly she stopped running, turned about and stared straight at the oncoming beast as if she'd heard me. By the Almighty One, she must be terrified. Yet incredibly, she made her stand, glaring at the vile creature while he inhaled deeply, preparing to Flame her into oblivion. She glanced not to us, understanding if she did, the beast would realize too soon that we were behind him. We tore through the sky while she kept her gaze defiantly locked on his, but just as we were within reach, he finally caught on.

Abandoning the girl, he banked sharply leftward to avoid being slashed. Gunnarr growled a curse in Dragon Tongue as he just missed the other's exposed eyes, but managed to score deeply into his neck scales. The pain and the jolt of impact made the Hoard Dragon miss a wing beat, along with his opportunity to roll quickly enough to present his own talons. But Gunnarr would have none of that, for the chase was on, and he shredded the back and neck of the loathsome creature, keeping him in defensive mode, unable to turn about. 'Twas raining blood, but the other's Healing was swift and Gunnarr couldn't seat a fatal gash. *"There is little time! His eyes!"* He was fatiguing, we'd been exhausted afore we'd rescued Walkyr, and we couldn't keep going much longer. This kill became mine to set up. *"Ready,"* I Replied.

Rising to my feet, my left hand upon his neck to steady myself, I resheathed my sword with my right and drew one of my boot blades. Gunnarr maintained his offensive attack, forcing his opponent to duck and dodge, while maintaining an even keel to the best of his ability. *"Now!"* I Heard Gunnarr roar, and I launched myself into the air without hesitation, landing on the shoulders of the other. As the foul smelling beast desperately tried to unseat me, I grasped my blade tighter, my left hand digging under his granite hard scales, seeking a solid grip. An old memory flashed through my mind and I was once again with Storrm, rock climbing up a sheer cliff near the timberline, in search of the Dragon whose Song had led us 'cross the plains. My tenuous purchase on the neck of this beast was just as good, and the quick descent should I lose my grip would be just as fatal, only this time the stakes were much higher. 'Twas not my own life I risked this day, and I pushed the memory to the background as I began the perilous climb. From where I'd landed I tediously crawled hand o'er hand, straddling his neck and pulling myself up by the edges of his thick scales. 'Twas similar to climbing an unsecured rope made slippery with lard. He twisted and turned in his attempts to rid himself of his unwanted passenger and the higher I climbed, the more slender his neck, making it harder to hang on as I neared my goal. Fortunately, as long as I didn't slide under his chin he couldn't reach me with his talons since he'd have to lower his head, which would also drop his flight and seriously expose his wings, giving Gunnarr a distinct advantage. If I slid around anywhere along the journey 'twould be my end, as he'd shred me in a candle drip. Gunnarr had to change his tactics to give me opportunity to complete my mission, without actually interfering or hurting me in the process. The only position he could take that would fulfill the need to keep me safe by keeping the other busy and not able to maneuver, was very risky and considered last ditch defense. For most Dragons, flying belly up, just leading the other, would be their Check Mate. But the evil creature couldn't get close enough to take advantage of his 'superior' position and gradually realized he was fighting a much more powerful Dragon than himself. Finally in position and unable to secure any other hold, I grabbed inside the corner of his jaw. Avoiding the sharp teeth, I locked my legs around his neck, reached out with my blade, and sunk it to the hilt into his right eye. Pulling it out, I stabbed again and again, trying to do as much damage as I could, while the adrenaline rush was rapidly dissolving my ability to think clearly. Quickly losing count of how many times I'd plunged the blade, I Heard Gunnarr yell, *"Return to me Warrior!"*

Clearing my mind, 'twould be mere moments afore the beast upon which I now rode, crashed into the barren fields below and if still aboard, we'd all die. Once again I launched myself as far into the wind and away from the thrashing beast as I could, watching as he dropped like a rock beneath me. Gunnarr flew in hard and fast under my free falling body, swooping in for the catch just afore I hit the ground close to where the other Dragon now lay in a crumpled heap. I'd hoped to land on my feet, but had the wind knocked out of me landing hard on my back just behind his wings. A small hand grabbed for my ankle, and although he couldn't actually hold on, his fleeting touch reminded me to grab on fast or let myself get swept off to plummet again toward the fields below. Sliding down Gunnarr's back, I frantically reached for any handhold, but his scales were even more slippery with blood than the one I'd just abandoned, and with my precarious perch and the momentum I'd achieved, I couldn't get a grip. Continuing my slide, Gunnarr banked and dove to assist me to gather my seat. Unable to land without losing me, I slid o'er, slid down, slid forward and back again, increasingly aggravated. 'Twas getting us nowhere. The Hoard Dragon was still alive and Gunnarr couldn't finish him as long as I was yet unsecured. Valuable moments were passing, and instead of wasting more time, I Shared my plan. Gliding carefully, I tumbled and slipped back along his scales, grabbed onto his thick tail and then dangled below with my hands locked together. Damn the Fates, I had to drop my blade to keep my grip. Slowing down and coasting lower, I waited for his signal, for I had no view beneath me. *"Release now!"* I did so, and fell through the air, trusting his decision. I hit the dirt hard, let my body relax as I crumpled to the ground, and then rolled, getting back on my feet with all haste.

Immediately dropping into Battle Stance, I rapidly assessed the situation. Gunnarr had purposely dropped me off closer to the forest edge, to allow me to gain cover if the Hoard Dragon was able to gather his wings again afore his end was achieved. But I wouldn't be excluded from the fight. Grabbing a boot blade in each hand, I sprinted toward the twitching creature, my arms pumping hard. Gunnarr dove in o'er me, easily winning the race 'cross the field. Flaming as he came roaring in, the Hoard Dragon lit up like the Magic fire on the night of the LifeBond ceremony. Furious, the beast reacted by rearing up upon his hind legs, screaming wildly in pain and disbelief, and reached out with his massive forelegs clawing blindly. As Gunnarr battered him with his razor-sharp talons and fangs, he ripped the other's still beating heart from his exposed chest, forcing him 'cross the Veil.

<div align="center">~~~~~~~~~~</div>

"He didn't think he could be slain." Gunnarr squatted afore me in the dirt, his massive tail curled around his feet in his characteristic pose. 'Twas long past dawn and the sun was warming the chill air as I struggled to catch my breath. Breathing hard, I'd stopped in the middle of the field and crouched with my hands on my knees. *"He was so astonished, he didn't even think to Call for assistance. And I believe we have just eradicated the one who killed the Runner, for I Shared his Memory of Flaming the boy just prior to his disappearance into the forest yonder. This should please*

your sire as well. We have won a great Battle here, Darque. You should be proud."

"Proud… (breathe)… oh… (breathe)… yeah… (breathe)… (as I shook my head up and down)… proud." Then fearing he'd been injured or dislodged during the battle, I looked for Walkyr. After all, Gunnarr had actually flown and fought upside down, while I was on the other. Seeing his tiny body, his huge eyes shining out from his blood splattered face in amazement and wonder, I found another burst of energy from some store house within. Rushing to his side, I climbed up on Gunnarr's proffered knee and untied him, asking him again and again if he was alright.

"I am not injured m'lady Darque! 'Twas amazing! I can't believe what you did! You flew through the air! You killed the Hoard Dragon!" Sputtering in an enthusiastic rush of ideas while I tried to wipe off enough of the blood to see for myself he was unharmed, I answered him. "'Twould appear so, my little friend." Then came the rush of fatigue. After all, we hadn't slept in how long? I couldn't seem to remember. 'Twould be bad timing to succumb.

Suddenly I remembered why we came here in the first place and jerking my head up to survey the area I caught Gunnarr's expression as he shifted his gaze discretely 'cross the field northward, toward the forest. Speaking to me, he ticked off his observations one at a time. *"She's gone aground. She ducked into the forest during the battle. She is close, observing our actions. She is amazed at the boy Rider. She has seen much this day and is traumatized. She will run if we try to follow. I cannot enter the forest, my eyes, my wings…."* and his Thoughts trailed off with the return of his gaze to mine. For the first time, Gunnarr emitted true distress. He was fine 'til he made reference to entering the forest, and 'twas apparent we had some history to explore later.

"How safe are we here? Can we reconnoiter? I don't think I can repeat this performance for a day or so…." I Told him with a slight smile, as I finally caught my breath. Walkyr instinctively stood quietly at my side, averting his gaze from the forest. Not wanting the girl to run, we had to make her believe we didn't see her or know where she was hiding, or we'd lose her.

His distress evaporated as he Replied, *"We are safe for now. I cannot continue to Cast about however, or the Magic this involves will Draw their attention like a candle in the darkness."*

"Walkyr," I said quietly, and placing my hand on his shoulder, "you've been very brave. Do you See any more of the bad Dragons? Do you See anything at all?"

"No m'lady. I've been trying, but I haven't Seen anything since afore the fight."

Casting out with my own senses, I felt nothing o'er the death and destruction of the entire village. "Alright then, let's go." Instructing Walkyr to stay 'tween us, I took point into the village while Gunnarr took the rear. Flying o'er would be pointless, as well as possibly drawing unwanted attention. We wouldn't find out what happened from the skies, even though the smoke was mostly cleared now. We had to get down and dirty.

Within a half candle mark we were standing amidst the smoldering ruins of the tiny village square at Kaddart Well. Sitting on the edge with Walkyr at my feet and Gunnarr squatting to the side, he Said, *"She has followed us."*

"I Know. We'll let her take her time. She's insightful. We'll soon see how much." Stripping out of my bloody leathers, Walkyr stood up and did the same. The bucket for drawing water was burned to a crisp but 'twouldn't matter, for the arm and the pulleys were also gone. At least the water wasn't fouled. 'Twas deep however, making it impossible to lean down and reach the surface. Gunnarr stood up and ambled closer to oblige my idea. Clutching the pile of clothing, I lifted my right leg up high, as Gunnarr leaned down, gently taking my foot in his mouth, a move we'd actually never practiced afore. *"I am happy you trust me, my sweet, but I'm not all that certain of your sanity. I have little idea how much pressure to apply and I'd never forgive myself if I accidentally separated your beautiful foot from your leg."*

"Now is as good a time to learn as any. She's watching. My trust in you and this maneuver should do it. Just don't drop me, by all the fires of Hades! I doubt I have the strength to climb back out and this Well has a smooth wall."

He rumbled in anger or laughter… wasn't always sure of that growl. I smiled and Gunnarr clasped down on my ankle, positioning me 'tween his front teeth and his fangs to secure my foot against his gum line. Then he lifted me carefully off the ground, dangled me o'er the Well and slowly lowered me 'til I began to splash at the water's surface. His great snout was just inside the Well, his eyes outside peering o'er the edge keeping guard on Walkyr and his huge head cut off the light, plunging me into complete darkness. I hadn't expected that angle, although my vision was sufficient. Wetting the clothing in one big wad, for if I let go I was afraid I'd lose them, I soaked and squeezed and repeated to clean them as best I could, then used them to clean the worst of the blood, sweat and grime off my body, after which Gunnarr hoisted me slowly back up. Once out in the open again, he dropped me about a foot to the char covered cobblestones and I was suddenly covered by a clear, slimy ooze from above. *"Ewwwwww! What is this? Drool? Flame it all Gunnarr, suck up that spit, I just washed. UGH!"*

"Apologies, little one, but you do taste divine," the Mighty Blue Said sheepishly, slurping up the thick slobber like strings of spaghetti, and then sat back on his haunches, undaunted. *"And don't let that child hear your stomach growl like that,"* I Chastised, as I wrung the clothing o'er my head to wash away the remaining slobber and dirt from the awkward landing. We really must work on that, I thought. Handing Walkyr his clothing, I was donning my damp leathers when I noted Gunnarr's gaze shift. Following it down the square, I saw the little girl standing 'tween two burned out buildings. Ready to seek shelter if we approached, she was bold for all her youth. Smiling, she reminded me of Storrm when she was that age. It seemed a lifetime ago.

"Are you not afraid of that beast?" She murmured. Interesting talent. Was she aware of the Push she added to her soft voice? "Will he hurt you, to get to me? The other one did. He hurt everyone. But you killed him." She moved forward a few steps and pointed, "Is that your Dragon? Is he a good Dragon?"

Projecting my voice as she had, *"'Tis a Gift to be explored,"* I Told Gunnarr, and answered quietly so as not to frighten her further. "I am Darque. This Dragon is not mine. We're partners. Together we fight the bad Dragons."

Cautiously, she took a few more steps toward us. "So there are good Dragons." Then she took a few more steps. "Did that boy get hurt in the fight? Why does he Ride with you?" She continued to move slowly forward, still keeping enough distance to bolt if considered necessary.

"Yes, there are good Dragons." I smiled but stood my ground, allowing her to set the pace. "What is your name, little one?"

She hesitated briefly and then replied, "I am Fryya." And suddenly making her decision, needing to be with someone, anyone, she ran to me and leaped into my outstretched arms. Clutching her hard to my chest, I rocked gently, running my hand down her long red hair. She pressed her face into my shoulder and began to chant in shock, "they're dead, they're dead, they're dead," and my heart near shattered with her torment.

CHAPTER 9

The Dragon's Eye

THE NEXT DAY

When dawn broke o'er the Raptor's Talons, 'twould then reflect up the cliff face off the waters of the Sea of Dreams, providing natural light within the cave openings. But due to the angles, they wouldn't be noted from afar except when lit from within by torch. Since the 'Bonded rarely required torches, the ones we did have were lit only in the deepest gloom of some of the caverns and passageways. Without waking Fryya, Gunnarr and I carefully made our way to my favorite cavern to clean up. We'd taken to calling it 'the Cave of Jewels' in reference to the sometimes eerie but dramatic lighting effects of the jewel encrusted ceiling and walls. I was pleased to find we were alone in the vast open space, as I stepped through the sand toward the distant wall where several cool streams of fresh water gushed forth through crevices in a pyramid pattern all the way to the ceiling. The largest stream created a waterfall with a force strong enough to knock you off your feet if you weren't prepared, and at least two Warriors with both their Dragons could fit under the running water at the same time. Reaching the far side of the pool, I climbed up and o'er the naturally terraced rocky ledge and made quick work of showering and washing my hair. After taking care of my own personal hygiene, I was refreshed, and diving off the ledge into the deep, crystal clear water below, I swam swiftly 'cross the pool to where Gunnarr splashed in the shallows. Picking up a handful of the fine white sand of the beach, I began to scrub his leathery hide briskly. Purring his satisfaction deep within his throat, he sounded like a contented cat. Usually a Dragon would simply roll or wallow in the sand, or in reeds or cat tails along a river edge, and then stand under a waterfall or swim to rinse off. Helping him had become a time of renewal for us, creating an intimacy that couldn't be compared with anything I'd ever felt with anyone else in my life. I didn't want to lose this, but sometimes I felt guilty about not wanting to share with anyone else. What if I mated? What if Gunnarr mated? With the two of us able to Feel the other's emotions and Hear each other's thoughts, I had to wonder how that was going to work out for us.

Raising my eyebrows as my mind strayed yet again toward that topic, I turned from the task of playfully rinsing his broad chest with handfuls of clean water, and caught him staring at me. 'Twas clear we were think-ing the same thing. His great crystalline eyes flashed and sparkled and the smirk upon his face made me giggle like a little girl. Shaking my head and dropping my eyes, I stepped out of the pool where I'd been stand-ing knee deep. Striding naked and dripping wet toward the exit, the heat of his emotions bored into my back, but I was concerned about staying here any longer for fear Fryya would wake up alone and be frightened. Gunnarr tramped out of the pool close on my heels, and shaking his mas-sive bulk to rid himself of most of the excess water, I barely missed the icy shower as I entered the passageway just ahead of him. In the few moments it took to negotiate the long systems back to our main living quarters, the cold air had me chilled.

Picking up my leathers in the darkness of the cave, I stepped quiet-ly around the still sleeping child, and went out to meet Gunnarr on the ledge. Just how did he do that anyway? 'Twas always amazing to find him ahead of me, and how had he not wakened Fryya? Sighing, I dressed, al-lowing her a few more moments of blissful sleep. She'd tossed and turned and cried out most of the night, but hadn't awakened, and I'd learned a great deal from her erratic dialog. Alas, not much of what she'd said made any sense to me, so I'd cataloged it in my memories and prayed it became clearer soon. We'd gotten no sleep the night of her rescue (had it been just yesterday?) and we'd attempted to reassure the girl and settle her into our quarters all day. I'd tried to get her to take a nap, but she'd declared quite firmly that she was too old for that, and if I didn't need to sleep then nei-ther did she. So last night we'd pretended for her sake to tuck in early and she had thankfully, fallen into a deep sleep soon thereafter. Of course, Gunnarr's Song might have had something to do with that.

By the time I'd finished dressing, Fryya had begun to stir, and when she didn't immediately recognize her surroundings, she leaped up quick-ly. I was pleased to note instead of panic, she'd quickly accelerated to Battle Mode, awake, aware and ready to flee or fight as the situation war-ranted.

"'*Tis her birthright, she reveals,*" to which I received Gunnarr's con-firming nod. She had to be Clan, but who was her sire? Obviously not the one she'd alleged.

"M'lady Darque?" Fearless, she merely sought to know if she was alone.

"Here, on the ledge. Come enjoy the dawn with us." With a smile on my face, I watched her step out warily, rubbing the sleep from her eyes with the heels of her tiny hands. Her copper red hair bushed out from her head like a halo. The sun's early rays reflected off the surf below to shine through it, giving her a surreal appearance when she leaned o'er the edge to look straight down upon the crashing waves, as the rough surf broke o'er the rocks. 'Twas deep water just off the cliff face, but no one who didn't know this for fact would dare take a leap of faith for fear of impaling ones' self just beneath the surface.

"We need to get a comb through that hair, little one," I said cheerfully, and then I took her hand and led her back inside. Reaching to light the torch for her sake, she shook her head. "There's no need m'lady. I see well in the darkness. I don't require a torch." Then walking straight to the corner, she washed up using the clean rag and water bucket I'd set there for this purpose. Not positive of her loyalties yet, 'twouldn't be wise to show her all our secrets. Mayhap another day.

Once ready to travel, we mounted up with Fryya in front of me so I could hold her and we headed for Drekinn. It didn't take long to catch up with Walkyr and Shayla, but I didn't tell the Healer much, despite being aware that she was near bursting to know everything. When we'd delivered Walkyr back home safely about mid-morning yesterday, she'd been so grateful she hadn't even thought to ask questions and now thankfully, she understood my silence. Walkyr had always been good at keeping secrets, instinctively knowing what should and shouldn't be revealed, so I trusted he'd said nothing. Making a simple request to leave the girl child in her care for awhile, I assured her that she and Walkyr were friends. Raising her eyebrows and biting her tongue, she agreed. After all, how could she refuse? Having secured the girl's safety for the time being, I remounted and we took wing. *"Destination Kaddart, my friend."*

~~~~~~~~~~

After spending near half the day investigating, I was as troubled as when we'd first arrived. Adding to the mystery, I'd stood in the middle of the burned out fields for near half a candle mark, Searching for an elusive thread of Presence, to no avail. I'd already been a'Flamed that we'd lost a whole day prior to returning but we'd needed the time to settle Fryya and get the most vital information from her initial memories. If only I could be in two places at the same time. If I'd secured backup, which I was quite annoyed with myself for not having thought about at the time, we could've had them find my blade and do a preliminary investigation while the scene was still 'hot'. Fates be damned, we had to get organized. Someone needed to take Command. Sighing, I knew the others be-
~~~~~~~~~~

lieved that 'someone' should be me, and shrugging it off I returned to the 'Presence'.

We'd thoroughly searched the entire village and the outlying areas as soon as we'd arrived, coming up with some disturbing conclusions, but no physical proof. Since there was nothing to confirm my suspicions, I chose to keep them to myself for the time being. Suddenly amidst my decision making process, I caught the barest hint of Allure. 'Twas as if an invisible being had walked 'tween us, without physically touching either, brushing past me as a puff of air upon my arm, leaving me with the sinister impression I was being watched. No sooner had I felt this Presence than it vanished, and I was beginning to doubt I'd felt anything at all. Glancing at Gunnarr, he appeared unconcerned although he remained quiet, simply waiting for me to decide how to proceed, and I wondered if he'd noticed the same thing I had. Unsettled, I could Hear nothing from him about the odd feeling, but I supposed he would've offered his opinion had it been warranted.

Accepting I'd found no proof, I stopped my Search and jogged purposefully to what was left of the carcass still in the field. The remains of all of the Magical Races were indistinguishable to non-Magic Bearers (Mankind being the only Race I knew of, in that category). But since the 'Bond, I realized I'd always been able to See more than my fellow humans, I'd just not understood the significance of what I'd Seen. 'Twas yet another Gift of The One and I no longer questioned His Gifts.

Squatting, I reached toward what looked like a talon, when Gunnarr placed a Hold on my arm, stopping me mid-air. Unable to continue moving my arm forward, he Spoke with concern, *"For what do you search, m'lady?"*

The Hold felt and worked like a woven finger puzzle, the more you pushed or pulled against it, the stronger it became. Without looking at him directly, I relaxed my arm, letting it drop limply, the only way to maneuver out of such a Magical grip, but I stopped just short of trying to circumvent it. Looking up at him quizzically, I Answered, *"A weapon,"* as if he must be mad, surely he Knew me by now.

"But we have Searched for the blade without success. Why look for it in the ash?" Gunnarr seemed unaware of my purpose, confusion upon his face.

Slightly confused myself, I Responded, *"I know. 'Tis not the blade for which I reach my friend."*

"I do not understand. What weapon do you seek within the ash?"

Was he being purposefully obtuse? *"See my thoughts, this should work. I wanted to try to get them fresh, but we hadn't the time then. Now we do. Surely the fangs and talons don't succumb to Flame."*

I'd not realized a Dragon could truly smile, 'til I saw the sun dawn upon him. And had I known how concerned he'd just been, not able to read my thoughts 'til I Told him to, I would've been quite impressed indeed. Gunnarr was not impressed however, but managed to keep this knowledge to himself, aware that my blossoming Gifts could yet be perverted by Evil and I'd need him now more than ever, to teach me to control the raw power growing within.

With relief evident in his sparkling eyes, he took control. *"Allow me, m'lady. The ash will be corrosive to your skin 'til the first rains."* He ambled his huge bulk to the pile of charred debris that had once been a Hoard Dragon, and raking his impressive claws through the rubble he sifted out the beast's talons and fangs, placing them in his great maw to carry, as they would need special handling so as not to slice through the leather bag that I'd brought along and tied around his neck. He was surprised he didn't find any of the creature's teeth, but 'twas possible they'd been destroyed in his Flame, although teeth were the least likely part to be damaged and therefore the most likely to survive the death. As an afterthought, he located several mostly undamaged scales. Sorting through them, he placed the best ones carefully into the bag, filling it to near spilling o'er.

'Twas then he recalled another token he could give her, although he knew she was different from other human females, in that she rarely wore jewelry or even owned any precious stones. Raking through the remains a few more times, he soon found that which he sought. Extremely rare, greatly desired, and incredibly valuable, the gem once known as the Dragon's Eye hadn't been seen since the Last Holocaust. 'Twas ironic that the gem was so named, because the humans knew not 'twas a real eye of a Dragon they wore. He pulled out the undamaged left eye of the beast, knowing the damaged one would have disintegrated in the Flaming, and cleaned and polished it by heating it 'tween his fore claws with a light breath of fire. Rolling it on the flat of his paw, he marveled at the sparkling crystal that had been condensed from its huge life size to about the size of a walnut, making it the hardest known substance in the world, even harder than his own fangs and talons. Yet there were many other traits associated with the gem. There were some among Man who could See through the eye. 'Twas told in Song of his Kind, that those with the Gift could use the Eye as a predictor or locator of the lost, and 'twas highly valued by the necromancers for its great Power to boost any spell. 'Twas in his Memories that such had once been used as external lenses to enhance human vision for those without the Gift. Wrapping the gem to prevent light from entering the edges while maintaining your focus through the middle, you could actually extend your natural eyesight to see far distant images as if they were within your reach. And when touched by firelight or the rays of the sun, 'twould display magnificent color and extreme beauty. Placing it under his tongue to hide it from Darque, he was delighted about having something special to give her.

Packing the fangs and talons in the middle of the scales in the stuffed bag afore he turned around, he still had his doubts, but knew if anyone could make use of this refuse 'twas Darque. He'd never considered recycling such, for Dragons used their own fangs and talons and didn't carry separate weapons. But humans were not as sturdily built and had only their formidable creativity to enhance their meager physical attributes, though Darque had more than proven herself physically. His thoughts shifted to the sight of her standing naked under the waterfall in the cavern this morning. Her blue eyes closed, head back, her fingers running through her long red hair, her flat belly, smooth fair skin, muscled legs… brought a rush of heat to his loins. Hadn't he just been thinking of her skills in fighting? How did thoughts of her so often stray in the other direction?

He shook his great head to clear it and began to realize that with the proper Spell, 'twould be possible to share the act they both desired.

Smiling wickedly to himself and shaking his head again, he was finally able to focus on Darque's current thoughts. 'Twould take Magic to alter the composition in order to forge a weapon she could carry. He blinked as he tried to keep up with her rapid thoughts. Yes, 'twas ingenious and indeed, it could work. So armed, the Riders would be a force to reckon with in the coming battles. When would Maahayyel allow the Draw? His Matriarch was stubborn but not petulant and if she waited, 'twas for a good reason. He could ask of course, but she'd come to him when the time was right. Still, if she didn't come soon, he'd take his petition to her.

His pride in his Rider's resourcefulness shining through his eyes, he half knelt for her to mount up for the return home. There was nothing more to be learned here, and what they'd Felt was most disturbing. If only they'd found her missing blade. It should have been simple enough. He couldn't be certain, but there seemed a hint of Allure in the air o'er the Flamed fields that didn't 'fit' somehow. Of course, 'twas dusted from the battle, but there was something else he couldn't quite sense fully. Did this have anything to do with the loss of the knife?

Looking about them, trying once again to scent more information, he abruptly recognized 'twas a Mask. Most wouldn't notice, but Gunnarr the Mighty Blue was not most. Someone or something, had been here afore them, and since the battle. Masking took much Magic and 'twould not be used lightly. Had they taken the blade, and if so, for what purpose? And if not, why Mask, why not simply hide? Had they actually walked 'tween them, nearly touching them in the field? If he'd felt the Mask sooner, he could have tried to break it down, but he'd been distracted… and how had Darque blocked her thoughts from him anyway? She shouldn't have been able to do that without training. Gunnarr understood that she wasn't even aware of her growing powers. He knew not how their future would unfold, but he wasn't one to question prophesy. All this and more did Gunnarr shuffle through in the blink of an eye, and when Darque was secure in her place against his neck, he gathered himself, took a mighty leap and left the ground far beneath them as he spread wing for home.

~~~~~~~~~~

The Predator was impressed as he watched the big blue lift himself gracefully off the ground from a dead stop, carrying the human Rider without effort. His restless eyes watched them sail o'er the woods and hills to the horizon, becoming a tiny speck 'til they disappeared into the distance. Only then did he release his Mask. 'Twouldn't do for the Hoard or the Clan to learn of his power. 'Twas not time. He raised his hand and gazed appreciatively at the blade lying 'cross his open palm. Quite unique and of the highest quality materials, 'twas unexpected in something Man made. The Dragon motifs were a special touch, and the workmanship was exquisite. He sniffed the edge slowly. For a moment, there was something… ancient. Then 'twas gone.

He alone had Heard the Death Cry of the Hoard Dragon when he'd been forced Past the Veil, but it had taken him much time to spirit himself away unseen. This Village had served well as a lair, 'til the youthful Princess had let her curiosity get the better of her. No, 'twas not entirely her doing. It seemed there were some good men amongst the Race of Man. That Runner hadn't gone along with the debauchery. No, 'twas not his escape that had spelled the end, either. Kaddart was doomed from the beginning and there'd been no chance to save them once the wheel of events had been set in motion. He let out a long breath.
~~~~~~~~~~

When he'd arrived, he'd found the Dragon's remains intact and had just pocketed all of the teeth when he'd felt the Team arriving and had been forced to Mask. He hadn't been able to sense their identities 'til this moment, despite having walked 'tween them in the field. Nicking his finger with the sharp blade, he released a tiny droplet of his Life Source upon the edge and inhaled deeply. Raising his eyebrows, he suddenly realized he'd been within touch of The Dragon and Gunnarr the Mighty Blue. He'd heard so much of these two recently. The Hoard hierarchy was near panic about some kind of prophesy involving them. He no longer believed in prophesy. The realities of loss, war and the Evil One were solid and credible. Listening to their petty fears was becoming nauseating, but had served in helping him in his mission. The girl had something special, he thought to himself, but he couldn't quite place it. She'd bear closer scrutiny soon. For now, there were other tasks at hand far more important, and would keep him busy for many moons. Palming the blade, he tucked it neatly into the back of his waistband thinking 'twould make a fine gift to either side. He was certain 'twould be profitable in whatever manner he chose to use it, and 'twould bring him closer to his ultimate goal.

CHAPTER 10

A Royal Revelation

THE NEXT DAY;
A MOON AND A FORTNIGHT AFTER THE 'BOND

"WHAT THE FLAME DO YOU MEAN BY THAT?" the Battle Commander roared in my general direction and I took a step forward, while anyone else in my position would've taken a step back. 'Twas safer to be closer than farther away. Stepping back positioned you in the line of fire of anything that might come flying toward you, still without control of the situation, while being closer allowed you to duck and tackle. Once again, I was glad I'd left Fryya at home.

Quietly, so no one outside the room would hear, "Exactly what I said, Aba. I Claim the girl. She is Clan, 'tis obvious from her appearance, although she clearly thought she was the Princess Fryya, daughter of King Shytin. At least she believed that 'til she stumbled onto a secret rendezvous outside of Evanntyr Castle less than a fortnight past. She saw her 'Aba' sneaking out of his chambers through a double wall tunnel. And yes, she was in the tunnel as well, she knows every detail of the castle. She did what any curious child would do. She followed him. His path led him circuitously out of Evanntyr and he met with minimal escort, which she found extremely odd. She said Shytin had stepped up his bodyguard o'er the past few moons and 'twas not like 'the cowardly ass', her words not mine. So of course her youthful curiosity got the better of her and she continued to follow. They wound up on the outskirts of King's Gate Village in the Port District. A rather seedy part of town for her, but she apparently was able to keep her presence hidden. She was also able to eavesdrop on the King with some outsiders who spoke of 'The Evil One' and 'Hoard Dragons' which, by the way they were talking, she deduced meant very 'bad' Dragons. She was almost discovered at that time and had to depart afore the sun dawned, but when she tried to sneak back to her mother's chambers she was captured. Apparently the King had been observing her actions for some time and they didn't concern themselves with where she'd gone that night, just that she WAS gone. They kept her in the dark, literally, with a hood, and left her for some time in the dungeons. She was disoriented by erratic meals and water, wasn't allowed to feed herself, as her hands were chained to the wall above her. She heard a few of her captors talking about the Evil Dragons and how they made them shiver in fear. Finally, unsure how much time had passed and still hooded, she was hauled away to an unknown village and dumped there. By the time she was able to get free of her bonds and remove the hood, the village was a'fire and had been under attack for awhile. There were bodies everywhere and many Dragons at first, but they eventually left and she realized she was being systematically hunted by the one Dragon who'd stayed behind. Early on she'd made a few attempts to seek assistance from the locals but as soon as she made contact, the Dragons would target her protector, and finally she gave up and just tried to hide. She worked her way slowly out of the village square toward the fields, attempting to make the dash to the forest, where she felt she'd have a better chance to escape. Shortly thereafter, Gunnarr and I arrived."

"Aba, what she encountered that night may have led to the attack on Kaddart with the intent to make her disappear, without involving certain parties. Of course you realize the timing?" Raising my eyebrows, my arms crossed in front of my chest, I continued, "Kaddart must have been chosen because of its remote location, as well as the fact that the Runner had escaped from there. Mayhap Kaddart was The Black's lair for awhile. I believe the villagers were not randomly killed, but were silenced in this attack. I know there's more, there are still too many loose ends."

He calmed down with visible effort and said in a low growl, "Of course I know the timing. Shytin's meeting took place just after my Warriors would have made report. They should've returned here by now. Forced ride a'horseback is a fortnight one way. They haven't been seen, there's been no communication through any channels, and even Shytin wouldn't have the balls to openly admit to ME, that he held them for ransom. We must conclude he sent them Beyond." Stilted steps took him back to his chair where he sat down gruffly and glowered.

I'd been here since early morning and had reported all the pertinent details of the rescue, keeping certain specifics, such as exactly how we'd managed to slay the Dragon, to myself. Telling him 'twas by Flame, I'd given Gunnarr all the credit. My senses told me there was something very wrong with him, and stress seemed to make it worse. But even this puzzled me, as my father had never been one to stress or worry, he just took care of business. I'd never seen him in this state of mind afore. He was a exceptional Commander, the best the Clan had ever seen, and he came from a long line of accomplished Commanders. 'Twas rumored the One True Liege had placed within him the skill, memories and understanding of each of his forebears, and that each one in his lineage had thus benefitted. It did seem at times that he was much older than he appeared, but that thought faded rapidly and there were more pressing issues.

He'd been accepting, if not completely satisfied with the given report. He was distracted. The girl was obviously Clan, but how had she seen near seven winters without anyone knowing of her heritage? There were Warriors stationed all o'er Kadoor and being a randy lot, half Clan children did occasionally surface, but in the Castle? No Warrior would be so stupid as to lay with the King's Consort. Would they? I'd racked my brain, trying to recall who'd been stationed there around the time of her conception, but nothing came to me. In fact, few male Warriors had been stationed anywhere near the Castle since Shytin had taken the Crown, just a winter afore my own birth. 'Twas sufficient for me that my father had never trusted him, but we'd been forced to swear fealty to his Crown after King Bryard, Shytin's father and King afore him, had mysteriously and suddenly Passed the Veil. The Battle Commander and his lovely life mate Aalanna, had attended the wake, as was considered proper. Shytin had spent a great deal of time with Aalanna and she'd been gracious as always, which had allowed Grifynn time to investigate the mystery of the old King's death. He'd uncovered much conjecture and extended their visit, justifiable as the need to discuss security and continued business with the newly crowned King, but no real evidence came to light and they'd been forced to leave or bring suspicion of treason upon the Clan.

In just two short winters after taking the Crown, Shytin had instituted many changes at court, and had soon thereafter wed a woman rumored to come from the Outlands. No one had attended the binding and the officiating priest had disappeared, despite much covert effort to find him. 'Twas certain my father knew more than he'd ever told, but to push the issue could have gotten all of our heads lopped off. He was a jealous man and kept his new mate in near seclusion. Point of fact, we'd heard the Royal Consort was with child, but after her birth seven winters ago, we'd heard nothing else, assuming the Princess Fryya had died, as had been vaguely indicated by the court. Finding the girl alive was a shock, finding her as we did, was a coup.

After taking Fryya home, we got her fed and washed, and since I couldn't get her to take a nap, we talked. Her words flowed as if she were a Warrior reporting to her Commander. Not for the first time, I felt a vague familiarity about the child. We'd spent the day gathering information and then had bedded down for the night. She'd fearlessly snuggled up to Gunnarr's massive chest 'tween his great forepaws and was asleep nearly as soon as she'd closed her blue eyes. The next morning, after leaving her with Shayla, Gunnarr and I returned to Kaddart. I was both disappointed and energized with our findings there, but I needed to finish this arrangement with my father, and so I tried to concentrate.

Redirecting the conversation, I began on an entirely different subject, the one I'd planned on presenting afore we'd Heard Walkyr's Call and mounted our rescues just two short dawns past.

"The Teams are frustrated. We're battle adept a'Dragonback, we're prepared for this war effort, but we have no designated rank system and no clear target. I've been chosen to speak for all, and we want you to assume Command and coordinate our efforts from the castle. We need to stay together and fight from Drekinn to protect our people. We've no idea where the Hoard is and in fact, they seem to be spread far and wide. We haven't been able to pinpoint a base or lair, or predict where or why they'll hit next. I don't think THEY know what they're doing. And while they figure it out, we run a defensive effort and miss all the action. We have only Walkyr's Visions to tell us what's happening, and they're not at his beck and call. 'Tis frustrating to have all this power and not be able to use it to push an offensive." Crossing my arms o'er my chest, I pursed my lips and scowled.

Although I could feel his approval of the request, he stared at me and said, "Don't change horses amid stream. What of Fryya? She's Clan, I don't doubt your word, but she'd also thought to be the daughter of the High King, therefore of royal blood, and keeping her will likely bring great danger to you personally, as well as to the Clan." He'd made his statement and I sighed.

"Yes, 'twill bring danger, but I don't believe the Clan can be much worse off than we are right now, and her life is in more danger than mine, as 'tis my utter belief she'll be killed within marks of being returned to Shytin, or made a Ward of the Court." Stepping forward and placing both hands on the desk, I leaned closer and took a deep breath afore I summarized. "I believe Kaddart was staged, all the villagers were killed to hide Shytin's relationship with the Hoard and to silence Fryya, and I believe the High King gave his Seal of approval."

Grifynn sat back in his chair and groaned. "I was afraid of that. I knew 'twas what you were thinking. Did you find any evidence?"

"We returned within a day of the attack. We found nothing." Aggravated, I sat on the edge of the chair and leaned back into its plump cushion. I'd loved this chair when I was a little girl. The wooden frame was hand carved with Dragons climbing up the sides, apparently sneaking up on the 'sleeping' one stretched out along the top. The ball and claw feet added to the ornate design, and the overall effect was one of power not delicacy. I'd always felt strong in this chair, despite the 'swamping' effect it gave most others. I closed my eyes; I needed to feel strong. 'Twas irksome to admit I hadn't found anything. I'd hoped for some kind of solid evidence, but in reality I'd known there'd be nothing that could ever prove the King was involved, with the exception of the information provided by his daughter, if she was his daughter… which was still in question as far as I was concerned. And Flame it all, I hadn't found my boot blade, either. That was nearly as infuriating as the puzzle about the girl.

"So, she is mine?" I asked, sensing the meeting was finally coming to a close.

"Yes, yes, she's yours. What do you intend to do with her?" Wearily, he sat forward again, leaning upon his elbows. The fatigue on his weathered face was as plain as his discomfort.

Presenting the arrangement I'd chosen, I stated firmly, "I believe since we took the 'Bond, we've been collecting our true share of wages. That means I have o'er a moon's worth of back pay. I want all of it assigned to Kallyr and Shayla. I'll meet with the Pay Master as soon as possible and make arrangements for allocation of my future pay, to defer continuing costs of raising and educating her." The look on his face confirmed my suspicions about our wages and he ducked his eyes from mine as I stood up. "I expect her to be accepted into the Clan with full Rights at the next Elder Meeting, after which she'll join the others of her age in Training. I've seen her skills and know her ability to adapt. I've no doubt she'll catch up very quickly. Do you see a problem with that?"

He sighed, leaned back again, folded his hard muscled arms 'cross his chest and harrumphed, shifting to sarcasm with a heavy accent, "Can I at least lay eyes upon the child for me'self, afore she's Accepted? Not that I doubt ye word that she's truly of blood. Me thinks we jes' might follow a wee proper procedure, me bein' the Battle Commander an' all…"

Turning about and striding for the door, I glanced o'er my shoulder. "Of course. I'll bring her with me on my next supply run…." My voice trailed off when I saw the fire in his eyes, and sensing some dark event brewing, I defused the stress with a grin and flippantly finished with, "… tomorrow?" He shook his head and smirked while I made a hasty exit. Pounding his fist for emphasis, he bellowed after me down the hallway, "Tomorrow! No later!"

[illegible]

[illegible] the [illegible] of [illegible] by Dr. [illegible]. [illegible]
[illegible]
[illegible]

[illegible]

CHAPTER 11

A Well Deserved Promotion

THE NEXT DAY; EARLY WINTER

"Fryya, don't be nervous, you'll be fine." 'Twas quite early, the sun just dawning. Shaking her hand lightly in my grasp, I continued, "He's already agreed to my Claim, you've nothing to dread." She'd been excited, holding no allegiance to the King, but she'd been restless throughout the night and I'd heard her talking about her mother. She missed her, but had yet to ask if she'd ever see her again and was trying to be brave. When she'd awakened, she'd gone straight about washing and dressing without a word. Gunnarr stood on the ledge and assisted her to mount up while they waited for me.

"I fear not, m'lady," she said in barely a whisper, her eyes riveted upon the heavy oak door that barred our entrance. Still, her little hand gripped mine tighter and she chewed fretfully on her bottom lip. Kneeling down to eye level with her, I was once again amazed at her beauty. I was going to have my hands full by the time she came of age. With long copper red hair and blue eyes that matched mine, her facial structure reminded me of Storrm. Her nose and chin weren't quite like ours, but she resembled someone I knew. Who was it? I'd been awake all night struggling with a notion that wouldn't come forth from the back of my mind, but I wasn't fatigued. Another of the apparent benefits of the LifeBond; we scarcely required any sleep, although 'twould catch up eventually, and when that happened we'd crash into a near coma state, with nothing but an act of the gods able to wake us for nearly half a day or more. This had happened to Kydra, slipping off her Dragon during aerial practice maneuvers soon after we took the 'Bond. She'd not slept in several days, and unconscious, her heavy bodied, red-bronze Ragnyrr had just managed to fly in under her plummeting body afore she'd have crashed to the hard plains below. 'Twould have killed her instantly and Ragnyrr as well, but the situation was salvaged, thank The One. 'Twas probably due to her being totally relaxed when she landed that saved her from more than just a few broken bones, organ damage, and some lacerations and contusions. At least we were all educated in how we Heal major injury. Not exactly what we'd assumed, since the minor injuries we'd all sustained, Healed so quickly we simple ignored them, feeling little. The process had been mercifully short, relatively speaking, taking only about a day, but it had also been exceedingly traumatic and painful. Most of the Warriors had sustained similar injuries in the past, but all of them together might have proven fatal and at the very least, would've caused retirement from active duty. But we'd never experienced the level of pain she'd endured with the Healing of the 'Bond. During the process, Ragnyrr felt Kydra's pain intensifying and in desperation to help her, he shared it within himself without thinking and out of sheer compassion, effectively Blocking much from her. 'Twas an interesting benefit of which the Dragons weren't even aware. I considered this trial and error discovery far too dangerous, and resolved myself to further research. Gunnarr also divulged they had no idea why our sleep patterns were so disrupted. Their Race had never needed much sleep. 'Twould be days, even moons if they needed to, afore a few marks sleep would be required to renew themselves, as their personal strength affected their Magic. But they'd never fallen unconscious, not able to awaken if 'twas necessary. Odd changes were becoming noticeable since taking the 'Bond, each of them reporting some similar and some quite different. Each Team had their own special abilities and ways of working together that were coming to light. The Magic of the Dragons was mixing with the innate instincts and personalities of the humans, morphing into something new 'tween the pairs. I was wary, since there was no way to predict what would happen once we were plunged into the stresses of battle. There were just too many variables. I wanted more information and we'd barely scratched the surface.

Impatient, I knew our time was running out. Shayla was treating the injured, but there were more arriving almost daily and she'd resorted to recruiting assistance from the villagers as well as the refugees. She'd begun teaching, and had several promising new Healer Apprentices. Our Teams were flying daily but individual patrols, and recently Nalwynn and Rolf had found a small group of wandering survivors of a particularly vicious Hoard attack. Nalwynn was a truly social creature and had discovered she loved to be around humans and her fellow Dragons. She'd Reached out to them when she'd felt their mournful emotions. Upon catching sight of her they'd been terrified, believing they'd be tortured and killed like the rest in their village. Nalwynn couldn't get them to understand she was with a Rider, a human partner. Rolf tried desperately to gain their attention, but their memories of the destruction and horror they'd experienced were so intense, it totally negated their ability to reason. Since there was no Seer present and they were not in 'Bond, Nalwynn's communications were limited, and in a panic they'd all perished by the hand of the eldest among them. There'd been nothing they could do. The Warrior and his Dragon were as disturbed as I.

"Of course you aren't afraid. You are the bravest little Warrior I've ever met." Heartened to see her beam in pride at the intended compliment, I took a deep breath, stood up, and knocked. The Guard was silent and mildly amused, since I'd never knocked afore. Lifting the door latch and easily pushing it open without waiting for an invitation from within, I marched into my father's domain with Fryya in tow.

~~~~~~~~~~

Less than a candle mark later, the sun full up, Storrm came to take Fryya for a Ride and a tour of Drekinn, after which she'd leave her indefinitely in the care of Shayla and Kallyr. As a Warrior now in LifeBond, I'd no time to spare, and the girl would be better off with someone who was around at least part time on a regular basis. Besides, Walkyr was there and the two of them had become close in a very short time. I'd check on her as often as I could. The message to come and get the girl had been relayed through Gunnarr to Mystynn and then to Storrm. This MindSpeak and MindLink benefit of the 'Bond was awe inspiring, but as I was learning, all Dragons were capable of Linking and therefore we might not have as much of an advantage overall as I'd initially hoped. Still, 'twas a very important tool in our weapons hold and I just had to make sure we all knew how best to utilize it. There must be a way to gain a solid advantage o'er the Hoard and find it, I would.

As I pondered these ideas, I stood in front of the Battle Commander's desk, my feet slightly apart, my hands clasped behind me, and waited for him to glance up from his report. My father had a flourishing long hand on the parchment and I'd always wanted my own writing to be as lovely, but though my words were precise, my penmanship was near illegible. With a slight smile I remembered how hard Kallyr had tried to get me to scribe more clearly. Just as suddenly I frowned, as I noticed that my father was beginning to appear older by the day. Thinking I must be mistaken, I impatiently began a slow rocking motion, which always helped me center and ground myself.

"You were never good at waiting," Grifynn grunted, as he placed his signature upon the official Claim documents and pushed them 'cross his great desk along with his quill pen, for me to sign as well. This last bit of official documentation cleared the way to the Claim ceremony, but 'twas the agreement just signed, that gave Fryya full Rights in the Clan. Straightening, I pushed it back and noticed his face again. The look was
~~~~~~~~~~

sad, which was quite interesting, considering the look he had on his face when Fryya walked in with me. When he'd first seen the child, the utter astonishment was blatantly observable afore he was able to cover it and once again become the stolid Commander. Shock wasn't one of my father's usual emotions, which left me slightly bewildered. He must've noted the child was familiar, mayhap he knew and the surprise of recognition had registered upon his face. But there was too much to do to be sidelined by this piece of the puzzle, I'd have to save it for later. 'Twould give me something to chew on, as if I needed the additional mystery.

"Now to more important business." Nodding his head for me to stand down, I took advantage and sat, making myself comfortable. I'd always had to sit on one leg tucked up under me, in order to feel like I wasn't being swamped by wood and leather upholstery in this chair, and it irked me that even as an adult, I still had to sit on my foot to see o'er his desk. Although I loved it, I believed the Commander had it made especially for the obvious intimidation factor. 'Twould be like him to seize every possible advantage in any situation. But I was no longer a child and I'd never been intimidated by anything, least of all, furniture.

Brusquely he began, "You requested I take the Teams. I accept. First order of business, I'll meet with them at mid-day in the Pits. I believe you can make that happen." And without even waiting for my confirmation, he continued. "Next, I want them listed in the order in which they took the 'Bond, and give me a comprehensive record of your abilities, 'Bond affects, and the way the MindLink works. I want to know how you're being affected individually, I want to know what the dragons think, I want everyone's individual strengths and weaknesses listed. I want all this complete and on this desk by dusk, three days hence, AND I need to be able to read it!" Staring at me, I tried not to squirm at the reminder of my sloppy script. "And Warrior…"

Feeling something notable was about to happen, I rose and took my stance afore him, with his huge desk 'tween us like some kind of emotional dam. "Sir?"

Leaning forward again, one elbow upon the leather writing surface, the knuckles of his other hand resting upon his opposite thigh, he cocked his head challengingly in my direction. Glaring momentarily, then apparently confirming his decision, he spat forth, "As of this moment, you are my Second in Command."

CHAPTER 12

The Blood Oath

LATER THAT SAME DAY

I was stunned. Barely a candle mark earlier, the Battle Commander, my father, promoted me to Second. Sitting with my back against the cold stone of the cave wall, I stared out at the far horizon 'cross the Sea of Dreams. The view made me nearly as breathless as the full realization of the impact of accepting my promotion. When the Dragons returned, bringing with them the LifeBond Magic, I'd thought that everything had changed, including any opportunity for my accession to the post for which I'd been groomed all my life. But here I was, Second in Command to the Battle Commander of the Dragon Clan, with all the responsibilities and duties that went along. I'd only seen seventeen winters, making me the youngest ever to hold the rank. But I was now in 'Bond with a Dragon, what the Flame had I done? What was I thinking? There were serious issues I couldn't even begin to discuss with Grifynn. For one, I still felt the same way I had when we first took the 'Bond, and he had his same issues as well. 'Twas a matter of trust and respect. I trusted and respected the Dragons. He did not.

"What troubles you so, my spirited Dragonet?" Gunnarr Asked as I pondered, sorting through all the available information, trying to understand what was happening, knowing I was missing something.

"I am now Second in Command of the Dragon Clan. Do you know what that means?" I frowned at the possibility I'd have to explain further what was really bothering me and I couldn't, because I wasn't sure. *"And I'm not even considering the duty of Death Avenger if he should be taken down as an act of war. Not that I can't do that, mind you, I just...."* At a loss for words, I couldn't complete my sentence. What was my problem? What had changed 'tween me and my father? Why did secrecy surround me, this sense that I'd been betrayed? I'd trained since birth for this position, I'd sworn to the Code, fealty to the Crown, and now I felt I'd been told lies all my life, or at the very least, much had been kept from me. I'd discovered enhanced senses didn't always clear up mystery, and seemed often to create more. I'd have to work harder to learn how to interpret them. 'Twas keeping secrets akin to telling lies? No, he wasn't lying outright. There

was an aura of deception about my father, and the realization that I didn't know everything was shocking in and of itself.

"I know the ways of War and battle. I know the turmoil, the loss and the responsibility. Trust me, little one, I understand conflicting loyalties." Quietly, he Spoke with a duality I couldn't place. I must dig deeper into his Memories. His lowered Voice gained my attention and I turned to face him. His massive head perched upon his crossed forepaws, the rest of him was stretched out, with his belly flat upon the cool stone. His bright eyes displayed a deep emotion I couldn't read as he watched me closely, his breath blowing in frosty puffs from his great nostrils. *"In the end, 'tis best each does what we feel is right, and not depend upon others to make our decisions for us."*

There wasn't enough information to discern duality, but I sensed no Evil about my father or my partner. From Gunnarr came empathy, and committing myself to his confidence, I poured out my fears. *"I find myself in a quandary. I have nothing solid to guide me, just bits and pieces of what would seem a huge puzzle in which we're all represented. I keep getting more pieces, but they're so far apart in the overall design that I can't predict the entire picture. 'Tis most frustrating. I feel I will lose something precious to me if I cannot solve this riddle, if I cannot fit the pieces of this puzzle together. I must gain full understanding soon, Gunnarr! I have a dreadful feeling we'll all suffer greatly if I fail. I must know what to expect long afore all the pieces come together to make the whole picture on their own. 'Twill be too late by then to prevent a major tragedy."* The outlook of doom was so strong 'twas momentarily crushing, and I swallowed hard.

"Center yourself, Darque. For one of your youth, you amaze me. You are wiser than your own Elders. You just need more 'pieces of the puzzle' as you say. You're a mighty Warrior and you were destined by prophesy to Lead. Truth be told, the others have already acknowledged your right to this accession." Noting the surprise on my face, he rumbled his laughter. *"No, I didn't throw the salt on this one, I am innocent! 'Twas my brother Mystynn and Storrm. She Told Mystynn, he Informed the others, and each Dragon Told their own Rider."* Then quietly, as if prodding me to question him, *"The Raven told her."*

"A bird told her I'd been promoted? What memory does that prompt?" I furrowed my brow even tighter, trying hard to recall some bit of trivia, when suddenly I remembered hearing Shayla talking to a raven in the hallway during the trials. She'd been seen several times chatting with the bird as if 'twas actually holding a conversation with her, and I'd heard her call it Corbyn. We weren't certain of course, but we'd thought 'twas the

same bird for that entire fortnight, as well as the same one Storrm claimed to have seen frequently since. I'd actually thought 'twas studying my sister, but had decided that was a bit odd even for me, and I hadn't seen it since.

"*Ahhh, the sun dawns for my Rider,*" he Stated, seeing my rapid leaps from bit to bit of information, as I deduced the only logical conclusion.

"*By the 7th Prince. Don't tell me the raven we saw was actually… no, it cannot be. 'Tis mere myth, legend… the Spirit Ones, the Changelings? Are you trying to tell me the raven is a Shifter? He is… FAY? And you knew this all along? Now this is a huge piece of the puzzle indeed. We shall have to chat about this further, my devious friend, for 'tis clear you know far more than you're telling me. But we've no time now, we have a meeting to attend at the castle!*"

Excited, I leaped up, stripped quickly and rushed to the ledge. Swan diving, I interlocked my fingers just in time to rip through the surface of the calm ocean water, taking me far under afore I turned back toward the surface. "*Come swim with me, we need the refreshment! We have much to do!*" Kicking hard and pulling with my arms, I broke free to the clean crisp air above just in time to get a mouthful of cold briny water when Gunnarr dove in. Sputtering and coughing, I laughed 'til I near cried, then Gunnarr hauled me out of the sea to make ready.

So much churned through my mind. The confirmation of the existence of the Fay led me to believe the other rumored Races might also truly exist, and we needed to know upon whose side they'd make their stand. As Second, 'twas up to me to secure the leads to ally ourselves with these other Races, for whomever shared our world, shared our enemies. Gathering my thoughts after our surf frolicking, we took wing to the Den.

~~~~~~~~~~

The Battle Commander had never been much for ceremony, insisting only that his orders were followed without fail and without hesitation, which he considered posting due respect. When he felt 'twas not posted quickly enough or in sufficient quantities, he increased the work load. Given his ideas on such it didn't usually take anyone long to attain a new found respect. Thus, at the appointed time of mid-day, I simply arrived at the Pits, along with twelve other Dragons with their Riders, and took my stance at my father's right side to acknowledge my new position and show my acceptance. If anyone had a problem with this, they'd step forward one at a time to work out the disagreement in the Pits 'til we'd reached an understanding.
~~~~~~~~~~

THE BLACK WAR BEGINS

My adrenalin levels were so high I could've taken them all on at once, and without a doubt I would've risen victorious. The workout would've done me good as I was nearly shaking with Battle Lust, but no one challenged. Still, I successfully concealed my anxiety, my actions and facial expression revealed nothing. Only Gunnarr was aware. After all, I'd threaten the Fates afore I'd betray my father, my Clan or my Dragon. Betraying the King was noticeably absent from my list. Once again, I wished I'd known his father. He'd been a good man, a good ruler who'd loved his only son with all his heart. Never admitting even to himself that there was something dreadfully wrong with his son's moral code, he'd defended his behavior, bailing him out of all wrongdoings, right up to his premature and baffling demise. I supposed no father wanted to believe the worst of his own son. We all had high hopes for our children. Would I ever have any of my own? Fryya was my Claim daughter and I already loved her very much but I still wondered whether I'd be able to continue the bloodline of Aalanna Grifynn.

"Second, get your grip on them. I suppose I'm to be forced to alter my ways to accommodate the dragons here." Grumbling out of the side of his mouth, he sounded somewhat disgusted at the prospect.

Winters of training and expectation kicking in, and failing to consider the changes the 'Bond had brought, I Told Gunnarr to stay put. Taking several steps toward the others as if they were any other Warriors standing inspection, I grimaced as he heaved a sigh behind me, followed immediately with a dramatic effort to plop his huge rump in the sun dried sands of the Pit, throwing up an enormous dust cloud.

"What the Flame are you doing? Are you trying to make me look bad?"

"No. 'Twas in response to HIS words. I'm trying to get YOUR attention. You're not thinking. You don't have to walk anywhere. Tell me, and I'll Tell them. Whatever you want us to do, we shall endeavor not to mess things up." His tone was sarcastic but 'twas not directed at me, rather, his blatant lack of respect was directed squarely at Grifynn. In my utter surprise of the moment, I snorted trying to hold back my laughter. Choking and red faced, tears streamed down my cold cheeks. 'Twas evident yet again, the inherent problems involved in sharing emotions with a Dragon. Standing upright as soon as I could regain my control, I was shocked by my actions, in front of my father no less. This had to be the most memorable and miserable day of my life.

Turning sharply on my heel to face him, I cleared my throat. "Sir, forgive my behavior. I'll accept any reprimand you wish to deliver, but I respectfully request your indulgence for the rest of this inspection." I waited silently, and when he nodded affirmation I turned and stood at ease. The Mighty Blue now slightly behind me and to my right, sat in his characteristic pose, his great tail curled about his feet. So majestic in this posture, I had to remind myself not to stare. Speaking calmly with him, no one would know we were Communicating by my expression or posture. *"Gunnarr, bring your Dragons to attention behind my Riders. I want them standing as we are, lined up in dress left formation, if you will."*

In the blink of an eye they began to form a dress left line up that became near perfect. When I say 'perfect' 'twas in the loosest terms of course. Warriors were rough, tough, randy and usually difficult to handle at the best of times, and although we did practice some martial standards, 'twas merely what was required to post our respect and to ensure everyone knew from whom they took their orders. But the lineup afore me at this moment was a thing of beauty, pulling my confidence up out of the latrine. In my peripheral vision, I noted with pride the quick flash of astonishment on the face of the Commander. Of course, the others would've caught that look as well and I bit my lip to keep from repeating my earlier indiscretion.

Silence permeated the Pits afore he gruffly snarled, "I wondered how you'd handle them. Impressive control and obedience. But will they comply with your orders when it means their own lives, and that of their partners?"

Afore I could answer, every Team stepped forward, half surrounding him, clearly indicating they would voluntarily offer up their lives to support any order I may give. Then as one they turned to face me, Dragons rising up upon their hind legs, Warriors in half kneeling in front of them, raising their drawn swords in their fists to present an age-old Battle Salute. In unison, their free hand on their raised knees, they pounded their fisted swords 'cross their chests, swung forward to spin their grips, presenting all blades down, and then thrust them into the sands, the dull brushing thud reverberating throughout the Den, as they swore without reservation, "I will fight 'cross the Veil with you at my back!"

That they made such a salute to me, with their backs to the Battle Commander, did not go unnoticed. When the dust had settled I had them return to their previous locations, expecting the repercussions to commence. Instead, the Commander cocked his head in my direction, winked at me, and then turned on his heel, leaving the Pits in a quick walk. He actually winked at me? Surely not.

"He tests us, feisty one. He wants you to meet him in his office within a quarter mark. Do we let on I have Heard this, or do we not?"

As I watched Grifynn stride briskly away, I Responded, *"Interesting. Did I know you could Hear others? 'Tis not a 'Bond benefit."* The Mighty Blue near closed his eyes to avoid mine.

"I can Hear your father." Gunnarr Admitted reluctantly, then grimaced in real pain, effectively ending the conversation at this time. Returning to the original question, I gathered my thoughts. *"I admit to nothing. We let him chalk it up to coincidence. I already know he'd want to meet immediately and in his office. Besides, 'tis obvious to me, he already thinks we can Hear him and he fishes for information. Still, if he could tolerate the Link, 'twould be good in battle. In the meantime, Tell the others to look around, get familiar with the castle. The Den may be our home at some point. If we need to make any renovations in order to have room for anyone* (at which time I pointedly stared at my huge Dragon) *'tis best to know now and get it done. We meet at the clearing above the eastern timberline at dusk. I'll be with Grifynn."* Gunnarr both agreed and approved, and my heart pounding with a strange satisfaction, I took my leave to follow the Commander.

<div align="center">~~~~~~~~~~</div>

Boldly striding 'cross the office to the desk and taking quill in hand, I grabbed a piece of parchment and began listing the names of all the Warriors and their LifeBonds as per his initial request. He made not a sound during the time it took me to scribe the list with a fairly clear hand and when 'twas finally complete, I replaced the quill in the ink well, pushed the parchment toward him and stepped back stating, "I included any familial relationships of which I am aware, Commander." He picked it up as if 'twas aged kitchen scraps and read the names, murmuring each of them under his breath, "Darque (sister of Storrm) and Gunnarr, Storrm (sister of Darque) and Mystynn (second brother of Gunnarr), Kydra and Ragnyrr (third brother of Gunnarr), Axyl (brother of Daxx) and Haniyyah (sister of Linayyah), Daxx (brother of Axyl) and Linayyah (sister of Haniyyah), Yanais and Shykiyyah, Rolf and Nalwynn, Rygyl and Tegrynn, Tyndall and Fyndarr (brother of Zaydarr, cousin of Gunnarr), Apryya and Dannyrkyn, Zoe and Kyrlayyn, Ethynn (brother of Daylyn) and Makayyd (sister of Makyyan), Ariel and Zayddarr (brother of Fyndarr, cousin of Gunnarr)." When he finished, he slowly lowered the parchment to the desktop and seemed reluctant to speak, as if considering his words carefully.

"You know I don't trust them. Nor you, since you're now in this 'Bond with one. Magic alters you, 'tis not natural to live near forever..." he stated with lowered voice, his commentary incomplete. I was dazed by his admission of a lack of trust in me, although 'twas mutual, but 'twas his last statement for which I wanted clarification. Afore I could question him however, his expression altered and he continued quite decisively, "I am pleased with your overall control and the loyalty they've shown you. No doubt you'll make a good field Commander."

My eyes opened wide and my chin near dropped with the unexpected praise. Looking in my direction for the first time, he appeared more fatigued than I'd ever seen him. He reached for a mug of ale and took a few swigs, then leaned back and closed his eyes. "I know you can Hear me. 'Tis imperative you give me your promise that my thoughts will not be invaded on personal issues. I want you AND your dragon to swear on that."

Gunnarr was concerned, as was I. There was something very wrong with the Commander. *"Tell my father we swear not to invade his personal thoughts as long as the knowledge 'twould impart to us, will not affect the mission, the Clan, or the safety of the Teams. I know 'twill mean more, and make him feel more secure, coming directly from you, than if I just say it aloud. Can you do that?"* How did my father know Gunnarr could Hear him, and what made him think that I could? But Hearing was only half the effort. I was afraid of hurting him and I wasn't certain he could handle MindSpeak, as he wasn't in 'Bond, wasn't a Seer, and as far as I knew, had never Spoken with a Dragon afore.

"I can, and will." Briefly, Gunnarr was silent. I felt an odd familiarity pass 'tween them and an edge to the Conversation I couldn't identify. Some issue was being debated, but what? Gunnarr exhibited nothing, however, Grifynn's expression was stern and 'twas more than a simple assurance being discussed. Searching his face for increasing distress, I saw none. 'Twas apparent he was having no difficulty with MindSpeak and 'twas more and more obvious that I knew less than I should about my father, and the history of the Clan.

Gunnarr Speaks ~"I will not mince words with you. It has been a long time. I Speak now for Darque. She gives you her word she will not invade your thoughts or your memories unless 'twould take from us the victory of the battle."

Grifynn Replies ~"I know for whom you Speak. What of you, dragon? What say you?"

Gunnarr Responds ~"Hear me, Grifynn of Man, I know your every thought. I am tied to you in a way none shall ever be. Despite your addictions, I've kept my Oath. 'Twill be mine to keep 'til one of us Passes the Veil, since you have steadfastly refused to release us."

Grifynn Responds ~"I shall never release you. I know of what your Kind is capable. Now Hear ME! If you harm my daughters I shall make good on my personal pledge to hunt you down and bring an end to this prophesy, no matter the cost. 'Twill take no Oath for me to finish this."

Gunnarr Responds ~"I am saddened by your lack of foresight and honor. You know not what you say or do. The Elixir fogs your mind and alters your senses. I care not for my own well being in the Oath. I have no difficulty keeping it and 'twould not have taken the Blood. 'Tis for you I plead, for the Oath was never meant to be borne by Man. Corbyn gave you certain warnings as well. Do you heed them or not?"

Grifynn Responds ~ "Do not speak to me of honor, just keep your Oath."

Gunnarr Responds ~ "We must have a truce, Battle Commander. We must work together to defeat the Evil One or we're all doomed. You know this as well as I. The Blood Oath stays as long as you maintain it, despite what it does to you, but we will work together for the good of both our Races, and of Kadoor. Understand that Darque is vastly quick witted and intelligent and she's nearing the truth. There will be no hiding this from her. Soon she will know all, despite. Even the Oath cannot keep another from discovery of the truth."

Grifynn Responds ~ "For their sake and that of the Clan, we will work together….as long as the Blood Oath remains intact."

<div align="center">~~~~~~~~~~</div>

We left shortly thereafter, the other Teams still familiarizing themselves with the layout of the castle. The only ones absent were Storrm and Mystynn, who'd gone to prepare for our dusk gathering. Flying home, I Asked Gunnarr, *"Will you tell me about Corbyn? There seems much you haven't told me and I think 'tis time for you to do so, starting with the Fay. We've several marks afore we gather; plenty of time for you to explain why you've kept such secrets."* 'Twas as good a place to start as any and I wasn't very interested in examining my first appearance as Second in Command as 'twas mortifying. But there was nothing to be done about it now. 'Twas akin to fealty they'd sworn to me and my spirits soared. But discussing the Fay would take my mind off other mysteries for awhile and I needed the respite.

We landed, and my slightly awkward dismount reminded me that we needed some kind of saddle arrangement to increase our effectiveness as well as our safety during the aerial acrobatics we'd already been forced to utilize. Riding a Dragon 'bareback' had little similarity to riding a horse bareback. Although the strong and rhythmic beating of the great wings created a similar, but much larger rolling motion, 'twould also shift without warning in multiple directions whenever we found or lost a thermal. While on wing the Rider was required to be constantly alert or he'd fall off. The cold wind against us, the wings beating, changing altitude and direction as well as banking and flipping, took every bit of our enhanced reflexes, balance reactions and strength. The straps I'd begun using were merely adequate, but had been adopted by the others for lack of anything better. They allowed me to extend myself from Gunnarr, to slide to the side of his neck and toward his tail, to surf his broad back during flight. I could also grab them as they trailed past me, to climb hand o'er hand to gain my seat, mounting from a fly-by o'er the water or the plains.

We didn't need aesthetics, we needed practical application and durability. A Dragon's saddle would have to be easy for both partners to don, doff and wear without encumbering flight or fight. We'd need straps, hand and foot loops, but not a full stirrup. Some initial ideas took shape in my imagination and I determined to meet with Ian the Den's Stable Master, and Drekinn's Leather Master, Toryn, to assist in the design and creation of the necessary equipment as soon as possible. No one would've refused me afore, but now I had the absolute authority to order anything I needed for my Teams. What should I call them? We were all still in training. Teams in training and transition constituted what? A Stable. Once we 'graduated' and became battle ready then we'd be….a Flight. The entire force, consisting of all battle ready Flights would be….the Fleet. Yes, I liked the sound of that. With the next LifeBond I wanted to have First Stable transitioned to First Flight so we'd not have two Stables running simultaneously and by that time I wanted an efficient training regimen in place. A few more decisions down….a multitude to go.

"Gunnarr, please tell the Battle Commander my request to meet with the Masters."

Gunnarr suddenly spurt out, *"Corbyn may well be the last of the Fay. He's seen no others since shortly after the Retreat."* Hesitating, he stared deeply into my eyes, imploring me to question what he'd not revealed. 'Twas the urgency in his Voice that helped me find the answer he so desperately wanted me to grasp. Once again, the sun dawned and fitting the pieces together, I was taken aback. To use our Link would've increased the pain of acknowledging, so I asked aloud, "Are you bound by a Blood Oath?" The grimace of pain upon his face and the slight dip of his muzzle as he affirmed, made me wince, sending chills up my spine. "You cannot tell me something important, correct? Is it about me? Is it about my father?" The pain in his expression intensified as he tried to lead me to the ultimate answer, 'til I made a huge leap that would cause him much pain to confirm. I had to take the chance, for 'twas clear he wouldn't survive much more of this. "You're sworn to secrecy, but can you confirm and answer if I ask the right questions?"

Gunnarr was in so much pain by now that any human would've been comatose, and he could barely stand up as he sought to distance himself physically from me in order to breathe. Practically crawling to the ledge, he sat heavily, his massive head hanging, his huge shoulders shaking, his great tongue lolling out, panting as if with fever. His nostrils flaring and smoking in distress, he stared at the far horizon o'er the waters. Just when I thought he couldn't answer, I heard his low growl, "Yes, I can confirm if spoken correctly. I cannot offer information. It causes great pain if I try to lead you to the knowledge you seek. I've no desire to deceive you. Know this Darque, I've held the Oath since long afore your birth and 'twas not I, who insisted upon its creation."

CHAPTER 13

Second Takes Command

THE FOLLOWING DAWN

It took most of the night for Gunnarr to start breathing normally again, and for the pain he'd endured while fighting the Blood Oath to finally subside. I couldn't bring myself to ask him anything more, and decided the best course of action was to deduce as much as I could independently, asking questions only when I needed definite direction. 'Twould cause him the least amount of pain, but I had three days to gather an accurate listing of our abilities, strengths and weaknesses and that didn't leave me much time for other concerns.

Due to Gunnarr's condition, the gathering was cancelled and I had Storrm relay orders. Afore the break of dawn I awakened and carefully dislodged myself from under the warmth of Gunnarr's left wing where he'd blanketed me, holding me tightly against him as if in need of comfort. Having been in need of such myself, I'd slept fitfully after we'd calmed his pain-induced chaotic feelings.

Naked and silent, I hiked deeper into the cave, sliding my right hand along the stone at hip height. A few long paces afore the cave appeared to end, I felt the opening which most would mistake in the shadows for a mere groove. Turning sharply into this depression, I stepped boldly forward several paces, ignoring the illusion that I was about to crash into the rock wall along with the warm tingling sensation that was so slight, I barely felt it anyway. Then I ducked my head, took several more steps and turned back upon myself to the right. Able to stand up now, I turned back to the left. As I continued winding my way deeper into the heart of the plateau, I ignored offshoot passageways leading to many other deep caverns and cliff side caves now shared by the Teams. When we were just children, Storrm and I discovered these caves were deeper and more complicated than they'd initially appeared. 'Twas hard enough to access them along the almost sheer cliff face, and attempting to carry in a torch was ludicrous. But, we'd no need for a torch and being ever the adventurers, we'd explored most every cave along the entire shoreline within a few winters and I was positive we were still the only Clansmen with this extensive knowledge.

The false end would stand up to all but the most intense scrutiny, the continuation unseen even with a lantern in the middle of the cave, forming what I decided must be an optical illusion, so influential even I ducked my head at times. Sliding and rolling and twisting, using his claws to pull himself along, Gunnarr would follow me, squeezing through the tightest sections and around the turns, hugging the wall to his belly, 'til the passageway widened and he could stand again. I wasn't certain he used Magic, but whenever I watched him I could only shake my head. It reminded me of seeing the twenty of them enter the Lodge and made me wonder how he managed to get back 'home' afore me so often.

As I wound my way through the maze of tunnels, I let my thoughts drift. The beauty of the Cave of Jewels was breathtaking. The ceiling within the main cavern was at least ten times as high as the Lodge, mayhap higher, and sparkled with more precious gems than were hidden in the Dragon's Den. Somehow self illuminating, the lighting effects seemed to increase with its own reflection off the water as well as the stark whiteness of the sand. Mysteriously waxing and waning with the sun, 'twould give the appearance of night with the stars shining above, then brighten with the dawn.

The waterfalls continuously fed the large pool and the fine sands of the beach front were soft enough to lie upon without irritation. The pool and beach together were easily the size of the village square and several alleys included. Storrm and I had paced out the vicinity as children and discovered the middle of this cave was roughly under the Dragon's Den. These had to be the legendary caverns blocked off from the dungeons. Despite many audacious attempts, we'd never found where they might have been, there was no obvious construction, patchwork, or masonry to even provide a clue. But I was now certain there were still more caves here that we'd somehow missed and 'twas possible they'd been hidden by Magic. After all, if you'd told me last winter that I'd be in LifeBond with a Dragon and fighting in a war today, I would've considered you in need of Shayla's calming herbal medications. Yet here I stood.

Only the Teams knew of these caverns, as only the Teams had traversed past the false ends to explore. Most of the caves along the cliffs had natural entrances to this same vast cavern pool, but unless the Dragons were using Magic, not all of them would be able to enter through their own living quarters. I remembered having to do some rather serious squeezing through a few of them, and that was when we were children. I might be small still, but I'm not that small. So far, only Storrm with Mystynn, and Kydra with her reddish bronze Ragnyrr, had shared this natural beauty, as we'd been swimming and bathing together at times since we'd moved in.

Thinking of Storrm and our childhood friend Kydra, who'd been like a sister to us, reminded me of a Vision Walkyr had recently revealed. He'd Seen Gunnarr, Mystynn and Ragnyrr together with three more 'big' Dragons and knew them to be brothers. He'd Seen these five Dragons solemnly hand Gunnarr a large sparkling spherical object resembling an egg, following silently as he carried it to the shores of the Sea of Dreams. With considerable effort, the Mighty Blue threw it to the horizon o'er the pounding surf during a terrible storm. As he described this Vision, I'd immediately felt the tingle of Magical Allure, and knew 'twas significant. Surely 'twas the Legend of the 7 Princes. 'Twould mean that Gunnarr was the High Prince who'd thrown the egg of his youngest sibling, the 7th Prince of a 7th Prince, to his cousins the Water Dragons. According to Legend Song, he'd done this to protect the Egg and to prevent his hatching just prior to the Last Holocaust, when most of the Magical Races had retreated to survive. 'Twould also mean that Mystynn was the Second Prince and Ragnyrr was Third, as I'd begun to suspect. If they'd survived, the Quad, Fifth and Sixth were still out there. That would explain a lot of mysteries. But why would Gunnarr not tell me this? And where was the Egg now? Had the 7th Prince hatched?

Yet another stray notion that came to mind as I made my way through the connecting maze of tunnels, the wintry breezes chilling my bare skin, was how to keep our thoughts to ourselves. I understood the principles of the Link, but still had difficulty with the finer points. Basically, if I was worried, Gunnarr would know and if he Cast for that thought, he'd Hear it. So technically, I couldn't hide but if that were the entire truth, neither could he. However, I knew he'd kept things from me. How was he doing that? Mayhap learning how to control the MindLink was as learning how to dance. I had the strength, coordination, desire and grace, but I knew not yet, the sequence of the steps.

Reaching my destination and stepping out onto the sandy floor, the beauty of the place made me hesitate as I gazed upon it. 'Twas as seeing it for the first time, every time. Crossing quickly to follow the widening incline of rocks, I threw my leathers into a dry alcove close to the edge of the falls, but protected from the spray. Then walking up a series of stair-step ledges to the main gusher, I stepped under the stream of cool water as it splashed o'er my body. Running my hands through my hair, finger combing the night's tangles, I made sure 'twas smooth and wet all the way through and then stepped away to wring out and braid the entire length of it by pulling it o'er my shoulder. Tossing the thick braid to my back, I dove into the deep pool. 'Twas odd, but as a child the water had seemed much colder. 'Twas obviously another 'Bond benefit that I was protected from all but the most excessive temperatures. Swimming to the opposite shoreline and back several times, refreshed me. At the edge near the base of the falls, I pushed myself up and out of the water, stepping forth easily. Squeezing the excess water from my braid, I tied it in a knot afore I finished dressing, my absorbent leathers being the only towel I needed. Returning to our living quarters, I passed quietly by Gunnarr as he snored softly.

I rock climbed up the bare face of the cliff wall straight o'er our ledge, a feat few outside the 'Bond could have accomplished without equipment. Less than a quarter mark later I reached the top and vaulted o'er the edge. My Teams were already there, following their orders with enthusiasm.

Cancelling the gathering last night, I'd made my first Command decision and promoted Storrm to my personal 'Second', her rank now Third Fighter, or Right to Second. I looked for her 'cross the rolling terrain and found her on the ground directing the practice session. Without thinking, I Called directly to her, as I had much on my mind and much I wanted to accomplish this day. We'd always had an uncanny ability to finish each other's thoughts, and seemed always to know what the other was thinking, almost afore they did. Some found it eerie that we'd known what they were going to say afore they spoke, and often finished their sentences. We'd even tried to Tell people what to say by thinking it ourselves and concentrating on them, and at times it appeared we'd been successful. As little girls we'd found these pranks quite entertaining. When confronted with each individual act of evidence that we were 'special', Grifynn merely became stone-faced, barely nodding his head in our direction, showing that he somehow recognized the truth of our behaviors. He'd then turn and leave without a word. Afore we'd sworn the Oath and joined the Warrior Brotherhood, we'd thought everyone could do what we did, knew what we knew and felt what we felt. We hadn't really been aware of how different we were. Fortunately, through some innate sense of need, I'd kept my gifts secret from others and taught Storrm to do the same. Of course, this made us more reclusive, while sharpening our differences. Of all the children, Kydra had been our closest ally, and the three of us would pretend we were Fay in human form, infiltrating the Clan and destroying spies. Many a hay bale was torn apart with our practice swords in our valiant efforts. Always knowing when someone was approaching long afore anyone else would have, we'd hide the evidence. Our barn animals had happily obliged us and so no one had ever been the wiser. Except of course, our father.

Taking a deep frosty breath to clear my thoughts, I Spoke, *"Storrm, have you the knowledge I requested? And I want to discuss new practice drills while everyone takes a short break."* Afore I realized she shouldn't be able to Hear me directly, she Responded, *"Yes, as much as they all recognize at this time. Like you, we're finding new talents daily, but we all have some similar as well. The most common complaint is the inability to Search for these skills. We seem to stumble o'er them by accident, a slow and tedious process. Even the Dragons are frustrated as they're also breaking new ground."*

Noting Gunnarr had just crawled up to sit behind me, I'd assumed this interaction had gone through the 'normal' route of me to Gunnarr to Mystynn to Storrm and back again. I continued to Speak, this time addressing the others. *"Kydra, you've healed well from that fractured ankle. How's Ragnyrr? By the way, good work on that rescue last week."* However, with this exchange came a delay. In what took more than twice as long, even though 'twas still just a fraction of a candle drip, I Heard, *"Thank you, Commander. Yes, we are well and ready for battle."*

When I mentioned the delay to Gunnarr, he Told me, *"I cannot say."*

Missing the double entendre, I continued, *"I like how this is working. 'Tis more efficient to simply Speak as if conversing with each of them directly. Can we continue to do that?"*

"Your Command is my wish, my Beauty," Gunnarr teased me with a snigger in his growl. 'Twas a relief to hear his quips again. I'd been worried. No, I'd been more than worried.

Afore joining my Stable on wing, Storrm and I set up maneuvers to push both our balance and our Links, hoping 'twould also help us discover more 'benefits'. Within moments the others were lost to my consciousness and Gunnarr and I were stretching our senses to the heavens. The ever-present strap in my left hand, I slid 'round to the right side of his long neck, hanging on with my legs, ducking back and under his wing as he descended rapidly toward a harbor buoy I'd positioned in the middle of the plains. As he passed the buoy I grabbed hold and lifted it just enough to clear the ground, then set it back again as close to the original position as possible. We worked it 'cross the field in precise, rapid increments, each of the Teams following my lead. When the buoy had been moved 'cross the plateau, we hung from the opposite side and repeated, this time flying in closer proximity, learning to tighten our formations without fouling each other. Being so near the ground at incredible speeds was initially intimidating, but 'twas easier once we let our Dragons actually navigate the fly-by, trusting them to help us achieve the goal. We accomplished much with the maneuvers, including raising our interactions to a higher level, strengthening our bodies and fortifying our trust in one another, not to mention teaching us how to perform precision extraction and insertion activities on wing. The Dragons gained new insight into their Riders' abilities as well as their own, how far to push the counter balance required and how to work together again.

Once we'd gained proficiency with this, we drifted apart to do some 'surfing'. Personally I'd found it to be more fun than water surfing, albeit far more dangerous. Gunnarr had grown fond of this, telling me it felt like a good rub down. Walking his back, neck and shoulders and the weight shifts required to maintain my balance as he'd dive, soar and climb, was nothing less than exhilarating. When I took a moment to observe the others practicing individual stunts, I noted some daring feats and tried to duplicate them. Yanais was using a modified version of a simple skill everyone performed at one time or another, but doing this on the scaled hide of a Dragon, and a moving one at that, was much more difficult. I watched him with some envy as he performed the 'kip' around Shykiyyah's long graceful neck, avoiding her wings. He slid around on his gut, pulling himself through the complete circle to the other side and twisting to regain his seat with apparent ease. Although 'twas a relatively simple movement around a tree branch or barn rafter, I quickly discovered I was too short to kip Gunnarr's thick neck in the same manner, but we made modifications and ended up with a whole new stunt. Mine began and ended the same, with a gut slide down and under, but half way through I had to use Gunnarr's forelegs as a stepping stone to get me far enough around to finish. While on his forelegs my grasp was tenuous at best, but with the straps I was in no real danger and Gunnarr would add a boost that would send me sailing up and o'er his neck with little effort on my part. It didn't take long for some of the others to attempt this added boost, but when we took this skill and added an extra twist, they actually landed or hovered, trying to get the best view in order to watch us work. Instead of using Gunnarr's paws as a stepping stone, I let the wind sweep me back to sit in the cradle of his forelegs upon his great chest. 'Twas difficult enough to accomplish with the assistance of the rush of wind and a slight incline to his flight pattern, but I wondered if 'twas even possible in hover mode. 'Twould not be explored this day however, as the others were having a hard enough time not falling, given all the advantages. When this happened, their Dragon was usually able to grab them afore they got too far away, although dangling by one's ankles upside down mid-flight wasn't the most pleasant experience. Occasionally they'd have to bank and dive to recover their Rider, so it became prudent they all practice at higher altitudes. 'Twas not the safest position but it most definitely had its reward, and how safe was flying or battle anyway? Stealth would be our ally. No one would be able to see the Rider in this position and there were very few people outside of the Teams, who could identify individual Dragons. As far as we knew, the Hoard had no Riders, so being able to fly unseen would serve us well. The only real problem being, 'twas not easy to complete, difficult to maintain and harder to get out of, but we managed to do it eventually. Well, all of us except Axyl with his beautiful green Haniyyah. Axyl was one of the biggest Warriors I'd ever seen, even bigger than my father, and Haniyyah was literally the smallest Dragon of the thirteen now in 'Bond. She had no difficulty carrying him during flight though, and they'd developed their own ways of doing most of the aerial acrobatics. She simply couldn't hover with him, or pick him up and take off without a run or drop of sufficient distance, and my instincts screamed 'twould be trouble in the future. However, she could do a very good fly-by and grab him off the ground, or out of the Sea, given she had enough speed and nothing to prevent her from full wing span. They assured me that she'd be able to pick him out of the air from a free fall, once she built up a bit more muscle and stamina. They'd been practicing off their ledge at home but so far, from what I could tell, they hadn't been successful, and Axyl had landed in the icy seawater every time. Nevertheless, they were determined to do whatever the others did, even if they had to alter it a tad. And in fact, Axyl didn't even ride in front of her wings on her shoulders as did the rest of us, he rode just behind them, upon her upper back. 'Twas more like riding a horse, and was the only way 'twould work for them both. She was a shy Dragon, and boisterous Axyl was good for her as he was bringing her out of her timidity. 'Twas evident how much Axyl adored her, and when they thought no one was looking, she'd nuzzle him, and then her bejeweled eyes would sparkle joyfully when he caressed her snout and whispered to her. The look on his face said it all. I knew that look. For those of us in the 'Bond, 'twas not hard to understand.

Probably the most difficult skill we worked on, the Teams teasingly referred to as 'skipping the scales', but for clarity I named them transfers and step transfers. In a simple transfer, we'd 'hop' from one Dragon to another mid-flight, and was practiced both with and without a Rider on the receiving Dragon. We could then perform another transfer back to our own Dragon. In the step transfer, our balance and timing were particularly hard pressed, as we'd jump from Dragon to Dragon, in a stair step pattern. So, a '3 step transfer' would have the Rider jumping from his own, then 'cross two others in rapid succession afore returning, and a 4 step would add another jump 'tween and so on. These skills would be needed in both rescue and battle, I was certain. I'd expected to find the differences in size and wing span of the various Dragons to be more problematic than the differences in our sizes. But I was surprised to learn that the Dragons literally found this more difficult for them to master as well, since they'd not worked or even lived together for many centuries, and these maneuvers required them to Link with their brothers and sisters to complete the precision flight patterns. 'Twas also the most fascinating part of the day and brought out more camaraderie and cooperation than I'd expected.

Interestingly, throughout the training session I'd discovered the Response delay was evident when Speaking with every one of the Riders except my sister. When Speaking with Storrm or any of the Dragons, not just Gunnarr, there was no delay. Another mystery. Gunnarr was in command of the Dragons and they had a good grip upon the Communication plan and they all followed through with Sending and Receiving, but I couldn't understand how that had anything to do with the inconsistency.

The Teams worked all day on discovery of their own abilities. They all tried various aerial stunts, pickups of Riders off the ground midflight and then dropoffs to the ground, which they'd certainly need to sharpen, as we'd been in that situation afore. Fighting techniques and swordsmanship a'Dragonback was not ignored, as 'twas great skill and balance required to avoid striking your own Dragon when swinging your sword, or even to avoid throwing yourself off with the momentum. Many suggestions were offered about some trial or variation that seemed to work for them. Having Trained near non-stop from dawn 'til dusk, we were all exhausted but had some beginnings of understanding of each other's fighting abilities and strengths, and some unique talents were being brought to light. This was very important information if we were ever going to be able to come together as a Flight. What this day had truly shown us was that we still had a long way to go, to fully understand the workings of the 'Bond. For me, 'twas exciting. For the others, 'twas frustrating.

By the time I called the session, dusk was upon us and hunger pangs filled the air. Dragons didn't need to eat often, if not expending much energy. They could essentially pass a full moon without food and with very little water, as long as they didn't have to fight or fly very far or fast. But this state of undernourishment would weaken them, and their Magic suffered as well. The Warriors had discovered by accident 'twas also true for us, and some had gone without food or water for several days, causing no consequence more serious than some issues with their Links. 'Twas my belief that we could extend this ability as did the Dragons, by placing ourselves in a meditative state, but we'd not the manpower to devote to such research to truly determine just how long that timeline could be pushed. 'Twas certain all of our abilities would eventually be tested in dire circumstances, and 'twas important to have some idea of what they were prior to the need. It seemed the real problem for both Dragon and Warrior was our amplified appetites when working hard, and having worked hard all day we were quite ravenous and needed to be fed.

Each Warrior Spoke with their Dragon individually, then they all took wing as one. Leaving us standing alone on the plains to go hunt, I realized this would be one of our most dangerous periods. We'd have to examine our partners' hunting and feeding habits. What if they couldn't leave to hunt? If we were under siege, we might have to find a way to feed them locally ourselves. Prior to The Black, all Dragons preferred to hunt far from Man, and consequently we'd never been in competition for food. I knew Gunnarr preferred to hunt in the Raptor's Talons or the Razor's Edge. There were plenty of large creatures there, along with many animals we'd never seen or even knew existed, and there was also much in the way of vegetation near the surrounding forests. I was learning that Dragons loved their salads, but I'd also learned that they didn't like to enter wooded areas. They would fly-by or fly o'er, but they'd not enter. I thought I understood; the forests were tight and for such large creatures 'twould be difficult to maneuver. But caves could be tight too, and they didn't have the same objections there. I couldn't help but wonder about this. Yet another mystery.

And that brought me back to how vulnerable we were when our partners were hunting. Surely the Hoard would have little difficulty catching us at that time and 'twould be done. This was simply not acceptable. I'd need to establish a buddy system so no Rider was ever completely alone. Sending my orders to Storrm to make this happen, I continued my line of thought. Mayhap we could establish a herd of beasts to feed the Team Dragons closer to home, raising them along with our own food animals. 'Twould also be wise to do some dedicated farming, and both endeavors would merely require breaking sod for additional land, as the manpower was already provided through the influx of refugees. Having these resources available during siege was optimal, but of course 'twould be wiser yet, to learn to hunt together. However, 'twould be dangerous, especially in the beginning, as Dragons in hunting mode didn't think clearly 'til their appetites were satiated. The hunt itself could be very grueling, and the Rider might be injured or even killed in the process. I wondered if these issues could be rectified, since there'd come the time 'twould be foolish to separate, and we all must make major lifestyle adjustments to accommodate our new partners. Even though Gunnarr was never gone more than a day at the most, 'twas risky besides being uncomfortable. The further away a Dragon was physically from his partner, the more anxiety was created, and that emotion would build with time as well as distance. And just to remind myself, of all these problems the most important was the binding of our Life Force. If one half of the Team died the other would follow, and once the Hoard understood this concept, the human half would be their foremost target. Add yet another problem to the ever lengthening list.

My Warriors gathered about me and still very fatigued, we sat in the winter dried grass near the cliffs. I called upon each in turn to give a summary of what they could and couldn't do and wherein lay their principal talent. Each reported their personalities amazingly parallel, or completely opposite that of their Dragons. Listening closely, I realized that each pair was perfectly matched. They each had strengths and weaknesses, were able to assist the other, and they'd all developed very close ties. Despite the necessity for trust due to the binding, 'twas not always a given in partnerships, but I was pleased to hear we'd all developed a depth of faith and respect equal to the need. 'Twas also confirmed everyone had the same feeling about the MindSpeak, in that 'twas far more comfortable than speaking aloud, and had to force themselves at times to vocalize due to an uneasy sense they might never again. I admitted to them how Gunnarr and I had stumbled upon an embarrassingly simple solution within the first few days. I sang with him. Since the dawn of time, Dragons had raised their voices and for some reason, 'twas easier than verbalizing, and most of us played some kind of instrument as well. Eager to incorporate this activity into their daily routines, I smiled, knowing there'd be a lot more music in the near future, my Warriors' voices harmonizing with Dragon Song.

There followed a major discussion on equipment, saddles and other needs. While we talked, Tyndall, Apryya and Zoe gathered wood, along with Rygyl and Ariel who began setting up a fire pit. It didn't take long, and we were ready to roast whatever may come. Gunnarr was the first to return and he brought with him a large, hoofed, furry creature with a huge rack of antlers. He dropped the carcass in front of Daxx and Axyl who quickly cleaned it, skinned it and prepared it for the spit. Mystynn was next, bringing a huge claw full of greens from some distant meadow, thoughtfully washed in the icy river while crossing the plains. Ragnyrr arrived soon after, and brought some species of fish I'd never seen afore, so immense he could barely hang onto the slippery dead weight of it as he flew. After he'd successfully landed and the fish given to be prepared o'er the coals, he sauntered his way to Kydra. His back to me, I saw her face light up with something he gave her. Later I learned that she loved sea shells and Ragnyrr had brought one from a distant shore to add to her collection.

'Tween the offerings of the hunt and our provisions, 'twas the best evening meal I could ever remember. The beast was succulent, the fish flavorful, the greens tender and the mead well aged. For the first time since afore we'd learned of the coming war and the Magic of the 'Bond, I listened to the enchanting sound of all my friends laughing and full of optimism. We'd been far too hard on ourselves, working so long every day that we fell asleep afore our eyes closed, beginning again afore the next dawn. We'd flown patrols, practiced fighting a'Dragonback, kept up with our swordsmanship upon the ground, made rescues, and strengthened our ties with our new partners. Although no one would admit to such, and all of the 'Bonded were single, we'd not had any family time since we'd begun this journey and our hearts had been heavy, missing brothers and sisters, fathers and mothers. I was still the only one who'd been in an actual battle with a Hoard Dragon, but others had been close. At least no one was feeling the fatigue from the MindSpeak any longer.

I enjoyed the stories being told around the campfire about the first morning after the 'Bond, and near snorted my mead at some of them. Storrm wasn't talking but she was listening. How had so much time passed afore we gathered like this? 'Twas in my mind to make sure it didn't happen again. 'Twas glaringly obvious how much this meant to all of them, how much stronger and encouraged they were with such solidarity. 'Twas also apparent we'd made our own 'serious tactical error' as Gunnarr had put it, by not clarifying how the Teams would work together as a fighting force, prior to taking the 'Bond, the martial aspects having been literally ignored as we'd focused upon the ceremony and then plunged blindly into the aftermath.

Despite all the activity, I couldn't help but notice Storrm and Mystynn spent most of their time sitting quietly, obviously Speaking much to each other. 'Twas also clear how close they'd become and I was pleased to note that Storrm was no longer lonely since our parting. I'd worried, as we'd been inseparable from her birth and aside from Kydra, whom we didn't have much chance to spend time with, she and I had never really had any other friends. Realizing I was no longer lonely either, I smiled at Gunnarr and saw that twinkle in his crystalline eyes, followed quickly by the crease that ran 'cross the top edge of one inner eyelid, which I now recognized as his wink. I understood what he was indicating. His Race was solitary, even reclusive, but his entire existence had changed as much as mine. He'd been lonely too, and now we had each other. I couldn't ask for a better friend or fighting partner, and 'twas in truth much more than that. 'Twas an emotion I had yet to identify, but seemed to be budding in the vicinity of my heart.

Deciding to test my theory and hoping 'twould not turn out horribly wrong, I Thought, *"The fact that Storrm and I have always been different, knowing things and able to do things that others couldn't, is related somehow to Gunnarr's Blood Oath."* As soon as my thought hit reality, Gunnarr snorted a slight haze of smoke and I peered anxiously into his eyes. Afraid I'd started something that might not end well, I was comforted when I felt just a slight unease as he nodded his confirmation. Pushing the issue, I continued, *"The delay in our Communication is significant and is also related in some way to the Blood Oath."* Again, Gunnarr snorted slightly as if clearing his throat and then nodded in affirmation. This time 'twas relief I felt from him. Yes! I'd discovered the way to find out what I needed to know, without causing him pain. He wasn't breaking the Oath by confirming my own thoughts, as long as I stated them and didn't ask him questions. This was very good news indeed and I was exhilarated. Now I just had to deduce enough of the clues to make logical statements. Hmmmm. Mayhap my celebration was a tad premature.

Not allowing my personal feelings to deflate the moment, since we'd all worked hard and long this day, I knew 'twas time and Gunnarr agreed. Calling their attention, I stood up, raised my mead roughly to the sky and loudly declared, "You've done well this day and have learned much, my friends. We're stronger and faster than our enemies, Healing any wound they're lucky enough to inflict. With our LifeBond partners, we forge a new era for the Dragon Clan!" Throwing down my mead for emphasis, the pottery shattered upon the ground and my Warriors stood cheering, slapping each other's shoulders, and thumping their mugs together in rough salute. Their increasing level of rowdiness was my intention and 'twas my next test as Second to time this perfectly. "We're near unstoppable!" I roared, my hands in the air as my words were met with excitement, and they rushed toward the peak I sought to attain.

Dropping from the frenzied optimism, I lowered my voice and seriously proclaimed, "But we no longer practice for competitions or trials. 'Tis war we enter." And suddenly I had their undivided attention. Gunnarr sat behind me in his majestic pose, my long red hair sprayed out like a halo in the nearly constant breeze. My feet slightly apart, my leather braced forearms crossed o'er my chest, I was silent with all eyes, both Man and Dragon, now riveted upon me. The moonlit sky o'er the Sea of Dreams glowing 'cross the horizon, made an impressive backdrop. Taking a breath, I spoke quietly but firmly, knowing they were hanging upon my every word. Pausing for emphasis 'tween each statement, I began. "We have studied and trained for battle all the days of our lives, but never have we been in a declared war. We have practiced and fought each other here and in the Pits, but never have we battled a gathered foe. Our Warriors have been bodyguards to the King, kept the peace in and around Kadoor, have fought individuals and multiple factions, but in our span of days we've never seen war against a sworn enemy." We couldn't win this war with delusions of grandeur, nor could we win fighting as if we'd already lost. The seriousness of our state of affairs shone in their eyes as the sun dawned upon them. My words dug a ditch and I could feel them sinking. Now I must turn them around and raise them up, just enough to transform this Stable into a strong, solid, Battle Ready Flight. If I could do this, I deserved my position; if not, I would resign. 'Twas as simple as that.

But afore I could utter a sound, came the clatter of sword on sword, chain mail and breastplate. Isolated, it began in the back and was quickly joined by hilt banging on vanguards and shields. Now striking out a pounding rhythm and chanting their Battle Cry, "Darque, Darque, Darque," they created such a din, I wouldn't have been able to hear myself, even if I'd not been speechless. And then the Dragons added their voices and each and every one of them roared out their own battle cry in their growling language, 'til all the Warriors who'd Passed Beyond must be wondering what was happening on the plains of Drekinn.

Breathless, motionless, speechless for several moments afore I managed to collect myself, I raised my sword, signaling for quiet. The sudden hush hit me like a charging bull and again, I was momentarily dumbstruck. Hiding my astonishment at this show of support and allowing only my fierce pride to show through my expression, Gunnarr Called his Dragons to silence as he towered o'er me. I waited 'til I sensed everyone was listening. "I haven't the right to declare a state of War. 'Tis the sole responsibility of the Battle Commander. But at this point, 'tis merely a detail and mark my words, such has been thrust upon us. We are at War with The Black." My fellow Warriors strongly approved my stance, their mood solemn. Gravely, I continued, "We did not ask for this War, nor did we cause this War, but we will not back down, for this is a War we must win. 'Twill determine not only our personal freedoms, but the very existence of Kadoor and our respective Races. We are the Warriors of the Dragon Clan, and in LifeBond with our Dragon partners, we will defeat the Evil One and his Hoard. The battles to come will be shared in Legend Song, for we are truly invincible!"

Their response was a renewal of the din from foot on ground, Dragon roar, the crash and thud of metal against metal. Now I was certain we'd be heard Beyond the Veil. I smiled as I thought about our ancestors who'd fought for our freedom in so many battles afore us and hoped they were watching us from the other side. Surely they'd be proud of their sons and daughters as we accepted the challenge this night. Soon we'd join the ranks of veteran Warriors in true battle and 'twas my intention that we be ready. My arms folded 'cross my chest once more, I held my head high and stood watching my Battle Ready Flight as they celebrated, and I did nothing to stop the revelry this time. Let them roar. Let Evil be afraid. The LifeBond Teams are coming!

CHAPTER 14

Darque Goes Shopping

THE FOLLOWING DAY

Navigating the back alleys of the Port District, the hustle and bustle of a new day promised excitement. The light of the breaking dawn at my back was barely enough to show me where to place my next step, but I knew well my way through this labyrinth. I was enjoying my return here for the first time since the 'Bond. Oh how I'd missed the smells of seafood fresh caught, of the taverns and inns, breakfast sizzling o'er the wood burning stoves and grills, kaafy brewing and bread baking. The chill in the air was brisk and invigorating, but the frost melted quickly. A multitude of emotions radiated from the working people, pushing their way through the growing crowds toward their destinations afore their pay was docked for tardiness. My hearing so acute, I had to Hush the brooms sweeping last evening's dirt o'er the thresholds into the narrow back alleys, and the inn keepers ordering fish, meat, dairy and vegetables from the mass of market vendors plying their wares. Lightly Casting, I Heard entire conversations, some humorous, some making me blush, and some I might have to consider discussing with the Battle Commander. Gunnarr wouldn't yet be at ease here, and so he flew high above, a dazzling opal in the sky, following my progress as I made my way to my appointment with the village Masters to tender my orders. I had shopping to do. This trip served a dual purpose, as did everything nowadays. Honing my skills, we Shared our vision, allowing him my sight and shifting views. 'Twas a bit unnerving at times, as I'd suddenly see myself winding through the Port from close to heavenly heights, and then switch back to the world through my own eyes, causing me to almost miss my next step. But my mind was on other things. We were scheduled for Rover Patrols within two dawns and I wanted to leave as fully suited as we could. The icy kiss of snow drew ever nearer and would soon envelope us.

I'd met with the Commander to make report late last night, and he was pleased. 'Twas good I didn't need much sleep, as my appointment this dawn came upon the heels of that meeting. Meandering my way to the Leather Shop, I was to meet with Toryn the Leather Master, some of his Apprentices, Ian the Stable Master, and Silas the Blacksmith, and had extended my own private request to Alric the Weapons Master, to grace us with his presence as well.

The finish processing for leather was not the most pleasant of odors generated, so his shop was one of the furthest away from the mainland Village, and was one of the first encountered when exiting the Port docks. Also, one had to travel through a veritable maze of narrow streets and back alleys to get there. If you weren't familiar with the area, you might get lost, but everyone who lived and worked here knew how to get around and we tended to be a friendly lot. Suspicious but friendly, as 'twas typical for a port village. People understood the needs of the trade and market, but were always aware who was Clan and who wasn't.

Drekinn was rather large for a village, and considered a major port along the coastal regions. We prided ourselves in having a rich variety of shops, inns and taverns, and I was hailed frequently as I passed them by. The closer to the docks, the more crowded the area became. All ports were set up in a similar manner, and most sea travelers and merchants never entered the village proper, spending all of their time, and a great deal of their coin, in the port districts. Port O'Drekinn was no different.

The harbor was situated along the southern edge of the mainland, aside and below Drekinn, and one had to pass through the High District 'tween the two areas to get to the village. The natural lay of the land provided a twisting and turning terraced rock wall slope to sea level on the southern edge of the plateau. The rocky gradient was perfectly designed to separate and protect the village from the port. Where the land met the Sea, the One True Liege had formed a long horseshoe shaped, deep water inlet that made the port possible as well as profitable. The North Docks on the mainland side were full of activity, ships arriving and departing quickly after transferring their loads. Along the southern length of the cove 'cross the harbor, were the South Docks, where ships tied up for longer stays and was usually less hectic. The Port might look to the unknowing eye to be difficult to defend in siege however, due to the War heritage of the Dragon Clan and unbeknownst to most, 'twas built in such a manner as to incorporate the rock terracing into the walls of the buildings and streets, and included a double level, the lower one concealed. The only way into the Village proper from the Sea was through this area, as the crossed water region was enclosed by cliffs and all South Dock traffic was vented around the eastern end directly to the North Docks and into the Port District. The huge timbers forming the rafters and central pillars or truss beams of certain key buildings, were rigged with iron rings threaded to attached pulleys, and could be quickly tugged out of their places with the assistance of a War Horse, or two or three stout villagers. This would bring down enough heavy beam to collapse the entire central portion of the district in a domino effect, completely blocking access to any of the buildings, and protecting them from looting as well, with most stock rotated through the lower level. It also blocked anyone getting through to the Village from the harbor. Ever brilliant was my father, as were his forebears. The rest of our seaside border was protected by the cave riddled cliffs we now called home.

Stepping 'cross the alley side threshold of Toryn's leather shop, I reassured Gunnarr that all was well, allowing him to See through my eyes as I entered. Never certain of the welcome I'd receive from Silas, (I hadn't burned half his shop down a'purpose), I was pleasantly surprised when he grabbed me up in a huge bear hug, as he used to do when I was a child. That would be afore the fire of course. I knew all of these men, had grown up around them, and they knew me. But I'd learned that having everyone know you, wasn't always a good thing. After exchanging greetings and hearty congratulations on assuming my new rank, I sighed in relief at their acceptance, determined not to let them down. We gathered at the large table in the middle of the main work area in the back of the shop, where hot kaafy, fresh baked bread and newly churned butter was laid out, along with my favorite jam as well. His mate Myrta, was a Master Cook and worked at the Den, so I knew we were in for a special treat. Picking up a still warm-from-the-oven loaf of the crusty bread from the platter, I eagerly tore off the heel, passing the rest along to the others. Using one of my boot blades, I slathered on a thick layer of the fresh churned butter and some strawberry jam, and ate ravenously. I'd not realized how hungry I still was.

When everyone had eaten their fill and had poured themselves another mug of the hot kaafy, Myrta cleared the table and we began to discuss my requirements in earnest. Nothing like this had ever been created afore, and I needed all of these respected Masters working together to help me design what I envisioned. Soon I had the rapt attention of every one of them and they were even taking notes. Pencils sketched furiously as I described my ideas for saddles, including connections, strapping systems and weapons holders. We discussed logistics, the need for comfort, sturdiness and stability, versus the need for quick tie on and release. I kept to myself the surprising dexterity of the Dragons, for all their animal-like paws, not wanting this to become common knowledge, allowing them to believe we only needed to design ties and releasing systems to suit human hands and fingers. After much debate, including input from all, we finally settled on a working version without stirrups, which would only get in our way during our maneuvers, but included straps we could curl up and tie on when not in use, and a small seat with a short leather flap to provide some protection to the Rider's legs from rubbing against the rough scales of the Dragon's neck and shoulders (or ribcage, as was the case for Axyl). 'Twould be lined with thick fleece to cushion their spiny backs and to prevent wear on their scales, as well as to help keep it in place, but I'd debated against a cantle. That edge at the back of the seat would be comfortable, but 'twould make it more difficult to surf or perform the multitude of aerial stunts required. Ian disputed this, confident he could give us a small flexible cantle which would assist us in our balance and still meet our needs. Finally I agreed, not really believing 'twould work. I'd originally visualized a bit more than a surcingle would provide, but not much, and it now seemed we'd be getting more saddle than I'd bargained for.

Reassuring me, he said he'd quickly produce one trial version using a War Horse stock saddle as a base. These were not yet solid and could be modified for width and length. 'Twould be easier than starting from scratch, 'til I'd tried it out and knew what worked and what didn't, and 'twould be ready for me to break in by the next dawn, if they could take accurate measurements of Gunnarr. I received his confirmation instantaneously and since I needed the saddle afore two dawns, I told him where Gunnarr would be waiting just inside the High Gate and they could go there now and get what they needed. His Lead Apprentice and staff darted out the door and ran for the High District afore another word was spoken. I shook my head in amusement, since they weren't all needed to obtain the measurements, but apparently none of them had ever seen a Dragon up close afore and they'd not miss this opportunity. I couldn't fault them their enthusiasm, for I was indeed fortunate.

When Ian left to supervise and assist in the design and creation of the saddle, I sat back down with Toryn for my next order of business. The few younger Apprentices stood fidgeting behind him, hoping the Dragon wouldn't leave afore they could sneak away. With Silas listening in, I described my ideas for a sling to be used by one or more Dragons at the same time, for carrying large or heavy loads 'tween them as they flew. Although I didn't want to admit to the real need for this device, we'd eventually use it for rescue and recovery of our own. This should be a simple project, its only other requirement was that it did have to be carried on the Dragon when not in use. Toryn and Silas discussed a few sketches and then Silas left the table followed closely by the remaining Apprentices, muttering something about lengths of leather straps, weight limits and grommets.

Mayhap 'twas not as simple a project as I'd originally anticipated. No matter, 'twas in good hands now.

Next, I described our clothing requirements with Toryn. So far we'd been spared hard snows, but Riding was always cold with the combined high altitudes and wind chill, and even with our altered senses, we'd need heavier gear soon. Magic would keep us warm of course, but 'twould be a drain of valuable resources, and if we needed that Magic to help in a fight we'd lose our warmth. So I ordered full length overcoats with hoods and thigh high heavy boots, with everything fleece and fur lined. The new boots included alterations from our usual horse riding boots, not needing the heels for non-existent stirrups, and for increased flexibility and traction for us to manage surfing, rock wall climbing, aerial stunts and the new saddles we'd just ordered. The boots would be cut high above the knee in front and then dip the cut below the knee behind, to allow for freedom of movement and the most protection and warmth. They would of course, have to incorporate our blades. The Master offered up a suggestion that would allow them to be unlaced and folded down to create a shorter boot without need to change. The cut above the knee would fold down o'er the top of the ankle and 'twould then be midcalf. I agreed to this, but I also ordered another pair of midcalf working boots for all of us, with the flat sole design as well. This would give us all two new pairs of boots, one with a dual purpose and quick change ability for the coldest temperatures, and one pair for warmer weather. He promised the orders for thirteen of everything would be ready within a few dawns. I was skeptical, but reassured once he told me how many workers he now had, following the Battle Commander's prior orders, affording additional manpower to my requests. Biting my bottom lip, I wondered when he'd issued those orders, for he'd told me not. Then I provided him with the necessary measurements which I'd obtained afore we broke up the gathering last evening.

Proffering the parchment with my scribbled notes, 'twas then handed off to his First Apprentice who'd been listening intently, offering whispered advice occasionally, pointing to one thing or another as his Master sketched. At that time I made one more request. Dragons could carry much more weight than we could, and I needed some sort of saddle bag for gatherings, however, this couldn't be directly attached to the topside of the saddle as 'twould interfere with their wings and our surfing during flight, if in use. As soon as I pointed out this stipulation I Heard Gunnarr's gratitude. *"You are most wise, m'lady,"* and then he snorted, as he was being tickled by the Apprentices crawling o'er him to obtain appropriate measurements for the saddle.

Trying not to laugh aloud, for those present wouldn't understand the cause of my amusement, I continued, "I like the bag I've been using, but 'twould be better if it hung in such a manner that the weight it carried when full was more evenly spread out and balanced 'cross the Dragon's neck, and mayhap attached at the bottom to the underside of the saddle to keep it from flapping about. 'Twould be good to be able to secure it close to his chest so as not to create as much wind drag during flight," I added, as I recalled the instability we'd encountered during our return from Kaddart with the full bag dangling beneath us from the single strap tied about his great neck. This had not only caused Gunnarr trouble with keeping level from the bag swinging hither and yon, but also created the wind drag to which I'd made reference, which dropped us like a rock at odd moments. All of which caused him to fatigue much quicker than he should have and finally I'd pulled the bag up to sit 'tween my thighs. This wasn't an ideal position either, but 'twas better than the alternative.

"I'll get my staff started on your requests immediately, m'lady Darque," he stated enthusiastically, nodding his graying head. I nodded my confirmation that we were finished for the time being and he bowed his respect, leaving the room to join the others above. I tried not to giggle like a school girl. The man had worked with the Dragon Teams for moons now but hadn't as yet actually seen one up close either. I could feel his impatience to get there afore the Dragon took wing.

"I'll wait for him," Gunnarr Sighed in resignation. The poor beast had never had so many human hands upon him afore, and his distress was evident.

"Hang on, my love," Trying to be encouraging, I hadn't even noticed the term with which I'd just addressed him. 'Twas from my heart and spilled forth in answer to his state of mind at that moment, and I could do naught but comfort him with my true emotions. I felt the impact of my words immediately as Gunnarr stiffened and sucked in his breath, and I Drew us into a state of Silence, similar to the dual existence we'd shared in the Magic fire of the LifeBond, closing down all outside interference, unable to Sense anyone or thing, nor could we be Sensed. *"Did I say something wrong?"* Anxiously I awaited his answer, my growing concern becoming more apparent.

Gunnarr's Voice was calm and warm, also from his heart. *"You can do no wrong in my eyes…."* he Stated clearly, and with such strong sentiment I could barely breathe. And then he Whispered into my very essence, *"…my love."*

Stunned, but reassured we were of one heart, it took several moments to return to the present and Release the Silence. It mattered not that I was of Mankind and he of Dragonkind. Even though I knew not how, I was certain our love had been growing since long afore the 'Bond and nothing could part us from this path.

My hearing cleared slightly afore my vision, but I was surrounded by stillness. Alric sat opposite me at the table and we were alone. As I shifted reluctantly back to Command mode, I realized the true meaning of the elongated hush. 'Twas protocol, and 'twas the first time we'd met since my promotion. I must gain his respect, or at the very least, his recognition of my rank. Suddenly, the small room seemed huge, and near bursting with anticipation and a sense of triumph, I waited for it. Finally he nodded his head in my direction seeking permission from his Second in Command to speak, and I nodded my authorization. However, any notion that I'd gained his full acceptance, was short lived.

"I must say m'lady Darque, I was most curious last night by your private invitation to this meeting," he stated firmly, while maintaining full eye contact, his challenge near palpable. My eyebrows raised at his use of the familiar greeting, acknowledging my familial status but not my leadership. 'Twas acceptable from the others, as they weren't technically a part of the Warrior Brotherhood. But Alric was Weapons Master, an integral component of our organization, and I would have his acknowledgement of my rank afore we broke down formalities and began our new relationship. I was his superior, and capable of giving direct and unquestioned orders to which he must immediately respond. He knew this, but he seemed surprised that I apparently knew this as well. 'Twas an eye contact challenge he could by no means have won, of course. I'd never lost a stare down.

Adding a hint of a Push to shorten the inevitable, he blinked his deep green eyes and cast his gaze to the floor at his feet afore clearing his throat. "I beg forgiveness, Second. 'Twould appear as if I've lost my mind as well as my manners. Think not that I dispute your promotion however, for 'tis nothing of the sort," and looking up again into my gaze he smiled at me and continued. "I merely test your mettle girl, for you are younger to take Command than I'd expected. I have long awaited your succession, and as you will find, I know of the prophesy." Then he winked at me and his face broke into a huge smile.

With his words my eyes widened and my jaw near fell open. The prophesy. Just what did it say? Seemed every time I tried to think on it, my mind would haze as if I knew the answer but 'twas subdued. Did everyone know it but me? My eyebrows furrowed, but I caught his look at that moment and chose to accept his apology, as 'twould do none of us good to hold anything against him.

"Fair enough. As long as I hold your allegiance. I know you're an honorable man." And with that simple exchange, we moved on.

Reaching down, I dragged forth the bag I'd carried into the room and shoved under the table upon arrival. Then I hoisted it up and opened the drawstring top, grasping the bottom and shaking the bag to spill the contents 'cross the aged and well worn work surface. The tough scales slid out and clattered o'er each other, forming a glittering pile. The off white of the fangs and the shiny blue black of the talons drew his eye instantly. Gunnarr had managed to pack them into the center and they now appeared on top. They'd traveled well.

"Careful my friend," I told him, as I reached out and stayed his hand, just prior to having grasped the nearest talon. "They're much sharper than one might imagine." As he drew back, I leaned closer and skillfully picked it up, turning it o'er in my palm to show him the wickedly sharp underside edge and the point that could shred our shields like a hot poker through a brick of butter. Yet I knew from experience that these same talons could be tender and exacting in their touch, without harm caused or intended, and had fantasized often about how they could actually bring much pleasure. Clearing my own throat now and feeling the warmth rising up my chest and neck, I quickly redirected my thoughts.

Gunnarr told me the fact these claws stayed sharp along the edge and not just at the tips, was a feature of their Magic, showing clearly how the beast had Passed the Veil. In battle the talons would be in fighting mode and would remain that way upon his death. Had he died in a manner other than battle, his talons would be as of the big cats now said to be repopulating the distant forests. Sharp, but easily handled, carried and even worn as decoration, as some nomadic tribes in the Outlands were rumored to wear. I'd heard of similar jewelry beginning to appear through the Black Market, several moons past.

One might also wonder why Dragon bits and pieces had never been found afore. Gunnarr reminded me that the remains of Magic Bearers were camouflaged, and that most of the beast would simply decompose eventually, but the teeth, non-lethal talons and fangs which survived the death, would simply be lost to the bottom of the Oceans, or buried within the sand and rock of where they'd lain and breathed their last. If a Dragon had been forced Past the Veil, and their talons and fangs were still lethal, these would've been removed by the battle victor in compliance with the Dragon Code of Life and Living, and placed where they'd do no harm. Some Dragons in the far distant past of even Gunnarr's Memories, had kept such as souvenirs and trophies, proclaiming their great prowess.

And there was the notion that mayhap they'd been found afore but not recognized. This gave me an instant thought and I quickly relayed it to Storrm, to send out a pair of Teams immediately in Search of such within the Markets of the Port Districts along the coastlines. Real fangs and talons would be readily identified by their impressive weight, luster, and a definite warmth to the touch, not to mention the fact that one couldn't scratch their surface with a blade, thereby not mistaken for any other substance, but only other Magic Bearers or one in 'Bond would be able to see and feel these differences. To others, 'twould appear as any normal substance. 'Twould take a full moon to do a proper initial investigation at least, but 'twould be worthwhile to know if there were any on the Black Market, if they were known for what they truly were by the ones doing the marketing, and for the fact that we'd soon need stock to create what I wanted. If they existed at all, they'd show up along the coasts, and if that happened, we could follow up further. 'Twas a place to start. If we couldn't kill for them, I wasn't opposed to scavenging. Gunnarr was unaware of any ancient stockpiles that might still be intact, and of course there'd been topographical changes during the Last Holocaust, however, he agreed to Inquire of his Matriarch or her elder sister. I sighed, and then Storrm Relayed that Ariel and Zaydarr, along with Rygyl and Tegrynn, would leave on their mission within the mark.

"Ahhh, I see now," Alric stated with appreciation, bringing my attention back to our current dialogue. "You've saved me a severed finger, I wager."

"Most likely," I responded with mirth in kind.

He stared at the talon in my palm, and then redirected his gaze to the pile on the work table. "Me thinks you don't present these victor's spoils for mere admiration, Darque. And are these actual scales? And would they be safely handled?"

"Yes, they be real, and safely handled," I said. Gingerly touching the closest one, it tipped slightly, the glittering effect flashing in his eyes as it caught the candle light from the chandelier at just the right angle.

Wincing, he blinked several times, then wiped the tears from his eyes and brought the scale closer in fascination. Examining it carefully, turning it in his hands, he saw the potential as had I, when I'd discovered what Gunnarr had brought home with us that day.

"This is remarkable. So lightweight and yet so sturdy. I know what you're thinking. If we can find a way to attach these to your shields, 'twould be near impenetrable. But the very characteristic that would make it so, also make it impossible to pierce for tying on, does it not?"

"But you o'er look the obvious, Alric. I just stayed your hand from the very thing that can pierce scale."

"You're most imaginative. Have you devised a way to hold such, in order to use it safely?"

"I haven't had time to make any attempts on my own yet, but I have more than a few ideas. Truly they'll work, I'm convinced. 'Twill take some experimentation, but I believe one need do little to mount the talons. See here?" Pointing to the root where the sharp edge ended, I indicated the smooth bulb like surface. "'Twould provide a safe handhold if one were strong enough to avoid slipping, stabilized against the palm and squeezed 'tween ones fingers in a fisted grip, since the region 'tween the bulb and the talon proper is narrower. But 'tis not that narrow, and 'twould be better if mounted with at least a guard to prevent loss of fingers, and then used as a blade. Then one could also use it as an awl to pierce the scales and mount them in a lapping pattern to protect the rivets or ties from being broken during battle. The fangs could also be mounted as blades or made into hair picks. You may need the assistance of Magic and 'twill be at your disposal, just tell me what you desire." Sighing, I dropped the scale onto the pile with the rest of them. "Just my initial thoughts, but I pray you'll be able to utilize these creatively to meet our need for more effective weapons." 'Twas comforting in some manner to see the seriousness with which he pondered my concepts.

"I understand. You've sparked some ideas, I just need time, of which we have little," he stated, still turning the scale in his hands. His eyebrows raised, he asked me, "You didn't react to my 'spoils' comment earlier. Am I to assume you came by this stock in battle?" When I simply returned his gaze stone faced, he dropped the matter and then proclaimed, "I'll have a working model of both a blade arrangement using the talons, and mayhap the fangs as well, and a covered shield within, say, two dawns."

I was delighted with this timeline. "I must have your pledge on that, Alric. I realize I ask the near impossible, but you're the best man for this and I personally believe you're the only man who can accomplish what I ask." Pausing briefly, I then added, "I've admired your work all my life." I said this with heartfelt conviction, and was rewarded to see the subtle rise of his shoulders, the puffing out of his chest as he accepted my compliment. Then breaking the mood once again, turning to the most serious tack yet, I instilled the urgency I felt by declaring, "This war has brought much change to our mainstream notions. Do not doubt that we are sorely outnumbered, my friend. The Dragon Clan has never afore faced such odds. We must adapt or we will lose. I cannot allow that to happen."

CHAPTER 15

A Mysterious Relocation

SOMETIME AFTER THE LIFEBOND CEREMONY

'Twas hot, and Graasyn struggled to awaken from a terrible nightmare. Wrestling with some immovable force, he could do nothing as Kaddart went up in Flames spewed forth by the Hoard Dragons. He was helpless to defend the little girl hunted mercilessly through the village rubble, the dream dissipating as she was chased into the open fields. Slowly, he regained consciousness, as the fiery heat of the Flames switched to a cold burst of wind, like a snuffed candle, in his present reality. Completely disoriented, he wasn't at all sure whether his eyes were open or closed, and couldn't even tell whether he was lying down or standing upright. 'Twould have been more alarming if he hadn't already experienced all that had occurred o'er the last few dawns, especially that final incident afore the fog had completely blanketed them. 'Twas suffocating, stole the very air around them, and they'd both lost consciousness. Groggily, he squeezed his eyes shut to determine that they were indeed closed, then attempted to open them and found 'twas a difficult task. Was he that weak, or were his eyelashes actually stuck together? Deliberately, he made contact with his own body, mentally locating his arms and legs, face and hands, and then focused on his current position. Pushing up on his elbows, which was no easy feat, Graasyn discovered he'd been lying on his back on a pile of evergreen branches, just under a slight overhang of rock. There was a hard surface beneath the leafy pile, and within reach of his fingertips, the ground was lightly covered with something cold and white. Bringing his hand up to his face, he managed to scrape the frost off his lashes and opened his eyes enough to be blinded by the sunlight. Blinking back the tears, he finally regained his focus and was confused by what he saw. Although the sun seemed excessively bright a moment ago, he was actually in the shade. Surrounded by woodlands with visible cloud cover showing through in various patches, he could smell and hear a brook close by, and noted the rock and leaf litter all about. 'Twas beautiful, but 'twas also disconcerting as he had absolutely no recognition of this region, and he'd traveled far and wide in his lifetime. However, he was quite certain he'd never been here afore. But where was 'here', how long had he been asleep, what had happened at Kaddart, and of more immediate importance, where was his son?

Afore he had a chance to stir, came the soft steps of a man moving in stealth mode, halting close behind him. "Are we in the Fade, or did we make it Beyond?" Quietly Bastyen asked just o'er his shoulder.

Without hesitation, and sighing deeply in relief, he responded, "Neither. But neither are we where we began our journey." Graasyn's words rang with the conviction of experience. He was a Warrior of many winters afore Bastyen was even birthed, and he knew of what he spoke. He'd heard many stories of what to expect, and had actually been quite close to the Veil a few times himself. No, they were most definitely still upon this side and certainly not in the Hades of the Fade. However, they weren't home or anywhere familiar, nor were they in the aqueducts of Kaddart being chased by a Dragon and that stranger….the flash of Battle Lust this memory produced had him rising to defend them both. Rapidly stepping back into Battle Stance, he collapsed onto the hard ground again when a stabbing ache in his right thigh gripped him tightly, forcing a gasp. By the Dragon's Breath, what was that? The sharp pain caused the remaining fog o'er his memories to clear rapidly, all of them returning like a flash flood, making him feel dizzy and near nauseous. How had he forgotten about the sword wound?

"Easy Aba, sit down. You've lost a lot of blood and should not yet be up and about. Let me find something with which to clean and bind the wound." Bastyen hurried forward to assist him upright. Seeing the stern look upon the elder's face, he continued, "I should've cared for your wound first, but I needed to secure the area, and I was afraid I'd wake you and you needed to rest. No, don't think to remind me of my duty, keeping you alive is part of it. We're quite alone here; I've already scouted around a bit. I found no trace of Dragons or Man or anything but small wilderness animals. I haven't gone far, as there hasn't been enough time and I wouldn't leave you alone for long, but there is naught to observe. What you see in front of you is the same as what you see behind you and beside you and in all directions, as far as we can walk in several days, 'twould seem. There's nothing to break the landscape but rolling hills, small rivers and some interesting rocky areas yonder, which I was in the process of exploring when the snow began to increase." The slim young Warrior sighed and knelt down to begin inspecting the wound. Scraping together a handful of what Graasyn now recognized as snow, the boy carefully pulled aside the cut fabric of the pant leg to reveal the dried blood and muck they'd acquired during their escape. Using the snow, he began gingerly washing the leg and then with a frown, his eyebrows beginning to furrow, he scrubbed more vigorously.

"How long…." Graasyn started to ask, then sucked in his breath as Bastyen probed the wounded thigh with his fingers. The youth stopped his ministrations momentarily, looking carefully at the leg, and then massaged briskly with several more handfuls of snow, 'til all the dirt and blood were gone, and surprisingly, the pain subsided. Looking up, he raised his brows quizzically and then sat back on his heels, resting one elbow on his forward knee. Turning his palms upward, his shrugged his shoulders indicating his bewilderment, as Graasyn leaned in to take a closer look at the sword wound he'd received in the alley.

Near speechless, he examined the area, for where there should have been an open slash near to the bone, there was naught but slight discoloration and a thin, newly healed scar. His eyes wide, he touched the now visible scar tissue and said with some incredulity, "The flesh is healed together. 'Twas good work. Did you do this, my son?" Graasyn tried to hide his confusion about the passage of time, knowing 'twould have taken at least two moons or more, to heal. And he had no memory of anything, having just woken thinking they'd been caught by the stranger in the aqueducts only a moment ago. Couldn't have been more than a few marks, certainly not several days, let alone a full moon. What was happening…. no wait, first he wanted to know just what had happened. Who was the stranger, what did he do to them, when did he do it, and where were they now?

"I can see the look on your face and I understand the questions, as they've all occurred to me as well, since I awakened," Bastyen affirmed, as he stood up to stretch. "I haven't been up long, a few marks at best, but 'tis harder to tell time due to the cloud cover. I woke lying aside you, out there on the ground." He pointed toward the base of a cluster of trees to their immediate left, away from the outcropping, and Graasyn could see a shallow indentation in the leaf litter now being covered with the gently falling snow. While Bastyen narrated his story, Graasyn stood up again, cautiously putting weight on his leg, stretching to work out the soreness, still amazed the wound that could very well have taken him Beyond, was already healed.

Bastyen carried on with his tale as he started moving out in a circle pattern away from where they'd been lying, gathering firewood and bedding material as he walked. Graasyn listened carefully, following just off to the side to cover twice the ground in half the time. He knew Bastyen well and if he'd said the area was secure, then 'twas. For now, their main concern was obviously shelter and warmth first, then food and water. The snow was falling in an increasingly heavy pattern of huge wet flakes, and if the clouds he saw blowing in swiftly could be taken for any indication, they were facing a severe storm, and soon.

"When I woke, 'twas to the same nightmare or Vision of the destruction of Kaddart that you also had. Neither of us have ever had a true Vision afore, but 'twas so real I was afraid we'd actually been there and experienced it, which was why I was uncertain whether or not we were this side of the Veil. When I finally could see clearly and realized we weren't where we'd been, I found you aside me, but couldn't wake you. 'Twas getting colder and I could see that 'twould soon snow, so I gathered some bedding and dragged your tall thin arse to that outcropping, making you as comfortable as I could. For some reason, I didn't want you to freeze to death and leave me here all alone," Bastyen chuckled. "Then I scouted as quickly as I could. I'd just secured the area when the snow began to fall a little harder, so I returned and noted your efforts to wake. I knew 'twould take a few moments, as I'd suffered through the same experience."

"Did you find shelter in your forays? 'Twould appear to be our immediate need."

"Yes, I found a series of caves that seem to be safe for emergency occupation, and we're heading in that direction now," the boy said with a wink. Turning and looking at the elder Warrior, he stated, as if pondering the probability of such, "They're not far from here, and in fact, we couldn't have found ourselves in a better location. We're surrounded with easily gathered firewood and large leafy branches for bedding. There appears to be an abundance of small game and root stock available. There's a running river not far, which can supply us with plenty of clean water, even through the coldest weather. There are enough trees to provide decent shelter from being sighted from above, and yet we shall still be able to see the night sky, once the cloud cover resolves. And as I said afore, not a trace of Man or Dragon anywhere near this area. Although I have found no indication of where 'this area' is yet, I have great faith we shall know our exact location as soon as the storm passes and we can explore. But there's more to add to these mysteries." And then the handsome youth laid down his armload of wood, reached into his tunic and pulled out his crossbow, holding it in front of him like an offering to the other man. Graasyn's eyes grew large and as he realized the implications of this, and knowing full well the crossbow had been lost soon after they'd used it in the alley, he patted down his chest, hips, low back and waistband, working his way down to this ankles, finding all of his previously used and discarded weapons, back where they'd been upon starting this mission.

There was a clear question even bigger than where they were at this moment, which hung 'tween them but went unspoken. How did they get here? The boy spoke again, slowly and uncertainly, "'Twas something afore I discovered my crossbow, that led me to search for what else we might have been Gifted with on this journey," and his gaze drifted from the ground to the eyes of his father. "I was distressed upon waking from the nightmare and…well…." he hesitated again, as if afraid the other would think him lost to sanity.

"Speak up my son, I fear we're together in this twilight of unreason, but I know we must both be sane. What's happened to make you so ill at ease?"

"I think I'd best show you." Bastyen put his fingers to his lips and blasted forth a shrill whistle, afore falling silent. Graasyn was near shock as he listened to the sound fade away through the forest, followed by the snorting and stamping of War Horses in full run heading directly toward them.

<p style="text-align:center">~~~~~~~~~~</p>

Sometime later, after the snow fall became too heavy to venture out any longer, they unloaded the last stack of firewood, bedding, and the small bag of edible roots they'd managed to gather, from the Horses where they stood at the back of the relatively large cave. The low ceiling was still high enough to allow them all to stand up without much difficulty, and was just out of reach of the tall men's raised hands, however they couldn't sit astride the animals inside. But 'twould be easier to heat in this coming storm, than a cave with a higher ceiling and for that, they were grateful. If they had need, both of them were skilled in mounting and riding in all manner of positions, bareback or otherwise, although that would probably not be necessary as they'd found all of their original tack was present and accounted for. It appeared they were only missing the horses they'd left in the stables in the village. All that they'd stashed under the make shift cover afore they'd approached Kaddart that day at least a fortnight ago, had been lying on the ground aside the two sleeping men when Bastyen had awakened, along with their saddlebags and supplies. The huge beasts were snuffling their faces and boots, apparently seeking reassurance, and had been very excited when Bastyen had finally opened his eyes. All War Horses were well trained and emotional creatures and would seek out their human handlers if they'd a sense of foul happenings, knowing instinctively to wake them for escape if needed.

Bastyen had quickly recognized his father was alive but non-responsive and determined he was in no immediate danger. He settled the big animals, blowing his own warm breath into their great nostrils, reassuring them of the solidity of their relationship and that all was well, then turned them out to free graze, knowing they'd come to his whistle from wherever they roamed. He'd then made the strange discovery of his weapons and the tack lying nearby. Amazed, he moved to secure the area and then once Graasyn woke, they could analyze the events together. So he went about gathering information without making any conclusions, and now that they had a decent shelter and fire, he laid all he had upon the 'table' for Graasyn.

"Twas Magical. I felt the Push there, and then we woke here. We have little to base a timeline upon, only the fact that your wound is healed, might suggest we were asleep longer than a few marks. However, he probably Healed you with his Magic, for had you not been so healed, you would surely have bled out in your sleep. He apparently didn't want that to happen, and he didn't want to force us Past the Veil, as 'twould have been a simple task. I don't think he wanted us to Pass here, either. He Sent us somewhere we could provide for our own safety, surviving the coming winter as well, and he Sent our Horses and equipment and weapons." Bastyen had to stop when he realized the enormity of that task and the Power the stranger had wielded so easily, afore he could continue. "However, not knowing where we are, we have little chance of finding our way home in time to prevent or alter whatever is going on." Bastyen sighed in awe as he completed his report. "And there's not enough information for us to deduce our location. I believe the stranger not only wanted to remove us from the immediate danger, he chose this precise location a'purpose. Our being here was no hasty toss on his part."

Graasyn sat cross legged close to the fire and laid a twig along the edge, near mesmerized as it took the heat, began to glow and then burst into a tiny flare, afore it died out in a puff of smoke. He carefully considered all that Bastyen had said, and together with his own memories, he joined his perspective to that of his son. "Agreed. I don't believe this was a relocation merely to remove us from the danger we faced. Also, he could have, but did not, simply kill us or take us to the Hoard. Why? He provided for our needs. Why? I believe the answers to those two questions are most likely similar, and are of relatively little consequence. Which leaves the only question that may stand out. Why did he not want us to return to Drekinn? He must know we shall eventually return, but he has established a significant delay. Why?"

Bastyen stretched out upon the branch bedding he'd just finished weaving and sighed dramatically. Then he stated as if he were in great pain, "I suppose finding the answer to that question will devour most of the next moon, or however long it takes us to find our way home. And I also suppose that 'twill involve the minute analysis of every memory of the entire mission, from the moment we received our orders to the moment we encountered the stranger in the aqueducts."

Graasyn smiled at his son's obvious distaste for this component of their profession, finished weaving the branches for his own bedding and laid down, his hands clasped together under his head as a pillow. Staring at the ceiling he replied, "I am of a mind the answer is far less complicated than is the question, and I don't think we'll learn much more than we know now, 'til we return. Tomorrow we hunt. We live, think no more upon it, clear your mind and settle your thoughts." He took a weary breath and closed his eyes. "Rest well, my son."

CHAPTER 16

This, That, and the Other Thing

O'ER TWO MOONS FROM THE 'BOND; DEEPENING WINTER

'Twas a mere double dawn past that I'd placed my orders for supplies and this day I was very anxious to see the results. My Fleet (for although we were the only Flight, we did constitute the entire Fleet at this time) would receive sorely needed gear and 'twould be encouraging at the least. Our spirits were waning since we began this venture two moons earlier and I knew that what we really needed was the taste of triumph in battle to boost our flagging morale. We were Warriors, and training for battles we'd yet to even see was causing much restlessness. All of us had done clean up duty, seen the decimation of the helpless, but few had actually laid eyes upon a Hoard Dragon. Gunnarr and I were still the only Team to have faced one of the evil creatures and although we'd been victorious and shared our strategies, there was a growing envy that could only be dampened for the others by their own personal battles and successes. I held naught against them, for I knew of what they felt. I was just as eager to fight again, to win again. 'Twas as if I were Brewing my own Flame, the heat of it burning a hole in my gut, and it must be spewed forth soon or 'twould be my undoing.

This morning the Teams were expected at the Den to meet with the Masters afore Gunnarr and I set out. I was eager to gather my new gear, test the weapons and get that report from Storrm afore we had to leave on our patrol of the Northlands, but first I had a sideline outing in mind. I'd not set eyes upon my own daughter since the day I'd formally laid Claim on her with the Clan Elders in the Lodge a fortnight past. Although nothing showed outwardly, my senses allowed me to Share her grief and seclusion, even though Walkyr was doing his best to be a good friend. Not a baby by any means, she was a strong child who'd survived much. But her entire life had turned upside down and she was totally out of her element. She'd progressed well in her studies, despite all the recent changes. Kallyr near shadowed the Battle Commander and Shayla practically lived in the hospital wing, falling into her cot behind her office desk, asleep afore her head hit the pillow. Neither of the children were allowed out into the village now, and I'd recently hired personal bodyguards for them, due to an abduction attempt upon the pair which we'd successfully thwarted. Both were heavily guarded for their own safety, yet even though their rooms were next to each other, they spent little time together outside of their studies. There was a spy within the ranks and 'twas maddening, but I had great confidence in Grifynn's ability to ferret out the culprit and then as Second, he'd be mine. That gave me much satisfaction and a deep gratifying rumble resounded from Gunnarr as he made known his utter and complete agreement. The spy would regret his actions and enemy allegiance. By the time we were through with him there'd be no doubt he'd wish he'd never been birthed.

~~~~~~~~~~~

With dampened eyes, I left my all too short reunion with Fryya and entered my current reality once again. Ten Teams were present when Gunnarr and I made our appearance, waiting in loose formation upon the Magically warmed sands of the Training Pits. 'Twas nice to have warm feet, but 'twas not warmed for us, as I'd found the Dragons hated to sit or stand upon cold ground, and when I'd questioned the change, they'd acted as little boys caught stealing cookie dough. We could see our breath, for the wintry air was brisk and frost covered the outer rim of the surrounding walls. The Masters and their Apprentices were scurrying around, the Dragons accommodating under duress but allowing the workers to climb upon them. I could only smile and shake my head as I watched the organized chaos, and I strongly suspected the ones doing the climbing didn't really need to be up there to complete fittings or get measurements. After all, Gunnarr and I hadn't even field tested the new saddle yet. In the meantime, my Warriors were trying on boots and coats and everyone seemed very excited. It pleased me to see them so.

Glancing about, I pondered how best to 'batten down the hatches' of the Dragon's Den. Not that I really believed anyone would besiege us but 'twould be negligent to ignore the obvious target. The Pits were the only major area of the entire castle that we felt might be at risk for compromise during an air strike, if Drekinn was attacked. There being no way to cover such a large area with rock, which was the only substance that could thwart Flame, Zaydarr and Fyndarr were designing a Lesser Magic Spell that would prevent entry through the two doorways from the Pits to the Great Hall and the one door directly to the hospital. If the Hoard managed to compromise the Pits, it could lead to full invasion of the castle through these doors. I considered these the only internal weak points, the only external was the main gateway. The ancient doors were wide, tall, arched heavy oak, studded and railed with iron, with multiple heavy iron
~~~~~~~~~~~

planks and panels, and would have held off any invading army, but would do nothing to stop Flame.

All Dragons could Brew Lesser Magic Spells, but it took a very powerful Dragon or an Ancient, to Brew Greater Magic. Conversely, the simpler the Spell, the stronger many Dragons working Lesser Magic together, could make it. Therefore, this Spell would be one that was an all or nothing Block, lying dormant 'til kindled, at which time the entries would be Sealed completely. That meant no one, not even us, would be able to get through the openings in either direction 'til the Spell was released. Designing and Casting of such a Spell couldn't wait 'til 'twas needed, for 'twould take much from the Dragons' store of Magic, requiring time to recover. By setting it aforehand, 'twould take a infinitesimal flicker of Magic, when and if they had to Call the Spell to action, leaving them intact to continue to fight. Details. I was learning a great deal in a minimal amount of time but oddly, with every new lesson I felt further from the goal. 'Twas most infuriating.

The Warrior half of the Teams were working on renovations to accommodate their partners in the Den, with special focus on the hospital wing. One might think a Dragon's Healing made it so they'd never require such however, once again I was trying to accomplish multiple goals. The Healer needed to learn more about the anatomy and requirements of Dragons, so having them available when they suffered any kind of injury, gave her a chance to study them, and my Dragons were using up their stores with all these changes in their lives. Therefore, I'd ordered them to save up their Healing Magic for times of dire need, of which I was certain would come too soon. If the Dragons could get to the hospital, they couldn't currently be treated because there was no room. Most of their treatments had been minor and occurring in a corner of the Pits, but 'twas not ideal. A whole new hospital would eventually need to be built to have room for them, but 'twas not in the immediate future. Nevertheless, my ultimate desire was to train Healers who could be transported to the Dragons, rather than trying to relocate the Dragons to the Den.

Thinking about the preparations we were undertaking for a battle that was unlikely to ever occur, I was reminded of my favorite story as a child. My father would read to us from a scroll he kept neatly stacked on the shelves in his office. He'd referred to it often, whenever we had doubts about our ability to continue, he'd use the story to shame us for even thinking about giving up. And when we'd succeeded at some difficult lesson, he'd compare us with pride to these ancient Warriors. 'Twas the Legend of 300. They were of a people who didn't believe, who ridiculed and hindered the only ones whose eyes were open to the coming danger. They were just 300 against the vastness of the world and although they all perished, 'twas enough to awaken their people to the reality of the conflict that was upon their very shores. They faced enormous odds and were extremely successful, forcing legions upon legions of their enemy Beyond. Even knowing they'd not survive, they fought to the very end, were ferocious and brave, and used every tactic they knew, to try to save their way of life and their people. I felt as if they were my own kin. I understood their mind-set and I knew despite the odds, I'd never give up, never stop fighting to protect Kadoor and the Dragon Clan.

After a brief 'inspection' mainly intended to ensure everyone knew what was expected of them, and that all was proceeding according to the plan set forth by the Battle Commander, I made a few revisions and then let the Teams continue their work. Due to some sensitive issues, the labor wasn't farmed out to the usual Clan contractors, but was being completed by the Teams and a few specially selected Warriors who were due to stand soon upon sacred ground to participate in the Second LifeBond. This time the Dragon Ancients and the Teams currently in 'Bond were hand picking the candidates, all fine Warriors, and all were volunteering to make the attempt. I'd felt the need to field more than enough candidates in hopes of making more than thirteen, optimistically covering every possible Dragon who might be Searching for their individual Blood Call. I had a feeling 'twas possible, but I had no proof. All of the chosen now bunked in the Barracks for their own protection, as much as for the specialized training they were receiving in preparation for taking the 'Bond.

After hearing the report on the renovations and the Brewing of Magic for the Spells, Storrm and Mystynn showed me the gardens they'd planted, along with the beginnings of a herd of animals that could sustain our Dragons for several moons, given they were each in self induced stasis part time, to stretch their rations. We'd chosen to do this in stages, keeping full intent of our projects secret due to our suspicions of a spy among us. I had no reason to be concerned about water, as we had the well in the dungeons, along with the pool in the caverns.

Storrm, Mystynn, Gunnarr and I, were the only ones who knew about the changes being made to incorporate the caves into the castle once again. We'd discovered the original entrances hadn't been sealed, merely Spelled, but these were ancient Greater Magic Spells and very complicated works that were proving to require the talents of both Maahayyel and Kaahayyel working together. They'd been able to begin the process of breaking down those barriers without anyone the wiser however,

Storrm and I would be the only humans with the ability to traverse the openings. This came as a shock to us but the Dragon Matriarch had been specific, steadfastly claiming that the Spells were very old and apparently the best they could do now was to alter them to safely allow through only those with 'untainted' Dragon Blood. This apparently meant the altered Spell would be able to recognize any Dragon who'd been lost to the Evil One (since the use of Magic for Evil purposes altered both them and their Magic) and if they attempted to walk through, they'd die a horribly painful death. Not a bad way to prove one's loyalties, in my opinion. But I'd balked at their claim of altering the Spells even further to allow only Storrm and I through and had near argued if so, then why not all 'untainted' humans. Maahayyel had satisfied me with her explanation that full allowance was not only difficult to achieve when unlocking a Spell Cast by others, but also not a good idea, and that limiting access was the only practical thing to do. Magic always exacted a price and tampering with an ancient Spell could make it unstable. We didn't want to pay with our lives, complications we could live with. The process had taken days, but they'd finally broken it to that end and were now refining the alterations to allow us the ability to bring others through. Knowing how Magic worked, 'twould involve some form of skin to skin contact, hopefully nothing more than a hand hold, but this was no time to be picky. I'd take whatever they could Brew, and be grateful.

Ariel and Zaydarr, and Rygyl and Tegrynn, had flown in late last night to report their progress thus far and to collect their gear. Their fittings completed, they'd gathered their new belongings, tucked away at home what they wouldn't need in the field and left again shortly thereafter to continue their investigation. Thus far they'd found no link to any real fangs or talons but they'd planned on following a new lead this very day and were confident this time they'd find that which they sought. What they were finding was that the Hoard influence was spreading, their evil insinuating itself throughout the coastal regions with more and more of the people arriving from distant lands, reporting personal confrontations with Dragons. The Teams had standing orders not to engage unless they were forced, for theirs was a stealth and recognizance mission. They'd seen no other Dragons as of their report, had only heard stories told in darkened taverns in the wee marks of the mornings. I found it particularly interesting that the people of the Ports seemed as though they were familiar with the sight of Dragons, even though they obviously didn't trust them. Given the prejudicial treatment they'd received, Zaydarr and Tegrynn were avoiding the human population as much as possible, keeping along the piers of the lower Port Districts, their back alleys and shadows providing enough cover to supplement a touch of Magic. They couldn't utilize too much Power as 'twould shine like a beacon in the night to those with eyes to see.

Their Link communications with Storrm had been business as usual this morning, but as of a mark and a half prior to my inquiry, they'd suddenly gone Silent. Storrm wasn't concerned, as 'twas protocol when not certain of their situation and potential for being Heard by others. This reminder only strengthened my personal mysteries as Storrm and I seemed to be the only Warriors thus far, capable of Blocking individual Dragons without going into Silent Mode. 'Twas also true that Storrm and I seemed to be the only ones who could break through another's Silence, if only to See through their eyes. We'd yet to find a situation in which to Push this Gift but 'twas becoming quite obvious that we were stronger than any of our comrades, even with their 'Bond effects, and our Powers were growing exponentially. But I couldn't help but note the gap 'tween us was also getting wider. I was only a winter ahead of my sister in age, but physically I was the smaller, and therefore I couldn't account for this difference. As children we'd been quite similar in our talents and skills but for some reason I was now coming into my own and rapidly leaving my friends and sister far behind. If it hadn't been for my Gunnarr, 'twould have been a very lonely existence.

We'd retreated to one of the conference rooms outside of the Pits after our inspection and I knew the time was nearing for me to meet with the Battle Commander.

"I will ensure the changes you ordered are being carried out appropriately, little one," Gunnarr Spoke.

Frowning, I Replied, *"You do that my love, and I'll meet with Grifynn to make Report. Then of course, I'll catch up with the Masters and gather our goods!"* Brightening my expression from a scowl to one of delight, made Gunnarr rumble in laughter at my quick change of mood as he ambled off down the Great Hallway to make his rounds. 'Twas amusing to watch the village staff going to and fro, looking up at the rumbling sound, thinking 'twas distant thunder they heard.

Afore I could formulate my thought, Storrm Responded to my unspoken query, *"I'll keep you posted on the Teams out in the field. As soon as I Hear anything, you will know. If I do not Hear from them within a reasonable amount of time, you will also know. Stop worrying, I'm no longer a little girl needing your constant care. Mystynn and I are more than capable of handling our position of Right to Second, and all the duties that go along.*" Laughing, Storrm and Mystynn set off to their own tasks, leaving me to mine. Raising my eyebrows, I noticed Storrm's tight butt filling out her leather britches, her snug chemise showing lightly tanned skin o'er her low waistband, a sword sheathed 'cross her hip, her long red hair swinging in multiple braids, both arms leather cuffed, her fur lined, thigh high boots making no noise as she walked beside Mystynn down the hard stone floor of the Great Hallway. Turning my head, I caught several of the resident Warriors standing aside as she passed, and noted the calculating expressions on their faces as they followed her progress with their eyes. Pursing my lips, I fought my desire to order them to stand down, 'til out of the corner of my eye I saw Mystynn's tail sweep 'cross, knocking the boots out from under a group of leering offenders, and they all hit the floor in a tangled heap. This had the desired effect of silencing them, and as Mystynn and Storrm (who hadn't even looked back at the commotion) continued on down the hallway, I glared without remorse as the victims got themselves up and looked about, trying to understand what had just happened. Catching my stern expression, they hastened to their tasks. When did she start looking like that anyway? Trying to remember the last time I really saw Storrm, I had to admit my little sister was fully grown, and I could do nothing more to help her along life's way. 'Twas time to let go. Well….mayhap later, I chuckled to myself, and then off I marched in search of my father. I found him in the first place I looked. His office.

"Oh don't bother knocking, or permitting yourself to be proclaimed by the Standing Guard," my father quipped sarcastically, without glancing up from the multitude of parchments lying 'cross his desk as I came barging in. The Standing Guard who blocked the portal to all other traffic, had long since given up on trying to make me follow any sort of protocol. They simply stepped aside when either Storrm or I approached, allowing us full access to my father's chambers as well as his office, at any time of the day or night. Since we'd grown up in the Den, nothing had ever been considered out of the ordinary with our behavior, and there was no one to whom we were unknown, nor anyone to whom we answered.

"Of course not. Why should I initiate such behavior now?" With a feigned look of extreme puzzlement, I braided my hair o'er my shoulder, then tied it in a knot behind my neck. Once this task was accomplished, I crossed my arms o'er my chest and stood impatiently for the Battle Commander's attention. I knew from long experience how 'twould transpire. If I didn't wait, he'd not respond, and if I tried to force his response, I could guarantee a 'no' to whatever request I had in mind. 'Twas the only form of his discipline that I truly despised, but 'twas also the most effective, and had honed my temperament for my present position. Although I might be impatient, I'd learned I could wait for a very long time to get what I wanted, as long as I saw sufficient need.

Finally he began his nightly ritual, and slowly gathering the parchments together, he laid one atop the other creating a neat pile which he then pushed to one corner of the huge oak desk, clearing the space immediately in front of him. Reaching to the opposite corner, he used two fingers to snuff out the candle and then leaned back in his chair. Raising his eyes to mine, I could see he was chewing thoughtfully on his bottom lip, shifting his attention from whatever he'd been doing, to our meeting and the business at hand. This simple gesture so mirrored Storrm's that I had to blink my eyes to keep from seeing double. 'Twas interesting to note that I'd been told I did the same thing on occasion and I knew my father once spoke with great fondness of how Aalanna would bite her lower lip when she was faced with a difficult decision.

Taking a stab in the dark, I asked, "Have you found any inconsistencies in the ledgers that might trace the spy?"

Although he didn't respond outright, his reaction clearly indicated I'd hit a nerve. Conversely the reaction itself was odd as my father had never been so open in his expressions. He'd made a lifelong habit of not allowing anyone to read him, and Storrm and I had worked to learn the subtle nuances he did display, in order to be aware of his mood. Even then, 'twas not always guaranteed we were even near the same trail, let alone on it. I decided my ability to read him so easily today was a 'Bond benefit and that his reactions were no more open than afore. They couldn't be, as that would mean my father was changing somehow. Since this was an unacceptable notion, I pushed it away from my daughter mind set, but in the mind set of Second, 'twas not to be ignored.

Nevertheless, there was business to conduct and I began by making full report. We discussed the castle renovations, defensive and offensive strategies, the current Team assignments and expectations, and then he gave me his orders for my mission. We were to patrol as far north as we could, to ascertain the level of infiltration and the Hoard influence there. I'd also be required to map all available landing sites in the most heavily forested regions. In addition, we were always hunting for a possible Hoard lair, and that would be my ongoing, secondary assignment. I was to get as much mapped and inspected as possible afore the coming winter snows fell, which would be quickly and dangerously followed by the Spring Melts, keeping even the Dragons from some areas as they couldn't fly forever.

Suspecting some kind of Spell, I was aware the Dragons were nearly incapable of entering the forests, but I'd made it a point to lead others to believe 'twas because the tree tops wouldn't hold their great weight and 'twould be too dangerous to risk long flights without known rest stops. Gunnarr and I would start as deep into the Far Northlands as we could go, where we knew the snow would be falling within a few dawns, and work our way back south. The entire mission would take us o'er a fortnight and by the time we returned, winter would be in full force and Maahayyel, Kaahayyel and the other Ancients would be in heavy preparation for the Draw. 'Tween the Magic embedded thusly into our main weapons, and the fangs and talons being made into short blades and picks, along with shields covered with Dragon scale, we'd have more than a fighting chance against the Hoard. Closely following the Draw would come the Second LifeBond ceremony. We were still choosing candidates to make the attempt, including as many as we could, and as soon as the Ancients recovered we'd stage a third LifeBond. There was unrest and speculation among some of the Dragons newly arriving, that not all of the Ancients would survive. Magic was difficult to control and was a give and take process. As much would be Drawn from the architect as they Drew from around them, and if the balance wasn't perfectly controlled, disaster resulted. 'Twould take much to Brew and control the strength of the Magic we were planning and then to jump into a second and a third ritual so rapidly would leave them weakened. We couldn't afford to lose any of them but neither we nor they, saw any options. 'Twould have to be attempted. 'Twas why they were preparing as never afore. They were trying to store great quantities of Life Force within themselves in an unprecedented attempt to use such to sustain their own life functions during the Brew, while also bolstering their strength for all that was to come. Should they fail, all they touched with their Magic at that time would become unstable and might also Pass. 'Twould be as a colossal whirlpool into which one could be trapped and drowned, pulling in those near them. We must succeed. To do anything less was simply unacceptable. I smiled in resignation. 'Twould seem there was much lately that I considered unacceptable.

"And Darque," my father's voice yanked me back to our conversation. He had that look upon his face clearly indicating we were near finished with our business.

"Sir?"

"There's no doubt your artwork is satisfactory, you've always been a good artist, but I have to be able to translate the scribing upon the map, for it to be useful," he said with some sternness. My brows furrowed as I tried to make sense of what he was saying, my thoughts having just been rather distant and scattered.

"The map? OH! The map. Yes Sir, translatable scribing. I shall endeavor to produce a legible scrawl," I replied and then winking, I turned about and took my leave.

Directing my path to the Master's quarters, I found Alric awaiting my arrival. He had a wicked grin 'cross his face and a small number of weapons arrayed upon the table. Picking up my shield, now covered with Dragon Scale, I could hardly believe 'twas not any heavier than it had been. "Remarkable! Truly, you've outdone yourself," I told him, as I admired the balance and the workmanship. Then I inspected the new blades made from fang and talon and was amazed at what he'd been able to design and complete so quickly. "'Tis superb, and I'm certain 'tis lethal as well, but I know not how you've managed to sheathe them," I said with respect, looking o'er the scabbards he'd included.

Proudly he answered, "I obtained some assistance from an immense blue Dragon we both know. He used his Flame to help form the scabbards. They're constructed of scales. 'Twas the only thing that would contain their edge. I've finished these two blades, or whatever we shall now be calling them, for I had limited time and wanted to be true to my word…however, I have more in the making." The look on his weathered face changed, and he frowned. "These weapons will certainly prove lethal, Darque. Be careful with their handling."

The tone of his voice gave me pause, and I saw true concern for my safety in his eyes. Yes, I was the youngest ever to hold the rank of Second, but I wasn't that little girl he once patted on the head as I skipped down the Great Hallway. Nevertheless, the offence I'd thought to take couldn't be sustained given the unease of his countenance, and so I was compelled to acknowledge in such a manner as to build his assurance in my skills, thus relieving his fears. As long as he still saw me as that little girl, I couldn't be his Second.

"Me? Take care?" Picking up the fang blade, I didn't need to draw from within to increase my speed and coordination. This I'd been practicing since I was very small. I palmed it, tossed it into the air, caught it by the hilt on the way down and spun it while expertly transferring from one hand to the other, all the while keeping my eyes upon the Weapons Master with a smug look upon my own face, 'til he near had apoplexy. Then I grinned, sheathed the deadly fang blade and tucked it away at my waistband, reaching for the talon to repeat my performance.

Leaping up and rushing toward me, he put his hand o'er mine afore I took my grip. Grinning, he said, "Take them and go, Second. I know you haven't long afore you should be on wing, and they await you in the Pits with your finished goods. I trust you're expert enough and fast enough to avoid slicing off your own fingers, but I wish not further demonstration at this time." Settling from the shock of my daring, he concluded sincerely, "Darque, you're one of the most talented and spirited Warriors I've ever had the pleasure of arming. Although some might think your exhibition here was childish, I see you, and I appreciate knowing you are as good as they say."

Nodding my acceptance of his admission, I hung the talon blade in its sheathe at my waistband, secured the shield o'er my long sword, and directed my path back to the Pits.

CHAPTER 17

The Blood of Life

THE FAR NORTHLANDS; THREE MOONS FROM THE 'BOND

We'd been out just o'er a fortnight and had delayed our departure as long as we could. We'd struggled greatly with the weather and the heavy forest, which had been a constant irritation for Gunnarr and left us little choice in landing sites. Had any of the others attempted such, they might not have returned, for Gunnarr was swift and strong and could maintain his flight longer than any of the others. Still, 'tween attempting to map potential rest stops and searching for possible Lair sites, we'd hop scotched 'cross vast sections of some of the thickest regions of Byndynn Forest and I was disappointed we'd not the time to do a more thorough search. We found no populated areas in the deep of Byndynn but suspected many existed under the canopy. And then there was St Swiftyn's and the Bog. I'd left the area to the last moment, a calculated decision I hoped I wouldn't want to kick my own ass for later. The Keep of St Swiftyn's was rumored to be haunted, without a living soul seen since afore Grifynn had taken Command. 'Twas a place once thought to be dedicated to scholarly pursuits and although 'twas ancient, the stone towers and walls that protected the inner sanctum should hold the weight of a Dragon and provide refuge if needed. 'Twas evident that none of the Evil One's Hoard had been there. Gunnarr had sensed no living thing without the great walls, but could sense nothing within, one way or the other. We believed 'twas due to stress but 'twas odd nonetheless. Wanting to include it in my maps, we'd chosen to fly one more time o'er the area afore we returned to our last campsite.

"I've heard stories of a Bog in this area, Gunnarr, why can I not see it?"

"I've traveled much in my lifetime my love, however, 'tis the first time I've been o'er these regions since the age of the Last Holocaust. The Forest was decimated, the landscape so distorted that I recognize nothing. O'er the past centuries, the flora and fauna have returned, and the Forests have Healed themselves. I do know the Bog of which you Seek, but I grow fatigued and can do no more this night. We must return to the ledge. I cannot stay on wing much longer."

"Oh my love, I'm so sorry! I know the forests cause you great stress and we've done much here. 'Tis plain the incoming blizzard will hit soon. Let us *be gone on the 'morrow, at least we have a place to start once the Melts have run."*

~~~~~~~~~~

The water in the stream was cold, but I had to clean up. It took me longer than I'd planned and when I'd hiked back up the trail, Gunnarr was snoring. Thinking it would take me awhile to catch up, I snuggled under his huge leathery wing and wondered about our future. The same problems kept running through my mind, "If only we had more time, if only we had more Teams, if only…." I soon fell fast asleep.

A sprinkling of snow had fallen softly throughout the night, covering the gently sloping trail leading from the outcropped rocky ledge upon which we'd spent the last double dawn, to the still flowing river cutting through the forest below, that I'd availed myself of only a few marks prior. Although 'twas freezing, I woke up sweating profusely, my heart pounding wildly. Slightly disoriented, I could say without a doubt, I'd just experienced wicked heat, and then it simply vanished, leaving me chilled by the glacial dawn air. 'Twas the sudden loss of all that stimulation that had me sweating, more than the Battle Lust it just pumped into my system. I sat bolt upright and struggled to slow my rapid breathing and hammering heart. "What the Flame was that? Gunnarr, what happened, are you alright?" Instantly aware 'twas not a fight or flight situation, 'twas also clear this high state of arousal wasn't mine and therefore it had to be Gunnarr's. But what could possibly throw my usually calm and focused partner into such a state? I'd never known him to lose control in any situation.

"Darque! You are well? Are you injured? I'd not forgive myself." 'Twas agonized sincerity that shadowed his Words, and then I felt nothing.

"I'm well, but concerned. What just happened? Why can I not Hear you now? You've withdrawn from me, have I done something wrong?" 'Twas a strange quiet, an unnerving mental isolation in which I was enveloped.

Again I felt the high level of his arousal when he attempted to answer, like a dam about to break, allowing the flood waters behind to trickle forth. His Voice was strained as he struggled for control. *"You've done nothing wrong, my little one. I did not maintain well. My Block weakened and I woke you."*

Immediately the emptiness returned, indicating he'd vacated my mind again. *"What do you mean? What Block? Why would you do that?"* My words tumbling o'er each other, I couldn't shake the sense of rejection gripping my heart. Sliding out quickly from under his wing, I was hit by a shock of frigid air against my bare skin. My breath came out in
~~~~~~~~~~

frosty puffs as I spoke aloud to try to sooth him. "'Tis well, I wasn't really sleeping anyway and besides, we keep no secrets 'tween us. This emptiness confuses me. I love you, I trust you with my life, do you not trust me with yours?" While talking, I ran my fingers along his brow ridge, using the flat of my other palm to massage the relatively smooth central portion of his snout from his nostrils to 'tween his eyes in long, slow strokes. He'd always taken pleasure in my touch in the past, but not this time.

'Twas contradictory and more confusing than ever, given that his burning arousal was plain to see in the flicker of his darkening eyes. Although we'd declared our mutual devotion, I'd little understanding of Dragon Lust and Love. We'd teased with playful innuendo, I'd felt the warm and tender touch of his lethal talons upon my body, but I'd never truly expected us to be able to fulfill the intimacies of a real relationship, the acts of pleasure that we both silently longed for. I'd accepted 'twas merely my own desire, my personal fantasy, to share his love. Still not certain of what was happening, I tried to Push my way back into Gunnarr's well disciplined mind. He withstood my gentle intrusion, but not afore I felt a powerful surge of sexuality. 'Twas barely a fraction of a breath, clamping down tightly and cutting me off again, but 'twas so potent I doubled down, clutching myself in raw need. This sense of rising excitement was stronger than I'd ever felt in my life.

Still technically a virgin, although that wasn't something I'd brag about, I'd never truly considered the sexual urges of my Kind. My sister and I had scoffed at the male Warriors, viewing their claims of 'need' as mere attempts to get us in the rack. Besides, we didn't have time to play the games, and when I did have a free moment 'tween Training and sleeping, 'twas not difficult to meet my own needs. Not that sex was frowned upon in the Clan. Sexuality was even more common 'tween Warriors, given our chosen professions with constant danger and stress, and we'd had no difficulty finding willing and talented partners. 'Twas that free time was scarce, being the Battle Commander's daughter, and quite frankly I was rather put off with the efforts of so many males (and more than a few females) trying to get me under their blankets simply to say they'd done so. I wanted more than that. I wanted a real relationship. I'd yet to find one in the human world, and had stopped thinking about it long ago. But with this flood of desire swamping me, I suddenly couldn't get enough fast enough, and my own hands weren't going to suffice. Gasping, I squeezed my legs together, hugging myself tightly in sheer bliss just remembering that fraction of a moment of masculine desire, and couldn't believe the drive I felt to seek out a partner now. By the Dragon's Breath! Is this how the male Warriors felt when they were trying so hard to get me to bed them? If so, then I had some mental apologies to divvy out.

"No! 'Tis definitely not what your male Warriors felt." Gunnarr's Voice was strained but his response told me, that even when he'd Blocked me from his thoughts, he could still Hear mine. Interesting, that. I'd not forget.

"Then Tell me," I Responded in my most heartfelt Voice. Turning around to face him, my chin resting on top of his nose, I gazed deeply into his eyes. And 'twas those eyes that revealed how much trauma he was experiencing. Why, it must be as painful as when I'd discovered the Blood Oath.

"I cannot," he growled and gently pried his head out from under my chin.

His retreat was offensive, and although I'd regained much of my emotional control o'er the past moon, I became angry, like a jilted lover. "NO!" I shouted. "You will tell me now! I demand that you tell me what's wrong. We are partners for life, and if something is affecting you, even some deep and dark Dragon Magic secret, I must know. We'll be tied together for our entire span of days. You can't keep anything from me, or we can't be true friends and we can't fight efficiently. One of us will make a grievous tactical error during the heat of Battle and we'll both slip past the Veil and that can't happen because I love you."

When I'd finished my slightly irrational miniature tirade, I stood in front of him all but naked, except for the bulky padding tied 'tween my legs with a leather thong, absorbing the erratic cycle of blood with which I was, as a female, cursed. I'd never been regular, and most female Warriors were the same. Shayla had by no means been concerned, and said it had something to do with how hard we worked. She'd said none of us were sterile, but we didn't require any birth control methods either. As a Warrior, having children was traditionally put off 'til we retired from active duty, but if we conceived, we were blessed. The child thus brought into our world to such parents, was fostered for his or her own safety, but the blood mother and father always helped raise them. We still bled, just not on a regular cycle as the Village women did. Most times, every other moon, but my last cycle had been afore the Ancients came. Must have been o'er three moons ago. I crossed my arms and stamped my foot in emphasis, and watching his great eyes nearly cross and his nostrils flare as he barely lowered his head toward me, I finally realized….

"I scent your blood. 'Tis not wound blood. 'Tis the blood of life." His growl strangled and harsh, Gunnarr the Mighty Blue spun his massive bulk around, spread his great wings and threw himself off the edge of the cliff into the icy winds.

Running after him, I was relieved to see his leathery wings beating, his huge body lift in search of a thermal o'er the forested terrain. Apparently locating one, he climbed rapidly into the cloudy early dawn skies. At least he was still airborne, and not in danger of taking us both past the Veil.

"You come back here! You can't run away! Or fly away, or whatever…" I grumbled as I watched him become a tiny glittering blue sapphire in the far distant horizon. I took a deep breath and got busy cleaning up the area and packing for the trip home. When Gunnarr returned from his snit run, I'd have a thing or two to say, and I wanted nothing left to do but climb on his sturdy shoulders and take wing.

Grabbing my change of clothes and the spare padding I'd created out of cattail plants, I headed to the water's edge. There I cleaned up, switched padding and rinsed out last night's bloody one as best I could. I laced up my chemise on the walk back, then spread out the wad of absorbent plant fiber in the sun to dry. 'Twouldn't take long. Damn the timing. I'd almost forgotten about this problem. 'Twas such a shock that I wasn't even prepared when it began, and had to go to the river to find the cattails just last dusk. I'd made the thong to hold it in place, from a strip of leather I'd cut off the bottom of my tunic. 'Twas adequate but not all that comfortable. I'd not even considered what 'twould do to Gunnarr. Ashamed I'd been so insensitive, I wanted to crawl under the ledge. I could appreciate how he must have struggled, as I had a good understanding of animal breeding and should've considered this response, but in my defense, I'd never thought of Gunnarr as an animal. He was simply my best friend, my partner, my everything, and I loved him with all my heart. I'd fantasized about some kind of Spell to make it possible for us to…. I pulled up short when a sudden revelation hit me so hard, I couldn't help but mutter out loud, "surely he doesn't want…ME?"

"By the gods, Darque, I'm not stupid, nor am I blind. Of course I want you! Do you think I've been lying these past few moons? You're intelligent, beautiful, sensual, talented and you're the finest swordswoman in all of Kadoor. What's not to want?" His Voice gained strength as he flew closer, and I was relieved by his amusement. *"But I've held back the strength of my emotions and commitment, as I am well aware of the unreasonable logistics of such. You are a woman to be respected. I won't hinder your life. I am NOT my brother."* And with that, he made a precarious landing on the narrow cliff edge.

"I wish I wasn't the cause of this trouble." We both stood very still, keeping as far from each other as we could. Fearful of pushing him away again, I prayed silently for a solution, anything to stop the cycles, to end this dilemma. Why was I so cursed?

"You are not cursed. The blood of life is a Gift, not to be thoughtlessly discarded. I hope to see you with child one day, and 'twould be a blessing of the One that it could be mine...." Gunnarr's Voice lowered 'til I could barely Hear him and then aloud, he continued uncertainly. "There is a Spell.... but I have no right to ask it of you."

"What spell? Will it stop my cycle? Do it!" I declared emphatically, excited at the prospect of a way out of this unbearable situation that had come 'tween us, wanting our relationship back, wanting his love back. I completely missed of what else he may have been referring.

Gunnarr didn't correct me. "I'll try to affect just this cycle, and we can then decide how to proceed. Are you certain?" he growled aloud, obviously unsure of himself, his distress once again building. The strength of his emotions still Blocked, I couldn't truly fathom what he was enduring, but his eyes told a tale of agonizing indecision and frustration. I didn't hesitate. "Yes, do it."

"We must be close, try not to bleed." He Spoke with hesitation, but I snorted so hard and unexpectedly I near choked. He lifted one heavy brow ridge and watched me regain my composure with suspicion. His eyes sparkled as the sun dawned upon him, and then he lowered his brow ridge and Said, *"Of course. You have no control o'er the blood, correct? 'Tis not so with females of my species, as they become fertile when they are so stimulated. But I should have known this. Once again I've made a serious tactical error."*

"Trust me, my love, if I had any control we wouldn't be having this conversation." I frowned. "Just where did you pick up your intelligence on Mankind? I think you should fire the one who had that duty." Gunnarr relaxed a bit as he almost laughed, then he became serious once more.

"You're not afraid?" He Spoke incredulously as he struggled to hold his Block, allowing me to begin to feel the raging turmoil within.

"Of course not, I've said it afore. I trust you with my life. And Gunnarr? I do love you. Are you ready?"

"Are you?" And as we both took a few steps toward each other, his Block began to fail and I sucked in my breath to avoid dropping to my knees under the powerful surge that swept o'er me. By this time, I knew what to expect. I'd witnessed the Dragons perform a few Spells and having gone through the LifeBond, I knew that when Gunnarr said we must be close, he meant close. I'd learned that all Magic stems from living energy, the Life Force within every organic thing in this world. For true Magic

to occur, it helped to be skin to skin, and adding strong emotion or blood, strengthened it exponentially. Of course, one had to be strong enough to handle all that power or things could get pretty ugly. Unleashed and un-controlled, raw Magic invariably caused mutation, and eventually led to death. Such was happening to The Black and his Hoard. Such was the root of this War.

Trying to make this easier on both of us, I turned around to unlace my chemise and let it drop. I inhaled deeply and closed my eyes to help me re-lax, as I stood with my back to his leathery scaled chest. His heavy breath-ing began to match mine and the rhythm of our hearts synchronized. 'Twas the harmony of our souls that astonished me, leaving me breath-less. Instead of pushing away the raw emotion flowing from Gunnarr, I embraced it as he spread his great wings with a cold gust of air that blew my hair o'er my shoulders, baring my chilled body to him. Gently he took hold of my hips, carefully avoiding sinking his talons into my skin, and as he dragged me closer he slid one great paw down to cup me tightly 'tween my legs, near picking me up off my feet. Then he wrapped his wings around me 'til I was completely enclosed and held on as if I were a long lost lover finally come home. I Heard his low guttural chant but didn't catch the words, and the tingling began in my toes and fingers, traveling up my legs and arms to my trunk, finally centering in the pit of my belly. 'Twas gently, nearly, not quite orgasmic, leaving me strangely satisfied. The warmth spread throughout my body, as the wave rolls up the sands and returns to the sea, leaving me with nothing. 'Twas done. The cold air gave me gooseflesh as Gunnarr slowly unwrapped me with some reluc-tance, and without making a sound, he backed away to sit in his usual pose. Facing him questioningly, 'twas then I realized without even check-ing, that my cycle had indeed stopped. Not that I hadn't believed 'twould happen, 'twas that Magic still held me in awe. Seeing his slightly glazed expression told me he was passing along the ordeal and our solution to the others. Apparently, we were the first to experience this. The other fe-males had been as I, so intense in the Training and transformation we'd plunged ourselves into, that none of us had started yet. I was glad we'd found such an easy solution, temporary as it might be. I ordered the Spell be performed as soon as possible, prior to the beginning of their Rider's cycles, if that wouldn't adversely affect anyone, and he nodded his affir-mation. No sense in anyone else going through this turmoil. I was sure I'd hear all about it at our next gathering. Was there a male Warrior to female Dragon equivalent issue? I was eager to return to the Den where I could see how Storrm was faring with her Green.

"You still don't realize the Power of the LifeBond, my love," Gunnarr Stated quietly.

"If you refer to the passion we hold 'tween us, I believe it's been growing since long afore the 'Bond," I Replied.

"For us mayhap, for Storrm and Mystynn as well, for you two are different from the others of your Kind," he Told me, not for the first time.

"How are we different?" I Asked again. *"I have the right to know. 'Tis something to do with the Prophesy?"*

"Soon my little Spitfire, soon. All shall be revealed to you."

Thinking about Storrm and Mystynn, I couldn't help but recall what Gunnarr had Said earlier, and was curious as to what he'd meant by, 'I am not my brother.' I definitely needed to talk to Storrm. And grudgingly I'd have to report this 'problem', along with the solution we chose, to the Battle Commander. I'd rather visit the Fade in the dead of summer, than to make such a thorny report, for 'twould certainly make us both uncomfortable, but doubtless, given the way things were going, 'twould not be the last such.

Caressing Gunnarr's face with my fingertips, I smiled and without a word, grabbed my change of clothes and set off back to the icy river to clean up again. The incoming blizzard was well on its way and I had to hurry. Slipping on the small rocks and leaf litter of the forest now covered with a steady fall of wet snow, I recovered my footing instantly but still glanced o'er my shoulder and caught the look in Gunnarr's glistening eyes while he watched me descend. A crowd of emotions clamored there, not the least of which were envy and frustration, even though I'd been unsuccessful thus far, in getting him to join me under the canopy of trees. Envious that I entered easily where he dared not tread, he was also frustrated that he couldn't protect me while I was there. Why were they so unwilling to enter the forest, what was preventing them, or was it just my Gunnarr? But then came to mind the reason I'd begun to suspect Magic. I could swear by the Flame, I'd felt the warmth and tingling that indicated Allure, whenever we'd neared the Forested regions, although 'twas oddly different somehow, than that to which I was accustomed. I'd been told in no uncertain terms 'twas not so, and all manner of excuse and justification were presented. *"The forest floor is mulch, and produces much heat,"* gave me a pained expression every time. And then there was the classic that made me giggle, turn beet red and usually allow Gunnarr to redirect the conversation. *"You always tingle when you have need, allow me to handle that for you, my love."* But in all seriousness, I was near convinced 'twas some kind of aversion Spell, as Gunnarr had been hard pressed just to land in the clearings we'd located. Something was very wrong and I frowned as an odd notion came to me. Surely the Dragons wouldn't have placed a Spell upon themselves to keep them from entering the Forests, 'twould make no sense. But if not the Dragons, then who, and why?

~~~~~~~~~~~

Darque finished her bathing and dressed quickly. The only reason she wasn't blue from the cold was the 'Bond and Gunnarr's Magic keeping her warm for this brief interlude, for which she was grateful. The snow was falling harder and they'd have to leave very soon or be stuck here indefinitely. Even Dragons had difficulty flying in a blizzard. 'Tween the use of Magic to keep them both from freezing in flight and the heavy snow falling upon him, he'd be hard pressed to stay a'wing. The onset of snow was long past due and would be hard and heavy, but 'twouldn't prevent Spring's arrival. Although 'twas morning, the skies were darkening as she climbed back up the trail to the ledge where they'd spent the night prior. Stopping momentarily, she looked around. She'd felt like she were being watched again, but as soon as she paid it heed, 'twould disappear. Shaking her head, she knew she had no time to do more now, and she continued up the slope. Gunnarr was restless 'til she touched him and then he calmed and his flashing eyes returned to a more normal appearance. He watched her with the intensity of a raptor in hunt. 'Twould be unnerving to another but Darque knew the true emotion behind the glare as she pulled on her full leathers, fur lined coat and thigh high boots without even unlacing them.

~~~~~~~~~~~

Her saddle in place, he leaned down for her to secure the gear, then proffered his bent knee to help her climb up. When she gained her seat, they turned to take one more look around the area. Had Darque felt that too? 'Twas as if someone or something were watching them from afar. There'd been something odd here since they'd first landed, but try as they might, neither of them could detect any foul Magic.

Gunnarr sighed with the fatigue that a fortnight of patrols and the distress caused by the proximity of the forest had caused him. Then as the snow mixed with sleet, he launched straight up into the gathering darkness, found a steady pace, and settled into his long distance flight. *"I should have been able to See that Magic, little one. I'm not as strong as my brother."*

"Which brother Gunnarr? I know you have several. Why have you not mentioned them to me? We've a long flight home and 'twill be hard to stay

ahead of this storm. I see no point in making another stop 'tween here and the Den, or we may be trapped. Mayhap 'tis time enough for you to tell me of your family ties, my love?"

"Are you warm enough, little one? The winds of flight do chaff your fair skin. I can keep ahead of the incoming blizzard, but 'twill be hard on you."

"I am fine, you great worrying beast! My skin is not so fair, and certainly not so soft, as the village women." I Replied with uncertainty evident to my own senses. Seemed even the Second in Command could be worried about her appearance. I snorted, as I'd never been concerned afore. What was making the difference now?

'Twas a smug satisfaction arising as he Answered, *"I meant not that your skin is inferior and in truth, I love the feel of it against my own. I merely wish not to cause you injury. 'Tis jealousy you feel. You're in love, little one. With ME!"* And his great chest shook with the deep rumbling of his laughter 'tween my thighs as he continued his hard flight to stay ahead of the incoming whiteout. I laid o'er his neck to decrease the wind drag, and pulled the fur lined hood of my coat o'er my head and face to keep the icy wind from blistering my skin. Every part of my body was covered in fur lined leather, with layers of leather underneath, and I had the warmth of my Dragon under the length of me, but the strength of the storm was already cutting through like an icy blade. We'd stayed far north longer than we should've, but we'd both felt something there and I was disappointed we hadn't identified the source. The only reason I'd not stubbornly stayed longer, was that we were also quite certain it had naught to do with the Hoard or any lairs or supply dumps, although we'd found some old abandoned sites and gathered some interesting evidence to return to the Battle Commander. No, the odd sensation was like a tickling memory. I was certain I'd felt it afore....but we'd no time to spare to try to sort it out. Mayhap after the Melts we could return and uncover the mystery.

<div align="center">~~~~~~~~~~</div>

Far beneath the huge blue Dragon and his Rider, the two Warriors watched breathlessly, as their only hope of being found afore the storm buried them indefinitely, flew away and disappeared above the tree-tops. Bastyen had run faster and farther than he'd ever run afore, trying desperately to gain their attention, but to no avail. He'd spotted the blue Dragon flying yesterday, followed the beast and found where he was staying. They'd needed to determine to whom this one held allegiance, afore they revealed themselves. Graasyn had joined in and they'd discovered the Dragon landed in the same area in which they'd originally found themselves. They'd gotten as close as they felt they could, staying upwind to avoid being scented by the beast, although they knew not how effective that strategy would prove to be with a Magical creature, and then they'd waited. But when the Dragon took wing again, a girl was perched upon his neck. Even covered head to toe in fur lined leathers, Bastyen was certain the girl was Darque, there could be no mistaking that small but commanding package. Nevertheless, despite their proximity, neither the beast nor the Warrior seemed able to see or hear them.

Graasyn leaned forward, huffing and puffing, his hands braced against his thighs as he tried to catch his breath. He'd chased Bastyen for at least a candle mark through the rough terrain of the wooded area, with the icy air making it near impossible to breath. He'd struggled to stop the boy, for they were leaving the protection of their latest cave shelter further and further behind and they'd need to return quickly to avoid being stuck out in the open when the storm hit.

"How could they miss us? They have enhanced senses!" Bastyen exclaimed in disbelief.

Graasyn caught his breath and stated brokenly, "'Twould appear as if we are invisible, my son, Masked." In answer to the other's bewildered expression, he continued, "What did you observe?"

"I noted nothing!" His angry response was drawn from disappointment, and feeling as if he'd failed his father by botching what should've been a rescue attempt. If he'd been able to get their attention, they'd be on their way home at this very moment.

Graasyn merely gave him 'that look', and Bastyen conceded. While he discussed what they'd seen (they hadn't been able to hear much), they began a steady jog back toward the caves. They'd stockpiled enough to survive for mayhap a fortnight, a moon if they rationed carefully, but 'twouldn't be easy. Still, if they couldn't get out of their current lodgings for awhile, they'd survive.

By the time they'd traveled back to the correct general location, the snow was falling so heavily they were unsure if they were even close, unable to find the entrance. Whistling to their War Horses, the animals exited the cave and trotted directly to them. Grabbing onto their long thick manes, they'd allowed themselves to be guided back as if blind.

After rubbing down the big beasts and getting them bedded again, they'd stripped and laid out their leathers to dry near the fire pit, donning what was left of their merchant's garb. Then they sat 'cross the fire from each other and munched on some raw wild carrots and onions they'd harvested in the woodlands o'er the next hill, sipping on clean water they'd discovered in the back of the cave, on the opposite side of where they were bedding the Horses. The clear water ran down the far wall into a pool, collecting along a ledge at about knee level to the tall men, and then spilled onto the floor below, running deeper into the cave system. The ceiling was significantly lower in that area, and the opening through which the water ran was small, but if they were stuck here for any length of time they might attempt to explore further.

"I agree with all your observations," Graasyn stated, "but what I don't think you're assimilating is the Magical element. The Dragons have returned and we must now consider what their influence may do to all our conclusions. We can no longer ignore their input, nor can we be erratic in taking them into account."

"I understand," Bastyen licked his dry lips as he attempted to reorder his initial thoughts toward the conclusion he knew his father was trying to lead him.

"Adjusting for that mystical component," Bastyen began uncertainly. As he continued he caught his father's smile of approval and his convictions became stronger. "I know they were looking right at us at one point, mayhap looked through us more than once. I believe they couldn't see us or hear us, but they should've been able to, given our proximity. I also suspect they felt something odd, mayhap thought they heard something, or felt they were being watched. They both had that appearance just prior to taking wing."

"Agreed." Graasyn nodded his head. "And you're correct. That was Darque, no doubt in my mind. And I recognized that blue Dragon she was riding, as being with the Ancients when they arrived. They must have made the 'Bond. Clearly they couldn't see us or hear us. I believe this must be part of what the stranger did to us when he Pushed us here, and it shows me his powers are at least as strong as the Dragons', if not more so. But what concerns me is there would seem to be no way to safely discover, that if own people aren't able to see us, does that also prove true for the Hoard?"

"Don't fret so Aba, we'll live to Sing this tale. And at the very least, we now know we're still in our own world." Bastyen smiled and then broke into laughter at the amused expression on the other's face, as 'twas always the father encouraging the son, not the other way 'round for this pair.

~~~~~~~~~~

"*I am known to my Kind as the High Prince of the Highland Dragons,*" Gunnarr confirmed, his Voice crystal clear in my mind, o'er the roar of
~~~~~~~~~~

the icy winds. *"Mystynn is Second Prince, and Ragnyrr is Third in our line. Then follows Kaygynn as Quad Prince, Synddarr is my fifth brother and Prince, and the last living brother is Shasynn, known as the Sixth Prince."*

Keeping my head down with my hood pulled low, I Replied, *"'Living brother'? What does that mean? Have you lost siblings?"*

"'Tis reference to the unhatched 7th Egg of my youngest brother, Bryynn. He lives, but not in this world as yet." And I was smugly satisfied that I'd already guessed his position and lineage correctly.

"Don't think, just because you're the eldest son of the Last Dragon Matriarch, that you get any special privileges, or that you outrank me now," I started to laugh, but had to stop because my teeth were chattering, and I fell silent to allow Gunnarr to focus on his lift.

O'er the next three dawns, we flew steadily southward toward home and the Dragon's Den. I'd tried to catch a last glimpse of the St Swiftyn's area as we passed, but couldn't see anything. I slept off and on as we managed to stay just ahead of the freezing blasts chasing us from the Far Northlands, laying a glittering coat of ice crusted snow o'er everything in their path. The regions would be snowed in for the next moon at least, making it near impossible to fly o'er, with nowhere to land or rest, let alone traverse a'foot or a'horseback.

"When the Melts have run, we should return and reopen those rest stops," I Said during one of my wakeful moments. *"'Twould be a good idea to scout around St Swiftyn's as well. I wish we'd had the time this patrol. The Bog is said to be well hidden and quite dangerous, but it could be used as a rest stop if needed, and no one would be the wiser."* He merely acknowledged with a grunt, putting all his effort into maintaining flight. I could feel his great hunger and when we returned, he'd need to hunt as soon as possible. When we were near enough I'd Call and have Storrm and Mystynn meet us with a herd beast or two, so Gunnarr would be strong enough to go on a proper hunt. Laying my head back down against his scaled neck, I knew 'twould be but a few more marks afore we'd be home. Grateful we hadn't encountered the Hoard, and with those thoughts shuffling among many others, I fell asleep fitfully, the gusts thrashing us up and down, Gunnarr's great chest expanding and contracting as he breathed deeply in and out, flying steadily onward toward the Dragon's Den, and home.

CHAPTER 18

Dragon Lust to Lorelei

THE FOLLOWING MORNING; DEEPENING WINTER

"What were you Singing just now?" I Asked, as I stood just outside on the ledge. Leaning forward, I squeezed out the excess water afore undoing my braid, and finger combed the thick mass to remove the tangles. Then standing up quickly, I tossed it o'er my shoulders. The rising sun reflected off the surf and glistened through the spray of water droplets thrown all around me in a misty haze. Taking a deep breath of the crisp air afore I stepped inside, I felt good about my workout. Body surfing the breakers, I'd dive and turn under the roiling waves just prior to crashing into the rock wall, then push off and swim against the current to catch the next one rolling in. Not only did it build my stamina and keep my muscles toned, it also helped me center myself. Besides, I'd always loved the sea.

Gunnarr had recovered well from his endurance flight, after consuming a half dozen herd beasts which Mystynn had thoughtfully provided when we'd arrived. He'd then left to hunt but returned shortly thereafter. The blizzard followed us all the way to the Great Plains but had soon lost momentum crossing the open farmlands surrounding the village. Now the snow glittered in the sunlight, a heavy white blanket spread o'er everything 'tween Drekinn and the foothills. Winter had finally arrived.

"Tis from Ancient Dragon Tongue, which was similar to the Ancient Language of Man, which has now evolved into what you know as Common Tongue. At least, I was attempting a translation. 'Tis difficult to create the words in Common while staying true to Ancient." His eyes sparkled with animation, his thoughts a jumble of emotions I had difficulty deciphering.

"What did you say?" I Asked, feeling quite flattered by the attention and his admiring gaze. I still didn't understand our relationship and lately I'd felt increasingly vulnerable. Standing there naked as usual, with the day's early light reflecting through the entrance making my wet hair glow, I grinned at his reaction.

"I love you," he stated simply, staring into my eyes.

Laughing, I replied, "I know that, you silly Sea Drake, I meant, what did the words you were Singing mean?"

"I love you," he repeated. His eyes half closed while he stared at me, and I melted, my heart in my throat, wanting so much to... be able to...

but then I realized he was telling me what the words meant. Slightly confused, not wanting to admit that I'd just thought mayhap he… well Flame it all, that would be near impossible anyway, what was I thinking?

Hiding my embarrassment o'er yet again assuming he thought more of me than was feasible, I Told him lightheartedly, *"'Twas beautiful, I wish to learn. Will you teach me?"* Walking past him briskly, having grabbed my clean leathers along the way, I reached out suddenly to tickle him just under his chin, as I'd recently discovered he was very ticklish, and then raced for the Cave of Jewels with him nipping at my heels.

<div style="text-align:center">~~~~~~~~~~</div>

"How do you say, 'I love you' in Ancient?" I Asked. Now lying on the sands near the falls, I relaxed, trying to forget what we'd been through o'er the last fortnight. Immediately after we'd returned, and while Gunnarr was ravenously satiating his appetite, I'd been grilled by the Battle Commander. He'd called it 'making report'. I wouldn't, but not to his face. I'd also handed o'er my maps, which he'd merely glanced at and then grunted his acceptance. I was a tad miffed, since I'd worked very hard on making sure he could read them, and my artwork was even pleasing to me. That said a lot, as I was my own worst critic. I'd also made arrangements to meet the next day with the other Teams, who'd all just returned from their own patrols. Finally, I'd been dismissed and arrived home just a few marks earlier. We'd been on patrol for a fortnight, then on wing pursued relentlessly by a blizzard, barely sleeping and half frozen for the last three days. I'd made report to the Commander, had a vigorous workout, the emotional confusion, then raced like the wind through the tunnels to the cavern and rough housed with Gunnarr afore we finally settled down to cleaning up, and I was still breathing heavily. Now as I laid here on my back, the rhythm of my breath slowed while I gazed at the sparkling ceiling, one hand casually resting 'cross my belly, the other pillowing my head. With one knee bent, I stared at the water droplets gliding down the pale skin of my thigh in tiny rivulets. Feeling out of touch somehow, I dared not look at the massive Dragon stretched out beside me, knowing intuitively that something was changing 'tween us, and I feared I was losing control. I couldn't admit to this, even to myself. I couldn't lose him.

Lifting his huge head, his Voice filled with an intensity I'd not felt afore, I listened carefully. *"Vit'Teyach."*

I made him Say the words again, and then again, so I wouldn't embarrass myself when I tried to mimic the sounds so foreign to my tongue. The first word was bitten off at the end, sharp and crisp, like 'twas spit forth, and the end of the second word was near a growl, from deep in the back of his throat. I was fairly certain my attempt would fail, but just as I opened my mouth he stopped me with, "But that's not what you'd say to me."

Waiting for him to continue, I grew impatient when 'twas obvious he wasn't going to say anything more. "All right, so what would I say to you, and why?"

"Feminine is '-ach' for a male to declare to a female. The masculine is '-okh' which is how a female would declare her love to a male. Vit'Teyokh."

Lying very still, I watched the droplets pool at the hollow of my groin, and then roll together into a single stream to puddle near my navel. "You jest, right?" But catching his stanch expression, I continued, "Apparently not. Fine, so could you repeat that once more, please?"

Suddenly he stood up and towered o'er me, his Voice guttural with desire. *"I will say this to you 'til the stars fall into the sea, for you are my heart, my very soul. I have Known you since my youth and have waited long for you to come into my life. I am patient, but by the Flame, you test me Darque. Your beauty engulfs my reason, my sanity."*

Gunnarr straddled me in the white sands. My eyes drifted from his hind legs up his belly, traveling to his great muzzle. His head tucked down, his nostrils flared as he sniffed my hair. Tilting my head back to follow his beautiful eyes, he took hold of my now outstretched arm, nicking me with the sharp tips of his claws in his barely concealed excitement, and dragged me up several feet, bringing my hips even with his forelegs. I was breathless with the force of his arousal pounding against me, as if I was one of the Battle Drums, and his emotions the hands of the player. He locked my gaze to his, stretching forth one great claw, and touched me softly upon my temple with the smooth top edge. I licked my dry lips, my tongue near stuck to the roof of my mouth, and tried to swallow, for I knew not where this would end. Caressing me from my temple around my ear and down to my chin, my lips parted and I was near panting. There was a burst of moisture 'tween my thighs, and the heat of my body climbed rapidly with the sensations he Shared with me through our 'Bond.

His eyes flashed wickedly, became darker than I'd ever seen them, while he continued his sensuous exploration of my bare skin. His touch sent shivers down my spine and I lost my ability to think or speak. A low growl rumbled deep within his chest and his scales glistened with a blood red tinge, while a delicious heat radiated from his body to mine, making my breath come in stuttering gasps. Nuzzling me with his talon, he moved down my neck to my shoulder, making delicate circles afore he continued down my arm. Hesitating mid-journey afore spiraling onward to my wrist, I could no longer lie still, my entire body was restless with need. When he touched the sharp tip of his talon to the center of my palm, I was drawn under a rising wave of long denied passion. Our eyes still fixed upon each other, his long tongue snaked forth to lick a single drop of blood from his talon. I was shaking with lust more intoxicating than I'd ever experienced, as his paw hit the sand by my shoulder and raising the opposite one, he continued the intense foreplay. His great body lowered and crowded mine possessively. My legs were sprawled apart, baring me to his mercy, and I could clearly see his masculinity pulsing as it filled with his Life Source, extending and elongating steadily, sensually. Even amazed and stunned at this clear display of his fervor, I couldn't stop my own reaction. I was hot, my blood pounding in my veins, quickening to the pit of my belly, the spasms rolling o'er me in rhythm to the beat of our hearts. His hungry gaze sought the glistening moisture 'tween my thighs, and then back to my face with an expression of unspoken promise that stimulated me further. Caressing my shoulder with his tongue, he licked slowly 'cross my upper body, lingering 'tween my breasts. 'Twas gentle and wet, barely touching me, encircling my hardening nipples. Making them peak in excitement afore moving further south, he took his time and gave zealous attention to my navel. Teasing me, dragging his tongue further still, he hesitated just above the mound of tight curls 'tween my legs. 'Twas no doubt in my mind, I trusted him completely and I wanted him as much as he wanted me. Cocking his great head, an expression of insatiable desire mirrored in his eyes, I silently pleaded with him to take me o'er this threshold. Hovering near the edge of release, I must find it soon or be driven insane! Finally, I could take no more, and having aroused me to the utmost precipice of yearning, his great tongue whipped forth. Firmly circling the tip 'tween my legs, I burst into frenzied spasms of pure pleasure. Through our 'Bond, Gunnarr Shared with me every sensation, our minds and bodies in perfect union. My orgasm spurring him on, he threw back his head and roared out in Dragon Tongue as he achieved his own potent release, his warm seed shooting o'er my body. Instinctively I knew 'twas his Claim upon me, as I continued to shudder in wave after wave of sheer ecstasy.

"*Vit'Teyach*," he Whispered, as the spasms gradually diminished and my breathing normalized. Brushing his talon along my bottom lip, I kissed its smooth surface. Tenderly he licked my entire body clean of his passion, as he'd done with my blood on the night of our 'Bond. His touch had me near rising again, but I felt abruptly selfish.

"No, my love, I didn't complete the act, for I won't hurt you. 'Twas sweet none the less." The intensity of his fervor made me sigh. His great crystalline eyes were near normal again, his own spasms weakening, both of us completely spent. *"My Race is obsessively sensual and this was but a minute taste of Dragon Lust. I can hold my own release for marks, for intimacy doesn't require orgasm as Man too often thinks. But regardless of what I feel, I have the ability to extend the pleasure for you as long as you desire. And through our 'Bond, you can Share mine as well."*

The Mighty Blue was telling me his deep and dark Dragon secrets. I was honored, but there was something he was having trouble saying. Gently stroking his leathery face to encourage him, he continued warily, *"We'll have to be careful, for once I've crossed that line, I cannot stop. I've struggled for many moons, for with you, 'tis not easy to avoid the full Lust."* His expression turned to one of pure delight and he continued, *"Foreplay for a Dragon can involve days, even longer. Fortunately however, once the line is crossed, Dragons are quick to peak, for we usually perform in flight."*

Laughing, I blurted out loud, "HA! If that's the worst you can tell me about Dragon Lust, I see nothing amiss." Then he appeared pained and silently I waited.

"There's one more thing," and his eyes locked on mine again. Suddenly I was afraid he'd Tell me the intimacy we'd just shared had somehow cost us the 'Bond. Noting my growing concern, he lifted his great head o'er mine and stared at me with real apprehension. *"I had no choice in this, there was never another for me. But for you, Darque... I'm truly sorry. Dragons mate for life."*

I tried to string together all the ramifications of our new status. "So what are you telling me? I don't understand why you're so anxious... oh wait," I said as the sun began to dawn on me. "You won't ever be able to have a relationship with a female Dragon? You won't be able to have baby High Princes?" As understanding grew, I was justly upset. I loved him, wanted his life to be fulfilled, for him to have the best of everything. Had I ruined that for him? Would he have to pay the price for my selfishness?

"You've ruined nothing. It's always been you, I've never wanted to take another as my mate and I've no desire for another in my lifetime. But Dragon females are also bound by the Claim and I don't know how your system will be affected. 'Twas a risk I shouldn't have taken and a choice you should've been allowed to make of your own free will."

I sighed. "I'm a virgin, Gunnarr, you knew this. I've loved no other in my life, but I've loved you since I first saw you. I may be only human," at which time I Heard Gunnarr snort and tried not to be distracted with wondering why, as I continued, "but it pleases me to be yours for life. We're partners for life, how could this affect me adversely? Besides, it's done and I'm glad. With the 'Bond, our Life Forces can't be separated and now, neither can our hearts."

Stretched out luxuriously and completely satisfied for the first time in my life, I opened my mouth to say the words he'd lovingly taught me. But afore I could utter a sound, he turned his ear toward the exit, at which time I also Heard the remote Battle Cry. Despite the distance o'er whence it had traveled, I was certain 'twas one of my Teams.

Gunnarr hastily arose from where he'd been lying, stepped o'er me while helping me up and then loped for the tunnels. Donning my leathers on the run, I quickly followed. Passing through our living quarters, I armed up with my new blade and shield, and although I'd had them through our patrol, they'd get their first test in battle afore end of day. The fatiguing effect of the tryst we'd just experienced disappeared with the blast of frigid air as I mounted up and we took wing.

Casting forth, I was confused. 'Twas the Voice of Makayyd that we'd Heard, but where were they? She and Ethynn should've returned from their patrol when we did, should've been at the meeting we'd scheduled for later this day, but they were clearly very distant and alone, confronted with multiple Dragons. Why hadn't my father told me last night they'd not yet reported?

Calling for backup to Storrm and Mystynn, they soon followed with Yanais and Shykiyyah, and Zoe and Kyrlayyn in rapid pursuit. There'd be four Teams to assist, but 'twould do no good if we couldn't get there in time, and we still didn't know where they were. *"Guide me, I must know where you are!"* My demanding Call crossed the leagues. After a slight pause I received in response a View through Makayyd's eyes. Three Hoard Dragons surrounded them, Flaming in from all sides while Makayyd banked and rolled in an awe-inspiring show of maneuvers to avoid being struck. But I needed landmarks, if not her Voice, to give me direction. After a near miss of a scorching stream of Flame, Makayyd spun backwards, taking her eyes fleetingly off the enemy, as she glanced toward the distant village and the nearby mountain pass in her effort to provide me the information I required afore shutting me down. If they were to survive they couldn't afford to divert their energies further, but that brief Sight was enough to give me their location. Afore my backup got close enough to see us, I Conferred with Storrm and urged Gunnarr to pick up more speed as we made haste to Lorelei.

~~~~~~~~~~~

Ethynn and Makayyd set out for long perimeter two dawns after Gunnarr and I headed to the Far Northlands. Since there were so few Teams, we were spread out o'er vast sections. They'd taken the southern region, patrolling the open plains and rolling hill country in the area that lay along the northern border of the Razor's Edge. Lorelei was a bustling trader village along the forest that fronted the treacherous mountain range. They were the last, or first community, to or from King's Gate Village, according to which direction you were traveling. 'Twas situated just to the north of the mountain pass known as the Razor's Cut, which was the only way for a traveler to reach Evanntyr Castle by land, as the range was otherwise impassable. 'Twas even treacherous for Dragons, as the mountains of the Edge were not only high but very steep, with near constant snowfalls in the winter, the peaks retaining their white caps perpetually. The lower levels were heavily forested down into narrow valleys cut through by raging rivers. Avalanches and rock falls were certain to occur with the slightest disturbance. In many ways there was no other range more dangerous. Unmapped and unexplored, Man and Dragon alike were at the mercy of the Fates. The Cut provided their only sure path, however this too, had its inherent risks as 'twas plagued seasonally with hazardous rock fall and avalanche.

Gunnarr flew at blinding speed, attributing the boost to our combined Battle Lust as well as a Drawing effect, Pulling us to the besieged Team. 'Twas extraordinary, and felt strangely as if we were standing still, but I could barely keep my eyes open against the rush of wind and could only tell we were moving, by the fur edging of my hood whipping 'round my face. 'Twas in the distance that I finally saw the scarlet bursts of Flame 'cross the horizon. Despite the marks we'd been on wing, they were still fighting, which was good, because it meant they were still alive.

As we neared the battle grounds, I noted we were far enough from Lorelei not to endanger the village. Even in full battle, they'd purposefully drawn the fight away from the heavily populated region, baiting their enemies further into the open hill country. But given the odds, they'd barely managed to maintain defensively, using the edge of the forest as their backup. As Gunnarr roared out his Battle Cry, Flaming in at full force, our distraction allowed Makayyd to get close enough to one of the creatures for Ethynn to land a solid strike against its eye, causing significant damage. Though the strike was glancing and didn't affect the brain, it startled the beast into responding reflexively. Hesitating, he
~~~~~~~~~~~

closed his outer eyelid, lost both altitude and his view of Makayyd, which allowed her to finally get above and latch onto his thick neck with her talons. Using her scalding Flame to slow his Healing, along with her slashing fangs combined with Ethynn's sword strikes, together they managed to sever his huge head mid-flight. All this took mere moments, while Gunnarr and I were attacking the second beast. The other saw what was happening to his comrade and attempted to protect his eyes from my fang blade using his wings. Throwing himself off level, thereby hindering his own talons, I managed to make several vicious cuts to his upper neck but his brutally damaged scales Healed amazingly fast. Still, his reactions allowed me time to slide sideways, tucking myself under Gunnarr's wing while he repositioned and locked talons belly to belly with him. In order to affect this kill, I changed both my tactics and my weapons.

Reaching out as far as I could, I sank my sword to the hilt into his heart with a forceful uppercut through the unscaled region where his great foreleg joined his torso. Of course this maneuver placed me squarely 'tween eight pair of massive legs, and immediately after making my strike I found I was unable to regain my seat. Having lost my sword, which embedded and Healed in place inside the wicked beast, I turned sharply, hugging my body against Gunnarr's like glue, keeping the lowest profile possible, while Gunnarr finished him with Flame and fangs, ripping his now injured heart from his chest.

Wasting no time, we turned to attack the third Dragon, to no avail. The coward had slipped away, affecting his escape through the Cut. 'Twouldn't be wise to attempt to follow, as 'twas a prime location for ambush, and we knew not if there were others nearby. Our ability to defend ourselves, let alone stage an offensive, would've been greatly mired in the confines of the relatively narrow Pass.

"The last beast ran with his tail 'tween his legs, when he Saw us 'cross the horizon, Second," my sister Called triumphantly from a distance, and I was grateful that she and the others would soon arrive. Confident that no Hoard rescue attempt would occur, and that we were safe here for the moment, I sighed in relief. Finding myself suddenly so fatigued I nearly fell out of my saddle, Gunnarr landed to give me a chance to rest.

Although he assured me we were alone in the area, I could tell the Hoard had been here in the recent past. When the other Teams arrived, they'd set to work trying to salvage the remains, gathering a multitude of teeth. I was still trying to decide what they could be used for but I knew in my heart, they'd be an important part of our arsenal one day. As for finding anything else useful, our difficulties here made me doubt that our Black Market search would bear fruit.

Gunnarr assisted in the salvage operations directing the gatherings, while I sat on the charred grass trying to catch my breath. My sword still implanted in the creature's heart when Gunnarr had ripped it out, Zoe returned it to me with unconcealed enthusiasm. "Nice strike force, Commander. Kyrlayyn and I can't wait to use that maneuver!"

The Mighty Blue poked about the ashes, but seemed unsatisfied. Apparently not finding that which he sought, he ambled back to me, his visage of concern for my welfare, his Voice chastising. *"What were you thinking, Spitter? You could have been slashed to bits. You should've stayed safe upon my neck; I would've destroyed him with my talons."*

'Twas clear in his eyes, and by the tone of his Voice, I had to make my stance in no uncertain terms. *"No, 'twould have taken too much time, and the third was still there. The Healing was fast on that one, your slash marks disappeared near instantly and you needed my assist. We fight as a Team, Gunnarr. I will fight for you, I will fight at your side, despite our love, despite our 'Bond, for 'tis my destiny to do so. I don't wish to put myself into harm's way, for as consequence I risk also your life, but if I'd not made that strike, we might all have Passed Beyond."*

Briefly he hesitated and then Said, *"You Speak the truth, but I did warn you of my possessive nature, did I not?"* Gunnarr rumbled his amusement deep in his throat and I couldn't help but smile.

"Did you find what you were looking for, my love?" I Asked him, changing the subject back to his odd behavior during the salvage.

"Undamaged stock," he Said, but there was a lustrous twinkle in his eyes, that I was unable to read.

~~~~~~~~~~~

Gunnarr was disappointed he hadn't found another Dragon's Eye for Darque. He'd been certain that Ethynn had done damage to both of his opponent's eyes, but he'd hoped at least one of the other's had been untouched. Alas, no such good fortune. He was also disappointed that he'd been unable to give her the gem that he'd tucked away for her back home. Deciding to give it to her this morning after he'd Claimed her as his Mate, they'd Heard the Cry and 'twas forgotten. There might not be another opportunity for some time to come. He sighed. At least he had his female. She was his!

Leaving Storrm and the others to finish, he persuaded Darque to mount and set wing. Makayyd had sworn she could still fly Ethynn and
~~~~~~~~~~~

he'd had no doubt, but they'd need assist on the long and painful journey, and there was always a chance they'd encounter trouble again along the way. They'd left prior to the salvage, but he quickly caught up to them. Setting his flight pattern slightly ahead and flanking them, Gunnarr's mighty wings cut the air resistance, allowing Makayyd to draft him, quickening and easing her flight. In this manner she was able to coast much of the journey.

~~~~~~~~~~

"'Twas near Lorelei, Commander, northwest of the Cut. We were flying our last long perimeter when she Heard an Unknown in the region close to the village. I made the decision to check it out. Could have been a Rogue, but 'twas too far away to Communicate easily, and I wanted to gather more intelligence afore I made report." Ethynn wheezed, having to stop to breathe and to reconcile the pain from multiple fractures and Flame burns. The Healing would knit his flesh and mend his broken bones, but 'twas an excruciating experience with the acceleration. Makayyd Blocked just enough of the pain for him to finish talking afore she'd Sing him to sleep through the final candle marks. 'Twas much easier for them as well, but they couldn't force what we wouldn't allow, and I knew that Ethynn's Dragon was in agony while she awaited his consent. She'd also received some major injuries, although the fact they both lived was a testament to their skill in battle, as much as to the success of the LifeBond.

'Twas ever odd to hear Ethynn address me so formally. He was the oldest Warrior in my Flight, although I wasn't certain by how much. I'd known the muscle bound fighter all my life. As an infant, my father had hired him as my bodyguard after discovering the Dragon scar upon my thigh, but for some reason he was soon convinced I was in no danger and let the big Warrior move on to his next assignment. Once I'd started advanced classes, he'd been one of my Survivalist Trainers 'tween duty changes, but had made his last deployment just prior to the time I took my Oath. Returning to answer the Call for the LifeBond, he'd fought his way through to join us in the ceremony. He'd laughed heartily when he'd heard how Storrm and I chanced upon the Dragon by hearing his Song that day in the meadow, his loud guffaws echoing through the Great Hallway as I wove the tale for his amusement. I told the truth mind you, but the account had been comical and the grin on my face as I enlightened my audience, added to the mirth of the telling. And when he learned how that chance sighting had led to our being taken afore the
~~~~~~~~~~

Council and questioned unmercifully by the Warriors in residence and the Council members, just to prove our integrity, well, he could barely catch his breath. When I'd finally related how we were accepted for Trials, the youngest ever to be so honored, tears had rolled down his face, he was laughing so hard. Ethynn was always up for an 'adventure'. Frankly, I still didn't know whether I was being complimented or sharped by his raucous reaction.

"Commander, the first Dragon had just feasted and was sluggish. 'Twas what Makayyd had Heard originally. I should've taken advantage but I hesitated and my indecision might have cost us all dearly. My only excuse was that the remains appeared to have been human. 'Twas barely an instant, but by the time I had a grip on the situation, the other two arrived and we were in full out battle. And Sir? Those two joined the first from the Cut. No offence Second, but you're still young and not well traveled. There's no place along the Pass that could benefit the Hoard. You know what that means."

Of course I knew what that meant. One would have to be blind not to see it very clearly. The only place that could serve as a Lair for the Hoard at the other end of the Razor's Cut was Evanntyr. If they came through there, they came from the Castle of the High King. I was no diplomat but even I understood that to openly accuse the King of having anything to do with the Hoard, would be to declare war against him and that was insanity. His influence was vast. Although the Dragon Clan supplied his Warriors, Warriors weren't the only forces that fought for him. We were the Elite, the strongest, best trained and most skilled, but the odds were against us taken as a whole. Had Bryard still been King, we could've sat down together in civil discussion of our concerns, knowing our alliance would be safe, for his word could be trusted. But then, if Bryard were still King, the Hoard wouldn't be anywhere near Evanntyr.

"As your Second, I expect you to offer up whatever intelligence you have that might be pertinent. As for your indecision, there are none who wouldn't have reacted in the same manner, seeing that for the first time. You fought well, Ethynn. Even untrained and undisciplined opponents can force one Past the Veil at such odds. This War has changed all the rules and we have to adapt. I'll return for a full report when you awaken. Now sleep," I said to the injured, and now much relieved Warrior. In scarcely a candle drip, he closed his sea green eyes, taking a shallow breath. Then Makayyd stretched out to lay her great head gently next to his shaggy blonde mane, closing her eyes as well. Very soon their breathing patterns slowed and synchronized and I turned and walked away, reassured in their recovery.

"*'Twould have been better had I given Ethynn the fang blade. They might have taken down all three beasts,*" I Grumbled in frustration to Gunnarr.

"*I am impressed with the expertise they displayed, fiery one, but I question whether they'd have taken all three with only the addition of a fang blade to their arsenal. The one who escaped us saw only the strategies used against them. Since the only Dragon who saw your blade and shield was forced Past the Veil by your hand, we can be assured that at least the knowledge of the special weapons is still ours alone.*" Gunnarr Spoke truth, his wisdom comforting. If any of them had escaped after having fought against our special weapons, they as well as our battle strategies would've been compromised and without sufficient stock, our efforts would be in vain.

Conceding his point, I dropped the issue, trying to summarize our situation. "*We cannot Draw our Strength soon enough, my love. We're in much danger against the Evil of the Hoard. We stand little chance of wounding them, let alone killing, and making a fatal hit will be nigh impossible now that they're aware of our strategies, even with the fang blades. With the Magic embedded in our steel, we'll be far more effective. We're snowed under 'til the next LifeBond and we need every advantage we can muster.*"

"*Agreed, Second. Maahayyel is also aware of our dire need and will execute the Draw as soon as she can make ready.*" Gunnarr's eyes flashed with his calculations. 'Twould take a Surge of incredible force to Draw for so many weapons from the heavens, and 'twould leave the Ancients drained for the following LifeBond ceremony. The Draw to non-organics required the Magic to merge within the object after traveling through the body of the one who'd be wielding such, and there was no guarantee that any of them had what it took to survive such raw power. Well, aside from Darque and Storrm that is. Truth be told, they needed not a special date to Brew for the Draw, just the correct numbers, powers, Voices and a clear night sky. It could be done upon the same sacred ground they'd used afore. As for the number of weapons so enhanced, 'twould take long and be painful for one, but thirteen? If the Warriors survived the process, 'twould be wise to have instilled the Magic into their most needed weapon, that being their swords. Thus the Warriors now in 'Bond would soon bear Dragon Swords, not seen in Kadoor since the Beginning of Time, since the creation of the High Races Counsel. Gunnarr knew through his

Memories what had happened after, and it gave him pause. Would this time be any different? Would they be opening Pandora's Box? Sighing, he conceded they had no choice, what would be, would be. He was unconcerned that he'd not been present at the birthing of the first Dragon Swords, as his Kind all Shared the Memories of their ancestors. Gunnarr was one of an elite few, which included his Matriarch and her eldest sibling, who possessed the strongest Magic of his Race. Sadly, he remembered the one who should be higher than all in this hierarchy. Even as High Prince of the Highland Dragons, his Magic was nothing compared to that which his youngest brother, the 7th Prince of a 7th Prince, would eventually Brew. Gazing toward the heavens, he Spoke earnestly into the silence of the deepening night, *"Where are you Bryynn? We need your Power, your Strength in these sinister days. 'Tis truth you've yet to enter Kadoor, but 'tis also truth you're not where I left you. 'Tis insulated darkness which surrounds you, or I'd be able to Share through your eyes. I'm not comfortable with this situation and by the Flame, this had better not mean you're endangered. I haven't been satisfied with the responses to my queries of your welfare these past few moons. With the blessings of the Mighty Maahayyel, if our cousins have lost your Egg I will spit their Reigning Matriarch o'er the blazing belly of Fire Heart Mountain alive, after feeding her bloody entrails to the Night Beasts of the Daggogh, while her entire Race is forced to watch!"*

CHAPTER 19

Playing Poker

A FEW DAYS LATER

"Regynn, isn't there anything pertinent to be found in the manuscripts? We know there were Dragons then. Were they invisible? How could such powerful Magic have been kept a secret? Wait… mayhap I answered my own question, yes?" I was frustrated, my instincts telling me we were lucky to have made all our 'Bonds at the last ceremony, but why should luck have anything to do with it? Surely the Ancients understood the parameters, after all, 'twas their Magic! But not a good point to make, since the LifeBond hadn't been performed in these Ancients' span of days, and they were working from their most distant Memories. But I needed all of the Warriors preparing to stand on sacred ground, to take their LifeBonds as we did, and I needed to make as many 'Bonds as we could. As 'twas evidenced by the recent Battle of Lorelei, we had to have more Teams and we had to have them now. Was there some reason we'd only presented thirteen candidates? Could we have presented more, and would they have taken? What would've happened if there hadn't been a Dragon to accept a Blood Call? Could any Dragon accept any Call, or was there some inborn match?

Too many questions. Not enough answers. After having endured the ceremony, we were all in agreement that not just any pair would survive. Those who'd succeeded were spirit-matched. They'd blended our Senses, our minds, our very heartbeat. I was in search of information. I wanted the why's and wherefore's of the Magic the Ancients were preparing to Brew again in less than a fortnight. Gunnarr couldn't answer my questions and Maahayyel was out of touch, deep in preparation. I didn't want to place so much stress upon them, but we had no other choice. And if anyone could find any scrap of evidence to lead me in the right direction, to ensure we were doing everything we could to assist them, 'twas the Clan Historian. Seeking advice, I caught up with him in his office behind the Library. 'Twas a large room which was horribly cluttered with scrolls, parchments, pictures and manuscripts stacked everywhere, including the desk in the corner. However, there was also a small bar with some tables and chairs along one wall, since the last Historian had been as much interested in entertaining as he was in learning. Finding Regynn there, I asked him the questions that burned in my mind.

"I've been researching the matter, girl, since the Ancients brought their offer to the table. I've found little from which to make any substantial conclusions, but I do think you're correct. Luck may have played a part, but odds played more. We might be constrained within some Magical parameters, but I believe we can stretch them a tad." The Elder Warrior raised one eyebrow and smirked at me, then returned to his parchment shuffling, sorting and separating them using some unknown reasoning, and instead of making less chaos, he created even more piles and then stacked more parchments upon the table beside him. Just afore I began to suspect he had forgotten me, he glanced up, focused upon me again, and I got the distinct impression he was about to regale me with a story. 'Twas his manner after all.

Pushing with one hand, I hopped up easily to sit on the bar. No simple feat for someone who stood about chin level to said bar. But even afore my strength and coordination were enhanced, I was able to accomplish this simple stunt. I just had to use both hands then. Noting the envy that gleamed in his eyes as he watched the ease of my actions, I was reminded of how much the Elders lost to Time. These great fighters, both men and women, spent their entire lives and long careers in battle and constant training, stressing their bodies well beyond any normal standards. Some never returned to the Den. He was envious not only of my strength, but of my glowing health. I knew his joints creaked when he trained now, his body hurting much when the snows came in the deep of winter. But although 'twould be unheard of for any Warrior to complain of pain, their difficulties showed them clearly slowing down in their Elder winters and my heart ached for them. In the 'Bond, I'd never suffer such. Of course, I'd probably not live long enough to discover that for certain. Crossing my arms o'er my chest, I smiled at my friend and comrade, then said, "Regynn, your horse is at the gate. Where are you taking me?"

Having received clearance to speak freely to his Second, he tossed his long blonde hair back o'er his shoulder and looked me squarely in the eye. Lifting one leather clad leg, he stomped his boot down on the stool afore us, crossed his solid arms o'er his knee and leaned forward, his thick mane spilling o'er his shoulders once again.

Regynn was a heavily built man, slightly above average height. His wavy hair had darkened through the years, but lightened to near white when exposed to the sun's rays for any length of time. Somehow he managed to appear as if he never brushed it a day in his life, despite his meticulous grooming efforts. It tended to give him a disheveled look that made people wonder if he'd just awakened, no matter the time of day. Having most people think him slothful would have caused another man difficulty, but Regynn was oblivious to what others thought of him and wouldn't have been concerned had he actually been aware. I knew for certain that the female Warriors, and even some of the village women, were attracted to his rugged appearance, but he never acknowledged them. He wasn't disinterested by any means; he was just so preoccupied in what he was doing at any given moment that he simply didn't notice. Whatever his focus was upon at the time, became his only reality. Nothing else mattered, nothing else existed. I always thought that made the women vie for his attentions even more, accepting what they thought of as a challenge from a man playing hard to get. Shaking my head, I thought to myself, if they only knew. He was so vastly intelligent that he quickly lost interest in the average and mundane affairs of life and had to keep his mind engaged at all times with multiple activities or he'd become more and more agitated to the point of self destruction. Toward that end, he had to struggle so as not to become bored, which was a state of being that he detested. Every Warrior and staff member of the Clan was extremely grateful when Regynn was occupied, trust me on that.

He was retired now, after a long career serving in the King's Forces at Evanntyr most of his active duty. This was followed by becoming a Trainer at the Den many winters past, and recently focusing most of his attention to archiving as the Clan Historian. There was no one I could see in that position who could serve better than he, with the possible exception of Kallyr, but the Seer couldn't do justice to both positions and no one else could be Seer. I'd never reveal this to Kallyr, but I was exceedingly pleased when his request was denied, after applying when the old Historian Passed two winters ago. I knew that Elder Warrior Regynn would be the best Historian the Dragon Clan had ever seen, 'twas a position into which he could truly sink his teeth and I was very happy for him.

I'd personally known Regynn all of my life, although no one truly knew his past or even where he'd been birthed and raised. Having come to Drekinn as an Outlander, he'd simply arrived at the Main Gate of the Den one day. He'd been my Martial Arts Trainer when I was a child and had been one of my hardest Masters. He was the only Warrior who didn't carry his own sword, although he did own one, usually found gathering dust in his Weapons Hold at the foot of his cot. Most times he didn't even carry a short blade or a dagger, although he'd never been bested in a fight. He was adept at disarming his opponent, and would usually just toss their weapon aside, forcing many Past the Veil during his lengthy career span, without benefit of cold steel. His unique fighting style involved using your bare hands and whatever you could find around you, and even now I'd be leery of facing him alone in battle. 'Twas a technique and set of skills he'd learned from some nameless nomadic tribe in his youth, and he'd honed his style by reading ancient manuscripts about similar methods. He had no use for 'rules of engagement', he fought dirty, he fought to win, and he instilled that same sense in each and every one of his students throughout the many long winters he taught. In this, we were in agreement and for that, I was thankful. If one Passed the Veil in the battle, what good were the rules? In both our opinions, there were but a handful of simple guidelines in battle. Stay alive. Force your rival Past the Veil afore he forces you. Protect your own.

Regynn stood staring at me, just as he had the moment afore and the moment afore that. His face took on a quizzical expression that turned to one of dismay, as if he'd been about to say something and then forgot. Even without the mirror I could tell my own expression must have mimicked his and when I could finally remain silent no longer I blurted, "What? Regynn, you're speechless? I don't believe that. 'Twould be an historical moment." 'Twas an offer of my own sanity to tease him, as you never knew how he'd take it, but I had to do something to help him find his tongue.

"No m'lady. Not truly speechless, and yes, I know you tease me." He winked, then continued. "I was just trying to decide how long I could keep you waiting. And after finally getting your full attention, 'twas frustrating to realize I had nothing more to offer than a simple suggestion. I've been waiting long for such a time with you. I'd thought to offer a speech of impressive proportions and I'm stunned to find myself deficient," he stated apologetically.

My eyebrows raised and my mouth dropped open. Uncrossing my arms and slapping one hand flat against my chest, I said, "I'm aghast! Are you trying to tell me you truly don't have anything to say?"

"Oh no, I have something to say, just not as much as I would wish, given the circumstances. I hate to waste such a moment. By all the fires of Hades, I finally have your full attention, I even get the official nod to speak freely, and I find I haven't anything epic to relate. The Fates can be cruel indeed, m'lady. But I do have something to impart." Regynn sighed, scratched behind his ear and then twisted his mouth as he sorted through his thoughts and reorganized them appropriately, altering his mode 'tween casual and formal. He'd never liked public speaking, mostly keeping to himself, and his social skills were somewhat lacking from isolation, due in part to others' misunderstandings of his idiosyncrasies.

Placing my hands on the bar beside my thighs, I leaned forward, swinging my booted feet gently up and down, creating a thumping rhythm against the old growth oak boards. Raising my eyebrows, I laughed. "I'm so relieved! I was beginning to think the Heart of Fire was about to blow again."

"The Heart of Fire has not had a full out 'blow' since the last Holocaust, m'lady, and in fact, has barely let off any steam at all, in several hundred winters, per rumor of course, since the written records of most tribes have long been missing..." and then he caught the look in my eyes and realized again, that he was being teased. "Oh, I see," he stated with a sheepish grin, and responding to my own smile, he continued, "I do have an idea, m'lady." And with that simple opening, he grabbed the back of a nearby chair, turned it around and straddled it, resting his forearms upon the top rail, while I jumped down and did the same. Facing each other thusly, he began teaching me a very old game of mixed chance and strategy known as 'poker'. This simple card game held much to compare with our current situation, and fascinated I listened, as he explained how one had to build a 'winning hand' with trades from the original hand that was dealt. Winning depended not so much on chance, but on playing the odds. One winning hand was built on matching pairs, and this particular aspect of the game was what he felt best bespoke his point. Starting with a full deck (many Warriors), one took the hand dealt (fixed number of Dragons), and attempted to pair them (sending out the Blood Call). Some cards might be eliminated in order to make as many pairs as possible and therefore, we needed a bigger deck from which to choose. Since the number of Dragons available was static, in order to ensure the most pairs we needed to offer as many Warriors as we could. The odds were in favor of more pairs if we did this, and there was nothing either of us could think of, which indicated this strategy would adversely affect the Magic to be Brewed.

"'Tis my conclusion that the idea of only offering thirteen candidates comes more from tradition than from need or ability, and by standing more Warriors for the Call, we're more likely to make all the 'Bonds available. Now, I can't be certain that more than thirteen 'Bonds can be made, for that part of the equation is still up to the Magic, however, we can help to ensure that all thirteen are found, and not come up short in the end," he said with confidence. "Of course, there's also the variable of survival. 'Tis still possible to lose pairs to the Power itself, as 'twas a possibility during your own LifeBond," he reminded me with a wink.

"'Twas exactly as I was hoping, Regynn, and your ideas have merely confirmed my own thoughts and strengthened my resolve. Tonight I put forth a Call for Warriors for the Second LifeBond," I told him as I rose, stretching to keep myself alert. The conversation had been interesting, as 'twas always with this Warrior, and I was pleased with the knowledge so imparted, but I had errands to run and needed to take my leave.

Regynn also stretched as he stood up, his joints cracking. His first steps toward the door with me were awkward and stilted. In a moment of compassion and inspiration, I spoke aloud what I'd been considering, for I knew the 'Bond would make us near equals in battle. "Will you Answer that Call, Warrior?"

He stopped and stared. Regynn wasn't the tallest Warrior, but he stood head and shoulders above me, and I had to raise my eyes to see his face. I saw the yearning there, and I struggled to maintain my composure. I moved not while his gaze bored into mine, calculating the odds mayhap. After a brief moment I broke the quiet of the empty office. "'Twill be my honor to have you at my side in battle, wingtip to wingtip with our Dragons. Don't underestimate your worth my friend. The 'Bond will change you in so many ways, you cannot imagine."

He took a deep breath, swallowed hard, and then he said quietly, "Yes m'lady, I can imagine. I have imagined every moment of every day since you took the first. I watched your Dragon pull you into that fire, my heart hammering, Battle Lust building, and then you were gone. As each of the thirteen Sent out their Blood Call, I felt a pull to be there, to stand upon the sacred ground, to take the Cut and grasp my own Dragon. I fell to my knees during the ceremony, my emotions were so raw I didn't even notice I'd scratched myself 'til the next dawn. My attention so riveted from start to finish, I felt not the blood upon my own leg. And I haven't slept a full night since, waking with vivid dreams of doing the same. I could Feel the heat of the fire, Hear my Dragon Speaking to me. 'Tis as if I've had Visions of my own, as if a Dragon Calls to me now. But I'd shrugged it off as an Elder's delusion of past glories, and 'til this very moment, I'd not a glimmer of hope I could return to the battle as a true Warrior, entering the War with something to offer my Clan and m'Liege." He swallowed hard again and I held my tongue for I was near choking, and had no adequate response. His need to join us was great, to be a Warrior once more, but there was a hesitancy I understood. 'Twas the fear of rejection.

"Then Answer the Call. We need you to stand ready upon the grounds, and if 'tis the will of the One True Liege, you shall 'Bond." Encouraging as best I could, for I dared not order anyone to the Magic, I then turned to leave. He stepped forward to hold open the heavy door as I slipped through. Surreptitiously I glanced o'er my shoulder, but I was forgotten and he'd already returned to his tasks. Wondering which path he'd choose, I pulled the door shut behind me.

~~~~~~~~~~

"I need to know how long 'twill be afore my life mate is Gifted a Dragon Sword. I cannot keep her out of harm's way forever. She is a mighty Warrior, highly skilled, and she has already succeeded in forcing two Past the Veil. But she's very small, with only cold steel to brandish, making her most vulnerable. We must Draw soon Maahayyel, or we'll lose this War. We knew 'twould be required afore we ever offered the Magic. I merely inquire with all due respect, what hinders you." Gunnarr near demanded the Draw, Speaking to his mother as no one else could or would. Although 'twas walking a fine line to garner favor and knowledge, as High Prince 'twas his duty to see this risky venture succeed. They had to defeat the Evil One this time, not just contain him, or the world as they knew it would end. All the Races held their breath, watching the Highlands in their efforts with the humans, praying for victory. The very idea of bringing in the weakest of the sentient Races had been amusing to the others initially. But Gunnarr had argued that Mankind was not truly weak; they had their own Magic and, although untapped and untrained, it did leak out in some on occasion. *"Have you never Communicated with their Seers?"* he'd Asked them, proving his theory. He'd also insisted Mankind had as much to lose, and therefore would be as highly motivated, if The Black and his Hoard should defeat them. Man was ignorant of the Evil engulfing them, not indifferent, and someone needed to open their eyes and teach them afore 'twas too late for them all. Hearing Gunnarr's arguments, amusement switched to outrage at his formal proposal to enlist Mankind, which at the very least meant divulging their own existence, and secrets held for millennia. But o'er time, Gunnarr had brought most of them to his way of thinking, and even those still in opposition held their tongues and actively participated for his cause once Maahayyel declared her agreement with the plan. The LifeBond would be invoked and the first Dragons to respond were volunteers, although all Dragons knew if a Warrior sent forth a Blood Call and 'twas meant for them, it mattered not where they were. If too distant to respond physically, 'twould only be a matter of time afore they found each other, both of them guided by the Call, neither able to fight the drive to unite with the other. 'Twas why Maahayyel had deliberated so long. It had been the most difficult choice of her extended life.
~~~~~~~~~~

But she'd been aware, given the prophesies to which she'd been privy, the High Prince was correct and 'twas their destiny. There'd been no further discussion or resistance once she'd revealed her concurrence. Only The Evil One had ever opposed Maahayyel or her lineage. Gunnarr sighed and chose not to think more upon the disastrous cascade of events that had thus resulted. 'Twas history after all, and he hoped his Legend Song would prove to be more positive.

In an uncharacteristically informative Response, the Matriarch explained, "*We need to build up our Life Force, and this we can only accomplish from home, in the Heart of Fire, where we've withdrawn. Kaahayyel lost much of her strength during the first ceremony and I fear for her survival through such a powerful ritual as the Draw. Although at full force 'tis arguable she is stouter than I, still I must have her knowledge and assistance, at least for this first attempt. But if she fails during the Draw, 'twould be untold damage resulting to all involved. You know this to be truth. Kaahayyel will be at full Strength by the time the Melts rush from the Raptor's Talons to the Dragon's Tears. She'll need as much time as I can give her. We store fire now. We strengthen our Life Force now. The Hoard will not be as active in the deep winter, but you must stay alive, you must protect Darque. Hold on my son. We make haste.*"

CHAPTER 20

Pastimes and Tapestry Designs

'Twas a beautiful morning, with the sun's warm rays reflecting off the white crust of snow and ice that dazzled all around the forested area in which they were now trudging. After making their original base camp within the caves close to where they'd awakened more than three moons past (by their estimations, given the weather, the stars and the positions of the moon and sun), Graasyn and Bastyen had branched out as much as they could, locating a likely place to camp for a few days and then trudging back and forth to supply it, so that they now had a series of campsites leading ever southward, toward home they hoped, like a skipping stone 'cross the woodland. This allowed them to maintain a safe place to wait out any sudden worsening weather and to let them map and secure an ever widening and lengthening region. It also gave them a much bigger scavenging range, for hunting, fishing and digging up root stock to fill their larder.

Graasyn sighed deeply and wondered what the others were doing back at the Den. Bastyen had been making a snare and glanced up curiously at the sound. They nodded to each other, knowing the others' thoughts were on going home, afore they returned to the task of survival.

~~~~~~~~~~

The end of winter was finally come, and 'twas near four moons since we'd taken the 'Bond. During the past fortnight we'd been mostly snowed under, unable to fly further than to the Dragon's Den and back. My Teams had spent many marks working with the new weapons made from fangs and talons, as well as getting used to the new shields, with the hope that enough stock would make itself available so that we'd all enjoy the benefits. Ariel and Rygyl were still out on their mission, but although they'd followed up on many leads, they'd yet to locate a source and they too, had been snowed in at times, having to hunker down, spending long cold nights under the wharfs. Alric had come through for me, creating the most effective and lethal weapons possible, using the minimal stock we'd compiled from the Kaddart battle. At Lorelei, I'd used the blade to our advantage but in the end 'twas my long sword that had effected the kill. The fangs were too short to reach the heart, but could be used to cut a
~~~~~~~~~~

path through the scales, as long as you didn't let your arm get severed by the Healing. Yes, the fangs and talons would prove beneficial, but 'twould still require skill.

All of us would be given at least one talon, but since there weren't enough fangs to go around, I'd divvied those out, taking into consideration their personal strengths and fighting tactics. After they'd all worked for awhile with the special weapons, they did a bit of trading amongst themselves, eventually settling upon what they each felt they could utilize best. All totaled there were eighteen talons, for a Dragon had five on each forepaw and four on each hind paw, and Gunnarr had found them all intact. 'Twas due to the quick kill of that one, whereas the battle with the two near Lorelei had been long fought with much damage resulting. Also, we'd salvaged all six of the long fangs from the Kaddart Dragon. The teeth had been missing and presumed lost to Flame, but we'd found plenty of those at Lorelei, which was odd in my opinion. The fangs were long and fairly straight, a lustrous pearl white in color. The talons were shorter, thicker and curved, with a deep blue-black gleam. All of us had at least one of the deadly talons, and five of us had two. They'd been Magically altered in such a manner that if you held the smooth end in your palm, the talon would slide through your middle fingers as if 'twas an extension of one's fist. My Warriors had nicknamed them 'Strikers' for the method in which they were most often used, that being in a forceful hook or uppercut. The fang blades, being referred to as 'Biters' in a direct and unimaginative reference to the fang bite of a Dragon, had gone to the Warriors who had only one Striker, and that still left Storrm and I with just one special weapon. Still, they were no substitute for a Dragon Sword. The special weapons were wickedly sharp and easy to use, but outside of a fight against a Magical creature, 'twould be little more useful than any good dagger, for one had to be in hand to hand conflict range, as opposed to using one's sword. But we were slightly better off with them, than without. The real difference was in the shield I now carried. 'Twas covered in Dragon scale and we'd found them still capable of Healing themselves of 'wounds'. Gunnarr had been as surprised as I was to discover this peculiarity, and had no idea if the Healing effect was temporary or permanent as they'd never attempted to reuse their scales. Like so many questions that had arisen since our union, only time would tell. But the number of scales had also been limited and only two shields had been covered thus far. My Warriors dubbed them 'Thumpers' because of the sound they made when hacked upon. Instead of the age old resonance of metal clanging on metal, it made a dull thump or huffing noise, like a man might make when he'd received a hard hit. 'Twas an eerie sound, but the Teams had taken to the peculiar effects, even speaking to the shields as if alive, and all of them clamored for one of their own as soon as possible. However, the few extra scales we'd collected from Lorelei were not enough to cover a third and I gave Storrm the second one. 'Twas my decision and she obeyed, although she'd initially been resistant. We'd made the sacrifice of having only one special weapon, which was part of my reasoning. Still, I was vexed, as we could lose the entire war without finding more stock or getting the Ancients to hold the Draw. We were not only outnumbered, we were out-armed as well. 'Twas in Ariel and Rygyl's hands, along with their 'Bonds, to find that which we so desperately needed.

Long days and nights with little else to do created much boredom and I'd encouraged the Teams to gather in the Cave of Voices frequently, and to practice their individual pastimes outside of their regular train-ing routines. I was growing used to waking to the sounds of my Warriors harmonizing with Dragon Song, accompanied by a variety of stringed in-struments, drums and pipes. Several of the females and a few of the males also dabbled in needlework, creating glorious tapestries adorning the cave walls. Storrm was quite talented in sewing and design among other things, and created colorful costumes for traditional dancing, as well as curtains and other effects, allowing each to personalize their own spaces. 'Twas her designs growing within the tapestries which, along with her other items, were quite coveted.

I liked to write and tell stories and I would dabble in painting, draw-ing, carving and scrimshaw. I also enjoyed making weapons, and had been told many times that I had some talent in that field. During our con-finement, the teeth we'd collected continued to perplex me. Aside from jewelry or as collector's pieces, I'd not been successful in thinking of how to mount them as a weapon. They were sharp, slightly serrated and would pierce scales, but although they averaged the size of my palm for the larg-est ones, they were not long. Mayhap some sort of spear tip? I shook my head in frustration. We'd not used spears for many centuries, relying upon the cold steel of sword and blade, dagger and pick. Regynn had been researching a stringed weapon that would force a small spear through the air, used often afore the Last Holocaust for hunting. 'Twas similar to a sling in my opinion, but to my knowledge he hadn't completed the project afore the chaos of the return of the Dragons. Mayhap a battle mace? I just knew not how to imbed them securely, and then how to carry it without self injury was confounding. 'Twas a guarantee the War Horses wouldn't appreciate such, slapping against their flanks. But there had to be an effective way to use them for more than trinkets. Fatigued, by the time I finally thought of some good use for them 'twould probably be so obvious I would think I'd been blind. In the meantime, I'd sat upon Gunnarr's forelegs while he watched, and using my Striker I etched elaborate scenes upon their flat sides. The work was tedious but the results were magnificent and I was well pleased.

I also visited the Kennels as often as I could, to see the newest additions. A beautiful litter of pups was sired by one of the new dogs brought to us by the Outlanders I'd assisted moons ago. I so enjoyed spending time with the massive brute, his glowing and soft brindle colored fur coat a tribute to his good health. Most of the War Dogs were a rich fawn color which would blend well into the scenery, but this dog had a black and apricot brindle pattern that made him a ghost in the night, and 'twas truly rare. Having near Passed the Veil in the attack at their farm, 'twas the will of the Fates he'd survived. If I'd still lived in the Den, he'd be mine.

His original owners had sold both of their dogs to the Clan, using the coin they received as their stake to buy into a business in the Port District. Bensyn was the elder of the two, and Bullaga, a huge apricot fawn, was close behind. Although they were not timid, displaying intelligence and courage as well as strength, stamina and great size, they did tend to keep to themselves and would quietly lie in their corner watching the world go by. But Bensyn, the one chosen to sire this new litter, held a special place in my heart. He was always glad to see me or Storrm when we came to visit, and would lope up to us, seeking chest rubs and playtime. War Dogs were trained nearly from birth and would be adopted out to work with their handler by the time they were weaned. This big baby was neither trained nor young, and wouldn't be placed on any list for adoption. He and Bullaga were leading lives of comfort, the addition of their excellent bloodlines and characteristics a much needed boost for which we were all quite pleased, but they would never enjoy the one on one relationship that such a social animal craved. Therefore, I made a special effort to spend as much time with them as I could spare.

<center>~~~~~~~~~~</center>

"Storrm, 'tis stunning! Where did you get the inspiration for such?" Asking my sister about her newest tapestry, I fingered the yarn she'd dyed a rich blue, admiring the workmanship of her weaving.

"'Twas of a great battle within a cave. Do you really like it?" She stared at her own work as though 'twas of another's skills.

"I know not this battle. 'Twas Legend Song? 'Tis not familiar," I said, as I tried to make out all the details within the barely begun work.

She was nervous when she responded. "Mayhap you'll recognize it when I get more finished, my sister. 'Tis hardly enough there now, for you to tell 'tis a cave." She sounded oddly serious and although she smiled and laughed, the mirth didn't reach her eyes. 'Twas somehow sobering.

She'd avoided my question, but I'd not be thwarted. "Tell me more, I wish to know about this great battle. I thought I knew them all." I stared at her, trying to decipher any hidden meaning behind her words. I sensed something was wrong.

She suddenly turned toward the cave exit where Mystynn came striding up protectively. Her face lit up upon seeing him, but there was a sadness I couldn't explain, in the depths of her deep blue eyes.

"Mystynn thinks I need some fresh air," she said, then taking my hands and looking into my eyes, she continued, "I've been given much in this life. Daughter to the Battle Commander, sister to the Second, live 'Bond with Mystynn the Green, Second Prince of the Highland Dragons. No matter where our destinies may lead us, together or distant, never doubt my love for you, Darque." And then she turned away too quickly for me to confirm whether or not that was a tear in her eye, and walked swiftly out with Mystynn, leaving me quite bewildered.

CHAPTER 21

Half Breed

FOUR AND A HALF MOONS FROM THE 'BOND

The short winter brought heavy snows, which held back the war effort. Now the Spring Melts had begun, causing much trouble in the regions far north and east, but the Battle Commander had other things upon his mind. Due to the Incident at Lorelei, Darque had ordered the Teams patrol only in pairs, but he'd violated that decision. He cared not, he could handle his daughter's wrath. He smiled to himself. She was beautiful when angry, but she also garnered great respect, for she didn't anger easily and didn't respond unwisely.

Grifynn sat at his desk, pouring o'er the ledgers listing the comings and goings of known Merchants, new Merchant licensing, new Warrior applications, arriving and departing ships, trading goods, as well as the latest bits of 'special' information from his various 'contacts'. He'd already gone o'er the Training schedules, the Trainers' requests for equipment, supply orders for the Den kitchens and Healer supplies, the candidate rosters, as well as the early childhood and adolescent education programs. There'd been subtle oddities in a variety of areas surfacing recently that were unexplained and mayhap focused upon the Port District. Or mayhap not. 'Twas just past midnight, as marked by the candle at the corner of his desk, and he sighed deeply trying to remember the statistics he'd just read. This used to be so easy, he had a perfect memory once, long ago. Afore he'd volunteered. Afore the night that changed their entire world. At least his instincts were still active, and still accurate he'd wager, and they were telling him there was a spy amongst the Clan. He just couldn't prove anything yet. He needed a break, just one small lead in the right direction and he'd be able to find him, to purge him. Toward that end he was considering a new 'contact'. Of course, that only added to the already enormous stress with which he was dealing.

But he was having trouble staying on task. His thoughts kept straying back to the missing blade. Why had Darque's blade not surfaced? He knew 'twas out there, but where? If 'twas taken, who'd taken it and why had it not been revealed? If so revealed, 'twould make it obvious that the Dragon Clan knew of the King's ill fated schemes and foul allegiance. If 'twere still at Kaddart, the Team he'd sent last evening should be able to find it, but he'd heard nothing so far. 'Twas the Warrior Daxx, and what did he call his dragon? He couldn't have sent a Warrior Team this early in the spring in the past, for Kaddart was in a region highly affected by the Spring Melts and would only be accessible a'Dragonback. He smirked as he considered how the Dragon Teams lent a new and useful angle to travel and held great promise of increased knowledge and communication. At least 'twas one good thing about them.

For all but one season, Clear Water Creek meandered lazily around the fields of Kaddart, but with the Spring Melts, 'twould become a raging river spilling o'er its banks, silting and enriching the soil, making their produce some of the best and most sought after in the region. Now the fields lay barren, burned out in the battle, with no one to replant. Could the blade still be there, buried in the silt, forever lost? But if the blade had been there, Darque and the Mighty Blue would've found it when they'd searched the day following the battle. Gunnarr would've been able to Call the steel, for these blades were special and his Magic was strong, almost as imposing as the Fay. Grifynn grimaced in pain with the conscious thought of the Raven. Seemed that Blood Oath was beginning to boomerang a bit. Lately, every time he thought about Corbyn, he'd endured shooting pains in his chest. Was it from the injury or from that damned Oath? He'd never believed in coincidence. 'Twas the Oath 'taking advantage' of the injury, although he had to admit, the Fay had been honest with what he had in fact told him. He'd been warned of the backlash of an unreleased Blood Oath after this many winters. "The Oath was never intended to last more than a few moons, a few winters, the span of days for a Magic Bearer. But for a human, 'twill be new ground we walk. I fear 'twill take advantage of any injury or fault and eventually deteriorate, given your blood, even though 'tis unique," Corbyn had said in his near monotone, devoid of excess emotion.

"I care not," was Grifynn's angry reply. "I will have this Oath on pain of death, or I will do what I must, to end the prophesy."

"You realize you are also bound to silence?"

"Of course I do. I held the highest security clearance my people granted. Don't worry about me holding up my end," Grifynn stated harshly to the one standing afore him. He'd broken eye contact and glanced around the area to ensure none of those who depended on him now, were close enough to see or hear this exchange. Lowering his voice, he painfully related, "I've seen many die horribly, some from wounds inflicted by other Men, but more from wounds inflicted by dragons. I've fought to survive and I've gathered many others, people who count on me to keep them alive. Now I've been told there are 'good dragons'? I'm told I'll have a daughter one day, who will be a great Warrior and will join our Kinds to lead us all? I've even been told what to name her! I've been a soldier all my life. I don't take anyone's word for anything. I must have absolute trust in that dragon and his Kind and there's no other way. If he's not willing to do this, then I will hunt him down with my last breath, and at least one of us will die. If he dies or if I die, either way, that prophesy also dies. You know this to be truth. This is the only way to be sure he will not betray me."

The Battle Commander gradually drifted back to the questionable location of the blade, as the pain began to ease. Taking a ragged breath, he slowly released his grip on the front of his tunic and braced his bare elbow against the edge of the desk. He'd never seen a reason to release the Oath, even after Darque was born. Even after the scar appeared on her thigh. Even after irrefutable evidence that the prophesy was indeed flowing into reality and that all the Mighty Blue had told him was truth. With the exception of The Black, Dragonkind had never betrayed them and they'd actually been strong allies. He finally admitted to himself that the Oath had not quelled his doubts and they still haunted him. Shayla had tried to convince him that his suspicions were a form of paranoia induced from the Blood, but he'd secretly doubted her word.

He leaned forward and rested his forehead upon his arms, just for a moment. Wishing he could sleep, not even sure when he'd last done so, he breathed deeply. Then raising his head once again, he started back through the parchments for the umpteenth time. There was something he was missing and he must find it.

~~~~~~~~~~

As Grifynn studied his lists, I was lying at home, Gunnarr at my side. I was exhausted after spending all day in preparation for our next mission, to check up on some rumors of more Dragon sightings to the East, which may or may not be the Hoard. We had yet to find a solid lead to a possible lair and my gut was telling me the Hoard wouldn't be so stupid as to keep to one place. 'Twas my growing belief the Hoard was plagued with psychotic depravity, but there was intelligence at their core. Going on that theory, I surmised they'd have many smaller lairs, located in a hop scotch pattern 'cross Kadoor, in keeping with their terrorist tactics of hit and run, and I'd long suspected that possibly the largest, if not the main lair, was Evanntyr. After Lorelei, 'twas no doubt, but also no proof.

Rolling restlessly, not comfortable enough to sleep, my eyes jerked open to Linayyah's ear piercing Battle Cry, as if the immense green
~~~~~~~~~~

Dragon was screaming in my face. Gunnarr had Heard the Cry as well, and already snatched the saddle off the hook as I'd leaped up off my blankets. Tossing his great head, he slung the recently revised leather contrivance smoothly o'er his neck even as I donned my boots, making sure all my weapons were secured. Hastening out to the ledge where he stood waiting, I seized the straps hanging down and made quick work securing it around him. He was already in motion, stepping off the ledge when I vaulted aboard, a maneuver we'd practiced to perfection. Remembering the first few attempts, I shuddered in vivid recall of hurdling headlong into the chilling water below.

Barking for backup, Storrm would follow us with two Teams of her choosing. Not surprisingly, she was already heading in our direction as I Cautioned her, *"Keep to the average speed of the others, I'm not prepared to divulge our secrets yet. And don't allow yourself to be seen behind us, I know not what we face. Secure our backs, assist as able, but your standing order is to survive. You must return to the Den to make report, if Gunnarr and I do not."*

Tracing the besieged Team to the southeast, Gunnarr set wing while I gathered my wits and checked my weaponry. My Striker at my belt in a specially made sheathe of Dragon scale and leather, 'twas camouflaged as a charm. The design was ingenious and I had to credit Alric for its creation, for 'twas not only lovely to look at and fully functional, but I could have the weapon in my hand and embedded in hide with blinding speed. At my back was my Thumper, and my short blade, wide and double edged, rode my right thigh.

Urging Gunnarr toward our new found speed, 'twould not take long to complete this journey. Frustrated and angry, I focused on the ensuing battle, Searching for Linayyah, praying she was still alive and we could reach her in time. I Called to the feisty Green, a stark contrast in personality and dimension to Haniyyah, her exceedingly timid and petite sibling, so that she'd know we were on our way. Merely Casting for their Presence in order to set our path to them as quickly as possible, I Asked no questions as 'twould distract them from the fight.

I quickly learned they were at Kaddart. What were they doing out there? Why were they so far away from home and who'd sent them? Surely they'd not ventured off on their own. I'd given no such orders to my Flight. Listening carefully, I Blocked the rush of wind in my ears as I leaned o'er Gunnarr's neck, but I couldn't Hear Daxx. Of course, if Linayyah was still alive so was the Warrior, but 'twas small comfort under the circumstances. 'Twas an ambush, as I didn't believe for a moment that they'd have been so careless as to have been found by strays. Was there a spy amongst our ranks? 'Twouldn't be possible for the Teams to harbor such. At least I didn't think so.

The fields were still flooded, although the waters were receding. *"How many do we face? Where are they? Do you Hear them? Do you Hear Daxx?"* My questions spat forth at lightning speed as we circled around to fly in from the south, trying not to forewarn those battling with Linayyah. They'd be expecting relief to appear from the West, from Drekinn, but I'd Heard precious little since the original Cry and this didn't bode well for them.

"I Sense the Presence of only one of the Hoard. There were several others here recently, then three remained, now two have just Passed the Veil." Gunnarr licked the air, his tongue whipping out to taste the Life Source of the rich organics surrounding us, and then continued, *"They were forced to cross by Daxx and Linayyah. Now I Sense mind-numbing pain, frustration, and anger. I know not what we face, little one. Be prepared for the worst."*

When the bridge came into view my heart near stopped. Once a slow running creek with a name so true to its appearance, the Clear Water had become a raging torrent of mud and debris, rushing just beneath the planks of the blood splattered bridge. Upon the western end stood Daxx, his arms held tightly behind him in the claws of a Hoard Dragon, who sat casually licking the blood off the big man as if savoring a delicacy prior to the feast. Without fear, Daxx defiantly held his tongue, which seemed to anger the beast further. His eyes flickered dangerously black and I could see Linayyah standing restlessly at the opposite end, helpless to rescue her Rider as 'twas obvious the intent was to behead him if she so tried. From the carcasses flanking the pair on the bridge, I deduced Daxx forced one and Linayyah the other, and he was captured afore she could pick him up. The very air around them held a disturbing sensation that made it clear the creature was holding Daxx to taunt Linayyah, but still waited for something or someone. For me?

Instantly, a noxious Voice broke and Shrieked, "I HEAR YOU HALF BREED! ABUSER OF THE BLOOD! YOU WILL NOT LIVE TO SEE THE DAWN!"

Gunnarr also Heard and at the same time I felt his massive bulk twitch 'tween my thighs. This gave me my only warning to hang on, while he pulled up so short and fast he nearly threw me forward off his neck as he chose a suitable landing site. I made no further effort to hide our presence as 'twas apparent we were being greeted openly. I barely had time to register what he'd said and wondered only how I'd Heard this conversation without the relay through my Dragon and why had he called Gunnarr a half breed?

Linayyah was itching to spring forward and finish her antagonist but Daxx was a human shield 'tween them and as much as she wanted revenge for such audacity, she also knew she'd have to kill one and save the other and she couldn't figure out how to do both at the same time. Her indecision was painful to observe.

"Hold your position, Linayyah. We shall not allow this one to leave this day." Encouraging her to stand down, I knew she'd relay the message to Daxx. His eyes were near swollen shut, his body covered with blood, his leathers shredded, and his feet dangled just above the bridge. The Dragon was holding him upright and now I saw that if he wasn't thus held, he'd be down on his face on the planks. Both legs were broken, splintered bone protruded at odd angles, and there was no telling what his internal injuries were. His eyes were glazed, clearly showing how much pain he was in, and the shaking and darkening scales of his Dragon told me how much she was Blocking. 'Twas mind-boggling how he'd maintained consciousness and I was humbled by his fortitude. He'd not show weakness to the Hoard, he'd given us every advantage he could to effect the kill regardless of his own, or Linayyah's safety. They desired only that I act as Death Avenger should this rescue attempt go awry.

Gunnarr Replied calmly, *"We are here. What is it you Seek?"* I understood that Gunnarr meant for me to keep silent, to let the beast think I Heard only what was relayed through the 'Bond.

The beast seemed confused when my Dragon answered for me, apparently thinking I could Communicate with him myself. How and why did he get that idea? The Dragon turned his attention away from me and Hissed his response to Gunnarr, *"Your Passing. Your deaths shall end the prophesy, and the Hoard shall rule Kadoor once again!"* At this point, my Hearing was no longer odd. 'Twas as suspected, and 'twas not the first time I'd noted my ability to Speak and Hear as the Dragons did. Accepting the phenomenon and determined to research it further, I'd learn how to use it to my advantage. With these thoughts came a rumble of approval from Gunnarr as we landed close to the eastern end of the bridge, upon the road surrounding the soggy fields. I didn't want to reveal my backup plan, knowing Storrm and her Teams would soon flank them. Having never shut down our Link, she'd followed the situation and we rapidly devised a plan as the dialogue continued with the enemy. 'Twas not a great plan, but 'twas the best we could manage under these conditions.

Linayyah was crowding her end of the bridge and the creature would think his back was safe with me approaching from the same direction. 'Twas in my mind to walk boldly up to him, distracting him with my own insolence, which would surely create confusion, and then once close enough, Storrm would make known her presence from behind, at which time I hoped to get my one and only chance to use my Striker to attack. If I could just free Daxx and wound the creature, he'd have no further chance 'tween Linayyah, Gunnarr, Mystynn, and two others of my Flight. This Dragon wouldn't return to his comrades to disclose our newest weapons and strategies, regardless of what happened to me. Oddly, this gave me all the determination and strength I required.

I dismounted slowly, stepping carefully upon the thick silt. Keeping my eyes riveted to the beast, I walked toward Linayyah, leaving Gunnarr upon the road. *"I don't care for the odds in this plan, my sweet,"* he Spoke softly, as if the other could Hear him if he was any louder.

Following his lead, I Replied, *"Nor do I, my love. But if you happen to think of another which may have better odds, please don't hesitate to share."* Gunnarr near snorted at my quip, as I tried not to reveal to the one manhandling Daxx, that I was thus in Link.

Of course Storrm added her thoughts to the conversation and Told us, *"Don't bother Gunnarr, she's always been headstrong, but she's also blessed by the One True Liege. She will not fail."* Gunnarr believed her, but I Heard the concern in her Voice. By the Fates, she'd better not be wrong, for to fail here and now would mean the end of everything. This feeling was so strong I was nearly inundated with Battle Lust. Not that I felt I was that important, for 'twas merely to boost our numbers that I was needed, but there was some kind of prophesy.

Storrm and those with her, Kydra and Ragnyrr, and Apryya and Dannyrkyn, would appear soon, and I had to move slowly to set this plan in motion with the best chance to succeed. They'd need sufficient time to get here, without being here long enough for the Hoard Dragon to perceive them. I also had to keep his attention upon me and not Casting about, or he might Sense them too soon. Added to this, I needed to keep him off guard and make him think I was arrogant, slow and stupid, in order to get close enough to execute my plan. I'd learned the Hoard had a bully's mentality, delaying their attacks to feed their egos, and they were surprised by our resistance. My plan depended on being considered an easy target. As I trudged from the soggy field toward the bridge, I was re-lieved he hadn't yet sensed my Striker and Shield.

Storrm kept a running but minimal dialogue of their location as I stepped onto the bridge, the roar of the rushing water beneath my boots making anything but the MindSpeak near impossible to hear. Linayyah, having been Informed of the plan, stepped aside so I could squeeze past and then crowded up behind me in her fretfulness. I had to stop and placed my hand upon her lowered muzzle to calm her. She Spoke, imploring me to Hear, *"We were taken completely by surprise. They anticipated our arrival. There can be no doubt they knew we were coming. They toyed with us, tried to force us to Call you, but we took down two of them afore this one captured my Daxx. I couldn't contain my Cry, m'lady, and he knew you were responding. 'Twas all a trap, they wish not your live capture. They want you DEAD!"* Taking my eyes briefly off the enemy, I gently pushed her back and then turned away. I couldn't acknowledge I'd Heard her, but Gunnarr kept her focused enough to stick to the plan. If the Green broke ranks early, 'twould get me killed for sure. When I was three Dragon lengths away from the massive, foul smelling beast, the aura of pain seeped through me from Daxx and I grit my teeth to keep from hurling.

"WHAT DO YOU WANT?" I yelled at the beast, just barely able to hear my own voice, and trying not to look at the broken Warrior. "WHY DO YOU HESITATE TO KILL HIM?" 'Twas a calculated risk I took, that he'd not simply do so now, with such provocation. Slowly I inched my way forward, covertly closing the gap. Deep in Battle Lust, his agitation was increasing. He could lose his reason at any moment and my plan would be useless, my Team gone, but this one wouldn't live to regret his stupidity.

"I want YOU, this one is of no consequence! And you will drop your long sword!" His growl was barely understandable in Common. I'd managed to gain near a third of the distance toward the beast without his noticing. Slowly, I unstrapped my long sword and tossed it behind me, hoping he didn't notice the short blade at my thigh. The plan had to work, for I'd no way to reach his heart without my long sword. Distracting him by glancing o'er my shoulder at Linayyah and Gunnarr, I not only covered my movements, I also made him think they were my only backup while I continued our dialog. He'd insisted I show him my hands and keeping them at shoulder level as I moved ever closer, 'twould take me a mere fraction of a heartbeat to arm myself. Daxx struggled to remain conscious, squirming just enough to block the creature's view occasionally, forcing him to change his grasp to continue to use him as a shield, and helping to distract the beast further.

Time stood still, but even though Storrm and her Teams were arriving, they were still too distant to pull off the original plan. The fetid brute was losing patience and when he made his move to decapitate Daxx, I went into action. Mid-sentence with the beast, and still one Dragon length away, I simultaneously dropped my left hand for my Striker, grabbed my short sword with my right hand, and charged. My Battle Cry upon my lips, the creature's eyes flew open. He was so entrenched in Battle Lust that he hesitated, fumbled with the killing strike on the Warrior and instead, lost his grip as I ran headlong straight into him. So stunned by this tactic, he jerked sideways to avoid me, which pushed Daxx off the edge into the freezing water. I barely managed to leap o'er his legs as he tumbled past, but I couldn't take the time to avert his plunge. As quickly as he'd submerged, I was 'tween the Dragon's forepaws, too close for him to step back and get a swipe at me afore I used my Striker, flaying his chest open with a vicious left upper cut quickly followed by a right drive, plunging the short blade deep into his heart, afore his Healing could stop me.

When he'd been struck, he'd near crushed me in his fall, managing to spit forth a tiny stream of Flame that was mostly shed by my Thumper, but my left shoulder was scorched. Gunnarr flew in to finish the beast afore he could take me with him 'cross the Veil. Unable to use his Flame or he might injure me, he grabbed the creature by his head just in time to keep me from being completely flattened. The strike had been true and he was weakened, allowing Gunnarr to haul him swiftly to the tree line of the nearby forest, ferociously slinging him against a huge trunk, the force separating his head from his body. I'd risen to my knees upon the bridge and watched this kill strategy with admiration.

Storrm and her Teams came into view and immediately searched for other Dragons in the area, making sure we'd not been detected and there was no rescue attempt in the making. Linayyah had rushed to save Daxx from the river almost afore he'd disappeared and she pulled his soaked and near frozen body from the rapidly moving waters with her strong jaws. The big man was dwarfed so carried, but she was gentle even in Battle Lust. Mercifully he'd lost consciousness from the pain when he was pushed aside, and was still not awake. The icy dip might have stopped the bleeding, but the only good sign was that Linayyah still lived.

Storrm and Mystynn sent the others ahead to prepare the Healer for our return. Then Linayyah took wing, not allowing anyone else to assist her in her efforts to transport Daxx home. Gunnarr and I had to head her off, ordering her to stand down and change her path to the Den, for she was in such pain she was not thinking clearly and had attempted to take him eastward. I could sense she was heading toward Fire Heart. In a way, I understood this to mean they'd completely accepted us as equals in not just the War, but in life. 'Twas sweet in its innocence and I was honored by her unconscious gesture. I prayed they lived so I could relate the story to them both o'er a fire pit at our next Gathering, for I knew that neither of them would remember much of this night.

Leaving Storrm and Mystynn to cover their retreat and ensure Daxx and Linayyah were delivered to the Healer, Gunnarr and I disappeared o'er the horizon ahead of them all and swiftly returned to the Den. I was going to have a Command discussion with my father.

~~~~~~~~~~

Barging into his office, pushing my way roughly past the astonished Standing Guard, I must have been dizzy with fatigue and pain. For an instant as I entered the room, I thought I sensed a third presence. But no one had passed by me on my way in, and there was obviously no one else in the room but the two of us, so I ignored the sensation as I stood at Battle Ease in front of his heavy desk. Still a Warrior, I impatiently awaited his nod to speak, my posture anything but 'at ease'. As a quarter mark dripped slowly past, my accelerated heart rate gradually returned to non-Lust level, significantly lower than those not in 'Bond. The red haze o'er my vision was gone by the time he finally deigned to acknowledge my existence. Why had he sent my Team out alone and what had he hoped to accomplish?

He didn't look up. "I sent Daxx and that dragon back out to investigate the Battle of Kaddart, and I hoped they'd find your blade." I hadn't asked aloud, 'twas still a thought in my mind. What the Flame was going on here? But my original focus was side tracked by the obvious disrespect for our LifeBond partners and the Dragon Race in general, thrust into the open 'tween us in his casual statement. 'Twas a disturbing development which he'd shown with growing intensity since their return. I stood afore him covered with dried blood and sweat, still trying to catch my breath. The battle had taken its toll, with multiple lacerations and rib fractures, along with a relatively minor Flame burn upon my left shoulder, all of which were Healing, and my emotions were still raw. Dragonkind was a sentient Race who'd given up much to help Mankind in the Black War, and they deserved to be treated with respect. I'd tolerated enough.

"Linayyah," I said, 'tween clenched teeth. My body temperature was rising as I purposefully stood my ground. Never mind that I should've been knowledgeable of that order, should've known that plan afore he'd sent the Team alone to perform a redundant investigation of a Battle in which I'd been intimately involved. 'Twas this increasingly troubling bigotry that had my temper flaring.
~~~~~~~~~~

"What?" He appeared slightly bewildered and looked up from his cluttered desk, peering at me o'er the parchment he held in his hand. Nevertheless, his deceit was plain. 'Twas an odd impression in the air that something was going on and I was missing out, but the easing of Battle Lust made me shrug off his subtle redirection. At that moment, I could handle only one concept at a time and making an attempt to Cast would require more focus than I was capable of giving. "His Dragon's name is Linayyah… Sir." I repeated. My ribs had Healed, but the Flame wound along my shoulder would take awhile longer. I sucked in my breath when yet another lightening like pain flashed up my neck to the back of my head. Hopefully, not too much longer.

He was first to break eye contact and dropped his gaze. Waving his hand in the air flippantly, he tried to dismiss the matter. "Oh whatever, it's a dragon. I can't be expected to remember all their names."

This had to stop. I couldn't understand this attitude, and I didn't care about any feeble explanations. Anger burned in my heart as a line was crossed 'tween us. He must have noticed it and actually looked up with some surprise, as I stepped forward aggressively, firmly stating, "Sir. You are the Battle Commander, with literally thousands of Warriors under your Command, and you've known every common name, surname, their siblings, their Horse, their Dog, where they were stationed, their favorite colors and pastimes, even what they preferred for evening meal." I felt his riveted attention and something else I couldn't quite make out, as I continued, "My Dragon Teams are unmatched in fighting skills and have pledged their lives for Mankind. I will not allow you, or anyone, to be disrespectful." I finished my rant with a snarl, my fearless resolve made clear in both my posture and the intense stare down.

Grifynn broke first, as he knew he would, his shoulders elevated, his broad back stiffened and for a long moment he didn't move, his eyes upon his desk. When had he become so easily angered? How had he lost his Battle Focus? His daughter stood afore him now, a strong leader in her own right, and having forced her to defend her Flight, her Teams, her rank, she'd done so admirably. How proud he was of her. He'd always been proud, but somehow he'd rarely found the means to convey the sentiment. 'Twouldn't be long now, and he was satisfied that he was leaving the Clan in good hands. If she managed to survive the next few critical moons, she'd be the Leader of whom the prophesy had spoken. There was nothing more he could teach her, no further wisdom to impart, he'd been the best father and Battle Commander he'd known how to be, and what happened next was up to her and the Fates. This war would not end quickly, as did the Last Holocaust. No, this would be the war of all wars, and 'twould take every bit of prophesy, skill and strength to win against the Evil One. His only regret was that he'd not see her bloom into her full potential, a far superior fighter and leader than he'd ever been.

CHAPTER 22

The Krakken

TWO DAWNS AFORE THE DRAW

"I'm positive we've uncovered something significant, Second. I'm certain 'twill lead to a cache of what we seek!" Ariel's excitement was contagious and I was encouraged. To have the Magical fangs and talons circulated into the general public was a ghastly thought, but to find a stash for our own use would be great news. She and Rygyl had just returned from their mission. They'd been hard pressed for the barest scrap of information o'er the past three moons, but had to return in preparation for the Draw, less than a sennight after establishing a viable lead.

Leaving Tegrynn upon the ledge outside the entrance to the Cave of Voices, Zaydarr had taken wing to hunt less than a mark prior.

"'Twas not so surprising to find evidence of Black Market dealings, as 'twas the increasing rumors of Dragons being seen in and around Lorelei," Rygyl exclaimed in disgust. "Ethynn and Makayyd may well have located a lair, Darque. And according to our findings, the Hoard is increasing exponentially. Even now 'tis unmistakable we're outnumbered by at least a dozen to one. Don't get me wrong, every Warrior has faced foul odds in one battle or another and prevailed, but they grow against us daily. We sorely need the Draw and the next 'Bond. If we don't reinforce our numbers soon, we stand little chance."

None of us could ever be accused of backing away from a righteous battle and our attitude of superiority had kept us alive in devastating situations. We were bred and trained to be our enemy's worst nightmare, but what had just been confirmed made me leery. 'Twas entirely possible for even the 'Bonded to succumb, if faced with such numbers. We were not invincible.

"I will fight 'cross the Veil with you at my back, Darque." The strapping Warrior bid me goodnight as he reached for my arm, and pulled me tight against his chest. I grasped him just as tightly in return, placed my other hand upon his shoulder and replied in kind, "'Til we are forced to cross together, my friend." Then he stepped aside for Ariel to approach, and in parting she hugged me saying, "Take pleasure in the night, for we know not what comes on the 'morrow." Searching her eyes, I suspected something had changed for the solitary Warrior. She'd always been reserved. She had no close personal ties, to the best of my knowledge she'd never taken a lover, and had no family outside of the Brotherhood. She'd been losing hope. Glancing at Rygyl, I caught the look of devotion in his eyes as he stared at her, and looking back at the pretty girl afore me, understanding that love grew 'tween them, I replied, "With the dawn, each day springs anew, my sister."

Encircling her wrist were several loops of tightly braided auburn hair. 'Twas Clan tradition for a male to make such a promise chain from his own locks, and she smiled when she noticed my quizzical expression.

"Rygyl has asked me to share vows, Second," Ariel said quietly. But then her expression matched mine and she continued in confusion, "but our Dragons will not allow us to…" and she blushed from head to toe as she peeked toward the cave entrance where Zaydarr had just landed and switched places with Tegrynn, allowing her to hunt, apparently not wanting to leave their 'Bonds alone.

Teasing her, I smiled wickedly as I kept my eyes upon Rygyl, who was now beginning to squirm himself. Then I said sweetly, "Won't allow you to… what?"

Her look of dismay was such that I thought to let it go, but afore I could ease out of the conversation she blurted, "Consummate!" Her hands slapped o'er her mouth and Rygyl burst into laughter.

We all joined in, and laughed 'til we cried. Finally regaining our breath, we sat on the rock floor of the huge cave, but they were exhausted and needed to rest.

Afore they made their leave together, Rygyl came o'er to speak to me privately. "Seriously Second, do you know why they feel as they do? We can't be intimate, for our 'Bonds will part us. For near three moons we've dealt with the frustration of not being able to do more than hold hands. Interestingly enough, 'tis not anger we feel from them, but a great sadness. 'Tis difficult to explain and most confusing. I love Ariel and I want her to be mine. She feels the same way about me, and we are promised one to the other. I just never thought about how 'twould affect our Dragons. I know not if this situation has occurred afore, but if the others have any knowledge that might help us, please tell me. 'Tis driving us both to distraction, Darque! With our enhanced senses 'tis not difficult to tell when the other is aroused. What are we to do?"

At that time I heard Tegrynn arriving on the ledge. I knew something wasn't right, for they'd both returned from their hunts too quickly, and seemed to have great difficulty being parted from their 'Bonds.

Assuring Rygyl that I'd confer with the Ancients about the situation and let him know of what I discovered, the love struck pair turned to leave in the company of their Dragons.

Suddenly, Rygyl turned back and exclaimed, "Oh! I near forgot to mention. I thought it rather unusual that at every Port along the coast we felt a strange Allure. 'Twas not to do with the Hoard, for it didn't have the taste of Evil. Still, 'twas a Presence along the docks that seemed somehow out of place, like a nagging memory that can't be brought forth when desired. If it hadn't been so bloody consistent, and had Ariel not noted the same phenomenon most strongly this night, along the entire length of our own Port District, 'twould have been disregarded."

~~~~~~~~~~

The Krakken arrived just prior to midnight, amidst a Magical haze produced routinely whenever they traveled off their homeland. No one noticed the huge ship tying up at the docks. 'Twas not invisible, 'twas simply… ignored. The shore from whence it sailed wasn't on any current map, and the ship wasn't registered at any port, but had weighed anchor at all of them at one time or another. Port O'Drekinn was the most frequented however and the crew was particularly familiar with the mainland of this region.

The woman's voice chimed through the chill night air as she crossed the quarterdeck, "Myrrdin, you've stood with me these many winters and it pleases me to name you my most trusted friend," Caleichante said to the striking Ship's Master. Her leather vanguards were old, and stained with the blood of many adversaries, worn as a badge of her courage and success as a fighter, as much as to protect her arms. Myrrdin's gaze drifted from them up to her pale bare shoulders, muscled from winters of specialized training. Her tight leather halter top and britches barely covered her willowy frame, and left little to the imagination. Her knee length white blonde hair was straight and heavy, pulled back in a single tail and tied with a plain leather strip, wrapped in a criss cross pattern. As tall as she was, the one to whom she spoke stood head and shoulders taller.

"It's been my pleasure, cousin, and there's none other I would entrust with your mission," he replied with an elegant bow in his equally melodic, but greater timbered voice. His long straight black hair was pulled back as was hers, the lustrous color matching his eyes. Lithe, ever youthful, the tall, pale skinned man saw her need, and reached forth to the Elite Body Guard for the Sprite Royals. Instead of merely sharing a warrior's grip, he pulled her close to him and whispered in her delicately pointed ear, "Your
~~~~~~~~~~

undertaking is righteous, there's no other who stands a chance, no other could survive and succeed. Dance through the Shadows, Drink from the richest Life Forces, complete your task and return home safely to us."

Grinning, she pulled reluctantly out of the embrace and replied, "You know I cannot Dance the Shadows with my charges, though 'twould be quicker. 'Twould be a beacon to the Hoard, with the cargo I carry. And the boy's injury is not Healing. If he should falter within the Shadows, well, 'twill be safer for us to go by land for now. 'Tis why I confiscated your horse!" And with that, she leaped lightly o'er the railing and hastened below deck.

Incredulously, he responded to her disappearing backside, "What? Demonseed will not allow another to ride him, 'tis insanity! There are plenty of others aboard!"

She reappeared a moment later, leading a spirited black stallion with flashing red eyes. The sleek horse restlessly scanned the pier below, his nostrils flaring as she mounted behind the child already upon his blanketed back. The frail looking boy clutched a camp roll and a saddlebag, and Myrrdin knew 'twas not for her comfort. She was the best of the best, and could live off the land without difficulty. But the boy was weakened, and there was also the cargo she carried, which counted as the other half of her duty. Without saddle or reins or need thereof, she hugged the fragile child tightly to her chest with one hand, and reached forth to ensure the saddlebag latches were secure.

"None as swift as yours!" She exclaimed o'er her shoulder, her pale eyes sparkling. Leaning o'er the snorting animal, she grabbed a handful of his thick silky mane and quietly implored him as if in prayer, "Go with the wind!" Demonseed reared up upon his muscular haunches and then he was racing off the gangplank and down the long dock, so fast he seemed not to even touch the timbers beneath his hooves. Her white hair flying behind her, he had no time to retort, and in an instant they disappeared into the Port District. Not a soul took notice as they raced past.

Myrrdin could do naught but shake his head at her daring. Quickly scanning the pier, he made certain no one had seen the dramatic departure. 'Twas a critical situation and had multiple hazards and assignments to complete against incredible odds, but even alone, he'd place his wager on Caleichante to succeed. His pride showing in the gleam of his eyes, for he'd been her trainer after all, he glanced to the heavens above and whispered, "Corbyn, if you can spare some time from that curse of yours, we could use a little help here…" Sighing, his piece in this action complete, he hailed his crew to ease out of port, and set sail. He hoped to reach clear waters by dawn, where he expected to receive information for their next assignment. Someone needed to arrange confidential and swift passage for another, within a moon. 'Twould take much Magic. He swaggered back to his cabin with a wicked grin on his handsome face. Magic was his very name.

CHAPTER 23

The Draw

TWO DAWNS LATER, NEAR END OF SPRING;
NEAR FIVE MOONS FROM THE 'BOND

My Sword is long, dual edged and light,
forged by the breath of my Dragon's Might,
with Dragon Strength and Dragon Magic,
drawn from the heavens as m'Liege would have it.

"So. There's no other demonstrating such?" I sat in the sand of the Cave of Jewels and faced my sister, as we continued our discussion on the effects of the LifeBond. Scooping up a handful and pouring it slowly out again, I watched it flow like a miniature waterfall, building up o'er my feet. Wiggling my toes free of the grit, I picked up another handful and repeated the process, while I contemplated the upcoming ritual. The Draw would be staged in mere marks and we'd been spending every moment for the last two dawns, in study and preparation for the expected trial. There was nothing more to be accomplished, nothing more we could do to get ready. Now we were trying to relax. My last stop had been with Warrior Regynn, who was hopeful he'd take the 'Bond in the Second, within the next fortnight. In my mind, his capacity to take the Magic would mean that no one was exempt merely upon his own skills or strengths. We'd opened the door for many more sources for our Teams. 'Twas heartening for certain, but Regynn wasn't the only Elder to make this attempt. Joining him would be Tannyr, the eldest brother of the murdered Runner, Tonn, along with his middle brother Daayn. The Elders making this stand alongside those younger and stronger, each had special skills and talents, each had been prime fighters in their careers, and the Magic would guarantee they were fully able to be such again.

Multiple quandaries ran through my mind and I ticked them off: survival through the Draw, First Flight had valuable experience and were being depended upon to raise and train the new Stables to come, 'twould weaken the Ancients, and the Second LifeBond was scheduled within days with the Third swiftly following. The issues left me fatigued and even at this late mark, my resolve began to waver. We risked much, but the rewards would be great indeed.

Storrm was watching our partners bathe in the cool clear water, with yearning in her eyes. I'd never seen that look upon her face afore and yet I was familiar with the emotion that warmed her and made her blue eyes sparkle. 'Twas love. Now I understood how much our parents must have struggled. His responsibilities left barely any time to devote to, or enjoy, a relationship. But where they'd been separated frequently and sacrificed much, Storrm and I were tied to the ones for whom we so cared. At least we'd always be close to each other, even if we had little else.

Shifting her attention from Mystynn's antics, she watched the sand flow from my palm to the ever growing pile o'er my feet. Then she lifted her face to mine and replied simply, "No, I've seen nothing to indicate there's another with such skills. We can fly faster than I'd dreamed possible; I don't know how to describe it. I can barely see the ground below me as it rushes past, the mountains and plains go by in a blur. I estimate we're now traveling twice as fast as the others, although we can't sustain this speed for long. But who knows how 'twill alter in the coming moons? And I've also noted this phenomenon which you describe, although not to the extent you seem to be enjoying, of 'lending' my strength. What's truly fascinating is that those I so benefit seem totally unaware. Mayhap they believe the boost is from their own Dragon." Instead of her usual exuberance, she spoke slowly, considering her experiences afore she continued. "Mystynn has no explanation for why the Dragons themselves haven't noticed, but we both feel we should keep these talents to ourselves for now." She smiled, adding, "I know what you're thinking, dear sister. Even prior to the 'Bond we were different from the other children. We've always been different, only becoming more obvious since taking the Magic." When she finished, she chewed on her bottom lip, an overt indicator that she had much on her mind.

After a slight hesitation, I responded. "I agree with your assessment, our flight speed has also increased rapidly however, I believe 'tis still a secret so far. As for the strengthening, I initially thought 'twas a 'Bond benefit, for 'twas similar to the Healing. But I've discovered since, that I'm truly able to assist others and I believe it comes from my own…" Faltering, I pondered whether or not I should admit to this, but seeing the growing awareness in Storrm's eyes, I finished, "….Magic."

Her eyes narrowed, her lips pursed. Looking briefly at her hands she nodded her head and then faced me with resolution. "I agree. I know not how or why, Darque, but by some means we bear our own Magic, free and clear of the 'Bond. Lately I've begun to believe we've always held such in our grasp." Suddenly her expression changed from wonder to confusion and she blurted, "Are we not Clan? Are we not of Man?"

Since I'd had the same ideas and had arrived at the same conclusions, I could empathize. Needing to comfort her as well as calm myself, I answered, "Does it really matter what we are, or from whence we came? Our hearts are Clan, our purpose is the protection of Mankind. We took the Oath and entered the Brotherhood. Our lives, our actions, our allegiance, carry more weight than our origins. There's much of which we're still ignorant. I'm led to believe the saga of our beginning is as deep and mysterious as the Wells, and we may never know the full extent. But fear not, my sister, for I also believe that all is unfolding as it should." Lifting my feet, I brushed off the sand and headed to the pool for one final rinse. I helped her up as I passed by, and pulled her along with me to the clear water. Lightening the mood with my laughter, I said, "We have to make ready. By dawn we shall be the first to wield a Dragon Sword since the Beginning of Time!"

~~~~~~~~~~

Circling high o'er the sacred ground, we flew in funnel formation, tiered one above the other like a Sand Demon upon the Dragon's Breath, or a Wind Demon upon the Great Plains. In helping to gather and concentrate the Magic of the area to this one point, three Teams each had flown in from the East, the West, the North and the South, with Gunnarr and I flying highest of all, spiraling in from above, to close the circular flight pattern. Looking straight up, each Team flew at their level, each circle tightened as we descended, and all of us were visible at the same time. The lowest Team landed, dismounted and stripped, giving everything to his Dragon but his sword and a thick piece of leather. Finally, each Dragon ambled off to stand in his assigned place, assisting the Ancients. In this manner we grounded and centered the area, increasing the potency of the available Magic for the Brew, as well as helping to acclimate our bodies. When all the Teams had thus entered, The Mighty Maahayyel stepped forth.

'Twas dusk in the waning light of the setting sun, and the thirteen Warriors of First Flight found themselves upon sacred ground once more, bare skin exposed to the cool early summer air. Winter had passed quickly, the Spring Melts had completed their full Rush from the mountains of the Far Northlands to the plains below, and from there to the oceans beyond. Now, Spring passed to Summer.

Maahayyel was awe inspiring as usual. 'Twas impossible not to feel the vast influence of energy that practically oozed from her scales. We stood
~~~~~~~~~~

flanking each other, near shoulder to shoulder in a rough circle 'round the Ancient Dragon, naked of all but our primary weapon, each holding the small piece of thick leather. That request had been cleared through Gunnarr earlier with the Matriarch, and the Ancients had agreed 'twould make no difference in the Brew, but I wanted to save our teeth. Each of us had a death grip upon our hilts that we dared not loose. Of course we'd been told of what to expect, and having survived the 'Bond, 'twas slightly more knowledge to garner our respect. Afore we'd mounted up to begin the gathering, I'd given my Warriors one last, though vital, piece of advice. "We may all face the Veil tonight, but you cannot be forced Past unless you lose your sword. Whatever else you may do, don't… let… go." Our usual arrogant manner cast aside, we made eye contact all around as afore battle, silently encouraging each other to hold on and stand firm. Storrm and I locked gazes for the briefest of moments, affirming our plan to assist the others if we could, but above all, we must survive. Although she'd initially opposed this order, 'twas necessary for the Clan and the war effort. She wasn't to extend her own strength to assist another, if 'twould put herself in danger. She'd argued we needed all to survive. I'd countered if we couldn't survive on our own, how would the Second Draw or the next, or the ones thereafter, fare? We couldn't possibly be present for every ritual, though 'twould be my preference. No, each of us would have to survive on our own, just as we'd survived the LifeBond itself. She'd been forced to see my logic and had agreed to my terms.

Above was the glimmering prism bubble of the Shield, concealing and containing the energy within. Gunnarr and Mystynn had organized this sideline effort, but weren't a part of the actual Casting or Holding, since they were participating in the Brew.

'Twas quiet as we waited, sword tips in the sand at our feet. The Ancients would Draw the Magic from every living thing surrounding us, and channel it simultaneously through the sand and the air to the Warriors. Even the air pressure would alter from the surge of energy, the atmosphere charged with the massive storm 'twould create. As if orchestrating a symphony, they'd guide this Power to clash in the middle, forcing it up from below as a geyser, and down from above as if struck by a bolt of lightning, to forge together within the cold steel. But 'twas more than just a simple Spell, and to bind this Magic to an inanimate object 'twould have to be 'offered' by an organic being, and that being's Life Force required protection from the enormous surge. To do this, our bodies would have to be completely immersed in the energy rising from below, a process that was excruciatingly painful, and just as this was completed, both ends of the object would be touched by the Power, ascending and descending at the same moment. Thus channeling the Magic 'twould keep it from centering upon our bodies, while it also dragged along a part of our psyche to be infused forever within the weapon. If anything broke this circle, 'twould disrupt the Power, resulting in a lightening like explosion that we'd not survive. Lost grip or imperfect timing, and the Ancients theorized we'd simply turn to ash with the released energy, similar to being Flamed at close range.

"Are you ready, Flame Spitter?" Gunnarr's pride prevailed o'er his fear for my safety.

I clenched the piece of leather firmly 'tween my teeth and Replied, *"I am ready. No doubts, no regrets."* The others followed my lead and as one, we took a two-fisted grip upon our swords, widened our stance, and lowered our heads. With our eyes upon the sands, we heard the soft chanting of the Ancients. 'Twas beginning.

I knew not what happened around me from that moment forth. The chanting grew ever louder and more insistent to my ears and I began to feel heat surround me, tiny wisps of steam rising at my feet. What had been a rhythmic droning during the LifeBond, became increasingly harsh and irritating. The sand began squirming as if something huge was crawling toward me just beneath the surface. Fighting my instincts to lower my sword and kill that which I knew wasn't there, the sand spider, the desert scorpion, or….no, 'twas Magic and I mustn't falter. Ignoring the nearly choking impression that I was about to be bitten by something noxious, I shifted my attention to the night sky. 'Twas a low thunderous rumbling, coming ever nearer. Darkness fell rapidly, the clouds loomed menacingly, the ever increasing flashes of lightening near blinding. I tried not to focus upon the churning sands beneath me, as my body grew warmer, tingling up my feet and ankles. The air was charged with the building storm, my hair began to float away, spraying forth in all directions. Casting to assess my Warriors, my effort was Blocked and I pulled back unto myself. The heat and crawling sensation became ever more uncomfortable, and then suddenly I was on fire as if standing in a pit of vipers, or within the anthills of the Dragon's Breath. The rolling thunder was deafening, the chanting roared in my ears, I was in more pain than I'd ever felt in my life, and I dared not move. The burning Magic from the sands traveled up my body to my hips, and I feared 'twould cause me to stumble and lose my sword. Standing firm, the fiery sensation climbed up my waist making me feel I'd soon hurl, yet my resolve didn't waver. This couldn't take much longer, I wasn't the only one struggling, so I held on tightly, renewing my Oath again and again in my mind, to help give me focus and strength. Engulfed to my shoulders in the upward spiral, I held my breath as it filled the rest of me rapidly, leaving me feeling as if I was being held underwater, suffocating. From out of the blindness came swirls of color, and in the distance I heard the unbroken chanting as the Magic surged up my arms to my hands. But as if alive, it hesitated to finish filling where my skin contacted my sword. Just when I could hold my breath no longer, came the loudest clap of thunder yet, and then an enormous burst of power hit the tip of my sword, at the same instant the Magic finished filling my body and then rushed upward to clash together within the blade! At the same time, I Heard Gunnarr Yelling through the tempest, *"HOLD ON MY LOVE, DO NOT LOOSE YOUR GRIP!"* As one, the Warriors Screamed their defiance into the night, and clenching my teeth upon the leather, fighting the powerful surges trying to rip my sword out of my grasp, I joined in the Battle Cry of my Fleet, *"This Dragon Sword is MINE!"*

<center>~~~~~~~~~~</center>

Blinking my bleary eyes, I discovered I was lying upon my back in the sand. My face was wet from the gently falling rain, which was all that was left of the storm. I could barely see my Warriors, still lying unconscious, their faces turned up, their swords still gripped firmly in their hands. Jerking, I was relieved to find I was still grasping my own. When I tried to sit up, Gunnarr held me down with one huge talon tip against my chest, and I lost consciousness once more.

<center>~~~~~~~~~~</center>

Much later I woke again, lying on my bed at home. Gunnarr was softly snoring, stretched out with his wing laid o'er me. I had the odd impression my Sword was hovering in the air by the head of my bed, but my vision was still fuzzy, and I was surely mistaken. There was a bag of water within reach and taking a deep drink I thought about what had happened and how the others had fared. Exhausted, I extricated myself from Gunnarr as he stirred to wake.

"How long..." I Began, but our thoughts crossed o'er each other with his Response, *"Last night. You've been asleep for a mere few marks. The sun just rises."* 'Twas both pride and fatigue in his Voice and kneeling in front of him, I caressed his snout. He sighed and after closing his eyes and briefly leaning into my touch, we stood up, gathered our supplies, and went to the cavern.

~~~~~~~~~~~

"Call your Sword, Warrior," Gunnarr Spoke, after reviewing the happenings I'd missed. Sitting waist deep in the water, I'd listened intently to how we'd all stood the test, and there were now thirteen new Dragon Swords in existence in Kadoor. The Draw had greatly weakened the Ancients, although they'd all survived. There'd been a tense moment when Kaahayyel had all but succumbed to the Power load through her system. Her near loss had weakened them further, and the Ancients and some of the others who'd assisted, retreated with her to Flight Of Fire Keep upon Fire Heart Island, to rejuvenate. The rest of my Flight were still sleeping off their grueling efforts, with Gunnarr and I the only ones awake and alert, but all were safe within their own caves.

Gunnarr reminded me that two of the Dragons who'd retreated with Kaahayyel were her own children, his cousins. Shraadarr and Krynnarr were up for the Second, and were siblings of Ariel's Zayddarr. I'd remembered these familial ties earlier, but it had slipped my mind. Sighing in consternation, I had to give my father more credit. Although I'd recently used his memory against him in an argument, 'twas no lie. He knew every Warrior and all about every Warrior, while I seemed to be fumbling with my own immediate 'family'.

Gunnarr Repeated himself, more clearly this time, *"Call your Sword, Warrior,"* and afore I could think about the fact that a Sword was an inorganic thing, I obeyed his insistent command and Called as to a friend I'd not seen in a long time.

Immediately, there was a whisper of air movement in my face, the palm of my hand felt the weight of the hilt, and I found myself holding the Sword as if I'd just drawn it forth from its scabbard upon my back. Delighted, I exclaimed aloud, "We shall never lose it! How far away can we expect the Sword to heed our Call, is there a limit of distance or location? Could someone hold it down, or bury it, or what if 'twas dropped in the ocean?"

Laughing in his Dragon rumble, Gunnarr Replied, *"There's nothing on Kadoor that can prevent the Sword from heeding the Call of its partner. The arrival time can vary depending upon all of the things you mentioned, mostly distance, however, may the gods have mercy on the one who attempts to hold it back from its Calling."* The image this invoked, of someone trying to hold my Sword down thusly, was such that it made me tremble. 'Twould be a bloody mess indeed.
~~~~~~~~~~~

"'Twill carve scale, hide, and bone, and I can Call it forth from whence 'tis, which is extremely useful. Is there anything else I should know?" I Asked with wonder.

"There's much to learn, my love. Dragon Swords aren't sentient, being inanimate, however they're as near to that state of being as is possible, through Magic and with the infusion of part of you within the steel. The Sword will never lose its Power, and it cannot be destroyed. There's nothing that can change what has been done. No one else can wield your Sword while you yet live, but others may or may not be able to, upon your Passing, for each has its own 'personality'. They react when they're close to kin, with other Dragon Swords considered the closest, however, there are rumors that some Swords were able to perceive other Magic Bearers and gave warning of such to their partners." I was amazed as he Spoke, relating the history of my Sword. Seemed the edge wouldn't dull unless 'twas angry with me, which had my eyebrows furrowed. Angry with me? What in Hades did that mean? "It's a Flaming Sword!" I'd said out loud, once we'd covered several more points about 'handling' and 'management'. "What do you mean, I don't have to sharpen the edge? What if the Sword gets upset with me amid battle? What then? Do I Pass the Veil because me Sword was upset?" My voice was rising, my anger heating, even my accent was more evident in my distress, and Gunnarr did his best to calm me down.

"No, the Sword would never let harm befall you by its own actions! 'Twill all be understood once you've shared bloodletting in battle. Simply think of the Sword as you would your Dog, or Horse, or even me." Gunnarr had such a smug look upon his face that I laughed out loud.

"'Twill be interesting, but we have Warriors to gather. I must know what happened, everyone's perspective, if I'm to coordinate the next Draw with efficiency."

Gunnarr put forth his Call and within the mark we were gathered in the largest cavern space amid the cliffs, the Cave of Voices. At various times, and for no logical reasoning, one could hear sounds as if someone was speaking or singing. Apryya, Tyndall and Kydra had mentioned they'd thought they'd heard several voices speaking at once, occasionally harmonizing in song. The cave was also known to the mariners of the Port Districts all along the coasts, for the voices were said to be heard at certain times of the season. 'Twas Legend, but in reality none of us had ever actually heard them 'til we'd moved in, and even now they remained a rare occurrence. No one had been able to hear them clearly enough to determine what language, if any, was used. But no matter, the Cave of Voices was a secure location that would hold all of us and we still had plenty of spare room. 'Twas connected to the Cave of Jewels, and to the dungeons of the Den.

At this gathering, listening to everyone's memories and perceptions of the Draw, I discovered they were surprisingly different in many ways, but with enough similarities to be certain we'd stood the same test. Each Warrior had felt or heard something during the ritual that had been unique to them and 'twas fascinating. Soon the Warriors drifted off on their own to discover more about their new Swords, leaving me to my own thoughts. And then I couldn't believe what I was doing. Taking time off? For myself? 'Twas not even deep winter. No work, no drills, nothing required of me. Unheard of! But Gunnarr and Storrm and Mystynn had agreed, and had made me swear to do just that for the rest of the day.

"Storrm, afore you leave, I want to gather the candidates. I believe they're in danger. Regynn and Tannyr have both mentioned incidents that at first appeared random. Now I'm not so sure. In each trivial mishap, had the candidate been less aware, or slightly later or earlier, or even slower, they'd have been injured enough to take them out of the ceremony, if not more. 'Tis my belief they're being targeted. I'm certain there's a spy among us."

"What do you propose, my sister?"

"Spirit them here tonight, and keep everyone silent. I intend to change the location for the 'Bond, find some remote area, but 'twill be necessary to use diversionary tactics and no one will be able to observe."

"You mean for us to sequester them for their own safety, and rush the 'Bond in secrecy."

"I do."

"'Twill be done as you say, Second," Storrm agreed with a wink, and then set forth to execute her orders. During the evening, the Cave of Voices filled with the addition of the candidates we'd chosen for the next two ceremonies, their arrivals erratic, 'spirited' through the Spelled doorway into a secluded chamber that butted up close to the Cave of Jewels. Quietly throughout the night, their blankets lining the far wall, they set up their gear for the unknown duration. Soon, our resident roster had climbed by thirty, including Regynn, sisters Tannah and Tiyya, Daylyn (sister of Ethynn), brothers Kayyd and Dayyd, Haleeyah, Barynn, Loryyn, brothers Tannyr and Daayn, Flynn, Raynah, cousins Kamdyn and Kamryyn, Alyyse, Paydynn, Kytahna, the 'bad boys' of the Warrior Brotherhood, Mikkal and Rakkah, Hannah, Cartyrr, twins Torstynn and Tyrrsyn, Prysym, sisters Astraa and Aspynn, Thorrn, Maddyx, and Mace, the twin brother of Mynx, Fryya's bodyguard. I'd hoped to have time to choose more, but with the threat of a spy, we were having a rough time keeping these thirty safe, and if we could only 'Bond thirteen per ceremony, we'd still have four extra. I almost felt sorry for those four. I knew how intense was the desire to 'Bond, but 'twas my goal that the Third wouldn't be the last either. My primary concerns now, were finding a safe location, delivering all of the candidates safely to said location, and staging the two ceremonies without leaking the information to anyone outside of those already involved. The fewer people knowledgeable the better, and I pondered how to complete my tasks without informing even the Battle Commander. If my deceit was discovered, I could face charges of treason or worse, but my instincts told me to beware his knowledge. Mayhap the spy had access to him? No matter, I couldn't push this off on Gunnarr and the MindSpeak, for Dragons were not capable of lying, and the Commander was one of only a select few who knew this. Although I meant not to lie outright, for 'twas forbidden of a Warrior who'd taken the Oath, I had a strong notion I'd have to execute some very interesting avoidance maneuvers in our communications o'er the next few days.

CHAPTER 24

Enchantment At The Bog

Graasyn was well pleased with how far south they'd trekked using the skipping stone method. They'd survived the wicked cold of the heavy winter moons and now stood upon a hill gazing down into the gorge of St Swiftyn's. He'd known 'twas near when they'd stumbled upon the Bog, and they'd decided to relocate closer. They didn't entertain the notion of attempting to enter the Keep as 'twould take several more days and 'twould ultimately be of no benefit. A remote and isolated village in the deep of Byndynn Forest backed by the Raptor's Talons, 'twas rumored to have been devoted to scholars, but 'twas said to be impenetrable. The entire village was within the confines of a huge fortress struck from the very stone of its surroundings, and 'twas enveloped in mystery. No one had ever returned from the Keep in his lifetime, and soon after Grifynn had taken Command he'd banned further exploration. In fact, there was no proof that any of its inhabitants still existed.

'Twould take several dawns, but this would be their last base camp. Although familiar, 'twas disappointing to find St Swiftyn's, as this meant they were off their mark of a direct line southward and had strayed east/ southeast instead, but at least he now knew for certain where they were. The Spring Melts had made it too treacherous to get this far earlier, with the rushing rivers impassible, and the journey around, even a'horseback, slower and far more dangerous than simply waiting it out. He'd been frustrated when they'd discovered they were within a triangle of rivers that created an island of isolation during the Melts, upon which they'd been stuck for sennights. The village and the bog were at the peak of this triangle, and since no one had been here for ages, Graasyn had insisted on mapping the region. They'd rested for a few days, finished their maps, and gathered as much as they could to sustain them for the last leg of their journey. He was confident once they crossed the river they could let the Horses follow, grazing part of the way, and at a forced march pace they'd be back to the Dragon's Den within two or three moons.

Graasyn saw the girl while setting out snares late that evening. He'd been very quiet, making no sound to disrupt their chances for a good meal. He was squatting behind a large tree when he caught the glint of moonlight off her long white hair. His jaw dropped open at his first sight of her ethereal beauty, and he actually lost his balance and sat hard on the damp ground. For one breathless moment her head cocked slightly to the side, listening intently, and he near choked when she turned to face him. Her golden eyes burned into his but briefly, and then she turned away again. No, she couldn't have seen him, 'twas impossible, he was just being paranoid. Still, he couldn't tear his eyes away from her. Stepping swiftly as if she'd been walking 'cross a meadow, she was sure footed and confident in the marshes. He knew any misstep and she'd be trapped, slowly sinking under the rank mud of the Bog. Who was she, where was she from; might she be one of the mysterious inhabitants of St Swiftyn's? He could do naught but stare as she continued to stride further away from him along the edges, moving deeper into the huge bayou. How did she know where to step? At any moment the stunning girl could slip into the depths of the muck and what could he do to help? With that thought rising to the forefront of his mind, he was desperate to find a way to assist her. Surely she wasn't out there to....

He sucked in his breath as she stopped and peered intently in all directions. Had she Heard him? No, she was merely ensuring her actions were unobserved.

Even in the growing darkness, he could tell the girl was tall, dressed in filthy torn leathers, her long, snow white hair caked with mud, partially pulled back with a leather tie, with bits of leaves and twigs stuck in the tangled mass. He couldn't help but stare at the most beautiful woman he'd ever laid eyes upon. He was enchanted, why, even her skin seemed to glow in the moonlight. At that point in his reverie, she dipped her chin and cocked her head slightly toward him once again. The timing of this action was remarkable. Was that an acknowledgement of what he was thinking?

Several heartbeats passed in silence, as neither of them moved a muscle. Graasyn's heart told him he'd lay down his life to protect this girl and if she meant to....no, he couldn't even think about that prospect. So swiftly he near jumped, she reached around and pulled open the saddle bag slung o'er her shoulder, and removed a large glittering egg shaped object. 'Twas obviously quite heavy as she promptly crouched down, then pushed it with both hands as far away from her as she could reach without moving any closer. The intriguing object laid for the span of a full breath upon the spongy surface afore 'twas sucked under the quagmire with a squelching noise, leaving no sign that it had ever existed.

As soon as it disappeared, she stood up, looked o'er both shoulders, and then turned and raced out of the swamp, her feet near flying 'cross the muddy surface to where she'd begun. There she was met by an ebony horse he'd not even noticed earlier, surprised he hadn't heard the beast snorting. The red-eyed stallion had stood still and silent as a ghost, awaiting her return. Mounting up, continually glancing uneasily all about her, he saw the child slumped o'er the neck of the animal. She grasped his shoulders, easily pulling his frail body to her chest, then turned to face him once again. 'Twas unnerving, but he recognized the sensation as the same as when he and Bastyen had attempted to get Darque and her Dragon to see them so long ago. He was Masked. How could he forget? She stared right at him and then past him, as if attempting to locate the source of her unease. Swallowing hard, he got up and climbed o'er the scrub brush near the tree to stand directly within her line of sight, praying she wouldn't challenge him, for he wished her no harm. Holding his breath, he waited, but 'twas as he'd expected. She stared straight through him, nervously aware of something amiss but obviously also aware 'twas not Evil. She was a hunter and a fighter for certain, and the two of them had clearly been through much to get here, the boy not faring well. Where had they come from and to where were they destined? But most importantly, who was she, and what had she just buried in the Bog?

She turned away and leaning o'er the horse's neck, she whispered to him. The sweat slathered beast reared up and then took off at a full gallop. Graasyn could barely breathe. All he could see was her beautiful golden eyes staring straight through his soul, her skin a'shimmer, her long white hair flying behind her, as they rode hard around the far side of the Bog, disappearing swiftly into the forest.

Unexpectedly, he felt the presence of the stranger once more. 'Twas as if he was standing at his shoulder and the sensation was as real as when they'd first encountered him in the aqueducts. His eyes darted all about to guarantee he was alone, but he heard the stranger whispering in his ear, *"Remember what happened here, for if she doesn't succeed in her quest, the Highlands will be lost forever."* This was why they'd been Pushed here. At least 'twas one reason for which he was certain. 'Twas imperative he retain this knowledge, for the desperation emanating from the girl had been near palpable.

In surreal wonder he returned to his snare, but he couldn't stop thinking about what had happened. 'Twould bother him for a very long time.

CHAPTER 25

Myrta Speaks Her Mind

EARLY SUMMER, A FEW DAYS AFTER THE DRAW; O'ER FIVE MOONS FROM THE 'BOND

"'Twas me mother's hand mirror, m'lord. 'Twas precious to me, a family heirloom. I know there's nothin' ya can do for me or me mirror m'lord, I just felt that I needed to explain me thoughts. These petty thefts and vandalisms are increasin' m'lord. They're not as other Villages sometimes are plagued, with destruction that makes no sense and comes from the perpetrator's mere boredom or actin' out his frustrations. No sir, we've no such quandary with our youngun's here and if we did there's plenty available for such to be targeted and yet, the damages are often a pittance, but close to one's heart, and with much meanin' to each of the ones to whom this has occurred. As well as the fact that 'twould have been near impossible for one not of the family to actually have gotten close enough to do such damage without bein' seen or stopped or at least remembered in the first place! No, m'lord, these are no ordinary happenin's. They aim to break the very spirit of the Clan. If ya don' mind me sayin' so m'lord, 'tis as if the perpetrator was tryin' to destroy us from within our very souls, by sinkin' us all into the depths of despair, and growin' paranoia amongst friends and family. After all m'lord, 'tis not that mountain you climb that taxes your strength, distractin' you from seein' your goal. 'Tis the grain of sand in your boot."

Myrta, the Master Chef and Lead Cook for the Den, as well as Lifemate to Toryn the Leather Master, finished her thoughts and stood back from the Battle Commander, waiting for his response. Having noted him walking near the back entry to the kitchens, she'd scooted out past the braziers and caught him in the hallway. She'd always heard the Battle Commander was a good man, and he'd never made her fearful, but still she'd been hesitant to bring forth her suspicions. She'd known his daughters all their lives, but she'd never spoken in such a manner to the Leader of the Clan afore, exchanging pleasantries o'er the many winters in which she'd worked here, knowing the man but not knowing him, and now she was anxious to see how this huge and intimidating Warrior would take her humble point of view.

Grifynn leaned o'er the fretful woman, and with his appreciation evident in his voice, he calmed her by saying, "Myrta, I can always count on you, to bring the recipe together. Now I just have to make certain I have all the ingredients." And with a wink, he nodded his head, and striding down the long hallway toward his office again, he offered his thanks o'er his shoulder. Myrta beamed, feeling her suspicions justified by the Commander's words and simple actions. Wiping her hands again on the towel she kept tucked into her waistband, she shook her head and muttered, "All the ingredients, indeed!" And chuckling, she returned to the kitchens, already making plans for the special pies she'd be baking the Battle Commander and his Warriors for evening meal.

<center>~~~~~~~~~~</center>

Darque was waiting for him when he finally came through the door. The air around her became warmer and he heard the slight buzzing as he passed her, as if the Sword she now carried 'cross her back was a living, breathing sentience. 'Twas a tad disconcerting, but he'd discovered no one other than himself could sense this peculiar phenomenon. Still, it made him take pause whenever he was around them, as it made him feel he was being watched. Immediately struck with the need to hasten past in a wide arc, he perceived the emotion originated directly from her Sword, and shaking his head, he continued walking slowly around them to sit down at his desk. 'Twas the principle of the thing, he'd not be bullied by an inanimate object.

"So, have you chosen a destination?" Grifynn stared at his daughter, defying her to evade the obvious question.

"Yes. We return to the St Swiftyn's region, to take up mapping where we left off," Darque responded. What she'd chosen was the truth, even if only partial truth, and 'twas the key to her plans. He'd never divulge her destination or her supposed mission, and she near held her breath waiting with uncharacteristic patience for his approval. She'd be gone for at least a full moon. There'd been no sightings of the Hoard since afore the Draw, and for all intents and purposes, no one knew when they were going to attempt the Second LifeBond. Technically, any Magic ceremony could be held at any time, some times were just more conducive than others, and the Summer Solstice was less than a moon from now. She'd told him afore the Draw that they'd have difficulty trying to manage that timeline, which was truth, and she'd left him with the impression they were targeting the Fall Equinox. 'Twas odd that he'd not questioned her further on that, but everyone had their hands full now. Given they'd be removed from a tried and true location and making the attempt with fatigued Ancients, she wanted to bolster their chances as much as possible, and being ready by the Solstice seemed wise as well as necessary. In that scenario, she had to get out of here with every sense of normalcy she could muster. She'd already spread the word that the candidates were taking part in a very intense training session involving meditation, that could last a fortnight or more, providing the perfect excuse for their absence as well as reinforcing the idea that they were waiting for the Equinox.

In reality, the candidates had begun spreading out erratically and in different directions, almost as soon as they'd arrived to the Cave of Voices. They'd rendezvous secretly near the border of Byndynn Forest, a day's flight for most of them, southwest of St Swiftyn's where they'd gather 'til Darque was ready. She'd decided 'twould be best in the Far Northlands, so the rendezvous point made sense, as once she'd found a site they'd have to move swiftly, and having them all at least in the same region would help. None of them had been allowed to return to the Den or to make contact with their families prior to leaving on their individual 'assignments', and none of them had asked. Warriors' lives and ties were ever unpredictable, and the entire Clan lived the Code. We fought hard, we played hard, we lived every day as if 'twere our last for 'twas wholly possible, and by odds we'd Pass the Veil hard.

"Good plan, I concede. I want no one to know what you're doing or where you're going. I expect you to leave immediately," he stated, and then dismissed her with a wave of his hand toward the door. If he were thinking clearly and his chest hadn't been hurting so much at this very moment, he'd have thought the casual manner in which she'd stood conversing during their exchange, most curious. Her usual impatience, which would normally permeate the very air about him, was not now evident, but he was working too hard on maintaining his composure, afraid she might question what he considered his own strange behavior, for him to make note of hers.

He gave his dismissal and she'd left without a word, not even a glance o'er her shoulder, as the Standing Guard shut the heavy door behind her. She'd been relieved, then felt a nagging disquiet. He'd said to let no one know where she was… that would totally isolate the Second in Command. It would also keep her out of the loop here at home. As she walked quickly down the Great Hallway pondering these irregularities, her Sword began to slap her shoulder with each step she took and for the life of her she couldn't get the scabbard to strap on tighter. She'd never had difficulty adjusting it afore. Reaching o'er her shoulder with the opposite hand, she pulled and yanked and when the offensive slap continued, she tried to adjust it from the other side, which only resulted in it switching from slapping her shoulder to slapping the back of her head.

Finally the sun dawned upon her and she stopped midstride. Yanking out the Sword, she glowered at it as she held it in front of her face and exclaimed, "WHAT?"

Quickly glancing about, she noted several people looking at her curiously. All they knew was that a Warrior had drawn her sword, yelling in the middle of the hallway, and they wondered if 'twas safe, or if they should seek cover.

Blushing deep crimson, Darque sheathed the blade and waved off the bystanders mumbling, "What? Haven't you ever seen someone talking to their Sword afore? Move on, 'tis done."

She continued on her way, picking up her pace as the Sword grew cold upon her back. 'Twas obviously peeved with her. 'Twas likely it tried to make her aware of something, but unfortunately she hadn't handled the situation very well, having been under great stress to pull off her clandestine mission and evade her father's all knowing nature, and 'twas the first time she'd encountered such a reaction from the blade. Sighing, she recognized her own perseverance and passion within the steel. She supposed she'd learn all of the peculiarities of its 'personality' eventually, hoping they'd not always be at odds with one another. If her Sword continued to display more of her own stubborn character, 'twouldn't be safe for either of them.

CHAPTER 26

The Second LifeBond

Gunnarr had flown Darque for days after leaving the Dragon's Den that night. She had less than a fortnight to relocate thirty candidates and to find a suitable site to hold the ceremony, but her mind kept drifting back to the last time she'd spoken with her father. Her Sword had tried to get her attention and now she wondered if 'twas something to do with him. He'd seemed distracted. His poise was dulled compared to his usual demeanor and she had only her suspicions as to why. Since she'd taken the 'Bond, he'd been subtly changing and she'd become very concerned. If the Clan lost Grifynn, they lost the most effective Battle Commander of the ages. She knew she'd make a good field commander eventually, but she wanted to enjoy the luxury of time to learn more from her father now that she held the rank of Second. Sadly she'd been unable to shake the feeling that 'twould not be so.

They'd actually begun their search near St Swiftyn's Bog, thinking to avoid a huge lie, but when they'd flown o'er, Darque was inspired. The swamplands afforded the perfect cover for the secret Training Facility she envisioned, as well as its ability to provide natural heat throughout the long winter moons that plagued the Northlands locale, and without a source of heat the Highlands became sluggish and their Magic suffered. The Forest was held at bay far enough to allow the Dragons within, but was near enough to discourage others from lingering or frequenting the area. Geographically, 'twas within a triangle of rivers, effectively creating an island during the Spring Melts, with the rush of waters impassable a'foot or a'horseback. Under the Bog, the Aversion Spell would hold no strength for 'twas specific to the trees of the Forests and not the land upon which they grew. Although 'twouldn't be the kind of environment anyone would expect her to use for what she had in mind, 'twould also be easily hidden as well as defended, and therefore 'twas perfect in every way.

They'd set up housekeeping immediately. Using Magic sparingly and in bursts so as not to create a steady beacon for the Hoard, the natural lay of the caves and the swampland required minimal alterations to create an entire Training Facility beneath the Bog. Leaving most of the surface untouched provided flawless camouflage and required little to Shield the entrances.

THE BLACK WAR BEGINS

The moment she'd made her decision all thirty Warriors were retrieved from the rendezvous point via the Dragons expecting to be present, and were now ensconced within. Darque had near choked on her own laughter when they'd first arrived, hanging onto the massive Dragons for dear life, and then struggling to dismount and stumbling away. They'd expected 'twould be like riding a War Horse and had discovered, to the amusement of the 'Bonded, 'twas not so. But that they'd even attempted spoke volumes for their guts and daring, and they'd learn soon enough. The prize within sight, their single minded determination to attempt to take a 'Bond with one of the huge beasts, supplied the audacity they'd require.

Darque decided 'twas most beneficial for them to mingle with the creatures prior to the ceremony and she couldn't help but wonder if this familiarity would actually bring the Warriors closer to the Dragons with whom they might soon forever share their lives. She recalled Gunnarr telling her so long ago that he'd known her when she was birthed, had actually found her and had laid talon upon her. Not that any of these Warriors had such a scar mind you, but during the construction process each of them gravitated to one particular Dragon, working together and forging ties. She'd tried not to notice the four who did not.

Darque hated that her communication was limited to emergency only, and only with Storrm. The Third Fighter held her own back at the Den and all was well, but she'd have preferred to be in closer contact. However, they each had a job to do and do it they would. She and Gunnar had felt a faint touch of the Hoard's presence in the distant past, but they'd clearly abandoned the Bog as uninhabitable, offering up prime security to locate their own lair here. She was learning that the Evil One and his minions were short tempered, short sighted, and impulsive. They could barely see what was in front of their own eyes, let alone fight cohesively with any form of strategy, and they had no work ethic. The Incident at Lorelei might have been planned to some extent, but 'twas set off by accident, of that she was certain. And Gunnarr had felt something new and peculiar when they'd made their first pass o'er the Bog this time. *"'Twas as if I'd been Touched by someone for whom I care greatly,"* trying to describe the sensation that had immediately disappeared. 'Twas not Evil, but couldn't be confirmed and therefore she'd been wary. She'd ordered him to Block all Links, even Mystynn's, 'til after the ceremony.

The Dragons who'd come to assist and to Stand for the Second and Third LifeBond included sisters Maklarynn and Lyrriynn, Taniyyah, Izayyah, and Kaahayyel's daughter and son Shraadarr and Krynnarr.

Her sons Fyndarr and Zayddarr were already in 'Bond, and the Highland Ancients had put out a Search for her eldest daughter Synahmarr, as she'd mysteriously disappeared prior to the Last Holocaust and hadn't been heard from since, although the Matriarch hadn't Felt her Passing. Kashiyann had come to Stand, sister to the Dragon Krydann, who was also missing, and hadn't been heard from since just after the Holocaust. Also present were Fyrrayann, Zymaalynn, Dylordynn, Delfyyan, and Varrdayyn as well as Daynahmyn and the rest of Maahayyel's sons: Kaygynn the Quad Prince, Synddarr the Fifth Prince, and Shasynn the Sixth Prince. No one knew where Bryynn was, but Gunnarr was certain he was still unhatched, as he could See only blackness, Feel only warmth, and Hear only silence. Arriving in time to participate for the Dragons were brothers Korriagg and Danniagg and their cousin, Radryagg. Radryagg had arrived just in time for the First LifeBond, rumored to have flown in from a great distance. However, after Speaking much with the Ancients, he simply flew away again mere marks afore the ceremony. Now he returned, but was accompanied by his cousins, as well as Shanndynn, and siblings Sydrayyah, Pelayyah, and Petrayyah, believed to have been recruited from the Rol Dan, an all but undocumented land mass beyond even the Wyrdritch of Darkling Forest, said to butt up against the far shores of the Dragon's Tears.

<center>~~~~~~~~~~</center>

"*Sydrayyah.*" The Mighty Maahayyel Spoke first, as was considered proper however, without actually Asking a question, she received no response, which was also proper. The one standing afore her appeared slightly nervous, which was to be expected under the circumstances, but Maahayyel felt justified with her discomfort. Finally, she deigned to Speak again, "*'Tis good to see that you and your siblings survived the Holocaust.*" Although the Matriarch had thought to chastise the other, she realized she couldn't. She was truly elated to discover the friend of her youth was still alive, but seeing her here now, well, 'twas a mystery. Surely she hadn't come to Stand for the LifeBond? Again, the imposing leader Spoke. "*'Tis unexpected to see you here at this time. I did not think that Radryagg would be able to find you, let alone recruit you and your siblings.*" No reaction. She sighed. No matter how she'd tried, she'd not been able to agitate the big Green afore her into Speaking out of turn. Throughout the entire conversation, all Sydrayyah had done was nod her great head, flashing her bejeweled eyes without menace, but with some unnamed emotion just out of her perception.

"Speak Sydrayyah," the Matriarch finally Commanded the Green.

"I Answer the Blood Call," Sydrayyah Replied matter-of-factly to the Ancient.

Maahayyel Heard no regret in that Voice. No apology. No recognition of wrong doing, nothing. Just a simple Reply, that avoided the events of their last parting altogether.

"You Heard the Blood Call of Man and you Answered not?" Maahayyel attempted to push the other into shame.

Sydrayyah was silent for a brief moment. Then she Responded reluctantly, *"I've made mistakes in the past, and it cost me dearly. My family, my friends, my Race. I near lost them all. Only recently have my sisters found me, and at first I was joyful in our reunion, but they brought with them the news of The Black's return and I was torn. Soon thereafter, upon the Winter Solstice, I Felt the Blood Call of a Warrior from a vast distance, but knew not from whence it came. I was pulled in many directions. Just as I determined to seek out this Warrior, Radryagg arrived with the tale of the First LifeBond and I knew that 'twas here I would find my destiny."* The Green lowered her luminous eyes and all was silent for several breaths. Then she quietly continued, *"I seek to make the LifeBond with this Warrior, but more importantly, I seek to repair our friendship, Maahayyel. I ask forgiveness for what occurred 'tween us that day. I place my future upon your mercy."*

~~~~~~~~~~

The date was rapidly approaching, giving us no time to think about the outside world. The Ancients had flown in afore dawn two days past and slept much. When up and about, selecting and preparing the exact location they'd require, Kaahayyel was relentlessly encircled as if she was the fire of the camp and they were keeping her well banked. Protected thusly, they hoped her Strength would not leach out, or be tapped unnecessarily. She hadn't appeared so frail prior to the Draw, and certainly had held her own during the First LifeBond. I was worried about her. If she failed during the Brew....I couldn't think like that. She'd not fail. 'Twas totally unacceptable.

Finally, 'twas the night chosen. The longest day of all the seasons, 'twas late when the sun finally dipped o'er the far horizon, but we weren't witness to the actual setting due to the surrounding terrain. When all was ready to begin, we stood thirty Warriors upon the grounds, under a Shield projected by Gunnarr. Since the Teams of First Flight were still at the Den, that left only the Dragons who came here to Stand and to as-
~~~~~~~~~~

sist the Ancients in the ceremony. I was concerned for Gunnarr's Magic to be denied them, but we'd no other option. 'Twould in reality have been more difficult to Shield the sacred grounds at Drekinn, since 'twas open, and here the Spell of Aversion o'er the Forests actually assisted and helped him to contain the power he used. In fact, the location lent itself to enhancing the power greatly and this Shield was the strongest yet conceived, but we could not spare an un'Bonded Dragon for such. There'd be no compromising this night. Once the Magic was Brewed and brought under containment, 'twas more concentrated than any of the others, and it actually pulsed as with a living heartbeat. Of course, all Magic did derive from the living.

I focused my attention upon the Ancients as they began their chant, and the Magic did Brew all around us. 'Twas fascinating, as I'd not seen the action from this side afore. Having no other to perform the task, I wielded the blade that released their Blood Call, and stared in wonder as each of them took the Cut. Regynn was the first and I gasped as he was dragged into the blaze by a Green female known as Sydrayyah. When they exited the flames clearly alive and well, tears of joy spilled o'er my cheeks. She must have been the one who'd Heard his Call moons past, the one he'd felt connected to since then, but was so far away she couldn't respond. They'd been working side by side on the conversions and had developed a very close relationship o'er the last few days. One by one, I drew their blood, all of them hopeful to find their true destinies. As each received the Cut, they willingly stepped forward to be engulfed within the flames of the fire, grasped by talon and dragged through to the other side, and I thanked the Fates and The Almighty One that we'd survived thus far. Mayhap we could make more than thirteen. We'd stood them all and we'd continue as long as possible. So far, this night seemed blessed.

After Regynn, Astraa paired with the Quad Prince, Kaygynn, then Tannah and Synddarr the Fifth Prince, after whom came Daylyn and Makyyan, followed by Tiyya and Shasynn, the Sixth Prince of the Highland Dragons. Quickly stepping through the fire one after the other, were Thorrn and Taniyyah, Barynn and Shraadarr, Hannah and Izayyah. The Brotherhood's bad boys followed suit with Daynahmyn dragging Mikkal through the flames while Rakkah partnered with Petrayyah. Everyone thought the two of them were brothers, but if 'twas so, 'twould be upon the maternal side, since I knew for a fact that Mikkal was the bastard son of King Bryard. This made him half brother to Shytin, but that was not to be revealed to anyone else, for he'd affirmed this to me in a sort of forced confidence when I'd guessed such, and he'd no way to dispute my youthful audacity. 'Twas a moment of confusion when Mikkal's Blood Call went out, as initially it seemed to settle o'er both Petrayyah and Daynahmyn, the hesitation evident to all. As I'd watched with widened eyes, my heart in my throat, the Call vacillated. The two friends faced each other and something passed 'tween them. Then Daynahmyn stood up and seemingly dragging the Call with her, she charged into the fire to pull Mikkal through, Petrayyah following immediately after, with Rakkah.

As each of my Warriors was successful, my spirit soared with renewed hope. But then I felt the ripple. Glancing toward the Ancients, I noted Kaahayyel's appearance was most peculiar. At first I thought what I'd seen was an illusion caused by the fire, but after sharing Magic with the Dragons for several moons now and with my enhanced acuity, I realized her image was truly flickering. While the chanting continued, I observed the Matriarch press her massive body against her sister's, as she attempted to bolster her strength. I hesitated long enough to catch two things happen almost simultaneously: I saw Kaahayyel's outline strengthen, the strange illusion less visible with her sister's proximity, and I caught the look in Maahayyel's eyes, pleading with me to make haste. Taking up the blade once again, I made the Cut for Loryyn, who took the 'Bond with Krynnarr, Kaahayyel's own son, and then Tannyr's brother Daayn was dragged into the fire. Kashiyann held onto Daayn tightly, but the fire seemed to grow pale and lost its heat with their presence. Try as she might, her muscular body heaving, her great claws seemingly digging into the dirt in her attempts to gain ground, 'twas clear she was losing the tug of war. 'Twas as if the fire now held the properties of quicksand, and Daayn was being sucked away from her grasp. Dropping the blade to the ground and running toward the fire, Tannyr stopped me, the blade in his hand. "You cannot help them that way. Kaahayyel is failing and the only thing we can do to strengthen her is to make her 'Bond. I am that Warrior! I Saw this many winters past, but didn't understand the meaning of my Vision 'til this moment. You must Cut me now! I'll take Kaahayyel and we'll help the Ancients strengthen the fire to save Daayn and Kashiyann!"

Staring into his eyes, I saw the truth of his words, and with a fleeting look from Kashiyann's struggle to Kaahayyel's, I knew 'twould be mere moments afore I lost them all. Taking the proffered blade from his hand, I made the Cut. Instantly, his Blood Call swept out, but instead of blanketing the others and then gathering to just one, the sparkling mist of his Call flew directly to the Ancient, covering her completely as a fishing net is thrown o'er the waters. It separated the two Ancients, pushing

Maahayyel aside roughly, as the elder sister exploded upright, her mighty head thrown back, roaring her Acceptance. With renewed strength provided from this joining, the powerful Elder was at the fire afore I could register she'd even moved, and yanked Tannyr deep inside. The Fire now contained two pairs of Warriors and Dragons, and I knew not how they would fare. But as the Ancient entered the blaze, it became a raging inferno with more heat than I could imagine, and I feared 'twould light up the entire forest. Quickly following, I watched breathlessly as Kashiyann and Daayn near tumbled out the other side as if shoved, and within moments upon their heels, Kaahayyel and Tannyr were spit forth. Instantly after they were clear of the blaze it turned cold and died, as if it had never been. In near shock, my breath stuttering, I fell to my knees in gratitude. They'd all survived, and we'd made thirteen new 'Bonds.

CHAPTER 27

A New Contact

A FORTNIGHT AFTER THE DRAW;
ABOUT SIX MOONS FROM THE FIRST 'BOND

Grifynn sat on the edge of his chair, pouring o'er the parchments that lay scattered afore him on his desk. What was he missing, why could he not see? 'Twas all in front of his eyes: the rosters, the inventories, his own secret forays and observations. Odd things had been happening and items reported missing or broken for no apparent reason. There seemed no connection 'tween most of the incidents, but his failing senses were screaming at him to pay heed. The most disturbing of all was what he'd referenced as 'the doppelganger infestation', with increasing rumors of people seen in two places at the same time. That was bad enough, but the latest incident had thrown the entire Den into an uproar within a half mark of the discovery. Teaka had bred an exceptional litter with one of the new dogs Darque had made available from a rescue effort. Although badly injured, their owners had nursed them back to good health by the time they'd arrived at the Den, and Teaka had been very excited to get hold of them. Darque had been much interested in these particular dogs, and they'd indeed been a great addition to the bloodlines, but the elder of them had taken to her and she to him, and had she been a Warrior free of the 'Bond, she'd have bought the beast then and there. Grifynn knew how much his daughters loved their animals and it had pained him to see how she'd reluctantly left the beast in the Kennel Master's care. But this very evening, just two moons after the birth of the dozen new puppies, the dog who'd sired them and had inspired such a strong reaction in his daughter, had been viciously slaughtered. Out on assignment to complete mapping the Far Northland regions, she'd not reported in near a fortnight so as not to compromise her location through any Link to the Hoard. He didn't look forward to telling her about Bensyn's death. It hadn't made any sense. The big Mastiff had proven a ferocious fighter, so he wouldn't have gone down quietly, yet nothing was heard and there was little evidence of a struggle. Also, the Kennels were secure within the Den. There was one kitchen assistant taking scraps to the kennel, who'd reported seeing Storrm leave the area just prior to his arrival. He later recanted the claim, stating he had no memory of having seen the Third Fighter anywhere near the Kennels for days, yet there'd been no evidence of obvious deceit. Such contradictions had his instincts screaming. Flame it all, he'd never had such difficulty ferreting out a spy. Once long ago, all he'd required were his altered Senses and his past training. Frustrated and fatigued, he bowed his head, squeezed his eyes shut and pinched the bridge of his nose. He needed to be convinced the contact was not the spy within his ranks. But if not that one, then who? If 'twere this contact, the Dragon Clan was doomed. Grifynn had felt the residual power dusted all o'er his Warrior, their only connection. He'd recognized the contact was a Magic Bearer, but held his tongue. Throughout his long life, he'd learned 'twas not always wise to state the obvious. Praying Dyrrk wasn't enthralled and therefore, helping a spy, he'd chosen to maintain his confidence. Keeping one's enemies close seemed a good idea.

'Twas getting late he noted, glancing at the candle that guttered in its lantern. He winced with the stabbing pain in his chest. 'Twas becoming more difficult by the day to control. The need to be close to his beloved Aalanna, drove him insane with desire to drink the Blood Elixir. 'Twould be so easy. Glancing at his boot, his left hand slid almost reluctantly down his leather clad leg, touching the slight bulge that reassured him 'twas still there. Had he not volunteered for this duty so many lifetimes past, he'd not be suffering so but then again, he'd be dead.

He'd been so young. A highly skilled, covert, elite Special Ops officer, he'd been idealistic and considered himself invincible. Had he known what was in store for him, for all of them, would he still have volunteered? Snorting, he thought to himself, 'twas no doubt, for had he not, there'd be no Dragon Clan, no life with Aalanna, no Darque, no Storrm. Did he still believe in the prophesy? What difference did it make if he couldn't now save the one he loved? For all his training, expertise, and strength, he'd been unable to protect those whom he loved the most, from the Evil.

In the beginning and for so long thereafter, he'd been ashamed for yielding to the burning need of the Elixir they'd given him in their attempts to create the perfect soldier. But even with the forced addiction, he knew 'twas the only way he'd been able to bring them this far, protect them all. And o'er the last seven winters, 'twas the only reason he yet lived and the only way he'd been able to stay in contact with Aalanna. Why had she not told him about Fryya?

Slamming his fist against the desk top, he squeezed his eyes shut and opened them again, trying to get the images to clarify within his mind. His woman was in danger, he could sense it, the Blood sizzled in his veins, Whispering to him of her dire circumstances. He had to get her out of there now or he'd lose her forever. He was past feeling shame for this, 'twas the only way he could keep going, he couldn't focus his attention, he needed the Elixir. "Aalanna, Aalanna," he murmured, the anguish contorting his handsome face.

The corner section of the bookshelves behind him shifted silently and slid back, as if pushed deeper into the wall. As the sweat broke out 'cross his brow, he shifted his eyes slightly downward and to his right, with the breath of air that sighed into the room. The shelves stopped, then slid behind the neighboring section to reveal a narrow passageway. The opening to the underground tunnels had been incorporated into this office several lifetimes past and to keep it wholly confidential, he'd done all the work himself. He'd made good use of the hidden doorway and none had ever been the wiser. It had provided him with much information he'd otherwise not have had easy or secure access to, and through the many winters he'd learned no one could be truly trusted. Its existence had never been discovered and 'twas only his great need to protect his daughters and his mate now, that led him to allow another to know of it and use it in this manner. The Warrior who stepped like a ghost through the narrow opening was his closest and most trusted ally, and best kept secret. Not even Shayla was aware of their relationship, as he'd never had real friends to anyone's knowledge. He smiled slightly and reminded himself that Corbyn had been most helpful. 'Twas the hand of the One that had led him to the Raven and to their ultimate 'arrangement'.

Grifynn didn't even lift his eyes to the Warrior who now stood quietly in the shadows o'er his shoulder, simply muttering under his breath, "You're late."

Without mincing words, the burly, battle scarred man stated succinctly, "My contact has foul news, m'lord."

"What could be worse than the news he's already conveyed?" The Commander sucked in his breath when yet another wave of pain rushed through his chest. Quickly regaining his ability to speak, he hissed forth, "And has he found a way to convince me he is in fact, trustworthy?"

"He tasks me with bearing a gift, m'lord. He avowed boldly that this gift would contain the only information you would require, although, 'twould not be well met."

"'Tis information on The Evil One's location and weaknesses that I require," Grifynn spat forth harshly, and then felt the regret that always followed the rebuke. He was in charge however, and everyone's lives had always depended on him, so he swallowed the emotion as he always did, to become the stalwart leader once again.

"He's closing in, m'lord. Just one more step and he'll be within range. He merely requires the right moment. Building trust within the Hoard while simultaneously creating chaos, is not easily accomplished, I can assure you. But even though they do not trust each other, the Evil One has his Right Hand in The Destroyer, and my contact intends to be The Destroyer's right hand very soon."

The Commander grimaced, struggling to control the emotional spike this information spawned. His body temperature began to rise, his control slipping. Surreptitiously, he reached into the desk drawer for the Life Crystal stashed there, unbeknownst to Shayla. Using his hardened and elongating nails, he scratched off a small amount of the porous blood red salt crystal and placed it under his tongue. Rapidly dissolving, he felt the instant effects, although 'twas becoming obvious they were weakening. He deduced the crystal would not much longer sustain his life functions. Switching to unrefined Blood as was the Elixir, he'd get an immediate boost, as well as stronger and longer term affect, but using it full time bespoke his impending doom. Softly, he uttered the thought that was now so clear, seven winters to see, "I'll soon Pass either way."

"Your pardon m'lord," Dyrrk stated in confusion.

"Nothing, just speculating the odds," he returned, and then gathering his resolve and clutching his chest, his back still to the one standing in the shadows, he barked, "I need the exact location of the Hoard lair, where and when The Black will be there. Does he provide this information or not?"

"I fear not as yet, m'lord, but I'm not privy to what this gift brings into the light." He stepped closer, making not a sound, holding forth the canvas package. The Commander turned to face him and reached for it, but afore his fingers even touched the oiled cloth wrap, he had a flash Vision that only strong Magic could provide, of what 'twas revealed in the gift so offered. His head jerked up and his eyes opened wide. His jaw dropped and his heart pounded. His breathing quickened, his mouth dried, as he grabbed the package and held it against his chest to try to ease the waves of pain, grunting, "No!"

Instantly realizing his mistake, Grifynn's eyes darted to the door, and noting the latch begin to shift, he threw a Hold against it as he called to the Guard, "I need you not! All is well."

"Yes, Commander," the Guard replied, and the latch returned to level. Grifynn released his tenuous Hold preventing the door from opening, and collapsed back in his chair with the effort, trying to catch his breath at the near miss. Twisting about, Dyrrk, his only link to the contact, had already disappeared the way he'd arrived. 'Twas no matter. The Warrior had standing orders to retreat with any possibility of being discovered, which superseded every other order. He was not to be seen alone with the Commander. Grifynn knew the man would never betray that order, or his trust. The Warrior would be found by now at the Barracks. Truly, Grifynn knew not how the man always managed to be in all places at all times. He sighed. His own secret was still intact, as the Guard hadn't pushed the Hold, and Dyrrk wouldn't have seen what he'd done. Even though 'twas clear the Warrior had dealt with Magic Bearers, Grifynn didn't consider himself such and he didn't want others to know of his meager 'talents'. Besides, he hadn't wanted to share what the 'gift' meant, either.

With trembling hands, he placed it upon the desk. Staring at it, he fought the urge to rip the vial from his boot and drink the thick, dark liquid. Reaching for the package instead, he shook with the effort to control his movements, untying the twine and carefully spreading it out 'til the content was revealed. There it lay afore him, upon the unfolded cloth. Darque's lost blade from the Battle of Kaddart.

So, Dyrrk's contact was trustworthy after all. This was absolute proof. He'd taken the blade, had kept it undisclosed all these moons. He could have used it against them, might have given it to the Evil One. Had he? Was this still a ruse? Was the Vision given by Magic, truth, or was it altered? Grifynn touched the blade cautiously, running his finger o'er the dark stain along the edge, and realized 'twas blood. Needing to identify it, he licked his finger with the tip of his tongue and closed his eyes, reaching for the truth. 'Twould leave no doubt. He'd expected the blood to be revealed as The Black's, or mayhap Darque's or Gunnarr's or the Hoard Dragon's from the battle.

As he ran the tip of his tongue along the roof of his mouth and then licked his lips to try to identify the Blood Call therein, he was shocked to discover yet another possibility. He felt a rush of misery and slid forward out of his chair to his knees in agony, as a Vision of the most recent Blooding upon this blade, struck him forcefully in his chest. Knowing these Visions were provided by the contact himself, 'twas understood that he risked much to reveal he was of a Magic Bearing Race, and not of Mankind. Hanging his head, breathing heavily through his mouth, he allowed the tears to roll off his cheeks to the wooden floor beneath his desk. Many, many winters had passed since he'd last cried.

As his vision turned crimson, he Saw his beloved life mate huddled on the floor, her back against the wall in the far corner of the Tower room where she'd been imprisoned for near sixteen winters. Her gown was torn and dirty, her beautiful face was battered and bruised, tears of frustration, despair and pain rolled down her flushed cheeks. She'd been beaten, and as she stared at the proffered blade from the stranger standing in the darkened corner, she cried out to the surrounding silence, "He mustn't know!" Still the stranger spoke not, the blade extended in place, unmoving. Regaining her control, she whispered quietly into the shadows, "If you take this to him, he will come for me. He'll not let this deed go unpunished."

The voice came from the man she couldn't identify, as he slowly lowered the knife. "'Tis true, you're being used as bait to lure him here. But they'll not expect him to come in time and prepared. 'Twill be his only chance as well as yours. You're to be sacrificed at dawn of a fortnight hence, and 'twill be ugly. Does he not have the right to know this aforehand? Would you rather he learn of this atrocity after you have so Passed?" His deep voice hung in the air 'tween them as if disembodied, leaving her chilled.

"Why would you do this? Why would you risk your life for mine? By warning Grifynn, you know he will come and 'twill be obvious the secret was leaked. 'Twill be considered an act of treason by The Evil One. You could be discovered."

He hung his head and then stated, almost too softly to hear, "Long have I battled The Evil One and many have I forced Beyond, both well deserving and not. My entire House has been torn asunder in this war. When I Pass, 'twill be to the gods that I answer, not to those I have wronged. I have risked much for what I believe, m'lady, and I've hardened my senses far more than any would think possible. If you were not who you are, 'twould be a simple matter for me. I could allow you to Pass without risking my place, as I have allowed many to do…" and apparently seeing the loathing reflected in her expression, he paused briefly and then continued, "No, do not think I care for your approval or lack thereof. I do what I must, for there is no greater need than to fulfill this mission. However, you hold more power than you understand, and your life is not mine to allow to end at this time. But the simple truth is that neither am I in a position to save you outright. 'Tis a daunting dilemma for which I have no better response." The stranger once again extended the blade to the lady, saying, "'Tis all I have to offer." And with these words the Vision began to waver.

Heartbroken, the Battle Commander could no longer see his beloved Aalanna, as his office returned briefly to his sight afore being filled with an otherworldly mist. The floor shook as if 'twould collapse and Grifynn felt as if all the air had been sucked out of the room. Suddenly unable to breathe, he didn't panic as most were wont to do in such circumstance, for he recognized the phenomenon from previous experience. He simply held his breath as he waited a mere candle drip for the air pressure to normalize. Gasping reflexively, he was then silent as he listened for the forthcoming message. If he could see anything, he knew 'twould be through the red haze of Battle Lust. Although he was angry and impatient to take action, he was still highly disciplined and needed all the facts he could gather. He'd not look this gift horse in the mouth.

The Voice returned from a great distance, as if the Vision had been a play and the director was now stepping forth from the background, narrating the epilogue. Deep and gravelly, hard and stoic, he felt some unfathomable turmoil within the man who spoke. "A'foot 'twould be a moon to travel at a forced march, a fortnight hard ride a'horseback, but you have only half those days in order to accomplish that which you must. If you would arrive in time to try to save her, you will follow my directions. I'm sure you realize the passage for this journey will not come about without paying a great price." He paused, as if sizing up the man afore him. Then with a touch of urgency he demanded, "Her life for yours. Do you so agree, Warrior?" Grifynn bowed his head without hesitation in his affirmation to this barbaric arrangement, for he'd already made his choice. "Then with the blade you must pierce your heart, adding your blood to hers, my blood to yours. Within a mark of the deed you must present it to Myrrdin, the Ship's Master of the Krakken, which will soon lie at dock in Port O'Drekinn. This must be accomplished by dawn on the second 'morrow or he shall set sail without you. I've made provision for your swift passage to Evanntyr, and once aboard, Myrrdin shall see to it that these arrangements are carried out. 'Twill be of Magical Allure for the entire journey, you'll be exposed to others of whom you do not as yet understand, but you're not a virgin to the other Races. Know this Commander, you'll speak to no one along your way, and no one shall learn of your mission. You must conclude this contract with great stealth and in total silence, for if your route is compromised at any point, your time is done and you'll cross o'er the Veil without ever seeing Aalanna alive again. Do you so agree to these terms?"

The Battle Commander strained to look upon the man speaking through the fog, but 'twas impossible. He suspected there'd be naught to see anyway, and most likely he was projecting only his Voice, for to allow himself to be seen would have placed them both in greater danger.

"When does my silence begin and when does it end? Surely I'll be allowed to speak once I reach the Castle. I will speak to my woman!"

The Voice was quiet for such a long moment that Grifynn feared he'd pushed too hard and lost the chance to rescue Aalanna. What seemed like a lifetime dragged by afore he heard, "Once you add your blood, set the Spell in motion, I can only Hold your presence upon this side of the Veil for the span of a few days. Your silence ensures that you remain long enough to finish the deed, or have gone as far as you can to so finish. I am not capable of more." Was that a hint of regret? 'Twas compassion spilling through? Grifynn's eyebrows furrowed and he admitted hesitantly, "I have my own means of extending my life this side of the Veil. If I make use of it, will I be able to break my silence once I reach the castle?"

Again the Voice paused and Grifynn Felt the tingling of Magical scrutiny throughout his body. Finally he heard, "Ahhh, I See of that which you now speak. I comprehend the lure of the Blood and the Call that is with you at all times. And now I understand the prophesy." He seemed to consider for a moment, then, "Yes. Use the Blood Elixir in your possession after you reach the castle. 'Twill give you voice, and strengthen you for what you seek but I warn you, 'twill not last for long." And with that, the Voice began to retreat from whence it had come, "She has a sennight at most, for we're at the whim of the Evil One in this. Do not be late to the Krakken."

Grifynn's sight began to dim 'til he could no longer see even the shadows. Gradually, he was able to gather enough control to focus within the room, but 'twas obvious he was in deep Battle Lust, his world crimson. Gritting his elongating teeth, he felt their razor sharpness nick the inside of his bottom lip, and tasted the familiar bitterness of his Life Source. These changes had never gone this far afore. He feared not for his own life, for he understood what was happening to him. 'Twas what Shayla had warned him against for so many winters in the early days. Why she'd tried so hard to get him to give up using the Blood entirely. 'Twould be so easy to just give in to it, to let the changes attempt to morph his human body into a form he was ill suited to assume and by so doing, force him Past the Veil. If only Shayla had been able to perfect her Life Crystals. If only there'd been more time. But no, they'd been given more time than any other and 'twas still not enough. 'Twould never be enough! He had to fight the transformation; he had to survive a little longer. There was one more battle to fight, one more personal war to wage. He'd need assistance however, for he knew he'd not return from this mission alive. He'd take the stranger's offer, his strategy already formulating in his once lightening quick mind. This would have to be played to the hilt. His acting skills throughout his unnaturally extended life had been honed by necessity and his current need was strong. He had one more extraction to perform.

~~~~~~~~~~~

At dark the following evening, a great ship surrounded by a ghostly mist sailed into Port O'Drekinn and tied on to the docks.

"Captain, your orders, Sir?" The First Mate asked the Ship's Master after making secure.

Myrrdin stood at the handrail of the quarterdeck and surveyed the port, his ebony eyes flashing. Briefly he wondered where they were now. Had she dropped her cargo? Was the boy still alive? Nothing to do but trust they'd succeed. Moving his thoughts forward, this duty was no less important or dangerous than was the last. He didn't wish it to fail, but 'twas mostly out of his hands. Even his great Magic would have little to do with the outcome of this night. "We await a fare. If he doesn't arrive by dawn, we set sail for home."

"Yes Sir!" The First Mate replied with obvious enthusiasm. Even though their last fare was of their own homeland, they'd not picked them up from home soil.

Yes, Myrrdin thought to himself, near a winter had passed since they'd been home. Sighing, he realized 'twould be even longer afore Caleichante and the boy saw home again, if ever. He'd heard nothing since he'd dropped them here. Where were they?
~~~~~~~~~~~

CHAPTER 28
A Deepening Deception

THE FOLLOWING NIGHT

Storrm had been running all day and was feeling the pressure of Command. Although she wouldn't shirk her duties, she half wished her sister would return early. They'd managed to shift all of the candidates out of the Den to the caves beneath, and then spirited them away o'er a few days under cover of darkness. The Dragons had simply flown away using their own stealth methods and all had gone smoothly, but she was worried. 'Twas past the time they'd chosen to make the 'Bond, but she hadn't heard the results. Although the ceremony itself shouldn't have been too problematic, Kaahayyel was weakened, and this let in an unknown variable. The Draw took more Power than the First LifeBond had, of that they were all certain. But to add to these concerns, their communications were erratic, the distance was great, and if their Link were compromised, the Hoard might discover them. They didn't have the resources to handle a full out assault and their intelligence so far, indicated this was just what was likely to occur. So Silence was imposed and 'twas nerve racking to the energetic sibling of the Second in Command. There'd been much happening at home and she wanted to share with her sister. Mystynn had been attempting unsuccessfully to establish a Link with Gunnarr but there seemed to be some kind of interference of unknown origin, preventing such.

She hurried to her appointment with the Battle Commander after her brief visit with Walkyr and Fryya. The children were too serious and they needed a distraction, so she'd purchased the top two picks from the litter last whelped. Sired by Bensyn, the slain dog of whom Darque had been so enamored, she didn't look forward to informing her sister of that event. But the youngsters had been delighted with the pups. During her investigation this morning, she'd learned there'd been rumors of a sighting of her leaving the area just prior to the grisly discovery, but no one had been able to confirm what they'd thought they'd seen. Of course, she'd visited the Kennels often afore and she knew the slain dog intimately. An enormous baby, he'd always bound straight up to greet her affectionately. 'Twas trust 'tween them and she'd enjoyed romping through the training area, although no one else except Darque could get so close to the beast.

But she was certain she hadn't been to the Kennel on the day of the slaying. Storrm recognized the possibility of memory Magic affecting the kitchen assistant who'd made the original claim of seeing her, and Mystynn conferred. But who'd done this and why? At any rate, the children's spirits soared with the gift of the pups, and the care and training that would follow would help keep their minds off the current situation, and just maybe 'twould keep them both out of trouble. They were constantly disappearing in the Den, and having the pups with them made her feel better. She sighed as she hesitated afore entering the Commander's office.

"Storrm, you'll lead the other Teams to the Eastland on maneuvers. I need updated information on the regions and how they fare after the Melts. I need the Runners to resume from the Outlands. Also, I've received intelligence on a possible Hoard sighting in the Darden region, multiple dragons that may mean a lair nearby." He was perched upon the edge of his chair, his hands clasped together, his thick forearms resting upon the well worn desktop, his shoulders forward, his dark blue eyes glaring at his Third Fighter, defying her to question his orders. If their positions were reversed, he'd certainly question them.

When it became clear he'd finished, Storrm stepped boldly forward. Bringing her hands around from at ease position, she crossed them o'er her chest and actually glared at him. Clearing her throat, she stated ardently, "Commander, I'm compelled to remind you that two of the Teams are out on mission now and we're not certain of their current location. Nor are we in communication, as they're attempting to infiltrate the coastal Black Market. Also, Darque and Gunnarr are out searching for a suitable site for the Second LifeBond." Pausing, she bit her lip to keep to herself the fact that the ceremony might already have occurred, afore she continued, "That leaves only ten Teams, including Mystynn and me, still at home. If we all leave, Ariel, Rygyl, Zayddarr and Tegrynn will have no backup or 'Link, as the distance from the coast will be more than doubled, and beyond even the Dragons' capabilities. Knowing not the precise location or direction of Darque and Gunnarr, they may well be in the same situation. And if my Flight did find a Lair, we'd have no ability to report such, nor would we have the ability to Call for backup, and they'd have no idea of our situation. Not to mention that Drekinn will be left vulnerable to attack. Surely 'twas not your intention?" Storrm questioned her Commander, unsuccessfully covering her growing sarcasm.

Grifynn was amazed at her impudence as well as the fact that she'd included that last point about Drekinn's vulnerability. As a hardened Warrior, the Clan being attacked had always been possible, though not probable, and he was proud she hadn't excluded it from her accurate summary of the situation. He tilted his head downward so she couldn't see the barely noticeable smile, and considered what she'd also just confirmed. 'Twas as he'd suspected and what he was counting on of course, but he couldn't allow his astute daughter to deduce such. He was so proud of her and her sister. He'd been blessed by the One True Liege, and despite the events about to unfold, the prophesy appeared true and his daughters and his people would survive through the coming catastrophe. His legacy would live. He could only pray his Legend would be honorable upon the lips of those who gave voice to his Song. 'Twould be sweet to hear it. Mayhap from Beyond? He'd heard those Legends as well. Nearly snorting at this evidence of his own ego, he brought his ragged thoughts back to his present situation, and the actor within him took control once again.

"I am quite aware of all that, Third Fighter. Although 'twas not necessary, I appreciate you're only doing your job and will let it go at that. This time." Having regained his composure, he glanced up at Storrm and was relieved, in an odd sort of way, that she showed no sign of shrinking from his rebuke. If he'd had any doubts afore, there were none now and he'd be leaving all in good hands, to her and her elder sister.

Presenting his trump card to convince her all was well and there was no subterfuge, he said, "I have a Link of sorts, with the Dragons. All Communication can be relayed through me here in the Den. 'Twas established with Gunnarr in the beginning of my Command of the Teams." Noting the look of betrayal that almost instantly disappeared from her face, he continued, "We felt 'twould be best if no one knew this at the time." Suddenly, his emotions got the better of him in his weakening state and he softened his voice, speaking to her with fatherly love, "Don't feel badly, girl. Darque doesn't even have this knowledge." And with this revelation, Storrm's eyes grew slightly wider, then gathering her wits she confirmed the reception of her orders, nodded her head slightly and stated, "So be it, Commander. We leave by midnight." Turning on her heel, she exited swiftly, her multiple braids swinging freely past her knees.

Grifynn wanted to stop her, run after her, give her one last hug. Silently, he watched her thick braids swing back and forth with each step she took, recalling another time, here in this very office. He could clearly see her youthful face peeking out from behind Darque's shoulder, her eyes wide, her long braids sweeping the floor as she waited for the fallout that never came, from some impertinence or other that had spouted forth from her brazen sister. As he watched his middle child retreat from his office, for 'twas certain Fryya was his get, he was grateful that he'd lived to acknowledge her strength and growth into her own, and accepted 'twould be the last time he laid eyes upon her, the last time he'd hear her voice. Wishing he had the ability to brief his family and say proper good-byes, he whispered into the gathering darkness, "I love you, girl." The tears that rolled down his cheeks to splatter on the floor this time, steeled his resolve yet again, and wiping the moisture away with the back of one brawny hand, he prepared for the next step in this foolhardy scheme.

Grifynn neatly stacked the parchments and pushed them aside per his lifelong habit. He wished nothing to make anyone suspicious, which could then lead them to discover him missing too soon. He noted the candle at the corner. This mission had a precise schedule and he knew exactly how much time each step would consume. Taking a deep breath, he worked to control the rise of Battle Lust. He needed to find his inner calm, and he forced himself to move slowly and methodically in order to do so, which brought a sense of déjà vu. He'd completed so many missions, but this one meant more to him than any other. He must not fail. Taking a deep breath, he reached into the desk drawer for the remains of his stash of Life Crystal, and then drew back his hand without touching it, aware 'twould no longer do him any good. Shayla would find it eventually and 'twould be useful to her, to continue in their efforts. He wished he could tell her how much he loved her, how much he needed her, and how much he'd appreciated everything she'd done for him throughout their lives. He'd always known she'd survive him. If only there was something he could give her, something to let her know how he truly felt. He'd never been good at telling others how much he cared for them. Glancing around his office, he was saddened by the fact that there was nothing left of their prior existence, nothing that he could give her as a memento. Then with sudden inspiration, he reached up to his collar, pulled out the silver chain with the rectangular tag that had hung around his neck, hidden beneath his leathers for many lifetimes. Dragging it o'er his head, he caught several strands of his auburn hair in the process, and wincing as he yanked out the clump of hair with the chain, he held the tag in his hand, rubbing its scratched plate with his thumb. 'Twas so long ago, the tag so old now, that the words he remembered having been inscribed upon the dull surface, were no longer visible. 'Twas strange, he thought to himself, for the first time he realized he couldn't even recall the name by which he'd answered then, the name which had been on the tag. 'Twas no matter, the meaning would be clear to her. 'Twas his most prized possession and he'd only removed it rarely, and then only to replace the chain. Although the chain had been replaced many times, the tag had survived.

Pulling the entire drawer out of the desk, he detached the false back and removed the two small vials of Blood Elixir, all that he'd been able to 'borrow' from Shayla. Stashing them into his boots with the one that he always carried there, he knew 'twould have to be enough. He prayed 'twould be sufficient to allow him to accomplish his task. Carefully, he replaced the drawer, stood up, brushed his hands down the leather covering his muscular thighs and considered whether or not he should wear his chain mail. No, he decided, 'twouldn't be needed. Leaving the necklace in the center of the desk, the clump of hair still stuck within the chain links, he knew he couldn't pen a note that might be seen by someone other than the intended, and he couldn't risk compromising this mission. But Shayla would understand his gift immediately and would know his intent. She'd always understood him better than anyone, 'til he'd met and fallen in love with his Aalanna. Thinking of her made him smile. She'd brought such joy into his harsh existence. He'd waited so very long for her. How he'd missed her these past many winters.

Stepping toward the far wall of bookshelves, he took up the roll of parchment that he'd often read to his daughters when they were very young. The story was the Legend of 300. 'Twas actually a favorite story of his own pre-Holocaust history and from memory he'd put pen to parchment, telling and re-telling the story of the fierce battle for his Warriors to learn and to understand, no matter the odds, never give up. Always do what was right. Always stand up and defend the innocent and honor your Oath to the Clan. Give your all for love and for your Brothers in Arms and never, never, never, give in to the Evil which may surround you or threaten to drown you, because 'twas not done 'til 'twas done and no one could stop you but yourself. He pulled the parchment out and stacked it 'cross the others at an angle, which wouldn't even be noted by the casual observer but his daughters would see, and finding the story they'd know his last thoughts for them. 'Twould not be easy and they'd need the encouragement as well as the lesson reminder. Satisfied, he walked to his weapons hold against the wall and armed up heavily. Then he licked his fingers and snuffed the candle on his desk. 'Twas time.

<div style="text-align:center">~~~~~~~~~~~</div>

The bookshelves sighed closed just prior to the spy entering the office in the guise of his own daughter, Storrm. 'Twas very potent, Evil Magic which allowed him to make such a shift. He'd not have been able to accomplish this had it not been for his master, The Evil One himself, boosting his Magic. But still, he felt he was the one in control. He could handle

THE BLACK WAR BEGINS

The Black. Later. Boldly, he walked into the office and looked about. He'd expected a confrontation with the Commander but strangely, the room was empty. His eyebrows furrowed. He'd have to do a better job of obtaining his information. Wait, what was that on the desk? Stepping closer, he picked up the chain lying there and gleefully snatched the clumped strands of hair, tucking them into his pocket. This was a coup, he thought, for 'twould be quite useful. Mayhap he could keep this find to himself. He sneered wickedly and then got down to work.

Scribing hurriedly upon a sheet of blank parchment, he rolled it and fastened it with the Commander's own Seal. Looking about, he could feel the Shift failing and he ran out of the office, brushing past the lone guard, and near forgot to alter his memory. His taxed powers weakening by the strength required to maintain this form, he wasn't as cautious as he should've been and burned the man with his touch. Caring not for this evidence of his sloppy Magic, he set out swiftly to find a courier to give the order to the resident Dragon and Warrior, the ones who'd come so close to discovering him recently. He'd tried to destroy the one known as Ethynn and that stupid Dragon of his, Makayyd, at what they were now calling the Incident at Lorelei, but they'd fought fiercely, refusing to give in or give up. The Fates were with them, for in the end The Black had lost two good Dragons and near lost another to the Veil. He hadn't been pleased with this one. Swallowing his rising bile, he remembered the punishment he'd endured and the whining and groveling he'd done, 'til he'd finally managed to get back into his confidence. He knew the Team on his trail here at the Den were an odd pair and couldn't possibly fight well. By sending them off on this 'mission', he'd be eating away at their numbers, getting them off his back and mayhap please The Evil One. There was yet another potentially beneficial end to this scenario. If anyone attempted a rescue, they might be eliminated as well. He could only wish 'twould be The Dragon and The Mighty Blue. He had some power of his own and as soon as he'd concocted this distraction he'd ensured his chosen ones could follow through without too much difficulty from the Spell of Aversion. Completing his task, he exited via the front gate of the Dragon's Den itself, the Change taking him so no one saw him as the Warrior Third once he was outside. Oh how delighted he'd been with his butchery at the kennels. Oh how he hated those sisters. In point of fact, he hated everything about the Clan, everything good. With every little jab, breaking their heirlooms, causing mayhem in the kitchens, and this latest mess in the Kennels, he was frustrating them and causing their morale to drop with growing suspicions of their own neighbors. The Clan had to be caught completely off guard. He'd been sent here to discover if they knew anything, and creating added mischief had been his own idea. Of what he could discern, the stupid humans knew nothing of the King's plans. He'd done well and The Black would be pleased. That royal idiot Shytin thought he controlled them, but he was so wrong. He smiled wickedly to himself. His eyes took on a feverish glow as he made his way to the outskirts of the village where one of the Hoard awaited him to make good their escape.

~~~~~~~~~~~

The Guard spoke not a word, merely stepped aside as Storrm pushed her way brusquely past him. He bit his lip to keep from teasing her as he'd have done when she was a child. He could tell she was angry, and although that was not her style, he knew that everything was uncertain lately. She hadn't even taken notice of him and they'd known each other her entire life. He found her behavior strange, but by the 7th Egg, he couldn't have provided any objective reasoning for that, so he ignored it. 'Twas not long afore she'd left the way she'd arrived, carrying with her a rolled parchment with Seal, touching him on his shoulder briefly and then disappearing down the Great Hallway toward the altered wing of the Barracks where he knew Axyl was temporarily staying with his feisty little green Dragon, Haniyyah. He liked that Dragon and they'd been most helpful around the Den, in their tightening of security and their search for the spy. The little green was timid and stuck to the huge Warrior like a newly whelped Dog. She was small enough to go near anywhere in the Den, and seemingly without trying, could sneak up on the best of them. He was beginning to think those two might find the spy afore even the Battle Commander. Suddenly feeling a burning sensation as if stung, his eyebrows furrowed and he reached under his leathers to rub the place on his shoulder where he'd been touched by someone. Hadn't someone just passed by? No, mayhap 'twas a bug bite. 'Twas shortly thereafter, he was relieved by the next on duty and he'd thought that he should report something to the other that had occurred during his watch. When he couldn't recall anything he shook his head and decided 'twas fatigue only, told him the Commander was still inside working and then headed to the Barracks for some much needed sleep.

~~~~~~~~~~~

Grifynn moved purposefully through the dark tunnels that honeycombed their way from his office to the Port District. The path he chose led unerringly to the North Docks. He'd traveled them often, through many lifetimes, and needed not the torch for his night vision was nearly as acute as was his daughters'. Running his hand along the walls, twisting, turning, up, down, counting the offshoot tunnels, steps and passages, he arrived at the hidden trapdoor beneath the wharf. No one would have or could have seen him in the darkness, but he took no chances: despite his great age, he could still sneak up on the best of them. He pulled the hood of his cloak o'er his head and managed to climb onto the docks, mingling unnoticed with the people there. 'Twas not as crowded as during the day-time, but the wharf was never still. Listening in on their conversations, he was initially frustrated that no one mentioned the Krakken. But using his enhanced senses, he struck pay dirt when he discovered the ship on his own. Slipping into the shadows nearby, he pulled Darque's blade from his hip sheathe, bared his chest, and taking a deep breath and gritting his teeth so as not to make a sound, he plunged the blade into his heart with one stroke. His eyes wide, he was astonished. There was no pain, no out-ward bleeding through the gaping slash and he barely felt the chill of the air, the sounds about him now muffled. Every sensation was muted.

Marveling at this unexpected advantage, he wasted no time and cov-ering up again, reminding himself that he had to remain silent from here 'til he reached the castle and drunk the elixir, he jogged to the Krakken. Walking straight up the plank, he was concerned how he'd find this Myrrdin without a fight, since he couldn't tell the crew his need. Sure enough, just afore he managed to reach the top of the access ramp, a handsome agile crewman appeared, blocking his way. He had very long straight black hair with sparkling black eyes, and his pale skin provid-ed stark contrast in the moonlight. Grifynn dwarfed the man, if man he were, for he appeared quite young. But he had to find Myrrdin, and so he prepared for the fight he thought was forthcoming, stepping back into Battle Stance, for no one was going to block his way onto this ship.

The seemingly young man cocked his head and gazed deeply into the Battle Commander's blue eyes. "Find him, you have," he stated simply, his voice as wind chimes on a clear night, but with far greater quality. The ef-fect was rather fascinating really, and took Grifynn quite off guard. When he near forgot his primary rule of silence, Myrrdin stepped forward and held up his hands in greeting, saying, "No words are needed, I know of your mission. You are my only fare; I was concerned about your timely arrival. 'Tis I you seek. I am Myrrdin, Ship's Master of the Krakken. 'Tis near dawn and we make ready to set sail. I believe you have a token to present me for your passage?"

Grifynn's pierced heart yet hammered in his chest as he stepped forward, offering the bloody blade he clutched tightly in his hand. He could feel the supremacy of the Magic this one wielded as he neared the Ship's Master, and he was grateful he hadn't needed to fight, for he was very much aware that even though this one seemed young and lean of muscle, he'd not have stood a chance in Hades of winning that argument.

Myrrdin took the blade, tasted the blood upon the edge, and inhaled its fragrance for good measure. When the other closed his eyes, Grifynn momentarily wondered how safe the Master would've been if he were not an honorable man, but glancing up he noted several others upon the decks, similar in build and skin tones. Even though their hair and eyes were pale as opposed to the one afore him, unspoken was the knowledge they were kinsmen and he was under close scrutiny. He could feel the Allure all about him, and he understood how well protected the Ship's Master truly was.

Myrrdin opened his eyes so quickly it startled Grifynn out of his reverie. He tried to retrieve the blade but the other tucked it into his waistband, maintaining solid eye contact. "You'll not need it on your mission, but I can assure you that 'twill find its way back to its rightful owner one day." Grifynn heard the sincerity and the regret mixed into the avowal, and he nodded his head in acknowledgement. Apparently this one knew 'twas his last mission. Somehow, 'twas comforting. Then Myrrdin did a remarkable thing, in his opinion. Extending his hand and closing the remaining distance 'tween them, they gripped arms in a show of mutual respect. Grifynn was once again impressed with the strength of the other and was grateful they were not enemies. Quickly, the Ship's Master broke the clasp, leading him onto the deck and then below, to a tiny room with a cot. "You may wish to rest here. Don't fear to sleep, your benefactor is very powerful and you'll be fine. Keep silent, sleep if you can, we set sail at once. You're free to wander where ever you like, but I'll come for you at dusk, as you'll be off from there upon the next leg of your journey." And with these simple but slightly confusing instructions, Grifynn was left alone. 'Off on the next leg of your journey' he thought? We'll be mid-ocean by dusk. Exhausted he laid down, unable to think, and shutting his eyes, was asleep afore his next breath.

~~~~~~~~~~

"I have me sealed orders, girl," Axyl stated. "We'll catch up with you in Darden as soon as we can." And with that, Storrm felt the gust of wind as Haniyyah bore her Rider off the high wall of the Training Pits, her sturdy
~~~~~~~~~~

wings pumping, soaring up and out of the Den toward whatever secret destination and mission to which they'd been entrusted.

Storrm chewed on her bottom lip as she attempted to make sense of this new hitch in the plan. Axyl had turned up with Sealed orders partially negating her own, which she'd just received from the Commander's mouth. Something was wrong. They were being fractured, divided into smaller and smaller forces, with little to no chance to obtain a timely backup for any of them. Mystynn had confirmed her father's ability to Communicate with the Dragons but 'twas with Gunnarr himself, which only made Storrm realize just how limited all of their communications really were, despite Magic. The Dragons had lived such solitary lives for so long, they seemed incapable of the kind of Link that Legend had Sung, with all of them aware of every other's thoughts and deeds. Mystynn revealed 'twas not a myth, but only the Elders now had that ability, and although he and Gunnarr were Princes with stronger Magic than most, they weren't Ancients, and were truly considered adolescents. This reminded her of the overall youthfulness and inexperience of the entire Fleet. The new Stable, if they'd taken, wouldn't be able to manage a full day of flight yet, not to mention they'd still be working toward coordination of their MindLink. They'd be safely secured by her sister, though she knew not where. Pondering her mission, she decided that if they did find a Lair, they wouldn't engage outright, in which case she'd have to control the urges of Battle Lust within her Teams, which would place them all in danger. Her lifelong training would soon be tested; she could feel great trouble looming upon the horizon as she and Mystynn, and what was left of her dwindling Flight, took wing toward the Eastlands.

CHAPTER 29

One Dragon Down

THE FOLLOWING NIGHT

The Standing Guard was the last patient of the day and had just left Shayla's care to return to active duty. She'd never seen anything like the burn on his shoulder. 'Twas in the shape of a handprint, but the man couldn't remember anyone having touched him or anything that might have bitten him. There seemed no explanation for the wound. After giving the guard some salve to ease the pain and avoid infection, she'd sent him on his way and then dutifully recorded the abnormal wound on her lengthening list of unusual occurrences. Wiping her hands on her apron after washing them for the hundredth time this day, she was so tired she nearly fell asleep walking back to her private quarters. Yawning, she reached for the door latch and began to pull off her apron when she heard the panicked voice echoing down the hallway.

~~~~~~~~~~

"The forest is ablaze!" Walkyr's youthful voice squeaked as he was inundated by a horrible Vision. "The Forest burns!" He screamed loudly enough this time for near everyone in the Barracks 'cross the Den to hear him, and they rushed to respond. All the staff and the residents knew of the boy's Visions by now. But even those who didn't hold faith in them, weren't willing to take a chance that 'twas a simple nightmare. Very quickly the first of the Healer Apprentices, who bunked closest to his room, came charging toward the door only to be met by his Body Guard. The arriving staff crowded at the threshold, peering curiously at the pair, but were soon dispersed by the other guard on duty, who cleared and secured the area.

Cayell was a big man, typically built for a born and bred Warrior, and was relatively young compared to his comrades in arms. He'd been honored to be chosen and hired by Darque herself, as one of two Warriors who shared the duty of protecting the young Seer and Darque's daughter. Walkyr's reputation had spread, despite attempts to keep his talents secret. Mynx had spent most of her time with Fryya, while Cayell had become quite close to the boy. He now felt as if they were family, even though the boy would never be a Warrior. This fact had made no difference to
~~~~~~~~~~

him, and he took his charge quite seriously. He'd lay down his life to protect the child, and not simply to follow orders. He truly loved Walkyr, had related to his loneliness, and even though he had professional reasons for being close, they'd grown closer still with every day they'd been together.

Most Warriors had thoughts of being a father one day, if they survived their careers, and Cayell had been typical. When the Dragons had returned and the Clan had been plunged into The Black War, he'd believed his chances greatly reduced, 'til he began his tenure with this child. Now, Cayell thought of Walkyr as his own son, stepping into his life, filling the emptiness created by the absence of his Claim father, Kallyr, as the Clan Seer was constantly working. How the big man's heart ached whenever he heard the dread that permeated the little boy's voice, screaming out his Visions into the darkness of the long winter's nights. This time, he'd just stepped out to relieve himself, leaving Mynx close, and was on his return when he'd heard the cry. Racing to his bedside, he'd still been the first one there. He'd frowned at Mynx when she arrived shortly thereafter, and she'd tried to compensate for her tardiness by securing the area and dispersing the onlookers. Comforting the boy, he knelt down and questioned him to extract as clear a memory of the Vision as Walkyr was able to provide. This information was very important and he'd become quite adept at helping the boy relate the finer details.

<center>~~~~~~~~~~</center>

Gunnarr and I Heard Walkyr's tormented scream near as soon as the words had left his mouth, and I was up and dressed afore the echo of his warning had died in the Great Hallway. Unbeknownst to any, we'd returned just a mark prior. We'd built an entire Training Facility under St Swiftyn's Bog, and the new Stable was already working out along with the hopeful candidates for the next attempt. The facility was functional and the Ancients were still there, recuperating from the heavy strains of the last few moons. I'd left Tannyr and his surprising 'Bond, Kaahayyel, as the ranking Team, flanked by Mikkal and Rakkah and their 'Bonds, to supervise the implementation of the Training programs and security. I'd not even taken the time to Communicate much of this to Storrm, let alone the Battle Commander, feeling an innate sense that I needed to keep all quiet for some reason. Upon our return, we'd merely lain down at home, falling asleep near afore we'd closed our eyes.

Now Gunnarr awaited me on the ledge, his saddle dangling from his teeth. As he tossed it o'er his shoulders, I helped him secure it. While he took the plunge off the edge, I vaulted aboard smoothly, gaining my seat a handful of heartbeats after the first alert. Locating Walkyr's essence at the Den, I Called for Storrm and Mystynn as my backup. I Cast for my father, but couldn't find him. 'Twas puzzling, and I felt something dark in the sensory trail 'tween us.

"I know not." Gunnarr Answered afore I Asked. He was worried, which steeled me to the worst.

"Then where is he, why can I not Hear him? And what is this fire? 'Tis close?" The Forests burning would be devastating, as they'd just recovered from the Holocaust. My thoughts were scattered, something foul was happening. Grifynn was protected day and night, and should be easily located, either in his bunk or his office. And why had Storrm not Answered immediately? What the Flame was going on?

Thinking back o'er our confrontation the last time I'd seen my father, I'd felt something was wrong then too. Several times o'er the past few moons, I'd tried to question him specifically about his erratic behavior, strange flashes of emotions, and the growing darkness within him. In typical fashion, he'd negated my concerns as little to nothing and no worry. By the time Gunnarr and I'd received our orders near a moon past, his emotions had somehow been 'contained'. My Sword attempted to get my attention and I was now certain 'twas about him and his distraction that night. I was positive he'd been struggling with some momentous decision.

Flying swiftly, we landed in the Pits and I dismounted afore Gunnarr managed a complete stop, dashed into the Great Hallway and raced for Walkyr's room. I was relieved to find him safe and sitting beside Cayell, who was just finishing writing down the details of the Vision. I liked that Warrior. He'd make a good 'Bond one day. The rest of the castle was quiet again. Once the staff noted the boy was safe, they'd returned to their own beds and to much needed sleep.

"'Twas the forest ablaze, Darque. I saw the trees burning. 'Twas one Dragon down in the forest, amidst the fire." Walkyr pleaded with me to believe him, for even he knew how much the Dragons avoided the forests. How would one of the huge beasts have gotten himself into that situation?

"'Tis well, my young friend, don't fret so," I said to him in a lighthearted manner, trying to ease his anxiety. But when I saw 'twas having the opposite effect, I leaned closer and placed my hand upon his trembling shoulder, forcing him to face me. "You are like a brother to me and I trust your Visions, Walkyr. You of all of us, have nothing to prove. If you've Seen it, 'twill happen. I just wish I knew when."

The boy stood up and gave me a hug. "I know not for certain, but this has the flavor of the present. I know the Dragons don't enter the forest, but this one seemed not to care! 'Twas as if driven, as if they'd been told to do so, or thought they'd find something important." Walkyr was puzzled, unable to adequately convey his thoughts.

I left him with Cayell, who could get him to sleep when no one else could. Remounting Gunnarr who stood ready in the Pits, I paused. I'd felt something, and there seemed an odd emptiness surrounding the Den. Was that a Cry? I closed my eyes and tried to place the direction of the sound. Thinking 'twas from a great distance, I Cast out, Reaching as far as I could, and Heard a scream of rage return rapidly, striking me with the force of desperation, coming from the north. I grit my teeth as the Cry carried with it such pain and fury, it racked my body to near convulsions. Calling to my Teams for reinforcement, I was shocked by the return silence. Casting forth in all directions, I Called again, more strongly than ever afore, and discovered Mystynn and Storrm were traveling to the far east, already too far away to Hear Haniyyah's Call for assistance. Why were they all gone from Drekinn at once, and who'd sent Haniyyah and Axyl north? I'd left them investigating at the Den, seeking the spy, how did this happen? I wasn't even supposed to return 'til sometime on the 'morrow and that would've been too late. I'd given no such orders for the Teams to go out and in fact, 'twould be foul judgment. What was happening? 'Twas obvious to me, that only Storrm and I had the ability to Reach 'cross such a vast chasm of distance and if not for our undisclosed skills, I'd have no backup for this rescue. As 'twas, we couldn't yet divulge our talents, and Speaking weakly 'cross the vast space, I Told her to turn and head in the direction of the battle now taking place, meeting me there as soon as they could. 'Twouldn't be half their return afore they'd all Hear Haniyyah, and she could then mount the backup openly. At least, I prayed the little Green would still then be Screaming her defiance.

All this Speak was completed as Gunnarr and I flew swiftly toward the site of the ambush. With our enhanced speed we were soon approaching the forested regions o'er which we'd patrolled mere moons ago. Little Haniyyah wouldn't have been able to fly blindly to a rest stop and the trees afforded no salvation. I couldn't imagine why they'd entered this region.

As we closed in, I could barely see through the black smoke, 'twas reminiscent of Kaddart, and once again I was the first to arrive upon the battle. This time however, 'twas the forest afire, not a village or fields, but 'twas not raging uncontrolled. A large clearing was smoldering and the Flames were heavy there, but I could just make out the diminutive

Dragon straddled o'er her burly Rider. Face down in the charred leaf litter of the burned out clearing, he was sprawled in such a manner that 'twas apparent he'd have been dead if not in 'Bond, but nothing was guaranteed at this point. All I knew for certain was that the big man still clung to life, as his feisty little Green roared out her challenge to the three Hoard Dragons surrounding them. They taunted her, hovering just out of her reach, battering her from all sides. Still I watched as she simultaneously struck out with her lethal talons, bared her wicked fangs and protected her Rider from the Flames of her enemies with her spread wings.

Haniyyah's leathery chest, legs and muzzle were charred and dripping blood. I could see that her wings had been systematically shredded as she'd protected Axyl. Unable to pick up her Rider and launch in such close quarters, 'twas obvious to me that this was an ambush well planned. The three Hoard Dragons were wearing her out, using up her Magic, waiting for an opening to finish off Axyl and thereby her as well, attempting to avoid any injury she might inflict, although I could tell she'd done some serious damage in return. But despite her success at holding them off, she was just one Dragon and when she could no longer Brew her Flame, they were done for. I was proud of her courage and the vicious effectiveness of her attacks despite the odds. I'd not imagined the once shy and apprehensive Green could step into Battle Mode this fiercely.

"'Twill come a time when we are not the first to arrive," Gunnarr Spoke in reference to my prior thoughts. We'd be close enough to engage within moments and I couldn't take the time to think about the underlying meaning of his comment.

"Ready my love?" I Asked and he growled his response in Dragon Tongue. We couldn't wait for Storrm and the others to arrive, we had to act now, and he not only affirmed my question, he also Spoke to Haniyyah, letting her Know we were coming. The instant she received this message, she took a long deep breath, then the Flame emanating from the Hoard Dragons engulfed her and I feared she'd succumb to the Heat.

Suddenly, from amidst the red and yellow licking blanket o'er her, she belched forth a long winded, billowing inferno that was brighter and hotter than I'd ever seen, forcing back that of the Hoard Dragons as they sputtered and then lost their focus against the onslaught of her rage. At the same instant, we sailed in behind the unsuspecting ambushers at full Flame, sandwiching them 'tween the firestorms. All I could Hear was their death howls as they were taken entirely by surprise, unable to react quickly enough to avoid being forced Beyond the Veil.

Haniyyah was in shock and slumped heavily to her side, making a gallant effort not to crush her fallen Rider. Barely breathing, she couldn't even Speak to Gunnarr.

"Will she live? What about Axyl?" I was terrified of losing them as we'd near lost their siblings not long past.

"They both live. We must get them to the Healer. They share severe injury and Haniyyah is not able to Heal herself while stabilizing Axyl's wounds, leaving their condition at a stalemate. Also, they cannot stay here in the open." Gunnarr's simple logic brought me back on board, for which I was grateful. Storrm was rapidly approaching from the East and despite the struggle against the Aversion Spell, we soon had a separate sling rolled under each of them, with two Dragons to lift each sling. 'Twas the first time we'd attempted this type of carry in real life and I felt mixed emotions, pleased it worked so well and aggrieved that 'twas required.

Traveling back to the Den took several marks, and the full of the day was gone by the time we arrived in the triage area of the Pits. During the transfer, I'd lent my Strength to Haniyyah, assisting her to Hold on. I Heard Storrm and Mystynn approaching as we landed in the middle of the Pits and dismounting in the back-beat of Mystynn's wings, I hurried through the sand to the spectators decks. Entering the Great Hallway, I ducked down toward the Healer's quarters while Storrm went to the Barracks for assistance. Finding Shayla with Fryya and Walkyr, I pulled them all away from the supper they were picking at in fatigue and hurried them back to the ambush victims. There hadn't been time to send anyone ahead and having no Communication Link with the other Warriors or the Healer, was a bloody nuisance. I had to rectify this situation immediately but I'd no idea how. We needed a warning system; someone had to be able to Link with the Dragons as relay. We simply didn't have enough Teams to leave one at the Den for this purpose at all times.

Gently, Haniyyah was lowered to the sands, with the other Riders and some incoming Warriors recruited from the Barracks, standing ready to assist her. But upon discovery of the severity of her wounds, they chose to simply leave her on the sling, spreading it out around her and pulling it as taut as possible. Then they moved to assist in extricating Axyl from his sling midair. Attempting to carry him into the hospital unit, Haniyyah aroused from her self-induced stasis and made it clear, no one was going to take him out of her line of vision. Given the ruckus that ensued, I had the cot brought out to the sands beside her and Shayla went straight to work on him there. Her Apprentices began working diligently on Haniyyah, providing what ministrations they could to stop the bleeding, thereby easing her pain while she focused her Magic on Axyl. As each of Axyl's wounds were cleansed, sutured or salved, Haniyyah's own pain levels began to lessen slightly. She'd stubbornly refused to Heal herself 'til she knew her Rider was in good hands, as this took her attention away from him. They were still Linked, but she was very protective and I had to reassure her through MindSpeak, reasoning with her that she had to start her process in order to be ready to take on his, and that he was being stabilized by the Healer. Still, she showed no sign of beginning the Healing, seemingly unable.

Under normal circumstances and in a safe environment, the Dragon could Heal herself easily, and the LifeBond Axyl shared with her would Heal all of his injuries as well, as long as both of them didn't share similar, severe injury. 'Twas when the Dragon had to stabilize his or her own condition as well as their Rider's Life Force in order to keep them from Passing the Veil, that caused the stalemate in which we currently found ourselves. In other situations, the best thing to do would be to put the Rider into a drug induced sleep to numb his pain levels, and allow his Dragon to heal. Once the Dragon was healthy enough to shoulder the load of the Healing for the Rider, then the Rider could be Healed while he slept. But in this case, Axyl was far too seriously injured, with severe loss of blood and Flame wounds that would have taken him Beyond if not for his stubborn Green. He couldn't be put into a drug induced state of sleep or he'd die, but it didn't matter, for he hadn't regained consciousness since I'd found them and this worried me greatly.

By the time Shayla had Axyl's condition under some tentative initial control, the big man was still unconscious but she felt 'twas better than drugging him. "The head injury alone makes him far worse than Daxx when he was brought in, but his Linayyah was not seriously injured and could shoulder much of the Healing. How did this happen? Axyl is bigger and stronger than any of the other Warriors and he was unconscious upon arrival. I understand he was so when you found him and he's not regained consciousness apparently since he was wounded. The longer he's been in this condition, the lower are his odds of survival."

I didn't want to hear that. I had to trust her, and she'd never failed me afore. Her Healer abilities were renowned and as I prayed for her to keep Axyl alive, she turned her attentions to Haniyyah. She was stunned to find the severity of the wounds the little Dragon suffered. Haniyyah had brutal talon slashing o'er most of her body, legs and muzzle, and more than two thirds of her wing span was shredded, pieces missing everywhere. In some places, the fractured bones were exposed and she'd endured long stream, full impact Flame o'er her body, her back and wings receiving the worst of the burns, as she'd valiantly protected Axyl. In addition, Shayla found multiple missing scales, leaving open bloody holes in her hide. Haniyyah had two of her sharp fangs ripped from her jaw and had also lost at least four of her talons on her front paws. Shayla had no idea if the Green could Heal from all this. What the ferocious Dragon had done for her Rider brought tears to her eyes. But Axyl had little hope of survival himself, and she'd lose them both if he Passed. The brawny man had severe internal and head injuries, and he'd most likely Pass without ever regaining consciousness. She bit her lip and thought about what she could do for them. The little Green had proven her worth and Shayla couldn't let her down. She must help her, there had to be a way. She had to try something, anything, for none of them had much to lose. She chewed upon her lower lip and struggled with a decision, then abruptly turned about and left the triage area.

~~~~~~~~~~

I watched in curiosity as Shayla left, only to reappear a short while later, and shooing all of the Apprentices out of the Pits, along with me and Gunnarr, she returned to Axyl's side. Just as I stepped into the long hallway, I glanced o'er my shoulder and thought I saw her place something in the big man's mouth. Ahhh, mayhap some Healer's secret that would turn the tide? Soon thereafter, she allowed my sole return and handed me a large tub of a recently altered salve, into which I'd seen her mixing a reddish powder. She hadn't known that I watched her do this, and I assisted her in applying the salve to Haniyyah while she worked on Daxx. It took quite awhile to cover the massive beast, and by the time I was finished, Shayla had also completed whatever she was doing with the big Warrior.

~~~~~~~~~~

Shayla would have preferred not allowing anyone to assist in this effort, for she hoped the results would amaze them and she didn't want word of this to leak out. But the effort was too much for her to handle alone. There were few who knew of the severity of the Team's wounds, and 'twas her intent to keep it that way as long as she could. Sending out her silent Call to Corbyn while Darque was busy applying the concoction, she Relayed her need for rapid response and identified the Apprentices who should be 'visited'. She prayed they'd not already begun to spread the rumors she'd tried to squelch, for the more who heard about this, the more difficult 'twould be to contain. She knew that Darque and her Flight would keep their silence.

~~~~~~~~~~~

While I helped Shayla apply the salve, I noted 'twas the consistency of cold honey, similar to aged Dragon saliva, but 'twas more of an almost clear blood red color, than orange or brown, and 'twas odorless. Axyl struggled just beneath consciousness several times during the process and I held my breath listening to his agonized moans. Mercifully, they both plunged into a deep sleep soon after we'd finished with the salve. I shifted restlessly, watching and assisting as directed while the Healer worked on the Dragon, making sure the salve was on every wounded surface, correcting angles, approximating hide and setting bones into proper alignment. Her expertise was astonishing for one who shouldn't have had any prior experience or knowledge of Dragons, and I vowed to learn more. One never knew what one might need in the field. I had some rudimentary Healing skills since she'd near raised me, but the level she'd displayed this day, had me in awe.

I'd have to wait at least 'til dawn for Axyl to awaken, now that 'twas more certain he'd live, and then I'd get some answers. Still, that seemed too long. Finally, Shayla shooed me out of the way, telling me to go to the kitchens to eat. She claimed she could hear my stomach growling from 'cross the Pits and wasn't happy with Gunnarr for allowing me to get so hungry. Securing her promise that she'd notify me as soon as Axyl so much as stirred, Gunnarr and I vacated, but not for the kitchens.

~~~~~~~~~~~

Shayla sighed in relief when Darque finally left, the sounds of bones popping and snapping, the evidence of new fangs and talons growing, becoming louder and more obviously unnatural, even for the enhanced Healing process. And she knew the astute Second in Command wouldn't be long in realizing something wasn't quite right. She was amazed herself at how she could see the bones knitting together, the lacerations closing, even to the point of watching Haniyyah's missing scales form, thicken, and harden afore her very eyes. Of course she believed she'd known the end result, as she'd attempted this afore, just once, but 'twas still a bold move on her part. She hadn't wanted to try to explain the acceleration and would leave that in Darque's hands for later. If she told her, that is. They'd be able to justify it to the enhanced Healing of the LifeBond and the Dragon's own Magic, and in truth 'twas just that, but without the boosting effect of her own Life Crystal the two would've perished, unable to get enough power to begin the process in the first place. The Life Crystal of her creation accelerated the accelerator. In other words, 'twas as if a wound couldn't heal due to an infection. The Crystal 'killed the infection' and allowed the natural ability of the wounded to begin the healing process. Her analytical mind struggled with that explanation. No, she thought, 'twas not that exactly, as there was no infection per se, but there was a point in which a wound was so severe, the ability to heal stagnated due to the level of the need, too much to do, and therefore it just quit. Her Crystal boosted the process, allowing it to begin again, only much faster than what it did naturally, as if 'twas pushed very hard to get it unstuck and then once released, nothing stood in its way to slow it down. Yes, she'd attempted this afore. Just once, upon a Dragon many lifetimes past. She hadn't let on to Grifynn and she'd no idea what had happened to that Dragon, but she'd felt the need to help him since he'd been injured helping them, and against Grifynn's specific orders she'd treated the beast. 'Twas too dark to tell his color, but he'd been enormous and he'd been heart struck. 'Twas similar to what Grifynn had suffered and had given her the inspiration to treat him the same way. She'd left the Dragon in the field where she'd discovered him for his own protection as well as hers, and there was nowhere to take him anyway. When she'd returned at dawn, the great beast had disappeared. She actually had never known for sure what had occurred, but watching Haniyyah Heal here and now, she felt certain the other one had done the same and had taken wing on his own in the night. She smiled at the memory. She'd always been too compassionate for her own good. "Ungrateful wretch," she muttered to herself, a smile forming on her lips.

<div align="center">~~~~~~~~~~</div>

"Where is my father?" I yelled at the Guard as I exited the Battle Commander's office. His confusion nearly swamped my senses, ensuring his truthful reply as he stuttered, "He's not there? I've not left my post! He's not left and no one has entered 'til you…" he trailed off, just shy of accusing me of barging in as I'd been wont to do throughout my life. He charged past me, nearly knocking me down in his haste to see for himself that his Commander was truly missing. The room was empty. His horrified expression told me everything I needed to know. Somehow my father managed to leave his office without a posted Guard knowing. I knew how. 'Twas the when and to where, I didn't know. And one more thing. Was his exit voluntary or coerced?

Pushing the Guard back out of the room, I stood just inside the doorway, my feet wide, my hands open and raised o'er head, as I closed my eyes and Reached for the answers. Quickly, a series of Visions flashed through my mind. The blade in my father's hand, a Voice telling him to go to Evanntyr, the anguish he felt. There wasn't much time, I had to try to stop him from reaching the King's Castle afore he was taken by The Black. Passing along the information to Storrm, I let my Battle Lust build. She'd meet me upon the Southern Plains.

Hurrying back to the Pits, I pushed past Shayla who was troubled by my actions, but I was out of options. I shook Axyl hard 'til he began to rouse, and finally attempted to open his eyes. "You were found in the forest! How did you make Haniyyah enter?"

"'Twas no problem, Second," he spat through fractured jaws, "she's never had the same issues with the forests as the others, but I can tell you it took much to get the Hoard to follow. 'Twas a special Allure about them and then they didn't actually enter, they merely Flamed the area to flush us out, which caused them great distress."

Gunnarr Spoke to Haniyyah while I was questioning Axyl. *"What happened out there?"*

"We received Orders to go to the border of South Byndynn, to meet a new contact who would have information about the spy. When we arrived, we felt something was very wrong. We just managed to avert the initial ambush, and the chase was on. We entered the Forest to lose them, but they had a protection Spell, even though 'twas not a well conceived Allure. During the chase, they forced us closer to the treetops, and we became entangled while trying to avoid Flame, the ensuing fire created the clearing in which you found us, and while fighting two of the Hoard Dragons, the third flanked us, knocking Axyl off, and he plunged to the ground below. I was barely able to cushion his fall, but he was unconscious from the time they hit him, to now."

"How did you shun the Spell of Aversion?"

"I've never been affected, m'lord Gunnarr. I can only say that I always thought 'twas associated with my size, or lack thereof, and that I've sought refuge in the Forests since I was newly hatched." Her Tone was eloquent, her demeanor noble, but Gunnarr could feel her anxiety at revealing this knowledge to him.

"Have no fear, for 'tis not my desire to chastise you, I merely wish to know how you succeeded. 'Tis time to dissolve the ancient Spell to allow us all to return to the Forests. As they now prosper, the need for such protection has long past and seems obvious now, 'tis more hindrance than help. However, the fact that you alone can do something the rest of us cannot, means there may be a way to selectively alter the Spell and if so, 'twould be a great advantage in the War, by keeping the Hoard at bay and allowing the

rest of us to freely enter. Not to mention that you must have intimate knowl-edge of the regions that we desperately require."

"Then listen well m'lord and I shall relate all that I know about the Forests, for I've traversed their length and breadth 'cross Kadoor since long afore the Holocaust. I know every tree, every creature, every tribe of Man within. I know what changed and what did not. I know the Wyrdritch." Haniyyah's Voice faltered as she fatigued, but Gunnarr couldn't contain himself with her Words.

"Every tribe of Man? The Wyrdritch? We do have much to talk about!" Gunnarr's enthusiasm was checked by Haniyyah's slowed breathing. The information could wait. She'd not be going anywhere for awhile.

<div align="center">~~~~~~~~~~</div>

"We'll discuss it in more depth later, but I still need to know why you went there and who sent you." I had to know the answers to my questions, but 'twas a struggle to keep him alert.

"We received an order to go directly to that location. 'Twas indicated we'd find the spy there," he spat past his still clenched teeth and then, taking a shallow breath, he near passed out again from the pain.

"And where is this Order?" I shook him persistently, trying to avoid the Healing fracture of his left shoulder. 'Twas a near certainty 'twould be gone, but I needed to verify his report for my own sake.

Seeing the look upon his battered face, my hopes were dashed. "I bore the Order with me, as you well know, lass. 'Tis gone now, Flamed, but the Order bore his Seal." Axyl spoke in a half whisper, one eye still swollen shut.

I was perplexed and my brow furrowed. "The King's Seal? Why would he send you an Order?" But even as I made the statement, I winced with what I was about to hear, trying not to listen, but forcing myself to accept the truth.

"No lass, 'twas the Seal of your father."

CHAPTER 30

The Battle of Evanntyr

We met Storrm and Mystynn upon the Southern Plains and took wing to King's Gate with all haste. 'Twas our fastest flight ever and within marks we were o'er the Edge. A few more marks and we could see the towers of Evanntyr looming in the distance.

The battle that ensued was surreal in its familiarity. 'Twas as if I'd been there afore, done this in the past. I knew from where each of the King's Agents would attack, could sense their strategies prior to their actions. Had I been in this Keep and fought this battle in another life? I knew the design of the castle, which entry would lead me to what room, exactly where I'd find my father, and yet I also knew I'd never walked this path afore. Fighting without having to think of where I was going or how I'd get there, I slaughtered my way from the Ward where Gunnarr had dropped me, through the gates of the Keep into the Great Hall, up the Grand Staircase and into the hallway leading to the damp stone spiral steps to the Tower. Storrm followed me, protecting my back, maintaining our escape route, while our Dragons perched upon the walls of the Castle, belching forth Flame upon the incoming forces beginning to arrive from the outlying Barracks and the Village. Through the Keep I fought like a mad man, without hesitation, for I was led by an eerie sense of déjà vu.

Fatigued as I was from fighting my way to this very room through the heart of the castle following in Grifynn's footsteps, I found there was one more obstacle to conquer. I took a deep breath, and crashing through the locked and heavy wood and metal door as if 'twere no more than stacked bales of hay, I found him up against the farthest corner of the room. He stood guard o'er a tiny woman like a human shield, facing a single swordsman whose back was to me. This was why he'd come to Evanntyr. That woman was my mother.

He was covered with sweat and blood. His sword was broken and his right arm hung limply at his side, a huge slash 'cross his shoulder exposing muscle and splintered bone, bleeding profusely. Aalanna stepped out bravely beside him, ripping her skirt for a bandage in an attempt to stop the steady flow. Even with old bruising evident upon her face, her long, copper red hair a tangled mess, she was beautiful. Grifynn maintained his stance 'tween her and the enemy swordsman and I noted as he shifted his weight slightly to move Aalanna behind him, he favored his right leg. Yet he still faced off unerringly with his rival. Although his gray blue eyes now seemed to flash and were almost black, there was no fear, just frustration in his inability to prevent what was obviously about to happen. I was barely walking the last time I'd seen my mother. Flashes of memories came unbidden to my mind. My father adored her, she was the most wonderful thing that had ever happened to him, he loved her more than his own life, even more so than the Battle Lust that now raged within him.

The King's swordsman glanced my way nervously as I came crashing through the door, then took a quick sidestep, keeping my father to his sword arm, he brandished his shield in my direction. All the blood drained from his face the instant he recognized The Dragon, betraying his rising panic. Reading his intent in his eyes afore he'd even completed his thought, I knew I'd still be too late. My forward momentum hadn't stopped but I'd been forced to slow down as I climbed o'er the fallen door into the room, while simultaneously assessing the situation I was about to enter. If I'd only arrived quicker, I might've been close enough to prevent his next move. Several things then happened at once. The Agent pivoted rapidly toward my father bringing up his broad sword in a swiping upper cut, my father had what was left of his sword in his left hand and used it to reach behind himself to push Aalanna away to the far wall on his right while I rushed forward 'cross the stone floor. Time near stopped, everything happening in slow motion. The Battle Commander and I locked gazes for the drip of a candle as he made certain his lifemate was out of the way of the oncoming attack, swinging his sword around in a wide arc. He understood he was about to leave us and he'd demanded I perform my duty as Death Avenger by slaying the one who was about to force him Past the Veil. I tried to prevent the inevitable but even with my enhanced speed, my Dragon Sword slashed through the Agent's short neck just as he'd sunk his blade to the hilt in my father's chest.

~~~~~~~~~~

"They besiege the Dragon's Den. Drekinn is in danger."

"They'd never attack us, they wouldn't dare to fight us on our own soil," I stated, as she carefully laid my father's head upon her lap. She'd just made the most incredible prediction as the first thing out of her mouth after I'd killed the ill-fated swordsman. She was a tiny woman, even smaller than I, but there was no mistaking her Clan heritage. Sitting on the floor with her back against the wall, she used her apron to wipe the blood from the Commander's face, but there was so much she soon gave up. Lovingly, she
~~~~~~~~~~

finger combed his auburn hair, murmuring to him as if he were a sleeping child. Keeping my Sword in my hand, I half knelt beside them. My emotions were scrambled, I was still deep in Battle Lust, my vision a red haze. My strategies shifted, from battling my way here to escape. There was a window behind me and I tried to work out a plan to get us both through it while deciding what to do about Storrm who was still attempting to hold the Grand Staircase, with Gunnarr and Mystynn waiting impatiently outside on the ramparts. My father was a big, brawny man, and would never have made it through that window. Clearly he'd have known this. I began to wonder what his strategy had been. 'Twas becoming clearer he'd not planned to survive this rescue. Just what HAD he planned?

Looking up at me as if she'd just noticed my presence, she said airily, "Darque, you're so beautiful. You favor your aunt, I would've known you anywhere." Her gaze drifted into some other world and time as she stated with a slightly lowered voice, "Not a day has gone by that I haven't thought about you and your sister. My memories have sustained me through these long, lonely winters." Rambling, she continued her flight of ideas, "I knew you'd come for me. I always knew you'd be the one who'd save me. 'Twas always you. You are the chosen one. You are the child of the prophesy."

I had an aunt? Although confusing, 'twas her last words that brought a chill to my soul, as I tried to recall why they'd seemed so familiar. I knew I'd heard this afore. I was privy to every prophesy of the Clan, why could I not remember this one? Her rambling continued, "I'm so grateful you rescued Fryya. You have to tell her who her real father is, she must be told she shares not the blood of Shytin, that vile bastard." She lifted her frail hand toward me and I leaned closer so she could place her small palm against my cheek. As she spoke in a slightly more serious tone, she searched my face, "Don't underestimate the Evil which permeates the King, or the power of the Magic he has at his beck and call. He'll stop at nothing to destroy you and the Clan. Now go! Don't let Evil succeed. With Grifynn gone, you are the Battle Commander. You will not fail. You must not fail…." Her voice trembled and as tears filled her eyes, I understood she wasn't leaving with me. I could Hear Storrm below the Tower, where she'd managed to hold her position all this time, but she'd soon be inundated by the steady influx of reinforcements. Before long, our escape route would be compromised, and I Saw her beginning to retreat up the stairs, flight by flight, fighting her way to join us. The Agents would be entering from above any time now and we'd have to make good our escapes separately in order to survive. If we'd had a plan when we came, 'twould have been modified a hundred fold by now.

THE BLACK WAR BEGINS

My mother's hand slipped from my face and she sighed heavily. Her eyes glazed as she leaned o'er my father, kissing him gently. There was so much blood I couldn't tell whose 'twas any longer, mine, hers, his, or the many Agents I'd left scattered in pieces o'er the Great Hall, upon the steps and draped o'er the railings of the Grand Staircase, down the long hallway, in front of the chamber door, and now in this very room. My adrenalin levels were still soaring and I struggled for control as I Heard Gunnarr from the ramparts, *"Mystynn reports for Storrm. There seems to be a never ending supply, but she's having little difficulty with the poorly trained swordsmen of the King's Forces, and in fact, she's enjoying the blood fest. I believe she seeks revenge. She retreats even now, to join you in the Tower, to make good your exit."* I let that worry leave me, but I seemed to be unable to decide my next move. Storrm and I hadn't even had time to think beyond following Grifynn, and my mind was reeling with the many discoveries thrust upon us this day. Nevertheless, afore I could formulate a plan, Gunnarr Spoke frantically, *"The Den is targeted and 'twill soon be under siege! We must hurry!"*

His words shocked me into moving again. Still not wanting to admit Aalanna's dire prediction was accurate, I urgently implored her, "Please Ama, come with me. Your home is with the Clan, your people are there..." I trailed off, hesitating when I didn't get an immediate response. Slumped in exhaustion, I thought she'd left us, but her skin was warm and she was breathing steadily when I touched her. "Ama? Let me help you. We have to go now..." I said as I stood up and tried to raise her to her feet as well, but she resisted me, and with more strength than I would have suspected, she squirmed out of my grasp. Slippery with all the blood, I couldn't get an effective hold without bruising her with my fingers. Briefly I was reminded of my first kill. It seemed a lifetime ago. I'd have to do something about bloody grips. Oh Flame it all, could I ever think about anything other than fighting?

Then Aalanna's authoritative voice rang through the night, cutting short my reverie, "Leave us here, you must make good your escape now. Shytin will return soon and you'll be trapped. There are too many of them, even with your Dragon blood. 'Tis what he wants. You must never let yourself be taken alive."

The full impact of what she'd said settled into my subconscious mind as I exclaimed, "I came for you! HE came for you and he DIED for you!" I threw my hands in the air, my Sword held tightly, as I blurted out these hateful words in frustration, afore I could stop myself. Seeing the resultant look upon her face, I was mortified at my outburst. But she only smiled sadly, and adjusted his head on her lap while choosing her words. Taking a deep breath, she calmly began, "No Darque, he died for you. He could've taken me with him seven winters ago, when he'd discovered Shytin's deception. And if he'd left earlier that night, as he'd led the King to believe, he'd not have been injured. He slipped away and found this tower by following his blood instincts. We spent several marks together and those memories will never leave me. They kept me alive. But the King would always be a threat to you and Storrm and the Clan. He was torn, but we agreed. If I went missing from the castle, you wouldn't see another winter. The King never knew he'd been to my chambers afore he departed that night. We thought to find a way to use my position to advantage, but Shytin sent away the Warriors stationed here, and kept tight rein on any new ones. He enlisted and trained more of his own Agents, thereby shutting us off from any effective form of communication through them. Speaking to me by the Blood was dangerous..."

I was puzzled. I knew there was more to her rambling story, but there was little time left and I let her go on without questioning. "I'd little access to the Blood, unable to get much information to him, and with every attempt he made, he risked his life further, especially after the injury. I never told him about Fryya because I didn't want him to try again, 'til you were of age. You needed time to mature into your role in the prophesy. I played my part well, and no one suspected Fryya's paternal status wasn't royal. Near seven winters went by and I was ready to reveal her to him, when suddenly two new Warriors arrived to report the LifeBond ceremony. I'd not been allowed to leave the Tower for so long and this news from home meant much to me. But Shytin was livid. I'd never feared more for my life than that night. Unable to sleep, I listened for marks to the sounds of the Warriors being tortured for information in the dungeons. I was proud of them, for although they knew they'd not survive to see the dawn, they revealed nothing. And even though they actually knew nothing, they managed to convince Shytin that his plans had been compromised. This was the only weapon they had, and they gave the Clan the only advantage they could. If Shytin had thought the Brotherhood unaware, then 'twould mean they weren't prepared and could be taken in a surprise attack. Since the Warriors had managed to convince him otherwise, he delayed his original plans to besiege Drekinn. Instead, he sent his own spy to reconnoiter and determine the extent of our knowledge. 'Twas this meeting with his spies which my beloved Fryya observed." She smiled with pride. "'Twas no worry for the Clan, for Grifynn could always identify a spy." I'd not the heart to tell her that her pride was misplaced this time, for the Battle Commander had failed to discover the identity of the spy and I was still searching. Caressing his face, she looked anxiously toward the doorway. The fight was nearing and I could Hear Storrm as she chanted her Battle Cry, keeping up her running, irreverent dialog to her victims. Her battle tactics always dumbfounded me, I believe she could talk non-stop.

"Mystynn Says she can," Gunnarr Told me, and I was reminded we must leave as quickly as possible. *"I don't like this. Numerous reinforcements are arriving and many with Dragons. You shan't depart the same way you entered, little one."*

"I'd already come to that conclusion, my love," I Replied, as at the same time, trying to get Aalanna's attention I said out loud, "Ama, Storrm approaches. Will you come with me?" Standing up, I reached out my hand, not really expecting her to take it. She looked at me weakly with a shine in her eyes and shook her head. *"She desires to remain with Grifynn, even to meet him Beyond. Darque, we cannot stay here any longer. You must come now."*

Taking a step closer and leaning down, I kissed my mother on the cheek for the last time. "I love you," I told her simply. There was nothing more to say.

Swallowing hard, she spoke wearily, "I am so proud of you, my daughter. Grifynn loved you both so much. He couldn't have been happier when I conceived. He said it made him a believer." She paused and I wondered briefly if she'd changed her mind. "I won't leave him here alone. I wish to be with him always. Please don't mourn. I've been waiting for this reunion for many winters." Silently, I handed her one of my boot blades, knowing that as the mate of a Warrior, she knew well how to handle a dagger and what to do with it should the need arise. "Do not let them take you alive, Ama." She nodded as she took the blade with gratitude, palming it expertly.

I turned away and without looking back, moved swiftly to the window, trying not to think about the circumstances which had led me to this place and time, and the situation into which I'd soon enter. As of this moment, I was the Battle Commander of the Dragon Clan, I was leaving my own mother in enemy territory to die alone, my first Battle was being waged on Clan soil, the other Warriors didn't know I'd assumed Command, and I wasn't even there TO Command. In full Battle Mode, strategizing on the move, I issued my first official orders, *"Gunnarr, advise Storrm and Mystynn of the situation. Tell her they're gone, we'll lose too much time if she knows Ama has not yet Passed. 'Tis not a lie, you don't have to Tell her WHERE they've gone."* Hesitating briefly, I suddenly realized that I had been Seeing what was currently happening within the castle as clearly as if Seeing through Gunnarr's eyes, but that was quite impossible as he stood outside upon the ramparts. Letting not confusion rein, I Spoke to Storrm. *"What the Flame are you looking at?"* She'd battled her way up the Grand Staircase and was currently alone awaiting the next wave. However, instead of continuing up to join me in the Tower, she'd hesitated on the third floor landing and would soon be sandwiched from above and below. She was against the wall, a mistake of monumental proportions and not like her. But she'd lifted the corner of one of the tapestries as if inspecting its workmanship, and I had to get her out of there. *"Morrigan! Get down that hallway afore you're blocked off, jump out the window and have Mystynn catch you! Now move your ass!"*

To Gunnarr I Said, *"I'm coming out the window of the Tower, are you ready?"*

"Yes!" I Heard his relieved affirmative. The arm's length thick stone walls of the Tower cell room that had been my mother's whole world for the majority of the past sixteen winters, held one tiny, narrow window. As I struggled to squeeze through it, I was astonished as I suddenly and clearly Heard Kallyr's words of prophesy, Spoken to me when I was very young, "You are blessed by being small, my child....one day 'twill save your life."

I could see little, there was nothing to hold onto outside the window, no ledge, no hand holds. All I could do was push away from the wall like a cliff diver and suddenly I was in free fall. Gunnarr was ready and plucked me from mid-air with his lethal talons afore I dove more than half the height of the tower, gingerly grasping me and carrying me away from Evanntyr into the darkness of a moonlit night. Extricating myself from his grasp, I climbed laboriously against the rushing wind, up his leg to his great neck. Hauling myself up to gain my seat, a chill once again passed through me, like a whisper in the night. 'Twas yet again a sense of déjà vu in my actions, but I had no recollection of why. Without looking, I knew Storrm and Mystynn approached to join me at my right wingtip, and making certain none of us had severe injury and we were all as prepared as we could be, I Declared, *"To the Dragon's Den! We Ride!"*

CHAPTER 31

Walkyr's Warning

EARLIER THAT NIGHT

Shayla barely slept anymore. Every curtain ruffling, every creak of a floorboard, every candle guttering in the sconces would bring her to full wakefulness and she was unable to halt the flood of ideas that would accompany. This night she'd finally collapsed into a fitful sleep, only to awaken a short while later in a sweat of fear and urgency by a nightmare. She was a little girl again, and all her friends were laughing and gathered around her. 'Twas an intricate dance they were learning and everyone was so caught up in watching their own feet and practicing the steps, that they didn't look up at the hills or the skies. Shayla looked. She saw a huge black Dragon at the peak of the highest mountain, the foot of which ran along the edge of the meadow where she and her friends now played. The Dragon was meticulously crafting a snowball, staring at her, a smirk upon his face. No sound did he make as he slowly lowered it to the snow covered ground where he stood at the very peak, and gave it a slight push. With an evil leer, he broke eye contact, twisted around and launched himself off the mountain crest into the skies, pumping his great wings and soaring away 'til he disappeared. She was mesmerized in confusion, gaping at the ever growing snowball rolling down the mountain. Suddenly aware of what was about to happen, but unable to prevent the oncoming disaster, she'd helplessly watched it roll faster and grow bigger, while she'd desperately tried to get her friends to leave, or at least look up and see the danger. They'd do neither. The amassing weight turned it into a huge ball of ice as it rushed headlong to the meadow, throwing snow from its surface and the path in all directions like a blizzard, so that even her face was wet. Just as she frantically tried to pull her friends away, and 'twas bigger than the Lodge and about to crush them all, she awoke in a panic with Walkyr's big, gangly pup lapping frantically at her face, Kallyr's Voice screaming for her to move!

Rolling out of her cot, she grabbed her well worn leather trousers off the floor where she'd dropped them less than a mark earlier, and swiftly pulled them on under her long, side-slit tunic. Kallyr's Voice had beseeched her to wake up, get the children to safety, but he was sleeping at home and had never been known to Speak afore. He'd kissed her passionately when taking his leave late last evening but wouldn't stay, despite her request. He'd mumbled something about having work to finish at home and instead of telling her he'd see her soon, as he was wont to do, he'd softly said, "I love you so much my dear one, never forget that. Now sleep, you're exhausted, and you'll need all of your strength very soon." Shayla had been too tired to argue or even consider there might have been another meaning underlying his words. She should've known. She was the mate of a Clan Seer, and she knew he'd Seen….no, she couldn't dwell upon it now, there was something very wrong and she had to move. She didn't take the time to don her boots, racing barefoot to the Hospital wing 'cross from the Barracks where she'd heard Walkyr's cry, his pup leading the way.

"They come Me'Shayla! You have to blow the Shyffah, I cannot, I'm too small!" Walkyr trembled with Battle Lust, and she grabbed his shoulders to face her squarely. Stooping o'er to his level and ensuring his attention with eye contact, she asked him, "Walkyr, WHO is coming? What did you See, what was your Vision?"

He opened wide his eyes and swallowed hard, then in a clear voice he exclaimed, "'Tis not what I Saw, Me'Shayla. 'Tis what I See." She shivered with the reminder of the power he wielded. Squeezing his shoulders, she knelt down in front of him. Now looking up into his determined face, she encouraged him to speak further. "Tell me."

"I See a great black cloud filling the skies, flowing like a living thing. 'Tis as the Highland Ancients appeared when they returned. But this cloud gets bigger and bigger as it nears Drekinn, and 'tis filled with Evil. 'Tis the Hoard, Ama. Too many to count, coming from the South, from the Razor's Edge!"

"How much time do we have?" She asked him, expecting at least a few days, trying not to panic, engaging her mental preparations for siege.

"Not long, mere marks, mayhap not." Walkyr was clearly upset and Shayla knew 'twas no dream. Now, not days from now? All her hopes and plans were cast aside as she shifted into Battle Mode. By the One, it's been so very long, she thought, please don't let me fail my people this time.

Shayla rose to her full stance, her shaggy, shoulder length auburn curls uncontrollable, as she pushed the child toward Cayell, who'd stood there tucking his tunic into his leather pants and strapping his sword 'cross his back. "Get Fryya and go below," she stated. "Then you and Mynx must choose. I have no authority o'er you, once they're secured. One of you must remain to guard them through the siege, 'tis all I ask. The other will be needed above." Shayla cast her eyes upon the male Warrior, silently imploring him to be the one to protect the children. Mynx was a good fighter, but in her youthfulness had been frustrated with the duty of 'babysitter' and had never made a tight connection with her charges.

Walkyr didn't even glance at Cayell, keeping his eyes locked on the Healer. "And the Life Crystal….the Blood Elixir?"

She was somewhat surprised at his knowledge, then silently chastised herself. For one so powerful, there'd be no secrets around him. "'Tis safe, many days ago I cached all that was left. Now get thee below. The Battle Commander will blow the Shyffah, 'tis his right and duty."

"He can't, he's not here," Walkyr near whispered, and Shayla swallowed her confusion, wanting to refute this, but knowing whatever came from his mouth was truth.

"Then Kallyr will do it, surely he's Seen this attack in the coming. He'll be on his way in from the village now."

No response came from the boy Seer. His blue eyes stared straight at her, locking gazes. When his frustration became palpable, she began to understand the enormity of the knowledge he held, and flatly questioned him, "What have you Seen Walkyr? You know what happens, don't you. Will you be injured… taken? Tell me."

"I live."

"What of me? I'll need to prepare the Apprentices if I don't survive…"

"You live." As he replied, his eyes began to fill with tears, as he willed the only mother he'd ever known, to ask the next question.

A long breathless moment passed. Shayla shuddered, inhaled again, and then asked the obvious, "And Kallyr?"

No response. Merely the tears spilling o'er his pale eyes. He pursed his lips in defiance of the outward display of unwanted emotion, but he couldn't say the words aloud to confirm her suspicions. 'Twas understood 'tween them.

Shayla lifted her head higher, licked her dry lips and cleared her throat, moving on to the next most important questions. "Darque? Storrm? How fare they?"

"'Tis unclear, they're even now distant… and they… change." Walkyr struggled to find the words to describe what he felt, when he connected to the Warrior sisters. There was something very bizarre going on with those two, but he hadn't received anything clear in his Visions to explain the phenomenon.

Nodding her head in agreement, for she knew there was much change in them, she calmly asked her final question. "And what of the Clan, Walkyr?"

His face displayed enormous compassion and bewilderment. He hadn't the ability to say more than, "'Twill be bad, 'twill be very bad."

With tears welling and threatening to spill, she stood up. Discovering her throat too tight to give voice, she simply hugged her Claim Son and gathering her wits, she pushed both children toward Cayell, then turned about and hurried through the dancing shadows of the torchlight down the Great Hallway to the Battle Commander's office. Finding no one there, she raced to the Tower and began her climb up the spiral staircase to the top, where she'd find the Shyffah.

~~~~~~~~~~

"Come! What are you doing?" Cayell tried to snatch the boy by the shoulder, but Walkyr wiggled out of his grasp and quickly followed Fryya, racing for the Kennels. Both their pups loped alongside them, already in protective mode, placing themselves 'tween their humans and the world. Cayell unsheathed his sword and followed the disappearing duo, quickly joined by Mynx when she arrived from her sleeping quarters fully armed, as they attempted to head off their charges and steer them toward the dungeons.

~~~~~~~~~~

Shayla lifted her long tunic o'er her thighs and trudged in all haste up the steps cut into the stone at the top of the central tower of the Keep, which was set on the northern most edge of the Training Pits, in the center of the Den. Prior to the return of the Dragons, this tower was the most protected place in the world. Now, she thought glumly, 'twas the most obvious target. But still, the stone was solid and could withstand even Flame. After all, Grifynn had designed the entire castle to withstand siege, including Dragons, but he couldn't make that too obvious. There was the Blood Oath, and if anyone had questioned him on some of the 'quirkier' aspects to the design, he'd have been in dire straits.

Despite her own Life Crystal benefits, she was almost out of breath by the time she reached the small room at the top. 'Twas built similar to a lighthouse, and in fact, the entire tower had always given her that impression. Instead of windows, the stone framed panels all around the top were open to the night air. The floor was surrounded by the stairwell, but there was sufficient room for the stone block in the middle. She took a deep breath, and then another, thinking she'd never done this afore, and the Shyffah hadn't been used for a true siege in many lifetimes. In fact, since settling here in Drekinn, it had never blown the sequence for such. 'Twas no matter however, for Grifynn had made sure that every man, woman, and child of the Dragon Clan, knew the sequence and what actions to take when they heard the ram's horn. 'Twas deep, mellow, commanding, and its voice carried 'cross the entire plateau, mayhap further. No one in the village or the surrounding farmlands could miss the blowing of the horn, and no one would mistake its meaning. There was a specific and unique series of notes like a song, which stood for different events; one for a Warrior Trial and a slightly altered one when a Warrior took the Oath, one for a Clan Elder meeting, one for the opening and the closing of the Faire. But 'twas the notes she must blow now, that brought the tears back to her eyes. The notes that told the Clan, 'THE ENEMY IS COMING, DREKINN IS BESIEGED! GET THEE TO SAFETY, GET THEE TO THE DEN!'

Shayla was operating in full Battle Mode and her adrenalin was pumping. She wasted no time in reaching for the pull, which moved the levers, which slid the top stone down and under the stone of the flooring, and then the platform upon which the Shyffah did silently wait, began to rise through the middle of the cold floor. She watched in fascination as the huge curling ram's horn rose, resting in its holder, for this horn was so big, 'twas difficult to carry, let alone hold steady to one's lips. Once in place, she stepped up boldly, took a deep breath and placing her hands around the end, she leaned forward and began to blow.

~~~~~~~~~~

The sound of the Shyffah broke the silence of the night, and as its deep resonant moan reverberated longer and louder, Cayell felt the hair on the back of his neck stand up. He'd never heard that series of notes, that Call to Arms, but he knew of what it spoke…three short blasts followed by three long and then three short, pause… and repeated, seemingly without end. 'Twas reality. The Clan was under attack.

Explaining her tardiness, Mynx spat 'tween clenched teeth as she began to feel the Lust building, "I woke Dayanah and Devorah in the women's quarters, and they'll wake the others…" She raised her head to the Call of the Shyffah and continued, "…not that anyone will need to be awakened now." Cayell and Mynx were Warriors, but they were working as private bodyguards, and their first duty was to their employer. That one just so happened to be the Second in Command and when she was absent they answered to no one other than Shayla, the Clan Healer. They'd received their orders and like it or not, they had to protect their young charges 'til they were released to go join the others in this sure to be epic Battle for the Dragon Clan. But waking her Warrior sisters hadn't felt as though she was doing anything wrong, she told herself. They were only warned a few moments ahead of the Shyffah's call.
~~~~~~~~~~

Mynx hoped her twin brother Mace was alright. It had been awhile since they'd spoken to one another and she liked it not. Adjusting her weapons, she hurried after the child. This would be her first true battle. She'd never even been deployed. But even in her youthful excitement, she was horrified that this battle was coming to Clan soil. Still, she wasn't as confident as some, in the boy Seer's Visions. If this turned out to be a'foul, there'd be Flame to purge. She hadn't experienced his accuracy, had spent most of her time making sure the girl child, Fryya, was safe in her comings and goings, which were mostly within the Den. Since she and Cayell had taken on the duty, there'd been no kidnap or assassination attempts and therefore 'twas a vaguely boring trial to her patience and not at all the way she'd dreamed of her first assignment. At least the girl was intelligent and of obviously good blood, but she was quiet and they rarely spoke to one another. She'd heard the rumors of course, that the child was the Princess Fryya, that she'd been rescued at the Battle of Kaddart, and instead of being returned to the King or even made a Ward of the Court, she'd been legally Claimed by the Second in Command. 'Twas difficult to ignore the uncanny resemblance 'tween the two, as if they could truly be of the same blood, although both Grifynn and Darque seemed oblivious to such. Yes indeed, rumors were flying since the little girl had arrived, but of course, no one would dare insult the Battle Commander or their Second.

Teaka had wakened and dressed immediately when she'd heard the alarm, and the children implored her to gather the pups and breeders, and to get the resident dogs to safety. All the Dogs partnered with Warriors lived and traveled with them, and only the breeders, pups and older 'single' dogs, left behind when their partners were taken 'cross the Veil, lived in the Kennels. Although 'twas one of the safest places to be during an attack, they'd only be safe if they actually stayed there. But they were trained to join in the battle, and although quite effective against an enemy a'foot or even a'horseback, they were still in training to develop strategies for battle against Dragons, for although they had no fear, they'd not last long in a Flame fight. So the children's idea that the breeding stock for the pride of the Clan needed to be secured safely away during the upcoming battle, was a good one. Teaka quickly recognized this wisdom, and calling to her assistants, they made short work of gathering up their charges, and with the children leading the way, and Mynx and Cayell bringing up the rear, they raced to the dungeons.

CHAPTER 32
Déjà Vu or What Once Was Seen

SAME NIGHT

Swiftly we flew, and I saw not the ground beneath us nor the retreating mountains behind. I'd not the energy to spare, to muse o'er what we'd just gone through. The reasoning and the sequencing of all these events would have to wait, for at this speed we'd be soaring o'er Drekinn afore dawn.

In the darkness prior to daybreak, I saw the Flaming of the Port District and knew Kallyr had breathed his last. My mind in full Battle Mode, I couldn't allow the heartache to swamp me with the realization of the loss of my second father and the only Clan Seer I'd ever known. My focus upon the siege to which we were traveling with all haste, I Heard the Cries of the Dragons and Warriors o'er my own breathing, and the whoosh of the air beneath Gunnarr's great wings. My eyes shone crimson and my heart hammered as I willed speed to his flight, to join them as they fought in the bloodiest battle staged upon Kadoor since the Last Holocaust. The wrath that had been building inside me through the last several moons dulled my emotions further still, and I allowed my Warrior Training and the Strength of the 'Bond to be my guide. The Battle for the Dragon Clan had begun.

The sun just rising, Gunnarr the Mighty Blue roared out his challenge to The Black 'cross the Southern Plains of Drekinn, his defiant growl echoed by Mystynn the Green. I became aware of the arrival of the new Stable from the north as we approached from the south, and my Sword leaped impatiently to my hand when I reached o'er my shoulder. Calling ahead, every Team and Free Dragon and Warrior knew we were coming and a cosmic Battle Cry echoed through the heavens. My enhanced senses located the 'Bonded and told me how they fared thus far, then giving my orders along with my blessings, we descended to join my entire Fleet and Clan in defense of our very existence.

I ordered Gunnarr to land when he spotted The Black perched at the peak of the northern ridge, observing his minions below. 'Twas my intention to force him 'cross the Veil or lose myself to the Fade in the effort, dragging his Evil corpse with me. Dismounting the length of the docks apart, for he was well guarded, I made my challenge clear, my eyes burn-

301

ing with righteous fury. While Gunnarr secured my back, I raised both my arms, one hand holding my Sword, the other grasping my boot blade, the universal sign that I was ready and willing to end this now. One of us would not live to see nightfall.

I'd locked his gaze to mine and finding himself unable to break the contact, I watched as his expression changed. My body temperature was soaring, which I'd always attributed to the Lust, either by Battle or sex, but this time 'twas as if I'd swallowed the very sun itself. 'Twas not pain, but a feeling from my gut similar to that of the release of my Blood Call, and something enveloped me of my own creation. I had the odd impression of enormous growth, both in size and power, and my vision was akin to Gunnarr's. As I found myself in the grip of a flood of emotions, The Black displayed his own, which I could barely read. If I'd not been in such a state, I would have seen arrogance, followed by hesitance and disbelief, then fear changed to true anger. Instead of coming for me, he wrenched himself free of my lock on his gaze to disappear o'er the ridge. Shaking my head as the tumultuous succession of sensations eased, I found myself again. 'Twas nothing more to do here, I couldn't chase his cowardly ass down, I had to join the fight. But just what exactly had he seen?

"No worries Flame Spitter, he'll not return this day," Gunnarr Assured me. 'Twould take some time for them to notice his absence, but even without their leader, the Hoard continued their attack with growing ferocity, and 'twas becoming a conflict of major proportions.

Remounting, we flew o'er the Dragon's Den, and from there I recalled only snippets of the fighting. My Striker slashed and scored scales, wings and eyes, my Sword cleaved bone and sliced through thick Dragon hide. My Thumper protected my backside from talon and Flame as Gunnarr and I ripped out hearts and beheaded the vile creatures. 'Twas as if the Sword could Hear me as did my Dragon, every strike rang true, and we fought like demons in our own nightmare. I saw hundreds of foot soldiers upon the ground, wearing the uniform of the King's Forces, and fleetingly I speculated as to how they'd arrived in time for this battle. The only answer that made sense was that they'd flown in with the Hoard.

It soon became clear we had no chance to save Drekinn and all our efforts would be defensive. Gunnarr and I stationed ourselves above the Den where the thickest fighting seemed to be, holding back the onslaught trying to compromise the castle, and protecting those of the Clan who were still trying to enter to escape the firestorm. Once we'd joined in, I trusted my Teams to know where they were needed and to do what was required. I couldn't think about Grifynn, Aalanna, Fryya, Walkyr, or Shayla. Slashing, cutting, striking, again and again, I hung onto Gunnarr's neck, ducking under his wings close and tight so as not to fall off during his twists, turns and rolls to avoid the incoming firestorms. We took down many, yet still they came. In the initial marks, for every one of the foul creatures we forced Past the Veil, six more appeared in their wake. After that, I quit counting.

"Gunnarr!" One of the tainted creatures tipped him o'er. Sandwiching us 'tween two others, its foul fangs gripped Gunnarr's wing and twisted him hard enough that I was thrown out of my saddle. Dangling beneath him by one strap as he struggled to free himself, my blood covered hands lost grip, and I plummeted toward the point of the Tower turret.

"Little one!" He Roared o'er the din rising from below, wrenched his wing free of the others' fangs, and tucking both tight to his flanks, he dove feverishly toward my falling body, like a stone from a sling. Afore he could catch me, and just afore I was impaled stem to stern, one of the Hoard was pushed in under me by Daynahmyn and Mikkal. The vile beast took the point through his groin and his Healing stuck him to the battlement afore he realized what he'd done. I landed on all fours upon his mid-back, and slipping off the bloody scales at the near roof top angle, I pushed forth from his thrashing body and skipped 'cross Daynahmyn to Rakkah's Petrayyah, who skillfully flew the stair stepping pattern as they continued their own skirmishes. Leaping off Petrayyah to the Plains, I rolled and ran swiftly, grabbing unto Gunnarr's strap as he picked me up and regaining my seat, we climbed to higher altitude to assess our injuries. 'Twas one of those moments one realizes they're not immortal after all. His wing was torn and the bone fractured but he'd not been able to set it, waiting to ensure my safety. After helping him yank the fractured limb to attain proper alignment, he Healed the wound and we descended again.

I watched with pride as my Teams rallied to one another's aide, engaging the Hoard Dragons using the techniques we'd practiced to perfection. Grifynn was missing, their new Battle Commander had arrived late and they'd started out slightly confused and slow to respond, but they'd picked up the ferocity and switched from defensive to aggressively offensive strategies once they Heard my Battle Cry. My Warriors skipped scales, rescued each other and took leaps of faith hundreds of feet through the air to attack the Hoard, causing much confusion amongst the beasts. Rivers of Battle Blood ran 'cross the Plains, the carcasses of Dragons piled high enough against the ramparts of the Den that the King's Forces began to use them to climb o'er the walls. I Sent out my orders and Gunnarr, along with some of the Free Dragons, Flamed the growing pile of remains to dust, salted with the Agents who hadn't yet fled the battlegrounds. My heart was stone, for none were Clan.

Even with so few Teams facing a devastating number of Free Hoard Dragons, we fought with vicious intent and within mere marks their siege fell apart, and soon thereafter they retreated. The Hoard had come in hard and fast but hadn't expected the Clan to be aware of their arrival and ready for them. Initially they'd seemed driven to complete their mission, which was odd since they'd always avoided every altercation afore. I could see the fear of the Mighty Blue as we were recognized, and once they became aware that they'd been abandoned by The Black, they lost momentum, despite the odds in their favor. Giving up afore they totally annihilated the Clan, they fled from us, refusing to engage any further. We'd proven too fierce to kill, too stubborn to surrender, and they weren't willing to lay down their lives for their own cause.

By the time the sun had reached its full zenith in the heat of the summer day, the Warriors of the Dragon Clan claimed triumph. Yet no one escaped injury and I was shocked at the numbers of those who'd Passed Beyond. Glancing around to make certain we were now alone, the Hoard in full retreat, I saw Shayla 'cross the battle ground, her back to me as she was searching for someone, anyone, still alive whom she could help. The Healer Apprentices and support staff came running out of the castle, and from on high they appeared as desert ants streaming forth from their hill. We watched in growing sadness as they stopped to give aide here and there, passing summarily by far too many. I'd commanded Gunnarr to land near Shayla and he did so, never wavering despite the fact that 'twas upon the dead he must trod in order to let me off near my destination. The Healer fell upon her knees and I knew she'd seen me and realized 'twas done, her own Battle Lust failing her, her senses inundated. Dismounting upon the blood soaked ground, I was near swamped by the pain and the Battle Lust emanating from the free flowing Life Forces combining in a miasma of Good and Evil. Hurrying to her, I noted there were still many yet among the living, who hadn't long this side of the Veil.

I jerked to a stop, my feet taking root upon the a'fouled grounds with another episode of déjà vu. Suddenly I wasn't certain if 'twas the reality of my present world or a dream. My sight blurred and I relived the entire Battle of Evanntyr, unfolding afore me. The subdued Vision of my youth lapped o'er the events of the past few marks and I was unable to prevent the repetition of the horror. My Sight shifted from the King's Castle to Drekinn, and the Battle for the Dragon Clan now echoed through my soul. 'Twas as if the past was rushing headlong into my present, and wouldn't slow down sufficiently to avoid running into my future, trampling me in the process. Once again, I Heard the cries of pain from both Dragon and Man, Good and Evil.

I'd never seen so much blood, so much gore, so much death. I'd never heard so many cry out for help, so many who didn't want to Pass, so many….there were so many. But somehow I knew I had the Power to save them. With barely a conscious thought I Reached deep within myself and Pulled from that place I'd found in my youth so long forgotten, grabbed onto the now burning and tingling substance without substance, and with Gunnarr's Magic to boost my own, I slammed a mighty Shield of Protection 'cross the battle field, covering my Teams and Free Dragons and Warriors who yet breathed the air on this side of the Veil. Purposefully, I excluded the minions of the Evil One, leaving them to the Fates.

My entire body shook with the enormous effort to keep all of them here, not allowing them to slip past this life to the Other Side. 'Twas a massive tug of war in which I struggled alone, but I couldn't let them down. They'd fought well, the Clan needed every one of them and I wouldn't lose them. They all depended on me, I was their Commander, and breaking out in a sweat, I near fell to my knees. Clenching my teeth against the growing fatigue and pain, my very Life Force, which I was using to sustain the Shield, was slowly and steadily depleting from my soul.

'Twas then the Vision from my past reached its pinnacle, and my present became clear again as I turned to locate the strangled voice from just behind me.

"Darque." Turning, I saw a Warrior lying in a puddle of his own blood. His Dragon laid beside him, her great jaws clenched, her eyes almost black and flashing with the intensity of the effort to maintain her Magic, trying desperately to keep them both alive. But 'twas obvious she couldn't Heal herself, let alone her Rider. As I looked closer I realized they were both old and horribly injured. The Warrior was near hacked into dismemberment, his guts spilled out of his belly onto the ground beside him, great chunks of flesh and muscle ripped away from his arms and legs or pierced by fractured bone, and he could control nothing but his voice and his eyes. The Dragon's wings had been slashed from her body, she'd lost more than half of her glittering scales, her chest and neck were flayed open, exposing the bunched muscle beneath, yet I was witness to this Team's successes as they'd done far worse to many of the Hoard, as well as the King's Forces who had come against them. Just as I became aware 'twas Tannyr lying there with Kaahayyel at his side, he spoke again.

"Darque, 'twas good to see you take Command, and you did a fine job of it, lass. But you must know, me Dragon can't Heal herself, let alone me. Her effort is barely enough to keep us from becoming entrenched in the Fade, and if you don't let us Pass soon, 'twill be our fate. 'Tis the severity of our wounds that drain you so. Without us, you can Hold the others. Don't force us to the Fade to be lost forever. Please girl, let me go." Tannyr sucked in another shallow breath, noted the indecision upon my face, and continued, "'Tis our time. Me destiny's been well served. Now our thread in this tapestry is cut, and yours just being woven in. Do you still not understand? You shall bring the Races of Kadoor back together and reestablish the balance. 'Tis unfolding as it should, and 'twill be a new beginning." The Elder Warrior coughed weakly and stopped to take another choking breath. He wanted to say more, but couldn't. The pain and fatigue of holding on was taking its toll and 'twas clear they'd run out of time. I was forced to make the difficult decision to let them Pass or I would indeed, lose them all.

The sun dawning upon me, I realized that I'd lived this afore, Heard his words afore. With this understanding I also knew there was not a moment to lose, and that I could do nothing else. There was no argument or reasoning that could change prophesy. Both Tannyr and I had Seen our own futures, and now I had to let him go. I couldn't deny him the Veil. His destiny had been fulfilled in having made the 'Bond to save another, and in having fought in this last great battle as a mighty Warrior once again. My destiny was just beginning. I placed his sword in his limp hand and held his fingers tightly around the hilt, as he had no grasp, and then I relaxed them out from under my umbrella of Protection, watching sadly as my friend and comrade breathed his last. With a smile forming on his lips, he Reached through their Link to his Dragon, the mighty Ancient, Kaahayyel, who gently laid her great head upon his chest, taking her last breath with his. 'Twas a Peace that defied understanding which surrounded me at the very moment they Passed. And yet, I knew I'd only been given a minor reprieve for the rest of them. The Shield would continue to drain me, although 'twas slower now. I couldn't keep this up much longer, but I wouldn't lose any more.

Given all that I'd learned o'er the last two days, I now recognized one person who could help me keep them alive. Although I was still uncertain of details, 'twas clear to me that the Healer of the Dragon Clan held the key to many secrets, and unlock that Pandora's Box, I would. As Storrm dismounted Mystynn in the midst of this field of death, she picked her way through the remains, searching for any signs of life within each body she passed or stepped o'er on her way to my side. 'Twas difficult to ascertain her injuries, her long red hair plastered against her shoulders and back, her leathers covered in blood and gore, but she yet breathed and walked and we'd many who were far worse. In her hand, her Dragon Sword still glowed in its fury, her eyes fiercely bright with the fevered red haze of Battle Lust, she met my stare and locked on. In a fraction of a breath, Storrm understood my actions and my plan, and turning in unison in search of Shayla, we discovered she'd mysteriously vanished from the battlefield. With no time to lose, we trudged our way as quickly as we could back to the Den in pursuit of her, while Gunnarr and Mystynn continued to secure the area, placing perimeter guards and Seekers to ensure there'd be no further attacks, gathered the walking injured and launched the initial rescue operations.

CHAPTER 33
Past Lives Breed Lies

THE INITIAL AFTERMATH

I knew where she'd go for solace. *"Gunnarr, we must Hold them 'til I secure Shayla's assistance. I know she can help us, she has many secrets and I must release them."* After Receiving his assurance we could indeed Hold the Shield for awhile longer, I left him to interpret and assist the Healer Apprentices to care for the downed Dragons and Warriors. Grounding and centering my innate Magic, ensuring the strength of the Shield wouldn't falter, I whistled for the first War Horse I saw. Ironically, 'twas Konann. Mayhap also seeking solace, he pranced straight to me and leaned his great head down to receive my touch. I wiped his bloody forelock from his eyes and checked him for injury. His saddle had been burned or ripped from his broad back and he had some lacerations, but nothing that would now be considered fatal. There was evidence of major claw and fang wounds, possibly how he'd lost his tack, but there was little active bleeding and he was nearly Healed. Must have been one of the Dragons who'd done this, and I was somewhat amazed that the War Stallion allowed himself to be licked by one of the same Race who'd inflicted his injuries. I made a mental note to try to Seek out the one who'd done this Healing and thank them, although the likelihood they'd Passed themselves, was great.

Grabbing a handful of his tangled mane and vaulting aboard, I reached out and grabbed Storrm by the forearm as we loped through the Pits, swinging her up behind me without slowing our pace. Racing past the Barracks, we entered the Great Hallway with Konann's increasingly heavy hoof beats creating an eerie echo in the uncharacteristic emptiness. The main gate of the Den was open, its massive arced doors nothing but slag and ash. At least the castle wasn't compromised, the Spelled entries having assisted to maintain the security of the inner sanctums. Once out of the main gate we were forced to slow down, and picking our way through the rubble, death and destruction, we arrived at my intended destination shortly thereafter.

She was there, fallen to her knees in front of the charred out remains of the house where she and Kallyr had lived for many winters. The home we'd once all shared together was totally burned out, with little to nothing left to see, let alone take with her as a remembrance. The hand carved headboard was gone as if it had never been, the ornate wrought iron bed frame was melted and twisted, unrecognizable if one hadn't known what 'twas afore. Scattered pieces of melted slag lay in the dirt and debris that must have been door hinges. The footings and hearth stone were intact, although most of it was buried under the ash from the rest of the place. Painfully, I recalled the last night we'd shared with Kallyr, the rich smell of the soup I'd handed him, how he'd told us of the coming Black War and the LifeBond the Ancients offered. 'Twas the beginning of this new life. But time was short. We knew not if the enemy had retreated this day in defeat, or was merely reorganizing for a new offensive. And I had no idea how long I could Hold onto the dying.

Dismounting, Storrm stood with Konann while I approached respectfully. Not knowing quite how to begin, I simply started with the facts. "Shayla? I know Kallyr is gone, and I cannot say how sorry I am. And you must have realized since I'm now Battle Commander, Grifynn is also gone. I know you were close to him. I wanted to be the one to tell you." Her posture and emotions passed through a gamut of changes as she listened. Weaving her fingers together, she dropped her hands to her lap. I placed my hand gently upon her shoulder to comfort her as I tried to help her focus on what I needed.

"My mother was alive, all this time. He tried to rescue her seven winters past, and beget Fryya. She's my full blood sister and I think you knew this all along." Her slight stiffening told me I was correct. "In his escape, he was attacked and had to fight his way out. He killed the guard, ensuring the King knew not, but was himself heart struck. Shayla, I know you've kept him alive all these winters, from what should've been a fatal injury." I was leery of pushing her too hard but we didn't have the luxury of time. Her puzzle pieces would fill in the whole picture, or at the very least, give me enough information to continue this War with an advantage. If Shayla had found a way to heal near fatal wounds, I had to know. There were many near death and we couldn't afford to lose them. Shayla had to function again; I needed her knowledge, her skills.

~~~~~~~~~~

She felt totally deflated, her hope gone, with the confirmation that Grifynn had Passed the Veil. She'd tried so hard to save Kallyr, to prevent his prophesy, but his natural lifespan was close to met and she'd dared not use her Crystal without his knowledge and consent. Had she been wrong? Guilt spiraled within her, but she was slightly comforted
~~~~~~~~~~

that Walkyr was still alive. When the boy had awakened with the Vision of the oncoming attack, she'd raced into Battle Mode. Sending the children and their bodyguards to the dungeons with hurried instructions not to reappear until she, Darque or Storrm came for them, she'd blown the Shyffah, rallied her apprentices, and started setting up a triage, even as she'd Informed the Dragons by MindSpeak of the attack and that Darque and Storrm were on their way. The Power that stress gave her had always been amazing. These Dragons had never Heard her Voice afore and were mildly shocked, but hadn't questioned what she'd Said, and the battle had soon followed.

When the strike began, she knew Kallyr was doomed. She'd felt him Passing the Veil when he'd been taken out in the first Flame while helping to set up the collapse of the Port District. He'd claimed to have Seen his death o'er a fortnight past and stubbornly refused to do anything to alter it. "Disaster will strike others if we try to adjust what is Seen, my love. You know this. But you and Walkyr weren't with me, so go. I'll not risk your lives for mine, nor will I exchange mine for yours. I love you very much. And Shayla? I know what you haven't told me, of who you are, of where you came, of why you never conceived. I've known for many winters, but it made no difference to my heart. I have no regrets." With that he'd kissed her passionately, and then pushed her toward the castle, saying he had no clue when the Fates would come for him, afore he turned and re-entered their home. They'd not been alone together again. She'd lain awake many nights since then, pondering what he'd said, but he'd never revealed or explained more.

She tried not to think about all that she'd lost this day. The Battle for the Dragon Clan had been the worst fighting she'd ever seen. She wasn't sure she could live with the sorrow she now harbored in her heart and soul. She'd always considered herself tough, but this may have pushed her o'er the edge, as she was now alone. She struggled to maintain her composure.

<center>~~~~~~~~~~</center>

Shayla's eyes were glazed, her breathing shallow, her focus shifted to some distant memory. Her sweat-dampened, disheveled auburn hair, hung like a shroud to her slumped shoulders, sticking in clumps here and there to her dirty face, her tunic torn and bloody. In barely a whisper she slowly began to tell me a story of long ago, and I listened intently, not understanding all of her words, but feeling the intensity of her emotions was quite enough to ensure the truth in the tale.

"'Twas so long ago, and I've lived many lives since then. I hardly remember the places, my own name. But what I do recall, I worked hard for many winters to forget."

Shayla wiped the tears from her face leaving dirty streaks, and sighed. Her skin appeared ashen from shock. I beckoned Storrm to bring water and towels while she took a deep breath to pick up her line of thought where she'd just left off. It appeared to take great effort on her part. She stared at the ash covered ground at her knees, and wiped her palms down the leg of her britches.

"'Twas just prior to the Last Holocaust," she breathed, and I stared at her, praying to the One True Liege that she'd not already fallen o'er the edge of sanity, but I remained silent. "Slowly things began to fall apart. The world was in turmoil, we knew not our true enemies. The military was meeting in secret with some 'foreign consulate party', and we knew little. Lies and lack of information bred apathy. People ignored missing neighbors, rationalized erratic technology breakdowns. For weeks, small sections of societies all o'er the world were shutting down and I feared 'twas systematic. Nothing would work in those areas, no information came forth, the people there disappeared, anything that made or required energy to run, just stopped. There was a name for it, a weapon. I don't remember." Shayla furrowed her brow and gazed up at me. I knew the look in my eyes revealed my concerns.

"I was a doctor, what we called our Healers. Everything was different then, not like now. Even the materials we used and the architecture, the weapons, the war. 'Twas a different time. Most people didn't even know we were in a war! Only those in the military or associated with higher levels of government…" again, she trailed off. I waited impatiently, trying not to lose her, as I could Sense her delicate balance 'tween rational and irrational ideation.

"I followed my brother into the military as soon as I became a doctor. Given my specialties, working with blood and DNA, the military scooped me up pretty quickly once he reached Elite in his field and recommended they recruit me for the Project. We'd been separated for many years due to his career focus and mine, and when the military made me this offer, I was excited. I'd thought we might be able to be together again. At least we could see each other more often. He did intelligence work, had been a special ops soldier and a sniper, and had been snatched up so high, I couldn't even begin to imagine his security level."

Holding my tongue so as not to stop her flow with a question, 'twas understood by the terms she used that her brother was a Warrior for his

Clan and a very good one indeed. But 'DNA'? And what was this 'Project'? Her story thus far was creating more mysteries than 'twas solving.

Storrm Reported on the wounded and I was gladdened that we'd lost no more, although 'twas not likely they'd survive without help. Squeezing Shayla's shoulder gently, I knelt beside her. My leathers were bloody, torn and Flamed to near shreds. Gingerly, I touched the wound visible through the tatters on my left thigh, already Healing. Grimacing at the sharp twinge of pain that went through me at the touch, I nudged Shayla to speak again. Her response was as if she'd Heard my thoughts, but I shook my head, assuming I was just fatigued. She couldn't have Heard me. Could she?

"DNA is the substance that makes us who and what we are, Darque. It's what makes a Dragon a Dragon and a Human a Human. And the Project turned out to be a study on how to modify Human DNA to enhance our soldiers' abilities on the battlefield. They were trying to create what you now experience through the LifeBond, only, without a partner. They were trying to create the perfect Warrior. Of course, no one knew about Dragons then, at least, not unless you had a high enough security clearance." Pointedly, she stared deep into my eyes, and I almost shivered. I knew what she was saying. Her brother had known. She'd learned. If she'd shared this knowledge, then no wonder my father had been so leery of the Dragons and the LifeBond.

"Of course, I wasn't told the real reason for the research, but something was odd about the Project from my first day. I'd entered a fully stocked laboratory with everything generically labeled, and nothing that would indicate from whence it came. In fact, how did I even know that what I was using was actually what 'twas labeled to be? I understood security, but I'd been told we were seeking a cure for radiation sickness, not the Ark of the Lost Tribe. Or were we? I'd always been stuck on detail, which was important in my field of research. I'd immediately noticed my surroundings and wondered why all the internal doorways were so wide, so tall. Not even the equipment I was using required that much clearance. Why the special latches instead of doorknobs? Why did the administrators for the Project meet at midnight and why were all the meetings closed? I was the only one with a security clearance at my level, but I'd never seen another person, not even my secretary, only hearing a voice when I made orders. I'd not been allowed outside the compound since I took the position, only out in the yard for fresh air and exercise on a scheduled basis, and I was always alone. Even though I was assured I wasn't being held prisoner, I began to feel confined. My own lab door was locked to me, the compound fence was as tall as four men, and had razor and electric wire along the top edge." I was again confused by her terminology and noted even her manner of speech altered, but her meaning was clear and what she was describing was just off beam. She was being held prisoner.

"I must admit that initially I was so excited to be a part of the Project, that I worked continuously and barely noticed being alone for hours and days at a time, but I finally noticed. I began to put the clues together. My work wasn't even the full research, just a part of it, or so I'd been told by the Administrators. We'd been set up in Sections and what I accomplished every week was taken to another location, for another researcher to build on. After a very short time, I realized I didn't like that at all. I believed it was done this way to keep any of us, if there were actually more researchers, from knowing the truth about what we were really doing. I began to notice more about my environment, and kept track of my supplies. I'd questioned some of what I'd been provided with recently and the answers were less than satisfying. I didn't let on that I no longer believed them, but with my few questions, they no longer trusted me. I knew what I should be working with and what it should be doing and I was certain this wasn't even human blood. As for the rest, I could only speculate. I began to detour away from my expected research as I attempted to discover the truth about what the hell was really going on. There were so many questions. What kind of blood was this? Where had the DNA come from? What was the Project really trying to achieve? But I had to be cautious since I knew I was being very closely observed. At first, this hadn't seemed all that strange. Security issues had been the excuse given to me when I started and it seemed normal at that time, but then I began to think it was more to keep tabs on me, than to keep tabs on my work. I decided I had to use stealth measures. I knew how to do some things, since my brother had taught me much before I got too deep in my schooling. Mostly it was weapons, explosives and survival skills. He'd taught me how to manage to do things and gather information without being noticed. Of course, I could never be as good as he was, but I was getting scared. I had to make him proud."

I could feel the intensity of her situation, the fear, the confinement. I wanted to console her, but we'd more pressing matters to deal with, and again I struggled to keep from being totally insensitive, trying to push her harder. Helping her to her feet, we moved to the Well, the only surviving feature of the square. She sat down heavily on the dirt and leaned back against the stone.

"That was when I pulled me head out of me arse, and decided I had to come up with a plan. I knew I'd been recruited immediately after my brother had recommended me. That meant there was a very good chance he knew exactly what I was doing there, and that meant he'd be trying to communicate with me. I just had to figure out how."

Storrm had returned and handed me a fairly clean towel and a bag of water. *"Return to the Den and send Konann back for us. Share my thoughts and my sight, for you will need to Hear this story as much as I, and 'tween us, mayhap we can make sense of the telling. I will bring the Healer as soon as possible."* Having Received her orders, Storrm mounted the big Horse and rode quickly away.

Wetting the towel, I began to wipe the grime from Shayla's face, 'til she raised her hands and assumed the task. She washed her face and wiped her hair back, tucking the strands behind her ears to keep them out of her eyes. Taking a long drink from the bag of clean cold water, she handed it back to me and bonelessly dropped her hands to her lap once more, but her voice seemed a little stronger.

"I got my first clue that very night. I had a dream so vivid, I woke up and 'twas still active in my mind. I Heard my brother and he warned me to be careful. I know now that he was using MindSpeak. He Told me he'd send me information. He warned me it would mean my life and his if we were found out, but that something very bad was happening in the world and he wanted me safe with him. We were all the family we had left." The knowledge that she was capable of enduring MindSpeak was encouraging for 'twould remedy some issues, but my heart ached for the woman who'd practically raised me. I could Feel her vulnerability, but didn't interrupt.

Shayla continued after a brief silence. "From then on, nightly for the next two weeks, I had the recurring dream of my brother Speaking to me. He'd tell me what to do during the day, how to appear to be completing my research as was expected, and how to complete a sideline project without being noticed. I was instructed to covertly stockpile as much of the blood and DNA samples as I could, and have them ready to run with at a moment's notice. Since I'd always trusted my brother, and had lost all faith in the Project, I did what his Voice told me and prayed I wasn't going insane."

She paused again, and I placed my hand upon her thigh to shore up her resolve. The pain these memories invoked was evident. I'd noted the mixture of terms, from her past and her present. She was near breakdown, but I had to keep her going.

"Please continue. 'Tis painful, but we need to know as much as we can. No more secrets. Please," I implored her, filling her with as much warmth and security as I could spare, and she took another deep breath.

"I don't remember much more, and what I did know wasn't much. I was sheltered in the Project and had no idea what was going on in the outside world. I was pressured to do more and do it faster. I'd created a serum for injection but the final touch was supposedly not mine to add. I was told it would be used in clinical trials after the next step with the other researchers had been completed, but by now, I knew what I was really doing. I'd created what they thought was a DNA modifier, using the provided samples that resembled a raptor or a lizard or some combination of both. Later I realized it had been derived from both live Dragon and egg. This serum, once injected, would have shifted the subject's DNA through the blood. It would have taken multiple injections to do this and I wasn't certain if its effects were permanent or temporary. I just didn't have access to enough information. I'd no idea what this was supposed to enhance in a soldier, and prayed my brother was not the one being used in the 'trials'." She shivered involuntarily with revulsion of the prospect that her brother would be the one to take the experimental drug, and I tried again to infuse her with strength and to ease the emotional turmoil I could sense.

She sighed, and looking up at me, she said, "In the meantime, I'd altered it as my brother instructed so that the injected serum became nothing more than a placebo, and would be sloughed off out of the system with sweating. Therefore I provided them with a useless product, with the exception of what they'd already been given. As I was altering the serum, I was simultaneously creating a crystallized form of the same product, using simple salt crystals as a base, since I could make those easily and without anyone noticing, that would do what they'd desired. But 'twas still unknown what the modified benefits would be, from a raptor and/or a lizard. My brother told me not to worry, just keep making as much of the product as I could, and don't let the Administrators find out. I kept up the pretense, becoming more confused and fearing I was going to get caught any day."

Shayla's voice took on an urgent tone and now she was truly reliving her past. I debated whether or not to break this memory, but the decision was taken out of my hands as she found her strength again and went on, "Then it happened. I'd just glanced up at the monitor when I heard a huge crashing noise not far from my doorway. I almost missed it before the picture was cut off. I couldn't believe what I saw! A huge black lizard looking creature was rambling up the hallway, with the Administrators following behind, and they were coming directly to my lab." Briefly, I heard the old Shayla return, her sense of humor and irreverence reminding me of my sister Storrm. She smirked, her next words causing me to snort in repressed laughter afore she regained her serious composure, and with great animation she said, "I had the immediate feeling that my contract was about to be terminated. I can't even tell you what I felt about seeing that creature. I did what my brother had told me to do. I went into what you now call 'Battle Mode' and grabbing up my bag of supplies and all the altered salt crystal I'd managed to produce, I reached under my desk, hit the make-shift battery that started a fire that would lead to an explosion, that would ultimately take down the entire lab, and if lucky, set off the series of mini-explosive devices I'd placed to make distractions throughout the entire compound, which would aid in my escape!"

I stopped her by gently grabbing her waving arms, "What's a battery? I know about explosives, they're fireworks, yes?" Shayla nodded her head affirmatively. We'd never used fireworks as a weapon afore. The notion was intriguing. I'd have to discuss this further with Regynn. Magic was far more potent but it extracted a price that usually involved fatigue or pain or even death, therefore anything that could give us an advantage without the use of Magic was welcome in my arsenal.

Settling back down from her near hysterics, she answered, "A battery was a device that focused power to set off the fireworks. Like a fuse." I listened intently to her explanation, and added yet another item to the list of what I'd be gathering in more detail later. Shayla seemed to know my thoughts, and with a clear voice she continued, "Then I climbed into the area beneath my desk I'd secured like a safe, with the aprons of lead sheeting and fire proofing that was used to protect me during part of the original processing. Since I'd refined my 'recipe', I'd not needed the aprons any longer, but hadn't let the Administrators know this, and therefore my order for more of them had not been questioned. I just prayed I'd built it well enough to survive the oncoming blast. I'd set up the explosives to take out my door first, and then it would circle around the building, go round the compound and eventually return to this very lab. And I'd better not be in it, when and if it completed that circuit successfully. I'd set the other explosives to do as much damage as possible, but wasn't really confident of the end results."

I was aghast. Shayla the Healer was a true Warrior. Even though I was unfamiliar with much of what she'd described, 'twas clear she'd fought a battle for her life, and had been quite ingenious in her creation of weapons. Untrained and alone, with nothing but a disembodied Voice to guide her at night, she'd done the impossible. I held my breath waiting for the rest of the story, knowing how it came out for her, but wondering what had become of her brother.

"I can't really remember much after that, how I got out of the lab and into the yard. I heard the first blast, counted to ten, and then just began to run. My brother had recited this sequence of events to me so many times, making me repeat it back, that I did everything by rote. Suddenly I found myself outside, everything was smoking and exploding, and I saw a few people in white lab coats running around. No one noticed me, I didn't see the Administrators and there was nothing of the lizard that I now know was a Dragon. They'd all just disappeared. No bodies, nothing. Of course, I don't really know if I would have seen them or not. I wasn't looking, I wasn't thinking, I was escaping! And being a non-Magic Bearer, I wouldn't have recognized the remains of anything Magical, even if I'd stumbled over them. I'd grabbed a few other items on my way out that I needed to recreate the crystal elsewhere, and my bags were getting heavy by the time I got to the fence. I saw an armored truck…"

At this point, I really had no idea what Shayla was talking about, but didn't want to interrupt her, and just decided to let her go on. "…that had crashed into the gatehouse, and the gate was open. I ran out and as I passed the truck, it caught on fire. The driver was trying to get out, but the door was jammed and he was stuck. Everything was exploding all around the compound and I was afraid, but I went back to help him. He'd obviously helped me by taking out the gate mechanism. I managed to drag him out of the broken window and 'twas my brother. Together we were able to get to the ditch opposite the gatehouse, where he pushed me down and covered me with his body, just as I thought I saw the heavens explode. 'Twas like a huge comet came hurdling toward the power plant, and the entire compound went up in flames. For awhile I tried to justify what I'd seen as mere shock. I told myself, 'twas my explosives that made the fire and took out the power station."

Was this what had happened to her brother? Was this how the man had Passed the Veil? So engrossed was I, that I near missed her next words. "I might as well tell you this now. It doesn't matter anymore. Grifynn was the man in the truck, come to help me escape. Grifynn was my brother." I couldn't hold back my sharp intake of breath as my mind ran quickly to the past, o'er all the odd facts I'd gathered throughout my life. The similarity in their facial features, the fact that neither of them appeared to age, how they'd acted toward and around each other. All innocent details that meant nothing to the casual observer, but now made perfect sense. The only part of this that I couldn't understand yet, was why they'd kept it a secret.

Shayla watched as I made the rapid associations, but didn't answer my unspoken question immediately. "It took me several days to remember I'd not put explosives anywhere near the power plant. I'd not had enough time or ability to get to the generators unnoticed to place anything there and in fact, what I had placed wouldn't have caused the entire compound to go up in flames." She gazed deeply into my eyes, daring me to understand what she was trying to explain. I was stunned with so much information, coming at me so fast.

"During those first few days, Grifynn and I merely struggled to survive. As we walked, we talked. We had to be cautious, for there was much looting, and danger was everywhere. He told me my research was about longevity, unnatural healing, as well as enhanced senses. He was the trial soldier, and had actually volunteered for the duty when it had first been proposed. A black Dragon had come to the top brass of the military and offered to assist them by helping to create the ultimate soldier. 'Twas this Dragon, along with his minions who appeared in human form, who'd supplied the DNA and the blood with which I'd worked. No one knew where he'd obtained the eggs or the samples from which the DNA was taken, or the Dragon blood, as there had originally been so much of the thick sticky dark liquid, it couldn't have come from this one black Dragon."

Again she sank deep into her past as she continued her story, "Grifynn explained the longevity he'd acquired was long term, and he insisted I use the crystal too. Initially I felt odd, and soon knew I was addicted to the substance. At the time, given the harsh circumstances, 'twas not so bad. I healed all injuries, I had more energy than I'd ever had, and there were other benefits as well. But the enhanced senses he gained were very short lived, having to mix his own blood with the blood of the Dragon, to get them. He'd been injecting himself with this in order to Speak to me every night, using the telepathy of the Dragons. But 'twas what he didn't tell me, that made me fear for him. It seemed the crystal wasn't so bad after all. The blood had far worse consequences. Although just as addictive as the crystal, 'mixing blood' seemed to cause him to age, and through the passing winters, I noted he became more obsessive and paranoid with each use. I feared for his sanity in the winters to come, and he agreed only to use it when absolutely necessary, switching to my crystals. 'Twas a promise I'd thought he'd kept, 'til Aalanna was taken. 'Twas how he'd

Communicated with her. But she somehow knew 'twas not good for him and limited this behavior by not answering. It devastated him."

Amazingly, I realized this woman had found a modified version of the LifeBond itself. I could only wonder at the effects it had on their lives, their health, their abilities. Quietly, she lowered her gaze, and I was fearful for her. I needed to hear the rest of her story. I needed to truly know my father, and suddenly realized she was the aunt of whom my mother had referred. It comforted me, as in the last day I'd lost my mother and my father, but had found a full blood aunt and sister.

Almost as an afterthought, seemingly in answer to my earlier question, "'Twas the Dragon I saw who'd Flamed the compound, setting off the generators, trying to kill me and destroy the research. He'd betrayed his own Kind, supplying us with eggs and blood, and I never knew where he got it or why he'd do this. I never found out who the Dragon was or who the Administrators were, although I now suspect 'twas The Black himself."

Pausing, she took another sip of water from the bag I offered. Her thoughts seemed to ramble. "In those early days we traveled constantly, trying to help the survivors. We saw much devastation, survived many skirmishes, entire cities were leveled and all communication and mechanical forms of travel were gone. Martial law was in existence, and there were dead and dying everywhere. I saw many Flame wounds, and what could only be the remains of humans who'd apparently been eaten by Dragons. We also saw many wounds of Man's creations. I did my best to help those I could, but we found this put us in much danger, as Healers were in high demand. We finally went underground, up in the high mountains of what is now known as The Razor's Edge, to wait out the Last Holocaust. During this time we met Corbyn the Raven."

I was shocked. She'd known the Fay all along. "He helped us off and on through the winters. It seemed that our changed DNA had Called to him, and he'd been curious. You know the Fay can alter memories. 'Twas how we were able to live so many lives, Darque. If people had known of our longevity and remarkable healing ability, they'd have held us captive, killed us for the secret. After we'd left the mountains and rejoined the world, we did what we did best. Grifynn was a leader, a fighter, and we gathered the survivors, building a society, a new world. But we'd outlive everyone and the only way we could keep that a secret was with Corbyn's help. We lived for a while at Evanntyr and I had a lab there but we were forced to leave suddenly. I had to abandon my lab, and we eventually settled here in Drekinn."

"With my Life Crystal we were able to survive illness and injury, and our life spans seemed indefinite, as long as we used it when stressed. Not a bad addiction, I suppose. Eventually it became obvious to me that we were truly altered. We'd become a new species, not completely human, and only partly Dragon. I discovered I could MindSpeak under great duress without 'mixing blood', but never let on to Grifynn. I used my limited talents to become a better Healer. I found I could plant simple suggestions in others' minds, making them believe 'twas their own idea. Mostly, 'twas to help them heal, to ease pain perception, or to gain confidence in themselves. Innocent things. Before fleeing Evanntyr, I'd created an improved Life Crystal that could be used in its purest form, under the tongue, as well as a Blood Elixir that Grifynn could simply drink." Shayla sighed as if trying to decide what to say next. "Just prior to the Last Holocaust, Grifynn heard a prophesy which he shared with me while we were living in the mountains. He told me he would sire a red haired girl child, of Dragon Blood and Dragon Seed, who'd receive a Dragon scar upon her right thigh shortly after her birth, and would eventually lead us into a new beginning by joining the Races and reestablishing the balance. He'd even been provided with a name. But by then I thought we'd both been rendered sterile. Even so, I took the description he provided, down to the scar that would appear on his daughter's thigh, and wove the prophesy into the tapestry that hung as a cover to my lab in the castle. But I didn't truly believe him until Aalanna was with child." Shayla hesitated, staring at me, daring me to rebuke her story, "'Twas you, Darque. You are The Dragon, conceived of Grifynn's Dragon Blood and Dragon Seed. You are the fulfillment of the prophesy."

So, this explained the tapestry in the Great Hall, on the Grand Staircase of Evanntyr Castle. It also explained the doorway hidden behind the wall hanging, and gave me much hope that Shayla's 'lab' was still undisturbed. Now I also recalled the Legends of Grifynn's life, and that he'd gleaned all his ancestors' knowledge and skills, and kept them. No wonder. He was his own ancestors!

I could scarcely fathom it all as I saw flashes of my Gifts shared by my full blood kin, knowing she was correct and that I was actually not fully human or Dragon, but a unique mixture of both. That explained my MindSpeak without the benefit of the 'Bond, my strong instincts and ability to convincingly change people's minds, my innate Magic, even the struggle to take the Link with Gunnarr when we first took the 'Bond. What else would it explain?

Chapter 34

The Shield of Protection

Through the chaos in my mind, I heard Shayla breathe, "I'm afraid I've provided few answers and only given you many more questions, my child." She'd run out of words, exhausted as were we all. But there wasn't enough time to digest all she'd revealed, and more would have to wait. We must hurry back, I must have the Healer fully functional, her secrets exposed at least to me, for I had Dragons down and the effort to Hold the Shield was draining me as well as Gunnarr, who'd Joined me to share the burden. I also felt 'twas another Sharing our burden, but only had my suspicions as to their identity.

"Storrm, how fare thee?"

"I am well, and they yet live, but you must hurry if we don't wish to lose the most badly wounded to the Fade," Storrm Replied to my query. Her Voice revealed her fear and impatience for me to return, to do something. I scowled at the mention of the purgatory neither this side or the other of the Veil, a place one could be wedged for eternity, a place I might be sending those I was trying desperately to hold onto. If I let them loose, they'd Pass without fail, for none of them could live with the injuries they'd sustained. If I hung on, and they Passed anyway, I was the one who'd failed them, for despite the power I wielded, I'd not the power of the One True Liege.

Shayla held the secret. After all, she'd just admitted to being nearly as old as my Dragon. She'd done it with some kind of crystal of her own creation, in something she named a 'lab', and if she didn't have more of the substance, then she could make more. She'd said the crystal assisted her to Heal all of her injuries, and given what I knew of the enhanced Healing of the Dragons, I prayed this meant even near fatal ones. During her story I couldn't help but be reminded of how well Axyl and Haniyyah fared after what should've taken them both Beyond, and I recalled seeing her place something in the Warrior's mouth. Had she already been using the crystal upon my Teams? Was that what she'd added to the salve? If I could just revitalize her, make her return to Healer mode, I was certain she'd agree to use the crystal. I cared not at this point about any ill effects. She'd mentioned the addictive properties, but I'd yet to see anything of the sort with Axyl and Haniyyah, although they were still recovering. But with so many of my Fleet wounded, let alone the free Dragons and Warriors who now lay near death at the Den, I cared not about any such problem. I needed to help them survive the coming nightfall, we could work out the long term issues later. What she'd told me about the Dragon's Blood on those not in 'Bond hadn't fallen on deaf ears, either. If all else failed this day, I'd take that risk, but only if they volunteered. I prayed I wouldn't have to ask, for there was no doubt every one of them would grasp onto the chance without a qualm. I needed Shayla back in charge of her staff.

"Get up Shayla, many lay in need of your help." I tried to get her to stand up, but when I looked at her face, her eyes were unfocused. Trying again, I raised my voice attempting to appeal to her passion and devotion, "Healer! You're needed at the Den! There are Warriors down, Dragons down!" Still no response. I knelt beside her and cupping her face in my hands, I stared directly into her eyes, imploring her, "I know not what to do, Ama'Shayla. You taught me much, but this is beyond my capability. If I cannot get you to return to us, I shall be forced to locate and use your medicine myself, and 'twill be mere guesswork." She simply shifted her eyes to the rubble of her home.

"*Shayla? Do you Hear me?*" I Spoke softly, in my last ditch effort to force her out of this self induced stasis. I feared she'd not be able to handle the MindSpeak in her current condition, but then I feared even more that she'd slip away from us forever. Choosing to risk it, I attempted to reach her at the Link level of her consciousness. "*Aunt Shayla…? I need you to come back to me, come back to us. Healer, I need your help, the Clan needs your help. Please, I've just found you, don't leave me now.*" Desperately, I tried to force my message, my heartfelt love and understanding, my urgent need, into her awareness through the windows of her soul. I ran my fingers through her thick mop of auburn curls that couldn't be tamed despite the sweat and blood caked in it, and no matter how often she'd tucked it behind her ears. Deeply, I stared into her dark gray blue eyes, the very match of my father's, and wondered how I, or anyone, could've missed that we were all kin.

As if in the barest whisper of her own Voice, she Spoke to me, "*I Hear you, my child.*" I clutched her face in my hands, sucking in my breath, my heart hammering in my chest, as hope was renewed. Her eyes cleared, she focused upon me and smiling the tiniest smile, nodded her head in acknowledgement of her return to the living. Raising my face, I cried to the heavens, "Thank you, m'Liege!"

I stood up swiftly, pulling her to her feet. Initially unsteady, with a grand effort she gained her second wind and without looking back, she hiked up her britches and trudged barefoot to Konann's side, grasped a handful of thick mane and vaulted aboard his broad back. As she mounted the spirited beast she reached down and hoisted me up behind her and we returned with all haste to the Den.

As we approached the castle, she grilled me with questions of the extent of the wounded, and how my Shield worked to Hold them. I did my best to answer, although I knew not how the Magic worked, 'twas as natural as the Speak to me now. I described it as best I could however, and she seemed pleased as she took in what I said, while making her own plans and creating a strategy to keep them all alive. 'Twas awe-inspiring to watch her mind work, to see how she rallied, how a true Healer ran in Battle Mode. I could imagine her as she and her brother had survived the Last Holocaust, how they'd fought and struggled, battling both Dragons and Man, back when the Fates had woven her so intricately into this tapestry of our lives.

"'Tis apparent you've seen battle afore, Shayla. I'm impressed." We'd raced through the Great Hallway, everyone backed up against the walls to let Konann lope through without slowing, to the Pits and the hospital wing where the injured Warriors and Dragons were hanging on for their lives. Anyone able to stand and carry anything, were helping the Healer Apprentices with the more seriously wounded, cleaning up the Den, as well as out on search and rescue throughout the village. There were many missing, much to be salvaged this day. No one, not even the injured, could be spared.

Having dismounted while Konann was still checking his breakneck speed, I had to admire the Healer's balance and skillful landing. Without stopping her own momentum, she ran through the sand to where the wounded Dragons were being triaged and tended. They'd been brought in by the less injured Free Dragons and deposited there along with the Free Warriors and their closer proximity giving me more time and strength to Hold the Shield. Gliding from one to the next, she examined them hurriedly, spoke summarily with each of the Assistants, giving clear and commanding orders that were instantly obeyed. With her respected and uplifting spirit, hope grew and people began to scurry about with purpose instead of floundering without true direction as 'twas just moments prior to our arrival. Storrm was good, but she couldn't be in two places at once. She'd followed orders to organize the recovery and search and rescue efforts, giving only slight attention to the wounded as she could do nothing to assist me and therefore she'd considered herself next to useless here. She'd well chosen her path and I commended her for her decision. I could feel the Life Force of each and every one of the mortally injured, ebb and flow around and within me. I couldn't sustain this much longer.

With Battle Lust fading, I folded to my hands and knees in the sand, just as Gunnarr ambled his massive bulk up closer. Nosing me gently, his beautiful eyes sparkling and dark in the sunlight, I could feel his concern.

"Can you climb up, my love? I'll carry you inside. Mayhap the strain will lesson there." The worry in his Voice was evident.

"I cannot lose them, Gunnarr, I will not lose them," I Said, as I laboriously found my feet once again and using a combination of both of us pushing and pulling, with a smidgen of Magic thrown in as a boost, I managed to get me arse o'er his neck.

"Who Holds with us in the Shield, Gunnarr?" I Asked, and he shook his head as a shudder of pain permeated through. 'Twas breaking down! If I lost any portion, I'd be able to feel everyone's pain as well as their anguish and fear. 'Twas but a fraction of one of them breaching the barriers, and given the effort to Hold it firm, I began to shake and sweat profusely as with fever. Then just as suddenly, the Presence patched the break, forcing the pain back under, and Gunnarr Confirmed my earlier suspicions, *"My mother is that Presence, Warrior. She assists us to Hold but we cannot do this for much longer. 'Twill continue to erode 'til none of us will be able to survive. 'Twill be then that you must either let them go or we'll follow them to the Fade."*

"What are you saying? If I let them go, have they no chance to Pass the Veil?"

"'Tis too late, my love. We've Held them here too long and they can no longer make that journey. If you loose them now, they Fade, most likely dragging us with them. Our only chance is the Healer." And with that stunning revelation, Gunnarr began to stride purposefully toward the hospital wing, following where Shayla had just disappeared moments afore.

<div align="center">~~~~~~~~~~</div>

Shayla sprung off Konann's back and barely felt the sand beneath her feet as she raced for the wounded Dragons. If either side of a Team Passed, they'd both Pass, and she knew that if the Dragon was the stronger, the Team had more of a chance to hold themselves this side. If the Warrior was the stronger, he had little chance of Holding a seriously wounded partner. If her decision cost them, she'd have to live with the results. She'd already chosen to use the Life Crystal, and even the Blood Elixir if she had to, for she couldn't allow any of these brave fighters to Pass, she couldn't fail them. Making her plans on the run, she grabbed the first Apprentice she saw and gave orders to bring out all the helpers to tend the Dragons first and get them stable. Again and again, as she moved swiftly from beast to beast, giving orders to set broken bones, approximate torn flesh, replace loose fangs and talons, suture lacerations, she was amazed they yet lived. But then she'd remember they were being Held under the Shield, and she was in awe of the power wielded by the new Battle Commander.

As more wounded were brought in from the battlefield and the fringes beyond, Shayla knew she had to get to her supplies. But they were limited. How was she to divvy them out? What rules did she follow? Memories of the aftermath of the Last Holocaust came to her, the rioting to get to her, her skills as a Healer, her 'medicine'. There might not be enough to give to everyone who needed it now, and 'twould take time to create more. So, to the Dragons go the last of her current stash, 'til she could replenish her supplies. Once they were stable, they could Heal their own.

"No need to see to that one Healer." The young Apprentice touched Shayla's arm, stopping her as she tried to climb up upon one of them to open its eyes. The look on Lowah's face was enough to tell her the Dragon had reached her Final Sleep.

"I don't recognize this one. Was she..." Shayla's fear was for the Warrior who may have been her 'Bond.

"We haven't been able to confirm a 'Bond. We believe she was a Free Dragon. We just don't know. She was already gone when they brought her in. We couldn't recognize her body 'til one of the others Cast a Spell upon us, allowing us to see their remains, and suddenly we saw many more of the dead, so many more still lying out on the battlefield. So many still incoming." Lowah hung her head in fatigue and defeat remembering when the Spell was Cast, suddenly revealing the dead. Prior to that, no one had realized the enormity of the decimation. She'd been working for marks, without rest, without food, feverishly tending to the injured, all of them in desperate condition. There weren't enough Healers around, even though Shayla had begun to train many new Apprentices.

Shayla looked up again, as yet another wounded Dragon came in via the sling, his Warrior lying atop him in a jumble of broken limbs and blood. Making up her mind, she grabbed Lowah by the shoulders and gave her orders to forget about bone setting and cleaning, they were to quick-suture the lacerations, stop the bleeding and then move on to the next beast. All else could wait. Lowah nodded her understanding and then turned to put her orders into action. Shayla left the Pits for her quarters.

~~~~~~~~~~
~~~~~~~~~~

Dyrrk fared well through the battle. He'd always been blessed by The One True Liege. He knew his friend, only known as 'the contact' to the Battle Commander, had been present during the siege. 'Twas good they'd not actually faced off upon the field, for the Battle Blood flowed heavy this day and 'twould be a cruel twist from the Fates had they added each other's. Many were lost, both Dragon and Man, both Good and Evil, and many more were still within the confines of the Shield of Protection. Would the new Battle Commander be able to Hold them? Would the Mighty Blue manage to keep her from failing? When she and her Dragon had arrived in the midst of the fray his heart did sink for 'twas obvious to all that she'd assumed Command and that meant Grifynn was gone. He'd never thought to see this day, despite the subtle innuendo the big men had bantered back and forth recently in their 'private meetings', however, Grifynn's words hadn't fallen on deaf ears. His vision still recovering from Battle Lust, he clearly recalled how the battle had abruptly turned with the arrival of the Warrior sisters and their Dragon partners. Their ferocious tactics and commanding presence rallied everyone to new-found strength. Still, the odds strongly favored The Black and his Hoard and had they fought with any kind of strategy, the end of this day might have been far different. Fortunately for the Clan, the Hoard appeared to be without direction, weren't well trained and didn't work together during battle. Even with some of the King's Forces fighting with the Hoard, there was no middle command system and they couldn't withstand the fury of the attack the Warriors mounted with Darque's arrival. His friend had done well to foster the Hoard's lack of discipline and structure, undermining their efforts from within, keeping their trust levels dismally low, working slowly and with great caution, as a ghost chills the ones he passes in the night, never observed, never detected, never blamed. Even so, the Dragon Clan stood little chance if they were besieged again afore they came up with a new strategy. But if prophesy was believed, there'd be a new plan soon, with Darque as the architect. Trying to stretch out the kinks in his battle weary muscles, he wiped away the blood of the few minor lacerations he'd sustained and looked about him at the destruction. At first glance, 'twould appear as if the only structure left standing was the Den itself, however, he knew as did all of the Clan, that the Port District was still intact under the rubble of its upper levels. They hoped to find more survivors there, but there wasn't time to ponder further, 'twould have to wait. He joined in the salvage efforts while others were organizing security, search and rescue and the building of funeral pyres. As the Battle Lust ebbed within him, 'twas not much different. There was so much blood that all was red despite his clearing vision. Mechanically he lifted, carried, stacked and stored all he could reclaim, the work performed without conscious thought. Once he realized a Spell had been Cast for him to see the remains of the dead Dragons, he began to gather undamaged teeth, fangs, talons, and scales. 'Twas a daunting task, and the Flamed ash was corrosive to his skin. He tried to focus, there was much to do. He had to be careful so as not to seriously injure himself, and the heat from the concentration of hundreds of Dragons' Battle Flame hadn't left as much to salvage as he'd hoped. His thoughts drifted to other matters. He had a meeting to arrange….soon. Although both he and his friend had been aware of plans to attack, making every effort to do what they could to prevent total annihilation of the Clan, they'd not known the exact timing and the assault had surprised both of them. If all went well, mayhap he'd found a reason to advance his promotion during the Battle. He couldn't have outright killed the Right Hand of the Destroyer, and he himself hadn't encountered him upon the battlefield. He sighed. 'Twould take the luck of the gods, but his friend surely had that. He'd have to confirm the Battle Commander had Passed afore they'd decide their next move. Should they trust The Dragon and The Mighty Blue? Did they have a Flamin' choice? He sighed again and then went back to work in the bloody rubble, shoulder to shoulder with his brothers in arms and the Clansmen not too injured to work.

CHAPTER 35

Parting Advice

A FEW DAWNS LATER

Darque sat behind the desk in her father's huge chair, and leaned back. Her diminutive frame dwarfed, her feet dangling, she wondered how she was supposed to replace a Legend. 'Twas the first time she'd entered his office since she'd discovered him missing. There'd been no time to do so afore now, but she'd known she'd find herself here sooner or later. Might as well get this done with, so the next time she entered 'twould be without the ghosts of the past so blatant. Her restless eyes roved the room, wondering what had occurred that night that seemed like a lifetime ago, but 'twas in reality, just o'er a moon. So much had changed. Contemplating the events, she tried to create a clear picture 'tween what she knew and what she'd deduced. What she knew was that the last person to actually see her father alive was Storrm. She'd arrived in this office, received her rather ambiguous orders and departed. The events that occurred after that were still being pieced together. She accepted that she may never know all of the facts. But she knew her father had arrived at Evanntyr just prior to her own arrival and that kind of speed would have taken a Dragon. She had yet to find one who knew anything about his trip. So who'd flown him, how had he accomplished that feat, and why did he go at that time? He'd known Aalanna was at the castle for at least the past seven winters. What had been the impetus to launch another rescue attempt now? She couldn't shake the idea that 'twas all a plot to get her and Storrm and the Battle Commander out of the Den at the same time, so that the siege could be staged without them. She knew he'd not have participated in such knowingly. He had to have a very good reason to abandon the Clan. 'Twas obvious his orders to Storrm were a diversion and 'twas clear the sealed orders to Axyl and Haniyyah were not by his hand. That was the spy's doing, and the only way someone could have access to her father's seal was if they looked like one of his daughters. Not even Shayla had access to the Seal of the Battle Commander of the Dragon Clan. Given the many rumors of Warriors having been seen in multiple locations simultaneously, even Storrm having been seen in the Kennels just afore Bensyn had been brutally slain, she deduced the spy had access to Shifter Magic. That meant that somehow, the Fay were involved. With this conclusion so strongly suggested, she had to wonder how much she could trust Corbyn. So far, 'twas confirmed that none of the known Races were immune to the Evil One. Which led her to wonder, how many more Magic Bearing Races were there? Where were they, and why were they hiding? There were many rumored human tribes scattered around the world. How many of them were being affected by The Black?

The Dragon Clan was in trouble. Not only had The Evil One and his Hoard attacked, but the King's Forces had participated, although not a single body had been recovered as proof. She couldn't trust Shytin, for 'twas obvious he was in league with The Black and that left the Dragon Clan on their own. But, if the King knew without doubt that she was aware of such, he could very possibly march against them. 'Twas why she'd sent out the new Stable to ensure the fleeing troops wouldn't return to him to tell the tale. Without any of his own to make report, he'd be in the dark for confirmation, and suddenly this became a diplomacy dance of ultimate intricacy. If he posted a Royal Decree against the Clan, they'd all abruptly become outlaws. If he had the Magic of The Black at his disposal….well, she thought, let's just say goodnight, for they'd all soon enough reach their Final Sleep. Hiding was not an option for a Warrior and besides, as she'd learned about the Races being infiltrated, so too would be the land itself, providing no solace. She was going to have to become very good at deceit, with all haste. 'Twould take strong leadership to continue and to thrive. Darque licked her dry lips and sat forward in the chair, leaning her elbows upon the huge desk afore her, continuing her mental assessment of the situation.

The retreat of the Hoard from the battlefield had provided a mere respite in her opinion. There was still the matter of a spy among their ranks and that one had yet to be uncovered, if he'd survived that is. There was no certainty in that, either. The Village proper looked to be nothing but charred debris and ash, with the exception of the Well. The Den had remained essentially intact, being constructed mostly of stone, but everything made of wood or hemp were gone. The Port District appeared not much more than rubble, but her search and rescue Teams were beginning to bring in good news of finding the lower levels mostly undamaged and there were reports of survivors. Had the Hoard known the upper ground level was not all there was to the District they might have Flamed deeper, but as 'twas, the upper level had been collapsed per Grifynn's ingenious pulley systems, protecting most of the lower levels and the people therein. Once the beams were pulled the entire district went down like a house of cards. 'Twould have taken careful timing to avoid detection, for the enemy had to think they'd somehow caused the collapse in the battle or they'd become wise to the deception. 'Twas confirmed now, that the ones who'd pulled the beams, including Kallyr himself, had sacrificed their own lives in the doing. She was hoping the Port workers and residents were still below when that event had taken place, as 'twould have been close to waking and getting around. As for the docks, well, they were gone, as were all the ships and boats weighed in at the time. Nearly half the Clan were now estimated to have been killed in the first Flame attacks or were still missing, a quarter could still be alive under the Port District, while another quarter had sought refuge in the Dragon's Den. All who'd made it to the castle had retreated to the caves beneath, for during the siege the Pits had been compromised, leaving the Den open to attack. The Spell to Block the entries would have worked, but 'tween the Clan still streaming through and Shayla standing in the doorway to prevent the activation, only two of the three Spells had been sparked. Darque couldn't fault her for doing her job. She'd helped save many.

Those taken under had been courageously and tediously passed through the Spell Door within the dungeons a few at a time, clinging to the bare skin of her own full blood sister (the only one who could have done so), and those who'd been so protected were still bunking there. Fryya and Walkyr had apparently discovered the secret of the Spell door soon after they'd moved into the Den fulltime. 'Tween the two of them they'd also managed to save the entire Kennel stock as well. This effort however, had near drained Fryya of her own Life Force, and exhausted from her part in the rescue, she was still in the care of the Healers. At least 'twas certain now, that with rest she'd recover.

Darque was receiving names of survivors and known dead as soon as they were found or identified, and she knew that Mynx, the beautiful and very young Warrior she'd hired to protect Fryya, was still among the missing. She'd fulfilled her duty of seeing the children safely to the dungeons and then taking her leave, she'd charged boldly out of the Den into the midst of the fray. She hadn't been seen since, but so far no one had come forward as eye witness to her demise, either. Darque had no delusions about receiving her shorn locks, as ransom wasn't in The Black's vocabulary, but if she'd been taken, 'twas near certain she was dead.

Cayell had fearlessly held the dungeons alone, helping the Clan to safety through the besieged Pits, past the hospital wing, through the Great Hallway, delivering them to Fryya and Walkyr below. There was just not enough room for everyone to take refuge in the dungeons and if the rest of the Den were severely compromised, there'd be nowhere safe except the caves. Besides, the huge Dragons could have Flamed the dungeons via the stairwell and killed everyone without even bothering to descend. Their plan had been at great risk to everyone, but in the end it had paid off, as all those who'd made it to the dungeons had survived. Cayell had been one of the last Warriors to be treated by the Healer and was back out in the Port District now, continuing with Search and Rescue efforts.

Walkyr had worked hard to help organize the Clansmen descending to the dungeons. He grouped them, lined them up, and got them to remain behind the rock walls away from the open stairwell. He instructed them in what was happening during the time it took for Fryya to walk them through the Spell Door, so they'd understand and not panic, which would cause them all to fail. He had to instruct them to keep their eyes closed as 'twould appear as though they were walking straight into the rock wall, and not to lose their grip on Fryya's skin, but not to hurt her in the process. He hadn't flagged, he hadn't faltered. He'd helped to save near a quarter of the Clan, staying upon the dungeon side of the Spell Door, risking his own life with each passing moment, only ducking behind the walls with the others whenever Cayell yelled to them to take cover. The two children were heroes in Darque's mind.

Shayla had blown the Shyffah, and 'twas the only reason any of the Clan had managed to make it to the Den in time. 'Twas Walkyr's Vision of the coming siege that had given them that time. She'd blown 'til she'd run out of breath, and then she'd gathered her Apprentices and organized their efforts for the coming siege. It hadn't been long after she'd done this that she'd heard the initial Flaming, followed soon thereafter by Kallyr's death call. She'd directed the wounded, tended their injuries, kept her staff safe and even gone out on the battlefield, assisting in the rescue efforts there. She'd risked her own life many times to retrieve the injured from the fields as well as to treat the injured Dragons, as they couldn't be moved during the siege. Darque hadn't had time to talk to her again since they'd returned from the village after the conflict. She was sure the Healer would have much to tell.

Gunnarr's family ties had made her proud during the battle. Mystynn and Storrm were everywhere at once. Darting in and out, swift and vicious was their strategy, and they rallied as many as they rescued, leaving blood and ash behind them as they sped away to where they were needed next.

Ragnyrr the Third Prince, had the kindest heart of the family, and she'd been concerned about his ability to kill with the ferocity required to meet their need. But her childhood friend Kydra, was one of the most passionate among them and she held his heart in the palm of her hand. Once her life was at risk, he fought with keen brutality. Through the thickest skirmishing, they took their stand alongside his brothers, Kaygynn, Synddarr and Shasynn, who were still learning the Link with their new 'Bonds. Their Teamwork not yet as sophisticated as First Flight, he helped direct them, secured their backs, and saved their lives, time and time again.

The Teams took a beating. Among the losses was a young duo who'd shown every indication of ability and desire to take the LifeBond, and were scheduled to stand for the Third ceremony yet to come. The Passing of the youthful Warrior Flynn, and his Dragon friend and counterpart Shanndynn, was a blow to all. Their energy, their enthusiasm and devotion, had already permeated the candidates set to create the new Stable, and had everyone's spirits soaring during their training time together. They would be greatly missed.

But mayhap the worst tragedy was the loss of the Ancient, Kaahayyel, and three of her five children along with their Warrior 'Bonds, Ariel and Zayddarr, Barynn and Shraadarr, and Loryyn and Krynnarr. The female Warriors, Ariel and Loryyn, had been best friends since childhood, and Barynn and Loryyn had been cousins. Zaydarr had taken the 'Bond with Ariel in the First, and both of the others took in the Second. Ariel's betrothed Rygyl and his 'Bond Tegrynn, had fought bravely beside them, never leaving her side, trying to protect her back. But despite taking down several of the Hoard and many of the King's Agents, 'twas for naught in the end. The Teams fought well and had all come to the aid of their Dragons' mother, Kaahayyel. The Ancient had been swarmed by the Hoard from above her, forcing them a'ground, with the Agents meeting them below, sandwiching them 'tween. Zayddarr and Krynnarr had attacked from above, and Kaahayyel's daughter Shraadarr had managed to sneak in from under. The King's Forces were Flamed to oblivion, their Hoard allies providing little to no protection, but finally, there were just too many of them and all had succumbed. Only Rygyl and Tegrynn, and Tannyr and Kaahayyel were still alive on the battlefield when she'd found them. The Elder's Magic was the most powerful of any of the Ancients except the Matriarch herself, but she'd been forced to let them Pass. She was devastated, but Rygyl would take longer to recover from his love's loss than from his near fatal wounds, and she feared for his well being. Despite the Healing of his body, there seemed to be nothing but time alone to Heal his heart. When last she'd seen him, he was wearing upon his own wrist the braided chain he'd given to his betrothed.

THE BLACK WAR BEGINS

Of the 26 LifeBond Teams, they'd lost four. In addition, the loss of the potential Team of Flynn and Shanndynn was felt deeply by all. The free Dragons had fared no better. The battlefield was strewn with literally hundreds of carcasses, but given their difficulty with plainly recognizing the remains, the Spell that was Cast to see them still hadn't provided a clear cut means of telling upon who's side they'd fought. But most interesting, although horrifying, was the reported statistics of the fate of the free Warriors. Of the probable 1000 Warriors fielded in this battle, the Dragon Clan had lost an estimated 700. That left approximately 300. She squeezed her eyes shut and hung her head. The 300. Her favorite Legend. 'Twas an omen. Shaking her head to clear her thoughts, she knew she shouldn't take the time to think on this, for there was much work yet to do.

Darque had ordered that everyone continue to hide the extent of their survival. Going on her gut instincts and flashes of Vision, she knew the Hoard thought them totally decimated. Being quite disorganized, mayhap 'twas why they'd not returned to finish what they'd started. Or mayhap, they'd just lost interest. After all, they really had no rational agenda that rallied them tightly to The Black, and of what she'd noted during the battle, they had no organized ranking system for giving or receiving orders on the field. They'd cut their own losses, mayhap thinking they could take out the sisters at their leisure, now that they had little known protection. The fatal wounds they'd inflicted upon so many should've left few this side of the Veil, who could be easily defeated at a time and place of their choosing. The Hoard also thought the Clan were wiped out, gone in the destruction of their farms and lands, and according to her recognizance Teams, had even appeared to be dismissing them as a threat altogether. They knew not that the Clan yet survived. Although it had been a struggle for a few days, all who'd been Held by Magic and assisted by Shayla's Blood Crystal, had lived. She thought back to Tannyr and Kaahayyel, lying bloody and dying upon the battlefield. An eerie sense of déjà vu crept up her spine whenever she thought about that scenario. She was going to have a long chat with that elusive Raven when she found him; she was positive he was involved somehow. She was certain now, that she'd been deprived of her own memories, including her own prophesy, and that was not acceptable. She sat up straighter and sighed. But did it really matter? She could only do what she could do, work with what knowledge she had, rely on her Training, her Warrior heritage. She was Clan and she was the daughter of Grifynn, the greatest Battle Commander ever to hold the rank. She was also blessed with her own Magic and she'd not fail.

She cocked her head as the flickering candle light set off a glint of silver sprawled 'cross the desk. Grasping the chain she immediately recognized as her father's necklace, she was puzzled. He'd never taken that off. Her eyebrows furrowed in disbelief at the careless manner 'twas tossed. Something was wrong. She closed her eyes, held the chain tightly in the palm of her hand and brought it close to her cheek. Opening her senses, she Saw her father pull it off o'er his head, wincing with him as his hair became caught, but yanking it off nonetheless. He carefully laid it upon the desk. 'Twas not how she'd found it. But he'd meant this for Shayla. She'd make sure 'twas delivered.

Sighing again, she thought to herself that she shouldn't be surprised. Her father had never been one to show such emotions, even to his daughters. Why expect a token now? Shayla was Grifynn's sister, she should have the necklace. She'd not begrudge her aunt this simple keepsake.

Darque didn't even bother looking for a note, she knew she'd not find one. 'Twouldn't have been safe to scribe something that could be found by another. Flame it all! She'd always loved her father's flowing script. How she'd have treasured... what was that? Her eyes had been surveying the bookshelves as she thought about the necklace, and they rested now upon the rolls of parchment 'cross to her left. One was surely out of place. Not like the Commander. And if she wasn't mistaken....she stood up, her excitement growing, her hopes rising, her steps hesitant, but she couldn't stop herself from hurrying to the roll lying 'cross the others at a right angle upon the shelf. She reached forward, her hand beginning to shake slightly, her eyes beginning to fill. She pulled the scroll off the pile, and knew it instantly. She'd seen this one so many times in her childhood, had heard her father's deep voice reading from the parchment. She'd unrolled it many times herself and admired his beautiful longhand, the pictures inked along the sides, and read the words. The Legend of the 300. She swallowed hard, her throat so tight she could barely breathe, her eyes spilling o'er with tears, and she let them roll down her cheeks unbidden but unstoppable. He'd remembered them. He'd left her a clear and concise message with orders to continue the fight. He'd made it apparent that he trusted them, that he loved them, that he'd miss them. How could she let him down?

"Darque?" Storrm entered the office without knocking, as was their way, and now she understood how annoying that must have been for her father. But he'd never done more than tease them for their disrespect. Again, she felt the love her father had rarely been able to say aloud. If only she'd understood afore 'twas too late. Still, the behavior had left them open to the spy and some old habits would have to be rectified. She'd take care of that as soon as possible, but not now. First she had to show her sister something far more important.

"Yes?" Darque turned and carried the scroll to the desk, laying it flat upon the surface. Then she caught her sister's gaze, beckoning her to come forward.

Storrm stepped up to the other side of the desk, and looking down at the parchment then back up to her sister, she asked incredulously, "Is this what it looks like?"

"'Tis. 'Twas apparently his last message to us," Darque confirmed her sister's thoughts.

They shared tears, laughs, hugs. "'Twas Fryya herself, who ferried the survivors to the caves through the Spell Door in the dungeon. She worked without break, for marks, making trip after trip, Pushing her way through, leading the others. She is a sister to be proud of, Darque." Her eyes twinkled in merriment. Then her gaze became more serious, and she asked directly, "What say you, Commander? We have few Warriors left, lost more than half our troops. The Teams fared only slightly better." She stopped, because she didn't want to give in to the emotion in which she could truly drown.

"Who did we lose? Name them to their honor, my sister. They'll rise again in Legend Song, for we may have lost many lives but we didn't lose the battle and we shall not lose this war. The Hoard ran with their tails 'tween their legs."

Storrm and Darque discussed the statistics of the battle, the logistics of the war, and shared a mug of whiskey from their father's stash. Sighing, they put down their empty mugs and knew 'twas time to return to their duties. Just afore Storrm left, she peeked around the door and asked, "Have you checked the drawer or the passage yet?"

"By the 7ᵗʰ Egg, I know not what's gotten into me. I've forgotten both!" And Storrm merely winked, replying, "Let me know what you find, Battle Commander. My curiosity is piqued!" Stepping back out into the hallway, she firmly closed the heavy oak door behind her.

Darque sat back down on the edge of the big chair and sighed. 'Twas going to take awhile to get used to being called 'Battle Commander' by anyone, let alone her sister. Taking a deep breath, she pulled out the desk drawer. Finding the Life Crystal within, she was surprised that he hadn't taken it with him. 'Twas another mystery. Of course, Shayla was going to be very pleased, for she was running dangerously short on her stock after having used so much in the Healing of so many and 'twould take time to create more, for now Darque actually knew what 'twas. But even not knowing its purpose, she'd always known of its existence. Then there was the other. Pulling out the drawer, she discovered the vials that had been there for the last seven winters, were now gone. Must have been the Blood Elixir, she speculated. She'd learned the Elixir was the more dangerous of the two substances. That was what had started them all down this road of destiny. 'Twas with certainty her father had used it in his last mission. He'd been desperate. Sweeping her arm under the desk and to the back of the empty drawer space, she could find nothing more and she replaced it carefully. *"Storrm? Tell Shayla she can come pick up the Life Crystal in the morning. There's a very large chunk here, I'm sure she'll find it useful. And Storrm? Tell her I have a gift from a loved one."*

Receiving her affirmation, Darque focused on a plan. She had to formulate a defensive strategy to allow them time to rebuild their forces, an offensive strategy to allow their small numbers to conquer the crushing odds they now faced, and a strategy to keep the Clan alive. After Speaking briefly with her Second (for Storrm had received Battle Field promotion once Darque had taken Command) explaining her whereabouts for the next few marks, she placed a Hold upon the door and opened the passageway. The mechanism was so quiet, 'twouldn't have been heard by anyone passing, but 'twas so loud to her ears, she felt as if she'd notified the entire Den of what she was doing. She shrugged her shoulders and quickly entered the tunnels beyond, closing the doorway behind her. 'Twas quite dark, but her senses bespoke volumes. She could feel her father's footsteps, his determination echoing loudly through the tunnel. There was a long walk afore she reached the first split that connected to the honeycombed caverns under the plateau where her Teams were patrolling even now. She could feel the direction Grifynn had taken in his escape and decided to track his flight. She silently and quickly walked, crawled and scraped her way, following his essence, his will to complete his mission, to the small opening that served as an exit under the North Docks. Prior to the destruction, 'twas well hidden and she wondered if 'twas still so, but it made no difference. Anyone who entered would become lost and die, afore they could navigate through the maze within.

She forced her way past the rubble partially blocking the opening, and climbed out to the full view of the moonlight. 'Twas difficult to look upon the extent of the damage, but suddenly she was inspired. She climbed up and o'er the wreckage, noting no one had yet come to this end of the port and the Search and Rescue Teams were still working down from the High District. Her senses told her they'd find no one to rescue here. Still she followed her father's path, thankful for the Allure that allowed her to do so, for any tangible trace would've been destroyed, and soon found a place along the waterfront where his path simply ended. She'd need to check the registry to find out who'd docked there. But even if her father had taken a ship that night, it still didn't explain how he'd arrived so quickly to Evanntyr.

<center>~~~~~~~~~~</center>

As I looked up along the rock wall and surveyed the damage, I thought about how 'twould appear from above. *"Gunnarr? What do you think of a Shield o'er all of Drekinn to make it appear as it does now, for an extended period of time? Like the one we placed o'er the Training Facility. Can it be done? Can it be Held?"*

Gunnarr Replied, much intrigued, *"You have a plan? The Shield o'er the facility is not that extensive. 'Tis well hidden by the environment, the Spell of Aversion surrounds it, and most of the facility is underground. 'Twould depend on the parameters. Just Tell me of what you desire my love, and I shall endeavor to make it happen."* His sense of humor was returning.

If he weren't so endearing, I'd be frustrated with his antics. As 'twere, I still felt his interest in the plan I was devising. All had been awaiting my direction. I knew 'twas simply a beginning, a first small step, but at least 'twas a step, and I began to take heart that mayhap I could be the Leader they all hoped I was. Laying out my ideas, Gunnarr became just as excited, and I was heartened even more. It could be done and it might just work. The Dragon Clan was not defeated. We would rise again!

As 'twas, during our Search and Rescue and salvage efforts, we'd been relying on the Dragons' sense of whether or not the Hoard was anywhere near. I'd given orders to remain silent, undercover, unseen. I wanted to give the impression that all were gone, my thinking along the lines of discouraging the Hoard from feeling the need to return and finish us off. Simple logic really. We had to Heal, gather our resources, and find the Flamin' spy! I'd ordered a complete lock down, no one entered, no one left. The Training Facility now housed all of the Stable who were Healed enough to travel, for they'd not move to the caves to join those of First Flight 'til they were Battle Ready and became a Flight of their own. With them were the Warriors who'd Stand for the Third, with the exception of Flynn and Shanndynn. My heart ached for them, their loss weighed heavy upon me. They'd not been near enough to the Den to be included in my original Shield and by the time we'd found them, they'd Passed.

Their story was one of Legend Song, they'd sacrificed themselves to save the rest of the Teams, leading the Hoard away from the Bog region, distracting them enough for the new Stable to arrive without giving away from whence they came.

Not having 'Bonded yet, they were not only inexperienced, they didn't have the benefit of a true Link. Flynn was young and restless, Shanndynn was similarly stubborn and the combination had worked against the pair. But although they'd lost their lives, their efforts proved successful, allowing the new Stable to join the battle. If not for their daring act of selflessness we'd likely have lost them all, as well as compromising their location. Now the Stable pitched in with the cleanup efforts, most of them working harder than anyone else in some kind of furious attempt to seek forgiveness for not being able to help more, and for losing one of their own.

I'd Blocked all MindLink in and out, with all Communication going through Gunnarr and me. Mostly, we Listened. Thus far, this strategy seemed to be working. No Hoard had returned. There'd been no sightings, no skirmishes in the Outlands, and the most important thing was that the new Training Facility was intact and secure. Thinking of the Shield that kept them from being detected, strengthened my determination to set my new plan into action. My destiny, and a new era for the Dragon Clan, had begun.

Epilogue: The Predator

"Do it!" Dyrrk hissed through the pain as he struggled to draw his next breath. The multiple rib fractures and internal bleeding were a bitch, but 'twas the Flame wounds he'd just acquired that locked his fate. By all the fires of Hades, the mighty Warrior had never felt such intense pain, despite a long history of fighting Dragons even prior to the recent Battle for the Dragon Clan. 'Twas a fact that 'til then most Warriors couldn't boast. But even he couldn't avoid that incoming stream, 'twas as if the Fates were against them this day. He'd spun rapidly around to increase the force of his sword strike, managing to avoid the beast's first fiery breath, when he'd heard it inhale again. Dipping and stepping forward, he planned to rise up under the creature to strike the tender hollow where the massive leg joined the torso, and was already committed to the maneuver he'd used successfully in the past. But this time, 'twas as if the beast had been forewarned, and too late the brawny Warrior understood the battle strategy had been compromised. When he swung his heavy broad sword, completing the upper cut with his full force driving the blade deep into the chest cavity, he found the beast had shifted and his sword was now imbedded to the hilt in the heavy ribcage, while at the same time he'd felt Flame hit him squarely in the chest.

He'd never been Flamed at such close range afore and had marveled at the fact that he hadn't just simply disintegrated into a puff of ash when struck. Mayhap 'twas not full strength, as the Dragon could've been distracted by pain. Still, he hadn't been willing to lose his grip on the hilt of his sword, now lodged in the bony shield surrounding the heart of the beast. He needed to ensure he'd done sufficient damage to the immense organ so that this Dragon would never rise again. Protecting his partner and stubborn to the end, they'd tumbled to the dirt together while he'd endured a continuous stream of the deadly Flame, as he struggled to release his sword and finally get the heart adequately damaged. If he could just breathe, he'd feel shame for letting his friend down by allowing himself to be so incapacitated. After surviving the bloodiest and fiercest battle within several known lifetimes, he was taken out by one stupid creature who was in the wrong place at the wrong time.

They'd been in many battles throughout his life, both together and as solitary fighters. Yet he'd never sustained more than the usual broken bones and lacerations, and had only required the assistance of a Healer on rare occasions. If one were able to see his bare skin under the blood, burns and dirt that currently covered him from the top of his head to the tips of his boots, one would see a multitude of scars, most of them having been sutured together by the very one looking down at him now. Running a mental triage upon himself, he knew 'twould take more than a Healer's touch this time, and that he hadn't long this side of the Veil. At least the other wasn't seriously injured and could continue their mission. Of course there was a tiny hope, since he knew his friend to be of a Magical Race. However, he'd always been leery of Magic and Magic Bearers in general, and despite trusting him to have his back in all situations, the idea of allowing him to use Magic to Heal his wounds went against the grain. Besides, he knew what would happen if he didn't escape now and he also knew he couldn't do so. Gazing into the eyes of his friend he saw a look he'd never seen afore, but needed no interpretation. 'Twas time for him to leave Kadoor. This had always been a possibility and therefore he'd been prepared to do what he had to do. Without further hesitation, the hefty Warrior steeled his resolve and afore Brannyn could stop him, he spewed forth his Pledge through a mouthful of bloody froth, "I freely surrender my life to you, so that you may continue my fight. Do it, Brannyn! You know 'tis a journey inescapable. Hurry my friend, The Destroyer comes."

The edges of Brannyn's human appearance momentarily rippled and shimmered. He tried to blame the growing heat of the mid-day sun for this minor loss of control o'er his chosen form. Not a display most humans would notice but 'twas not the heat that caused this waver, as he became faintly cognizant of some emotion with which he was unfamiliar. Regaining his form's stability with slight effort, he was torn but knew well what he must do and didn't require his friend's Pledge to clarify the issue. Still, he stayed his hand as he stared down at the fading Warrior.

Dyrrk had been his only comrade since he'd forced his own exile from his people many long winters ago. They'd met when the human was but a child and Brannyn recalled how they'd forged their friendship, developing trust and skills together through the winters, as he taught the Warrior as much as the Warrior had ultimately taught him. They'd suffered through many a battle with both misfortune and glory resulting, but the stout fighter had never betrayed him, even to his own people. This one human was mayhap the only person alive today who knew his real name, although there was much he didn't know. Not even this one friend could be trusted with the depth of history and the truth to which Brannyn laid claim.

'Twas fact, the human had always disliked taking credit for Brannyn's deeds and glory, but the need for secrecy 'twas understood and never questioned. Besides, the fighter was nearly as good in battle as he was, and had earned his place in the Warrior Brotherhood on his own. He was vaguely aware that he didn't have time for reminiscing and wondered just what was causing him to detour his usual focus. He gazed down upon his companion who lay dying, his Life Source soaking into the dirt beneath him. Kneeling, he placed one hand upon the stricken fighter's chest. Skin to skin, he could feel his Life Force weakening, but 'twould take longer than they had. 'Twas now or never, yet he continued to hesitate. He tried to ignore the unfamiliar sensations that whispered through his soul like a spider weaving a web, infiltrating his will as if the strange emotions were developing a life of their own. Brannyn attempted to justify the increasing emotional chaos as mere frustration, since he knew his powerful Magic could Heal his friend but 'twas already too late to prevent exposure. Sadly, 'twould be insanity to attempt to alter the memory of his superior.

This day's clandestine meeting 'tween the two fierce fighters and swordsmen had begun typically. They'd met at the break of dawn, at the prearranged time and place, being as careful as they'd always been, but Brannyn now felt the Fates must still be angry with him. The human had very important information to deliver, which affected them much. The Battle Commander of the Dragon Clan had been forced Past the Veil during the recent Battle of Evanntyr, which of course Brannyn already knew. But what he'd needed confirmed was that his daughter The Dragon, who was in LifeBond with Gunnarr the Mighty Blue, had taken Command and had survived the Battle. Was the prophesy being fulfilled? Mayhap this shocking information, which included the obvious, that now no one in the Clan knew the truth of what the two of them were doing, had dulled his senses and precipitated the next disaster.

In the midst of their hurried information exchange, they'd been accidentally stumbled upon by a roving pair of Hoard Dragons who weren't where they should've been. Flame it all, 'twas infuriating. They'd been prepared for every contingency and 'twould be an accident that may now see his undoing. Why had he not felt their presence? With this blow, he faced losing his only link to the Battle Commander as well as his tenuous position in the Hoard, a position he'd fought long and hard to gain. Of course, losing that position would be a painful process without doubt, but pain meant nothing to him. He was far more concerned about losing the Black War to the Evil One. Although he'd count the loss of his friend this day as just as great a concern, for this human male was the only person of any Race who'd proven to be a trustworthy ally. What to do now?

Fortunately, the two of them had been more than able to handle the Dragons, taking them both down afore they'd realized exactly what they'd seen. Unfortunately, the Dragon his friend battled didn't go down quickly enough and had managed to Call to The Destroyer afore his life had been completely extinguished. The Right Hand to the Evil One was even now traveling to this very clearing to see for himself what had occurred here.

Brannyn was stuck. He didn't want to throw the salt prematurely by using his Magic to Heal the man. Such an act would leave glaringly obvious clues, easily read by any Magic Bearer, and therefore would be questioned by The Destroyer. He'd been very careful o'er the winters, managing to maintain complete mystery, and so far no one knew his Race or capabilities, having expertly handled all their questions when he first entered into their service. 'Twas why he'd gotten himself exiled. Even his own people knew not that he was fighting against The Evil One. Starting at the bottom of the Hoard hierarchy, he'd ruthlessly done whatever it took to rise to his present position. His true identity needed to remain a mystery for awhile yet. He had one more place to usurp, one more promotion to gain. 'Twould require assassinating the one now holding that place, but he'd done worse things. Even the Hoard followed certain rules however, and he couldn't kill a superior without Flaming good reason, or The Destroyer's approval. Disgustedly, he recalled how he'd actually had to defend the prick during the recent Battle, after having plotted and planned and awaited his chance to acquire that reason or approval. Regrettably, the Right Hand to The Destroyer, although quite depraved, had proven to be no idiot and no reasonable excuse had ever presented itself….yet.

Once Brannyn took his promotion the stakes couldn't get any higher. There could be no stain of mistrust about him or he'd not see another dawn, and the undertaking he'd worked so long and hard to realize, would fail. No one else had ever come this far, infiltrated this deeply, no one else had what it took. He'd given up everything, his people, his home, his family, his succession, his friends, his reputation, any chance at a real relationship. His life was in constant danger and he lived with the knowledge that any moment could be his last and that if he failed, no one would ever know the truth. There was just this one Man.

His attention returning to Dyrrk, dripping out his Life Source upon the soil, he realized the most frustrating idea was that he'd not be able to explain allowing this human male to live, unless 'twas for more information gathered through torture. Healing him and letting him escape was obviously not an option. No human could stand alone against him and escape, the very notion was absurd. And the outcome that would await the Warrior in the dungeons of the Hoard was not pretty. The Destroyer seemed to revel in the pain of others and in fact, Brannyn had begun to think he was actually feeding off such emotion. This thought gave him pause as he considered the clues briefly, trying to determine what Race had ever fed in this heinous manner. He knew Evil changed the essence of one's Magic, but from what Race had this deviation sprung? 'Twas as if he couldn't see his hand in front of his face, 'twas all there, why could he not see the answer? He was confounded.

Brannyn's attention returned abruptly to the present once again, upon hearing the big man cough while painfully trying to suck in yet another shallow breath, and he knew he had to help him Pass the Veil. Although he didn't like having no other options, 'twas time and he needed to act swiftly.

"You promised me, my friend. I have no doubt we shall meet again Beyond the Veil. Now deliver." The big man spat out his last words with a spray of blood and wiping the corner of his mouth with the back of one Flamed hand, he stood up unsteadily, stumbling away several paces. Raising his broad sword with a double hand grip and a mighty effort, he dropped into Battle Stance and prepared himself to die.

The surprise forgiveness proffered in those words, the acknowledgement of their camaraderie, was almost more than Brannyn could bear. He lifted his eyebrows and pursed his lips together as he admired the human's tenacity, his fortitude, his character. This one would be missed much.

With no time left, he threw his head back, spread his arms wide and Cast out, opening his senses fully. Feeling a sudden flood of emotion hit him like a crashing wave upon the rocks, he roared in anguish and anger, "ARRRRRRGH!" Rising to his full height from his knees, the one known only as The Predator, took a two fisted grip upon the leather wrapped and metal studded hilt of his long sword, rushed forward and attacked with a vengeance.

Brannyn's only link to the outside world attempted weakly to meet the vicious sword strikes now raining down upon him, but even with his great skill and strength, he couldn't begin to slow the furious speed and power emanating as a result of the deep emotion the situation had invoked. His Magic so fueled by the boost of energy, Brannyn's sword beat back his friend's now feeble efforts at self defense and knowing toward what end his actions were bound, Magic fueled anger and anger fueled Magic 'til exhausted, he sunk his sword into the bloody dirt afore him.

Crouched with one hand upon his knee and the other gripping the hilt to steady himself, he must now look upon the carnage. As he slowed his breathing and heart rate, the red haze of his Battle Vision dissipating, 'twas unbelievable what he'd just done. Gazing upon the butchery, he'd never felt such despair. Holding back as best he could, his heart near shattered, he was amazed to discover a single tear running down his dirt streaked face. Using his finger, he wiped the tear from his cheek and stared at it in disbelief.

"Your mission….my mission, will not fail," he near whispered to the bloody mess. "By the gods, you alone have managed to unlock my psyche, giving me the Gift of deep emotion, opening my senses to the cosmic influence contained therein. I understand now why my people shunned its power in the past, why my Race attempted to eradicate such from our lives. I feel the strength of it growing within me, urging me to let loose my restraints." Brannyn grimaced, causing his eyebrows to furrow as he endeavored to leash the intense, new found power. "'Tis quite stimulating and I fear 'twill be most addictive. 'Twas also forced upon Corbyn, yet despite tragedy, he lost not his control. The echoes of our ancestors say I can do no less." His eyes still dark and sparkling with Magical residue, he finished swearing his Oath to his friend, "I will avenge you. We will meet again."

Pushing aside the immediate concern of establishing a new link to the Clan, he regained his stoic demeanor with concentrated effort and returned to face his present predicament. He used his Magic to Mask his new found emotions and alter his anguished appearance, as he casually kicked at the blood soaked dirt surrounding what was left of the Warrior, in feigned contempt. There wasn't enough of any one thing to reveal what once was, no leathers, no boots, no identifiable bones or body parts, not even the big man's sword was left intact. Catching his breath, he stood upright again, drew his blade from the ground, wiped it on his leather britches and sheathed it at his back. All the while, The Destroyer watched his actions from somewhere behind him, with nauseating approval.

He felt many emotions emanating from his superior, not the least of which was overwhelming hunger. Sorting through them with finesse so as not to alert him, he learned much. Slipping past the other's attempts to feed from the death shroud aura of pain and terror lingering through-out the area, he discovered his berserker performance most certainly had given him that promotion and he'd finally have more than just his foot in the doorway. What was one more execution in the general scheme of things? 'Twould be too easy. The one he must remove to gain his new rank as Second to the Destroyer was merely human, a pawn who'd lost his use-fulness. Brannyn would soon be in a most powerful and yet compromis-ing position. Dyrrk would've been well pleased, for 'twas the end toward which they'd been striving for many winters. Ensuring The Destroyer knew nothing about him or what had happened here, he sighed in relief at the near miss and Pulled out of the other's barbaric thoughts. With slight difficulty, he regained his focus. The truth of The Predator's identity re-mained a secret and he'd avoided detection once again. But at what cost?

~~~ THE END OF THE BLACK WAR BEGINS ~~
~~~

Author's Bio

Born in Connecticut and raised in the Midwest, Derrien Relyea grew up fascinated with mythology, Viking lore and Dragons. Her vivid imagination was kindled by her highly creative family, encouraging a love of writing and fantasy. She worked her way through Oklahoma City Community College with degrees in Occupational Therapy and Therapeutic Recreation, and later graduated from The University of Oklahoma Health Sciences Center with a degree in Physical Therapy.

Taking her cue from an exciting genealogical history and such authors as Anne McCaffrey, Edgar Rice Burroughs, and Sir Arthur Conan Doyle, she has embarked upon a new adventure in her life. Please join her at:

http://thedragonwarrior.com/

Kudos and credit to my friend and accomplished artist, Lisa Dixon:

http://lisadixonfinearts.com/

www.ingramcontent.com/pod-product-compliance
Lightning Source LLC
Chambersburg PA
CBHW030655120726
47905CB00001B/225